FOREVER MY
SAIN†

FOREVER MY SAIN✝

A DARK ROMANCE

VOLUME THREE

International Bestselling Author

MONICA JAMES

Cover Design: Perfect Pear Creative Covers
Editing: Editing 4 Indies
Formatting by

emtippettsbookdesigns.com

Follow me on:

authormonicajames.com

OTHER BOOKS BY
MONICA JAMES

AUTHOR'S NOTE

CONTENT WARNING: *FOREVER MY SAINT* is a DARK ROMANCE containing mature themes that might make some readers uncomfortable. It includes kidnapping, captivity, strong violence, mild language, and some dark and disturbing scenes.

Welcome to the beginning of the end, my ангел. It's time to fuck shit up.

CHAPTER ONE

Day 92

I am swathed in silence.

The type of silence that has you wondering if you have succumbed to the darkness for good.

It's peaceful here, and after experiencing nothing but noise for the past ninety-two days, I never want to leave. But as a voice flashes in and out of the abyss, demanding I wake the fuck up and fight, I know this reprieve is only short-lived.

"He's alive...I know where he is...and I need your help to get him out."

Those words play on a loop, taunting me with everything they represent. It's hard to believe they're true, and a big part of me believes this is Zoey's revenge. She knows *this* is the only thing she could do that would really hurt me beyond repair.

She's insulted me, hacked off my hair, and beaten me until I bled, but each blow was nothing compared to this. This is what I've wanted to hear since I witnessed something so horrifying, it changed my world forever.

I'm afraid. I'm afraid of every possible outcome.

If Zoey is lying and I accept her words as truth, I don't think I can handle losing him again. On the flipside, if what she says *is* the truth, then God help him. Her statement has me believing that wherever he is, he's there against his will.

It's getting harder and harder to breathe, and the tattoo on my flank begins to burn, singeing his name onto my very soul.

"I don't have time for this. Wake the hell up!"

"Calm down!"

"Don't tell me what to do! You gave up that right the moment you traded me in for a shinier toy."

"Do you blame me? You're fucking insane! You blew up my house!"

The atmosphere contains so much tension, I'm certain it will explode in seconds. But would that be such a bad thing? I've known nothing but sorrow with glimmers of hope since this nightmare began, so maybe ending it all wouldn't be so dire.

But his image, combined with his words as well as everything he did to save me, crashes into me, and I know there is no choice. All of this can't have been for nothing because I've been given a second chance. A second chance to make this right and save *him* this time.

Hurdling over the roadblocks in my mind, I stagger toward the finish line because it's time I won this race once and for all. The man whose name burns my very existence is all the fuel I need to pry open my heavy eyelids and gauge where I am.

I'm lying on the cold floor of a small room, *my* room. Since I literally had no other place to go, this room has been my sanctuary. I'm a fugitive. We all are.

As I meet the steel blue eyes of my once captor, everything comes to light, and I wince. If it wasn't for him, none of this would have happened. But on the other hand, if he had never brought me into his world, I wouldn't have met the man who shook my world beyond repair.

And that man is…Saint.

"Where—" I inhale and exhale deeply as I come to a shaky, half-sitting position. "Where is…he?"

The room falls silent, and if I didn't know any better, I'd say everyone thought I was dead.

Aleksei Popov, once the most feared man in Russia, has now become the most wanted. And that's thanks to his former plaything blowing his castle to smithereens. "Are you all right?"

When he tries to help me stand, I wave him off, not interested in his help. He's done enough.

Sara, my only friend, bites her nails as she watches on nervously. I can only imagine what being here does to her. It's because of Alek, her former "boss," that the man she loved is now dead. That she isn't throttling him to death reveals she's a bigger woman than I am.

"Are you sure you're not going to faint again?" And that leaves the last gameplayer.

Zoey Hennessy—Saint's sister, my arch-nemesis, and all-around psychotic bitch.

"Fuck you," I spit in a winded breath as I wearily come to a hunched stance.

Zoey stands her ground with her arms folded over her chest. How she's changed from when I saw her last. From when she was Alek's pet.

"Just making sure," she quips with a slanted grin while I grit my teeth. "Are you ready for the truth?"

Am I? I honestly don't know.

Suffocating in this small room, I push past Zoey, desperate for some fresh air. I need a clear head to deal with what she's about to share. The light streaming in from the large window burns my eyes. I shield them as I stagger down the corridor toward the glass door leading to the tranquil gardens. But the serenity does nothing to calm my nerves this time.

The moment the cool air hits my cheeks, I hiss at the bittersweet kiss. Regardless of the temperature, I tip my face to the heavens and take a moment to gather my thoughts. Clutching at the cross around my neck, I close my eyes and beg for divine intervention.

I know I don't deserve it, but here, in this Godly place, maybe He will cut me a break. "Please, let it be true."

Instead of being comforted by the hand of God, I'm assaulted by the tongue of the devil. "You need to get your shit together because you're all I've got."

My last tether snaps, and I swivel around, marching toward Zoey. Ready for war, she matches my stride. "How can I even believe you? You're hardly a credible source," I cry, stopping mere inches away from her.

She curls her lip, shaking her head in disbelief. "Do you

really think I'd come here if it wasn't true?"

"Honestly, I don't know!" I spread my arms out wide, eyeing her something wicked. "You'd do anything to get back at me!"

She snarls and lunges forward, ready to rip the hair from my scalp. "Not about this! I would never lie about this." Her anger simmers when she adds, "Never about *him*."

And just like that, Zoey and I find common ground.

I take a step back. She does the same.

With the tension still pulsating between us, we take a moment to calm down. However, I never take my eyes off her, and neither does she. We are thrown into this without a choice, but to save him, we will have to do something blasphemous—we will have to work together.

"You can hate me all you want, but we want the same thing." Her determination reveals she's telling the truth.

A heavy staccato rules my heart, and a wave of adrenaline overtakes me. She's right. To help Saint, we will have to put our differences aside. But the thought of us being on the same side leaves a bitter aftertaste because I will *never* trust her.

"Tell me everything," I demand, uncaring that my teeth chatter from not only the cold but also my fear.

"So you believe me?"

"I'll decide that once I hear what you have to say."

Zoey's cheeks billow as she commences her tale. "Alek discarded me as if I meant nothing more to him than trash. Do you realize how that made me feel?" she says, her tone filled with hurt and anger.

I fold my arms across my chest, hinting for her to go on

because I'm not here to console her.

When she reads my disinterest in her sob story, she continues. "But it was the best thing he ever did because Saint took me into the mountains and helped me heal. He brought me to а знахаря."

When I arch a brow, she clarifies, "A healer. Or some may even call her a witch doctor. He didn't take me to a clinic or rehab because he knew I'd escape. He knew I'd bribe my way back to Alek." When her eyes drift over my head, I realize we're no longer alone.

"бабушка was a tough bitch. She didn't take my crap. I hated her, and I hated Saint for taking me to her, but neither gave up on me. No matter how many times I tried to escape, Saint found me and brought me back. The terrain was cruel, so without a map or a soul in sight, I had nowhere to go.

"At first, I refused any help. When бабушка forced her disgusting home remedies down my throat, I fought with every ounce of strength I had in me. But after a while, I knew I was no match for her, and I gave in."

"What does that name mean?" I ask, watching as something foreign happens to Zoey—she smiles.

"Grandmother. But don't let the name fool you. Nothing is grandmotherly about her. Anyway," she says, clearing her throat, disregarding her obvious sentiment for this woman. "Once the drugs were out of my system, I was left to deal with what I had done. With what was done to me."

She casts her eyes downward; the first sign that a broken girl lies beneath her venom.

"There is no remedy to cure the damage done to your

head. And heart," she adds, lifting her eyes and locking them on Alek, who stands behind me. "But after all this time, I remembered who I was. And that's a Hennessy. I'm a daughter. A sister. I matter. And regardless if I didn't matter to the man I loved, I will never forget who I am ever again."

"Zoey…" Alek's voice cuts through the air like a knife, but she holds up her hand, proving that the lessons learned have shaped her into this fierce woman before us. He no longer has any control over her.

Kudos to her.

"бабушка helped me to heal my body and soul. She helped me find the person I once was. And so did Saint. He never gave up on me. God knows he should have left years ago, but he never did. And now, I owe him the same.

"He told me of his plans to save you," she declares, her anger almost burning me. "He said he'd made a deal with those monsters to protect you and grant you safe passage back to America. In return, he agreed to be their little bitch."

I close my eyes, wishing to black out the memory for good. But I can't. I never will.

"I knew it was a death trap, but he wouldn't have it any other way. He said he'd be back." When she scoffs, I open my eyes and focus on her tale. "Deep down, he knew their agreement wouldn't stick. Which is why he had a plan B. I didn't know how he expected to survive blowing himself up. And when he left his personal belongings behind, including the details of his fortune, he knew it too. But I couldn't let that happen, so with бабушка's help, I followed him. She told me where to stay hidden so he wouldn't know I was following.

"As I said, there is nothing grandmotherly about her."

I'm beginning to believe бабушка's part in all of this was a lot bigger than I originally thought.

"On the night of the masquerade ball, I entered through the secret doorway."

"That's impossible," Alek spits, challenging her story. "It was locked."

It's true. I saw him unlock the trapdoor in the kitchen with my own two eyes.

But when Zoey's tsks him, I realize she isn't referring to that one.

"Oh, sweetie," she coos, patronizing him as she smiles sweetly. "I meant the one in your study. The one you thought I didn't know about."

A huff leaves Alek, and I don't need to look at him to know he is seconds away from losing his shit.

"Anyway"—she flicks her hand, indicating it's now her turn to talk—"I couldn't stand by and watch him destroy his life. It was my turn to save him."

"How?" I never thought one word could carry so much hate, but Alek's wrath doesn't faze Zoey.

"You know what the best thing is about having criminals at your disposal?" She levels Alek with an unbending stare. "They never say no to a little violence. Turns out the reason Saint knew бабушка was because you convinced her son to 'work' for you."

"Who?" Alek seems limited to minimal wording, but it's enough.

Without a pause, Zoey replies, "Pavel. I believe you

acquired him because of his incredible knowledge of explosives and weaponry."

A string of Russian leaves Alek.

My brain takes a moment to catch up to speed. "So it *was* you?" I gasp while Zoey stands tall. She just confessed that *she* was the reason the house crumbled down around us and not Saint. Could it be possible?

I never saw Saint die. Could it be that he never pressed that button after all?

She doesn't answer my question just yet. There is more to her tale. "I knew your men were turning against you. Saint told me Max was going to help him, and that alliances were wavering. I knew it wouldn't take much to convince Pavel to help me."

I'll give it to Zoey—she had everyone fooled.

"I planted the explosives with the help of Pavel and a few other men."

"Disloyal bastards," Alek mutters under his breath. "After everything I've done for them."

Zoey recoils, appearing stunned by his ignorance. "Are you serious? You imprisoned us all. Pavel helped me because he wanted to go home. His mother was getting older, and you wouldn't even allow him to visit her. *You* are the reason for all of this, Aleksei. You only have yourself to blame."

And for once, Zoey and I agree on something.

"The plan was to catch everyone unawares. Pavel would detonate the explosives around the house before Saint could detonate his. But then that bitch Astra shot him, which really fucked things up."

Panic overtakes me, and I lick my suddenly dry lips. "So did Saint's bomb go off?"

Zoey shakes her head. "No, thankfully it didn't. Ours did, though. But Astra did shoot him. I saw it on the surveillance cameras. Pavel and I waited for the explosions to go off, which we planted away from the den so there would be minimal damage to all of you. The plan was to grab Saint, who would be most likely stunned thanks to the commotion around him. Then the cavalry would come in, saving you all. The result would ensure those three bastards never left that house alive."

"Your plan was dangerous. What if he got hurt? What if he died in the explosion?" I cry, angered she would endanger his life that way. "Why didn't you just tell him about your plan in the first place? It would have saved a lot of trouble."

"You clearly don't know my brother," she sarcastically taunts. "He is always taking it upon himself to save others. He wouldn't risk my life or Pavel's. In his mind, this was the only way to save your sorry ass."

I want to argue, but I don't. She's right.

"And besides, he hardly gave me any time to plan. If I hadn't intervened," she snaps, clearly thinking this through, "he wouldn't have just gotten hurt. He would have died. It was all I could do. When he told me about his 'deal,' I knew he would end up dying to save you. If, and that's a big if, the plans went off without a hitch, I still would have blown that fucking house to the ground. There was no way I would allow those animals to use my brother that way while you rode off into the sunset, forgetting everything he sacrificed for your freedom."

There is much distaste to her tone.

"I would have *never* left him," I spit, not appreciating her take on this situation. "I would have come back. Even if my freedom was granted, it means nothing, nothing without him."

Zoey seems unmoved. "Say what you want, but if it wasn't for me, you'd all be dead."

There were a million other things she could have done, but truth be told, she did what I couldn't—she saved him. Or she had hoped to because what she says next has a gasp leaving me.

"But when we got to the den, he was gone."

The world tilts on its axis. "Gone?"

"Yes. At first, I thought he had escaped, but I knew if he had, he wouldn't have left you behind."

The fact has me frowning because she's right.

"And besides, with the shot he took to the chest, he wouldn't have gotten far. I saw Borya's body. He was definitely dead. But…"

Her pause has the hair at the back of my neck stand on end. And when Zoey drops yet another bombshell, I know this is where the real story begins.

"But Astra and Oscar…they were both gone."

I blink once, robbed of breath.

"Impossible." Alek breaks the silence. "If that were true, then we would have heard."

"Heard from who?" Zoey challenges. "What alliances do you have left, Alek? None. No one will dare help you after everything you've done."

When the grass rustles behind me and Alek marches

forward, I expect Zoey to drop to her knees and beg for forgiveness as I've seen her do countless times before. But that was the old Zoey, and just like Borya, that person is dead.

She stands her ground as he lunges for her, gripping her bicep and shaking her violently. "You blew up my fucking house! You destroyed my life. And all for what? For revenge? Is that it?"

Alek shakes her harder, but she only laughs in response. "You destroyed your own life the day you threw me out like I was nothing!" She rips her arm from his hold. "And the house? That place was a prison to everyone who was trapped within those walls."

I couldn't have said it better myself.

Zoey rubs her arm as she continues her story. "Pavel and I escaped back to the mountains where he and his mother were finally reunited. But it was here where the real plan was hatched. Unlike you, Alek, Pavel has people who respect him. It took us a while, but we found Saint."

My legs threaten to give way. "Where?"

She inhales heavily, which hints that wherever he is can't be good. "Oscar has him. He's holding him prisoner."

And just like that, my worst fears have come to light.

"No," I cry, shaking my head because there has to be some mistake. But there isn't.

"Pavel has tried his hardest to infiltrate his house, but it's like a fort. Especially because of what happened. So without a plan, we're screwed."

I remember the picture; the evidence Zoey has. It was of a man who looked like Saint being shoved into the back seat of a car. The quality wasn't great, and now I know that's because Pavel's informant was attempting to remain hidden and not rouse any suspicion.

But there is a reason Pavel's snitch was able to get a photo of Saint in the first place. Oscar isn't careless, and now more than ever, you'd think he would be more careful to conceal his crimes. But he's not, and the reason for that is…Oscar is using Saint as bait. He's using Saint to lure us out of hiding.

They know Alek and I are not dead.

Oh, my god. I'm going to be sick.

The thought of Saint being held captive by that monster… and knowing the things he would do to Saint.

"Why are you only coming to me now? What took you so long to get here?" I can't keep the anger from my voice. She has wasted so much time.

"'Cause I tried every other option we had before I was *forced* to come here. I don't want to work with you, but it appears I have no other choice. I knew Alek had close ties to this place, so I knew where to look. You're lucky you kept your *kindness* a secret," she mocks, glaring at Alek, but she's right. No one has come looking for us here because they don't know Alek has connections to the orphanage.

But none of that matters. "We need to go. Now," I affirm, ready to flee this very second.

When Alek grips my forearm, preventing me from moving an inch, I'm prepared to fight until one of us is dead. "Don't be stupid!" he shouts, attempting to subdue me as I fight him. "This is a trap."

"Let me go, Alek, or I will kill you myself!" It's not an

empty threat. I won't allow him to stand in my way, not when Saint needs me.

"Please, listen. If what Zoey says is true, then there will be eyes all over Russia. This is worse than I thought. With Oscar and Astra dead, we had half a chance. But if they're not…"

There's no need for him to continue. I can fill in the blanks.

"They will do anything to find me." He's pleading for me to see reason, but he's shit out of luck. I refuse to stay hidden when I know Saint is alive.

Just as I break free, Zoey starts a slow clap. She catches us both unawares, unsure what has sparked a round of applause. "Your arrogance knows no bounds, Alek," she explains, stating the obvious. So what does it have to do with Saint?

I watch as she saunters toward him, maintaining total control.

"If there's a point to make, then get to it," he snarls, not appreciating her bravado.

She smirks, reaching up to run her fingers through his mussed hair. He doesn't flinch, and neither does she. It's the ultimate standoff, one which won't end pretty.

"They're not after *you*, darling," she mocks. His lips part, but she yanks his head back, refusing him speech. "They're after *her*."

And there it is. The truth wrapped in a big red bow.

"Wh-what? Why?" Alek's stutter is an uncommon occurrence. This can only mean one thing—he believes her.

With her fingers still threaded in Alek's hair, Zoey turns over her shoulder, pinning me with nothing but hatred as she declares, "Because she is the one who brought down a kingdom, and now…it's her turn to pay."

CHAPTER TWO

Day 92

"You lie," Alek snarls, seconds from imploding.

"No. I'm not." When Zoey releases Alek, he launches for her, furious she had the gall to manhandle him.

But she doesn't flinch.

"How dare you come here! Leave. You're not welcome." Alek clutches Zoey's bicep, jerking her in warning.

She stands on tippy toes, glaring without a trace of fear. "I am the only *friend*, and I use that word loosely, you have. Let go of me."

There is no way this will end without one of us getting hurt because after what she just confessed, I realize she is the reason for all of this. "You did this," I snarl with pure spite. "You are to blame. Saint did all of this for nothing. And it's your fault. He is god knows where, and it's because of you."

Alek freezes, watching me closely. He knows I am seconds

away from killing her with my bare hands.

"If it wasn't for me, he'd be dead," she says without remorse. Yes, she may be right, but where he is now with Oscar holding him prisoner—is this the lesser of two evils? "Don't you dare act a martyr."

During this ordeal, I blamed myself, believing Saint blew himself up to save me, but this entire time, it was her. It doesn't lessen the part I played in all of this, but I can't help but wonder what would have happened had she not intervened?

We will never know.

Even though I despise her with every morsel of my soul, I inhale deeply. Looking at the crucifix attached to the brick wall, I ask for strength and hope this is the right thing to do.

"Alek, let her go," I spit, unbelieving I'm defending her. "You're wasting time."

Alek's lips fall into a deep frown, confusion and anger plaguing him. "You don't honestly believe her?"

Zoey arches a brow, awaiting my answer.

"I don't have a choice. If there's a possibility that what she's saying is true, then I have to do what she says. I won't leave Saint to the mercy of that asshole."

Just thinking of him in the hands of Oscar causes my skin to crawl.

Zoey breaks free from Alek's hold, her grin revealing she enjoys having the upper hand—finally. As much as I hate to rely on her, she is the only ally I have.

"So what's the plan?"

"дорогая, no. Do not be fooled by her. She would do anything to get back at me."

The small tic beneath Zoey's eye betrays her newfound attitude. She may think she's rid Alek from her system, but the term of endearment he used for me still gets to her. But I can't blame her; he was her heroin once upon a time.

"That may be true, but I have to find that out for myself."

Alek sighs heavily, clearly annoyed by my stubbornness.

"When do we leave?" I want to ask a million other questions, but they can wait. This is the only one that matters.

Zoey nods once, happy with my choice. "I have a few ideas, all of which are dangerous and will probably get you killed."

Reining in my anger, I focus on the task at hand. "I'm okay with that."

Alek, it appears, can no longer stand this discussion and turns on his heel to go back inside. I don't know why he cares. It seems he's been given a get out of jail for free card as his life will be spared. But from his reaction, you'd think he was the one whose neck was on the line.

Once he's gone, Zoey reveals her plans. "Pavel has studied the blueprints of Oscar's home. Just like every villain, he has a secret tunnel leading from the master bedroom to the greenhouse. The garage is close by, allowing an easy exit."

"Good, let's go." I attempt to turn around, but Zoey shakes her head.

"Did you not listen to a word I said?" she asks, looking at me as though I'm an imbecile. "The place is like a fort. We wouldn't get three feet without being killed. And what good are we to Saint if we're dead?"

"What then?" I question, unappreciative of her tone.

She tongues her cheek, as if mulling over what to say. "The easiest way in…is for you to walk up to the front door and knock."

I blink once because I'm not sure if she's serious. She is.

"It can go one of two ways. They either let you in. Or…" But there is no need for her to elaborate.

I do what she proposes, and there is a high probability that I'll end up dead.

"But if you're too gutless, then—"

There are no buts in this situation. "I'll do it," I interrupt, not wanting to hear another plan of attack because there isn't one.

This is going to be the best way into the lion's den because deep down, I know Oscar won't kill me. Torture me, yes. But kill me, no. What good am I dead? I provide more interest for him alive. He said so himself.

"I need to know what makes you special."

That's what Oscar said to me when he tricked Max into taking me to his home. But this time, I come willingly.

Zoey appears to weigh my response, unsure if I've heard her correctly. "You know what this means, right?"

"Yes," I reply without wavering.

"And you're okay with whatever the outcome may be?"

"Yes," I repeat, staring her straight in the eye.

"Oscar will probably kill you," she says without feeling.

But I shake my head. "No, he won't."

Zoey doesn't hide her surprise at my confidence. "If that's true, then I won't need to tell you the rest of my plan."

That piques my interest.

"Enough, Zoey."

Our attention turns to the imposing man standing in the doorway. Alek is at his back scowling, so it's safe to assume he was once a loyal subject who has now turned rogue.

"I'm Pavel," he states with a sharp nod. That explains Alek's rage. "Saint is a good friend of mine. We both want the same thing."

I like that Pavel doesn't have time for small talk because neither do I.

"Good. So when do we do this?"

"We have to be smart about this. I have tried to devise a way to break in without getting caught, but thanks to красная долина going kaboom, security everywhere has been amped up tenfold."

Zoey grins at the fact her former prison no longer stands while Alek grits his teeth.

"We wouldn't get in, even if I were to plant explosives and cause a distraction. It's too dangerous as I need to have eyes on Saint. Which is where you come in."

I wait for him to continue.

"From what I can tell, Saint hasn't spilled who Aleksei's new supplier is. He knows this is the one and only leverage he has. So my plan is for you to get into Oscar's home by using your knowledge of Aleksei's empire."

"I don't know much," I confess, hating to be the bearer of bad news.

But Pavel, it seems, is two steps ahead. "You know enough, more than they do, which means we have the upper hand."

"How?"

Pavel walks forward slowly. He towers over us, but even if he didn't, his commanding presence would have most cowering in his shadow. "Once you're in, you will tell Oscar you know who the supplier is and will hand over the information on the proviso that he lets Saint go."

His plan may work, but I know Oscar; Saint is far more valuable to him than knowing the supplier's identity. He's clearly obsessed with Saint and won't let him go that easily.

"He values Saint more. It won't work."

It appears Pavel is well aware of the fact. "You're right. But he values his life more." I arch a brow, utterly confused, so Pavel clarifies. "You reveal that you know Astra is alive and will tell her everything. He knows that Astra would do *anything* to get her hands on that piece of information. He will agree to the terms, trust me."

It seems like a long shot, but when I hear the final piece to the puzzle, I soon change my mind.

"You request a meeting with Astra. If he says he won't arrange it, then you tell him you'll do it yourself, ensuring Astra is made aware of Oscar's reluctance to cooperate. He fears her and her wrath, so in the end, he knows Saint won't be worth the hassle. As I said, he values himself more."

"Do you know where Astra is hiding? If this doesn't work, do we have a backup plan? If Oscar won't give Saint up, maybe we could use Astra? She could force his hand."

Pavel sighs, clearly frustrated. "I *think* I know where she is, but I can't be certain. So you cannot fail. You must convince Oscar that you know where she is."

In other words, we don't have any other choice. We need

Oscar to set Saint free because if we knew where Astra was, we could go straight to the source. She would no doubt force Oscar to hand over Saint in return for the information we have.

Alek decides now is the time to intervene as the once ruler doesn't appreciate being spoken about like he doesn't matter. "Aren't you forgetting the fact that none of this will be possible without my assistance?"

Pavel's dark eyes turn murderous when he hears him speak.

Alek enjoys seeing him squirm as he walks over to where we stand. "My contact won't talk. No matter the circumstances, he won't deal with Astra and Oscar after everything that's happened. However, if I were to talk to him—"

That's where Alek's speech ends.

Pavel turns slowly. "Do you really think I would hand him over to another monster?"

Alek is taken aback as it appears Pavel has thought this out.

"There is no way I will allow that to happen. This ends now."

"And how do you intend on doing that? Astra isn't stupid. If you come to the table empty-handed, you'll all pay."

"Who said anything about going empty-handed?" Pavel challenges. "Thanks to the fact you kept me hidden in the shadows, no one knows who I am. I could be anyone, and I plan to be."

Zoey gazes at Pavel with nothing but respect while my mouth parts in understanding.

"I go in, pretending to be the supplier. It's all I need. I just need clearance to get into that house. Once I'm in, I'll take care of the rest."

A small bubble of hope simmers inside me because this might work. Breaking into Oscar's home will result in our deaths, but to be invited—that'll give us a fighting chance.

"Willow, I need you to understand that once you're in, Oscar won't let you leave. He will ensure you pay for what you've done."

"I understand," I say with conviction. "But it's a risk I'm more than willing to take."

"No, absolutely not!" Alek exclaims, his cheeks turning a blistering red. "I will not allow it."

"Allow it?" I question, shaking my head at his audacity. "This decision is mine to make. Not yours."

"This is suicide!" he presses, tousling his hair further as he runs his fingers through it.

I still don't understand why he's so concerned for my well-being. I thought he would be grateful this plan doesn't involve him, but when Zoey's lips twist into a smirk, I know how wrong I am.

"Don't worry, sweetie. If this doesn't work, then we will use plan B."

Alek's fight soon dies. "Plan B?"

She nods, pursing her ruby lips. "We give you to them, which is what I voted for."

This plan seems far easier than the deception as so many things can go wrong, but Alek won't go willingly. He would betray us all to save his ass because let's not forget that Astra and Oscar were once his friends. I have no doubt he could win them over again.

So for now, this will have to do.

"I know it's not foolproof, but it's the best option we have."

Alek scoffs at Pavel, folding his arms across his chest.

"It'll work," I assure Pavel, ignoring Alek. "I'll make sure that it does."

And I will.

Pavel is right; because of what happened to Alek's home, sneaking in would be nearly impossible. Being invited in is the best way to infiltrate his empire and attack it from the inside—Trojan Horse style.

"Oscar won't make it easy for you. You may need to do things you aren't comfortable doing."

It appears Pavel knows what a sick bastard Oscar is.

Standing tall, I never falter when I reply, "It can't be any worse than being sold by my husband to a Russian drug lord."

Pavel nods, my point being read loud and clear by all. Alek, however, averts his gaze, appearing wounded by my comment. A twinge of regret overcomes me because I did say it with intent to hurt him. But I must never forget that he *is* the bad guy and the reason I am here. No matter the circumstances now.

"When do we do this?" We are wasting precious time.

"In two days," Pavel replies. I open my mouth, amped to protest that that's two days too long. "We must prepare you on what to say. Your story has to come naturally. If any hint of deceit is detected, the plan will fail."

Even though I hate that we have to wait, he's right. If I

were to go in there now, I would be charged with emotion, and I can't allow my feelings to rule me. Saint is relying on me, so there is no room for error.

"Okay." Pavel can sense my distaste at waiting, but I'll make sure I'm a convincing liar once we leave here. So much so, even I'll believe the lies.

"Excellent. You'll say you have no clue where Alek is. You passed out after the explosion and woke up in the care of Sara. For all you know, he's dead."

On cue, Sara appears around the doorjamb. She really has done so much for me, and I honestly will never be able to repay her.

"I want to explain," she says in a small voice, wringing her hands together nervously. "Saint was never going to let me get hurt. He asked me to trust him, and I did. I was to take your place for only a little while, but he promised if anything went wrong, he would get me out of there immediately."

Max confirms her claims as he too appears. "It's true. Saint asked me to ensure her safety. Both of yours," he adds, alerting Alek to the fact that every single one of his confidants had turned against him.

How that must sting.

But Alek doesn't allow his emotion to show—that's what got him into this mess to start with.

Pavel isn't one for sentiments as he continues to detail his plans. "Oscar won't believe you because he saw you leave with Alek. You must earn his trust. But whatever happens, you mustn't reveal that Alek is alive."

Alek pales.

"Why?" I ask, wanting to iron out all the details and possible outcomes.

Pavel takes a breath, then continues. "Because he is our ace in the hole."

"I will never help you," Alek spits, standing tall. "You are a traitor. You all are." That includes me.

Pavel isn't bothered in the slightest by Alek's insults. "Be that as it may, I don't need you conscious to deliver you to the wolves. I'm not under your command anymore. I don't owe you a damn thing."

A burst of Russian bounces between the men, each word getting more heated than the one before it. This will not end pretty.

"Enough!" I cry, placing my arms outward to stop them from advancing to kill one another. "You can whip your dicks out later. Now, let's focus on what's important, and that's getting Saint out."

"Finally, we agree on something," Zoey says, examining her short nails, clearly bored by the testosterone-filled outburst.

Alek backs down first, surprising me. But I don't mistake his retreat as weakness. He is simply biding his time. "Get out. All of you."

Without a doubt, I know that includes me.

"With pleasure," Pavel replies, running a hand over his shaved head. "You can hide under Mother Superior's habit while we clean up the mess you've made."

Zoey giggles while Sara's lips twitch. How times have changed.

A small part of me, a part I wish would go away, feels sorry for Alek. This is a big shock to us all. We're all grieving. The cause of our grief may be different, but we've all lost something. Alek has gone from hunter to hunted, and he now feels how I once did—imprisoned.

I don't know what his plans are because we haven't spoken about what the next step would be. I never believed we would be brothers in arms, but for so long, he was my only ally. My only chance at getting out of this country alive.

But now, I'm given an out. An out which doesn't include him.

Swallowing down the sudden lump in my throat, I quickly excuse myself. "I'm going to pack."

I don't wait for anyone to reply and brush past Alek, who senses something is off. Being thrown together in such dire circumstances gives you an insight into the other person's psyche. I don't know how or why—I just know I don't like it.

Getting out of here can't come fast enough.

I can barely keep up with my own two feet as I race down the hallway. When I get to my room, I slam the door shut and lean against it, catching my breath. Once my hands stop shaking, I walk over to the dresser and pull out my things.

Even though my belongings barely fill a backpack, I doubt Oscar will allow me to keep any of it anyway. He will degrade me and punish me for what I did, so the luxury of wearing clothes will most likely be a thing of the past.

As I'm folding a sweater, my door opens, and the pine-scented cologne hints Alek stands at my back. "Please, don't do this."

My hands tremble once again, but I tighten my grip on the material to stop myself from wavering. "I have to. I can't leave Saint there."

It's been the giant elephant in the room since the night we escaped. Alek hasn't spoken about Saint or acknowledged Saint's feelings for me. But he also hasn't addressed the reason Saint let him live.

"I need someone who…loves you…as much as I do."

That's what Saint said.

Saint acknowledged Alek loving me as much as he does, but that's absurd. Just the notion leaves my stomach in knots. However, Saint wouldn't leave me with Alek if he had any doubt. Of that, I'm certain.

He believes Alek loves me…

"I know that, but this is just plain crazy," Alek says, interrupting my thoughts. "We will think of another way. I will get him out."

Spinning around, I pin him to the spot where he stands. "Why? Why do you even care? This doesn't involve you. This might even be your way out. I surrender to Oscar, pretending you're dead, and you can slip away to someplace where no one knows you. You can start again."

Alek inhales sharply. "I will not run away like a coward. And I most certainly will not hand you over to Oscar!"

"Why not?" I cry, not understanding any of this. He doesn't owe me anything. He never did. This is his chance to wash his hands of me, once and for all.

"I made a promise to Saint," he replies, but he's using that as an excuse.

"That promise was made when you believed he was sacrificing himself to save me," I stubbornly argue. "He's not dead; therefore, you owe him nothing. You've held up your end of the bargain by keeping me safe here, and I thank you for that. But now that Saint is alive, I'm going back to him. And you can't stop me."

Alek interlaces his hands behind his neck and tips his face to the ceiling. He clearly needs a minute. "I didn't do it for him. I did it…for you."

He speaks in barely a whisper, but I heard him, loud and clear.

When he finally meets my eyes, the sincerity I see unsettles me beyond words. "The reason he left you with me was because he…" Alek pauses, wetting his lips. "Because he could see that my…feelings for you are—"

But I quickly intervene, not wanting to hear whatever he has to say. "Stop!" I thrust my palm toward him. "I don't want to hear any more."

Alek's frown reveals my admission has hurt him. But hearing him use the word "feelings" has left me uncentered, and I can't afford any distractions. The only thing that matters is getting Saint away from Oscar.

Nodding firmly, he suddenly appears thankful for the distraction.

"You are making a big mistake. Oscar will see through your lies."

"Well, it's my mistake to make," I reply, turning my back so he can't see my lip quiver.

"How can you trust her? After everything she's done."

There is no need for him to specify who. And he's right. But what I say next cements my decision. "I trusted you, didn't I?"

Silence.

But it speaks volumes.

"Very well, I can't stop you. But know that if you leave here, I won't come and find you. You're on your own." A bitterness accentuates every word as though he's hurt I've chosen Saint over him. However, it was never a choice.

Saint will *always* win.

"Nothing has changed then," I reply, folding my T-shirts as I need to do something with my trembling hands. "I've always been on my own."

A heavy sigh fills the room, hinting this conversation is over. Alek can hate me all he wants, but nothing will change my mind.

What he says next, however, has me wishing I'd kept my mouth shut. "If you really think that, then I've failed you, дорогая. I wish you all the best."

And just like that, the man who imprisoned me and changed my life forever walks out of my world for good.

It's what I've always wanted.

So why do I feel so guilty?

CHAPTER THREE

Day 94

The autumn hues will soon be replaced with blankets of crisp white snow, thrilling my inner child. When I was younger, I was desperate for a white Christmas. The thought of being bundled up tight while sitting by the fireplace as I unwrapped presents was my perfect Christmas morning. But being from Texas, I had to settle for sunny mornings in December instead.

But now, being in a foreign place, the thought of seeing snow by Christmas utterly depresses me. I want to say with conviction that come December, I will be out of this place for good, but I can't.

The truth is, I don't know where I'll be or if I'll be alive to see my first white Christmas. The future is uncertain.

Shifting in the back seat of the car, I appreciate the deep orange hues in this magical landscape since I don't know when I'll see it again. Pavel made it clear that Oscar will ensure I pay my dues for what I did. But it's nothing I didn't already know.

I want to prepare myself for every possible outcome, but truth be told, I don't know what's headed my way.

"You have everything?" Pavel asks as he peers at me in the rearview mirror.

"Yes." By everything, he means do I have the tiny bugs he asked me to plant around the house as, no doubt, Oscar's paranoia will prevent him from allowing me any communication with the outside world.

And he has every right to feel that way.

When the familiar neighborhood comes into view, Zoey peers at me from over her shoulder. She's been quiet for the ride, staring out the windshield, so when we lock eyes, I wonder what she's going to say.

I know we're not friends. We merely want the same thing.

"Don't fuck this up."

"I won't," I reply with conviction. Even though my racing heart and sweaty palms contradict my confidence.

Pavel clears his throat. "Make sure you stick to the plan, all right? No going rogue. As I said, I don't even know if this will work. He may not even want the details of the supplier, but—"

"But as long as I'm in, that's all that matters," I interrupt because I don't need Pavel to list everything that's wrong with this plan.

For the past two days, Pavel has talked me through the plan until I could recite it in my sleep. It seems simple enough— play dumb when it comes to Alek. Trade information for Saint's release. And do the one thing I haven't been able to do since this nightmare began.

Submit.

Oscar isn't like Alek. He won't tolerate any misbehavior. If I step out of line, he'll make sure I pay. Or more accurately, he'll ensure Saint pays. Oscar knows I'll do anything to set him free. But this time, we're leaving together.

"Okay. I'm going to park here. We can't be seen," Pavel says, turning in his seat to look at me.

Pavel has parked the black car three blocks away, which allows me time to settle my nerves and get my head in the game.

"Make contact as soon as you can. He will most likely take your cell, but try to reach out when you can. I'll be listening. Make sure you plant those bugs discreetly so they remain undetected."

I nod, wiping my palms onto my jeans.

"Good luck."

Zoey doesn't say a word.

I take her silence as goodbye, so I unbuckle my belt and reach for my bag. Just as I'm about to open the door, she speaks. "Bring my brother back."

This is the first time I have ever seen emotion from her, and her raw and heartfelt plea was exactly what I needed to hear.

Regardless of our past, she is the only person who understands this loss I feel. Every day, I wake with this gaping hole in my chest, and I don't know how to fix it. Coming here may be suicidal, but living with this feeling will eventually end my life for good.

Nothing but respect passes between us as I affirm, "I will." With those parting words, I open the door, and following the advice Saint once gave me, I don't look back.

Each step takes me closer to the unknown, but I don't feel scared. For the first time in a long time, I feel like my fate lies in my own hands. I know how ridiculous that sounds, considering my circumstances, but this decision was mine to make alone. And that's something I haven't been able to do in a very long time.

With that as my mindset, I hold my head high with no expectations and don't look back as I walk toward Oscar's house. A car drives off in the distance, alerting me that Pavel and Zoey have left. When the tall steel double gate comes into view, I push aside the memories of when I was here last and only focus on the now.

I measure my breathing, going over the rehearsed story in my head one last time. I know it like the back of my hand, but I'm worried I'll mess it up somehow now that I'm here. But that isn't an option. I can't fail.

Tipping my face to the heavens, I inhale deeply and gaze into the gray skies one last time because I don't know when I'll see it next. So much is about to change yet again. My life is a constant merry-go-round, and I wonder when it'll slow down.

Gathering my thoughts, I take a deep breath, then put on my game face. I ignore the tremble to my finger as I push the button on the intercom. Even though no one answers, the flashing red dot on the camera above me indicates someone knows I'm here.

After a few seconds, static crackles before someone speaks to me in Russian. He could be saying go away for all I know, but I don't let that deter me.

"Hi, I'm here to see Oscar." I can only hope he understands me.

He does.

"Oscar isn't here."

Before he has a chance to tell me to beat it, I quickly press the button. "Just in case he is...tell him Will—" I quickly backtrack. "Tell him...ангел is here." I raise my chin firmly, staring into the camera so he can see me.

The blinking light is hypnotic as I focus on it and pray that this works.

My heart begins to race as one minute turns to two. If this doesn't work, then I will scale these high walls. Even though I won't get far, I sure as shit will get their attention. Just when I think the plan has fizzled even before it had a chance to flourish, the gate slowly whines open.

A small jubilant bubble explodes inside me, but I rein in my emotions.

I don't wait for further instruction and slip in the moment the gap is wide enough. I measure my pace as I don't want to seem too eager. Pavel told me I need to remain calm and collected because Oscar needs to think I have the upper hand for our plan to work.

The gardens are dull, a harsh contrast to the flourishing vegetation I saw when here last. I suppose even the flowers have gone into hiding, not wanting to witness the shitstorm about to unfold. The house reeks of wealth, but it's cold and unloved. It appears to be more a museum than a home.

The moment I am within a few feet of the front door, it opens and out marches three armed men. I've never seen them before, but my guess is that they are the muscle. They yell at me in Russian, and when I stand dumbfounded, they yank my backpack off my shoulders roughly.

Tossing it to the ground, they rifle through it without care. There isn't much in there, but when they pull out a pack of gum, I hold my breath. They look at it closely, passing it around, while I do what Pavel told me—stay calm.

That's a little hard because what they hold isn't just a pack of gum. Inside is what will save Saint. Hidden inside a stick of gum—the first and third in the pack, to be precise—are five tiny bugs. I don't know how Pavel acquired these, but he said they would work.

However, when one of the meatheads hunts through the packet and retrieves a stick, I worry the only thing Pavel will be listening to is the goings-on of his digestive system.

I try to think on my feet, but stopping them will rouse suspicion. So I simply watch on without any emotion.

The three men each help themselves to the gum. They examine me as they remove the wrappers and pop the green gum into their mouths. There is no way for me to tell if they've eaten the bugs or not.

After a few noisy seconds of chewing, they nod, then toss the gum back into my backpack. Just when I'm about to sigh a breath of relief, one of them gestures for me to turn around. Without hesitation, I do as he requests.

He commences frisking me, straying a little too close for

comfort. But I never waver, even when he lifts my jacket to examine the small of my back and runs his hand over my ass. I just envision breaking every one of his fingers. When he's satisfied I'm not packing, he then turns me by the shoulders and frisks my front.

He fondles my breasts, acting if this behavior is all part of his "job." He watches for any signs of fear. In response, I roll my eyes at his clumsy groping. Once he's ensured nothing is strapped to my legs and ankles, he stands and grunts.

"Come," one of the goons says, gripping my bicep and dragging me up the stairs. Once I step foot inside, I am hit with a wave of nostalgia. But it's not of the good kind.

I shrug from his grip, not interested in playing nice. "Where is Oscar?"

The man who frisked me tosses my backpack at my feet while the one who manhandled me is far from impressed with my demands. "Wait here."

That suits me just fine.

Two of them disappear, leaving me alone with my groper. He leans against the wall, chewing his gum loudly. While he makes no secret of his ogling, I am also forthright in my response that being near him repulses me. I shift to the left, folding my arms over my chest.

Looking around, most would be impressed by their opulent surroundings. The walls reek of wealth as no expense has been spared. But just as Alek's home was, this place is merely a prison with golden bars.

The thought of being imprisoned once again makes my skin itch, but I stand tall, not showing weakness. I instead focus on where I should plant the bugs. As the loud chewing continues, I can only hope and pray that they're still in the pack of gum.

If not, I have no idea what I'll do.

Minutes pass and no Oscar, which is not surprising because I wasn't expecting this to be easy. Honestly, I wouldn't be surprised if he leaves me waiting all night. This is a game to him, after all, and right now, he's the frontrunner and will do anything to ensure it stays that way.

Finally, one of the men reappears, but without Oscar. "You wait in there." He gestures with his chin to a small room off to the right.

Without debate, I nod and gather my bag from the floor. I'm surprised however when they allow me to venture alone. When I turn the door handle, I see why that is. Claustrophobia grips me tight because this parlor room is tiny, and it's also stained a bright red.

The wallpaper is red. So is the velvet cloth which drapes over the fireplace. The fire burning brightly doesn't provide any warmth. Instead, it sends a shiver down my spine. A circular red rug decorates the middle of the room, but that's it. No furniture. Just a small red room.

How bizarre.

Once I take a cautious step inside, the door slams shut behind me, and the distinctive sound of a lock clicking in place cements my future as a prisoner inside these walls—these red walls. The small confines and the devious color crash into me, and I lunge for the handle, tugging on it frantically because I suddenly can't breathe.

I need to get the fuck out. Now.

"Let me out!" I scream, banging on the door when the lock won't budge. But my pleas are in vain. No one is coming to get me.

The direness to that thought has a fire burning up my neck, threatening to set my skin alight. The harder I try to escape, the more frantic I become. The crimson walls seem to grow smaller, threatening to swallow me whole.

Thoughts of being suffocated as Kenny defiles me rob me of air, and I wheeze. My breaths are heavy, echoing through my ears as the blood pumps rapidly throughout my body. My heart races so quickly, I'm frightened I'm moments away from having a heart attack.

"Open the door!" I cry, my banging on the woodgrain growing sluggish by the second as the fight in me soon dies.

The room is spinning a deep crimson, but I measure my breathing and focus on inhaling and exhaling. I was brought in here for this exact reason. This red room is a mindfuck trip, intent on breaking those who are trapped under the scarlet hue.

With that thought, I will myself to calm, refusing to fall victim to Oscar's psychological torture. To survive this, I must stay strong. I cannot show any weakness. This was a test—one I failed terribly—and it mustn't happen again.

It takes me a few moments, but once I'm composed enough to breathe without wheezing, I scope out my surroundings, wondering if there is anything of use inside. I search under the velvet cloth draped across the mantel in hopes to uncover a weapon.

I don't.

There aren't any fireplace pokers either. I kick the rug away, hoping for a trapdoor, but all I'm confronted with are wooden boards. I feel my way around the walls, looking for any inconsistencies to indicate a secret passage.

Again, I come up with nothing.

The light fixture is a single bulb hanging from the ceiling. All in all, this place looks like a torture chamber. The simplicity indicates it isn't used for comfort. Well, not in the conventional sense. And the color scheme wasn't chosen by chance. I can only imagine what atrocities it conceals.

My legs grow heavy, but without any place to sit, I'm forced to stand. Again, the unfurnished room isn't accidental.

Have I bitten off more than I can chew?

There is only one way to find out.

With that as my mindset, I take my position in the middle of the room, standing tall, and face the door. When it opens, I will be ready because I've already made the mistake of being caught off guard.

But I will ensure it will never happen again.

Every muscle in my body aches.

Many hours have passed since I was locked in this cage, but each minute, each second has only strengthened my resolve. I know what this is. It's a test. Without a doubt, Oscar is watching me because like a lab rat under a microscope, he is waiting to see what the results of his experiment will be.

However, I've not wavered. As each claustrophobic second threatened to choke me into submission, I pushed down the urge to scream and the urge to claw at these walls, desperate to flee. Being locked away in a room with no windows gives you the sense that you're all alone. Just like in the movies where an apocalypse has struck, the world has succumbed to the darkness, and you've only got yourself to survive.

And this is what Oscar wants. This is just the start of things to come because he won't hand over Saint without a fight. He wants to break me, hoping he can control me too, but it's going to take a lot more than that.

And when the lock pops, it seems Oscar has realized this too.

The door swings open, revealing the man I hate with every fiber of my being. He saunters into the room without a care in the world, wearing a black silk robe. A glimmer of a smile spreads across his full lips.

Rage overtakes me, but I rein it in. I lock eyes with him, staring him down. But he doesn't waver in the slightest.

"What a pleasant surprise," Oscar says, opening his arms wide and feigning shock to see me here. "I'm so sorry you've been in here for so long. I was…attending to other pressing matters." His pause for effect has me clenching my teeth because no doubt, those matters involved Saint.

"Cut the bullshit," I snap, not interested in playing games. "I came here to talk. You know what I want."

Kudos to me. Oscar appears taken aback by my candor.

His façade soon fades and, in its place, twists a perverse

grin. "Why would I want to talk to you? You have nothing of value to me. You're yesterday's news. You and Aleksei both are."

He watches me closely for any signs of emotion. There are none.

"I wouldn't know," I reply, uninterested.

Now I've really piqued his interest. "Don't be coy. I know you and Alek are shacked up somewhere cozy, discussing your *feelings*." A word has never sounded so polluted before.

"Please," I mock, folding my arms to stop the tremble passing through me. "I'm glad to have finally gotten away from him."

Oscar purses his lips, tilting his head slightly. "Are you telling me you have no idea where Alek is?"

"No idea." I scoff. "And thank god for that."

"I don't believe you," Oscar replies, a hint of something lacing his tone. "I saw you leave with him. I saw you leave *us* to die."

Ah, now I know what it is—bitterness that I allowed him to burn.

Rehearsing the speech in my head, I put the plan into motion, hoping he buys my lies. "Yes, you're right." He stands tall until I add, "I did leave that room with Alek. But we all suffered in that explosion. We made it, I don't know, only a few feet before the ceiling caved in around us. The last thing I remember was Alek being hit on the head with a beam before I passed out, suffering a similar fate to him.

"When I came to, I was stowed away on a farm somewhere. Sara, yet another pawn in Alek's sick game, had saved me. If she hadn't dragged me from that mess, I would have ended up like Alek."

A tic under Oscar's eye reveals I've hit a nerve. But I hold back the premature celebrating for now. "Like Alek what?"

Taking my time, I exhale slowly. "Dead."

"You lie," he gasps, shaking his head.

But I stand my ground. "No, I don't. For all I know, Alek perished in that explosion."

"His body was never found," he rebukes, but cracks are beginning to show.

"I'm sure a lot of bodies weren't."

Clearly, Oscar wasn't anticipating me delivering this news when he opened his door and allowed me in. A small win for me.

He takes his time digesting everything I've just said. "I don't believe you." *No surprise there.* "Alek would never leave you. Not after his heartfelt promise to be the hero of this story."

His patronizing tone wins him back a point because I almost lose my shit—almost.

"Believe what you want. That's not why I'm here."

"Then why are you here?" He's angry, and that's good. I can work with that.

Taking a step toward him, I pray I'm a convincing liar. "I know Astra is alive. Borya, not so much. But Astra is."

His mouth parts slightly, revealing his surprise that I'm privy to the truth.

"So, as I said, I have something you want. And you have something I want."

Oscar's eyes turn murderous while I gloat at the sight.

"I will give Astra what she's wanted this entire time… what she risked her life for. The details of Alek's supplier." When Oscar pales, I use it as fuel to continue. "I will tell you everything on the proviso that you…that you give him back to me."

He's soon to recover, and his poker face slips back into place. "Astra is alive?" he mocks, pressing a hand over his heart as if expressing surprise. "This is news to me. The moment everything turned to mayhem, I gathered what belonged to me and left. Thankfully, my men are loyal. Unlike Alek's."

I leave half-moons in my palms as I dig my fingernails into the flesh to stop from lashing out and throttling him to death. How dare he refer to Saint as belonging to him?

He belongs to me.

But I don't allow it to affect me because it seems Pavel knows this vile creature after all. He knew Oscar would deny knowledge of Astra surviving the blast.

"Oh, well, I suppose it's up to me to tell her the good news then. Although, I'm sure she won't be too happy knowing you denied her the knowledge she risked her life for."

His hands curl into claws while I smile confidently. "You're lying."

"I guess there's only one way to find out." I attempt to push past him, but his hand snaps out, and he grasps my forearm in warning. I don't allow him to intimidate me, though, because I can see it in his soulless eyes.

I've won.

"You don't expect to just walk out of here, do you?" His grip is punishing, but it gives me the strength to go on.

I giggle manically in response. "Of course not. What do you take me for? You're bad for letting me in."

His face drops, unsure of why I'm laughing. "What's that supposed to mean?"

Once I'm done cackling at his expense, I level him with nothing but utter hatred. "It means, I have friends of my own. How do you think I knew about Astra? And how do you think I know that…Saint is here?"

His grip falters.

"Give me what I want, and this doesn't have to end badly for you. You can run to Astra like the good little dog that you are and attempt to worm your way back into her good graces." God, that felt liberating. My confidence spurs me on. "I'm sure she isn't too happy with you for allowing Saint to get under your skin. Maybe if you were a little more…focused, he wouldn't have slipped a small thing like a bomb past you."

His breathing is deep. He's seconds away from killing me.

It should scare me.

It doesn't.

Standing on tippy toes, I close the distance between us, and whisper, "But it's okay. I know what it's like to have him under your skin."

Oscar snarls, my comment hitting home.

I'm awaiting some form of punishment for my insolence, but none comes. Just as quickly as Oscar turned murderous, his demeanor changes, and he smirks—a cat got the mouse kind of smirk.

"Well, look at you. Talking big. But can you back your words?"

"You know I can," I bite back, still on tippy toes.

He's the first to retreat, which thrills me.

I watch as he begins to pace the room, clearly deep in thought with what to do next. "How?"

Tsking him, I shake my head at his stupidity. "Oh, silly lamb," I patronize. "You didn't think I'd come here without a foolproof plan, did you? I may be your prisoner, but we're both prisoners to our wants. If my friends don't hear from me, they'll tell Astra everything."

He stops pacing and strokes his chin in thought.

"And when she finds out..." I whistle, indicating shit will hit the fan for him. Keeping this from her is a death wish on his behalf.

For the first time ever, Oscar appears at a loss for words, and the reason for that is because he believes me. My knowledge is too vast to be lying.

How do I know these things if I'm not telling the truth? Alek's pride wouldn't allow Oscar to be standing here as he would have sought revenge on him the moment he could. But Alek isn't the man Oscar once knew him to be.

Oscar believes Alek is still the ruthless leader, and if he were, he wouldn't send me here, putting me in danger. Oscar saw us together, and he knew that Alek had feelings for me.

The thought weighs heavily in my belly.

So my tale is believable because the Alek Oscar once knew would burn this house to the ground, not seek refuge in an orphanage. How the times have changed.

But it's evident Oscar doesn't completely trust me, leaving him caught at a crossroad. If he doesn't believe me, then I could ruin him by alerting Astra to his disloyalty. Yet if what I'm saying *is* true, then handing over the information I know could put him back in her favor.

He pins me with those cruel eyes. "If what you say is true, we both need to trust one another. You may think you have the upper hand but…my house, my rules," he states, indicating a world of pain is headed my way.

Standing tall, I refuse to buckle under his intense stare. "I didn't think otherwise."

"So, let me get this straight. You have no idea where Alek is?"

"That's right." And watch my nose grow…

"And you have somehow managed to acquire the allegiance of someone who clearly knows the goings-on of my business?"

"Yes."

"If I play by your rules, you will hand over the name of Alek's drug supplier to us?"

"Very good. You paid attention," I belittle, but I'm internally crossing my fingers this works.

"And you're doing this, all of this, because of…Saint?"

Just hearing his name has my façade almost slipping, but I nod firmly.

"How do you know he's even here? He could have perished in that explosion?"

"We both know that didn't happen," I reply, my patience wearing thin. "Yes, he was shot, but his bomb never went off."

Oscar's chest rises and falls steadily, betraying his thoughts. "For someone so…insignificant," he settles on, "you have caused so much trouble to us all. Fine, I accept your terms."

He can insult me all he wants, but right now, I am one step closer to bringing Saint home.

"But as I said before, we form some kind of partnership, so I need to trust you. I can't have you here if I don't trust you."

And there's the catch. I don't doubt Oscar will make me work to earn that trust.

"Or I could just tell my friends to contact Astra. It's going to be a lot easier doing it this way. But if I have to get my hands dirty, then I will." That'll never happen because we both have a bargaining chip the other wants. But I need him to know that I'm not playing.

I have information, and he…he has Saint. We need the other to get what we want.

"There's no need. I will give you what you want, but it'll take time."

"Time?" I question, caught off guard as this was not part of the plan.

Oscar nods, finally realizing his charade is up. "Poor Astra, she suffered dreadfully in the explosion. She is wounded, mending her face, and you see, she is intent on revenge for anyone involved. You included. She is very paranoid these days. Your *friends* won't get within three feet of her. *If* they even know where she is."

He's calling my bluff.

Thinking on my toes, I reply, "I can be very persuasive when I want to be. Who do you think planted those bombs? If Saint's bomb didn't go off, then why did the house explode?"

"It was you?" He gasps, appearing to have solved a mystery.

"I guess you'll just have to trust me." And I mean that in every sense of the word. This entire plan is based on my ability to lie and earn Oscar's trust.

He trusts that I haven't gone to Astra yet because he has something I want. Or maybe he's just toying with me. I honestly don't know.

"Very well then," he finally says. "I will speak with Astra about this. No doubt, she will want to be there for the meeting."

Pavel mentioned I was to request a meeting with Astra, which means when he does this, he will ensure no witnesses are left alive. This ends once and for all. I have no idea what he has planned, but I can't imagine things will end well for Oscar and Astra.

"Which is why I need time. She isn't herself just yet. She is still gathering her strength. Once she's well enough, I will meet my end of the bargain, and you will do the same. The information in exchange for your beloved's release."

I hate that I have to trust his word because he isn't honorable, but there isn't another way. He has to trust that everything I've said is true while I have to believe that once I deliver Pavel, he will let Saint go. The plan is far from perfect, but I'm in, and I have a fighting chance at saving Saint inside these walls, rather than outside of them.

Oscar eyes me suspiciously because so much of this is based on blind faith. But for now, he believes me. Or rather, he'll humor me. "So do we have a deal?"

He extends his hand, appearing to want to make this official.

I peer down at the offering and wonder if this is the equivalent to signing my death warrant. But the thought of Saint being trapped in here has me placing my palm into his. "We have a deal."

"Excellent."

I yank my hand from his, not interested in touching this asshole unless I have to. "Where is he?" I go straight in for the kill, but Oscar merely laughs at my naïvety.

I understand why that is when two men enter the room and link their arms through mine. There is no point in fighting. Oscar hums at the sight of me being flanked by two giants. "We need to set some ground rules, ангел.

"As I said, trust is something we will need to work on, and until I trust you, Saint remains under lock and key."

"You asshole," I snarl, struggling with my captors to lunge for Oscar. The fact he opted to use the term lock and key enrages me further.

Oscar is unaffected by my insult. "Name-calling will not be tolerated." He grins, revealing this is just a fucking game to him. "Take her to her room."

The men drag me, kicking and screaming, while Oscar waves in victory.

Swathed among the red walls and draped in his black silk robe, he looks right at home as the devil.

CHAPTER FOUR

Day 95

The only comfort I have is knowing Saint is somewhere within these walls.

Once Oscar's goons took me to my "room," they locked the door, and it's stayed that way ever since. On the plus side, I suppose I can be thankful this room wasn't decorated by Lucifer himself. The walls are white, and the simple furniture is below average for a house such as this. But I guess that's because I'm not a guest.

I'm a prisoner.

I have the necessities—a bathroom, some toiletries, and a bed—but no windows. At least when Rapunzel was locked high in her tower, she could look out at the world, longing for her life to begin.

Oscar has ensured I don't have the same luxury.

Pavel taught me how to spot hidden surveillance. No surprise, there was a hidden camera in the smoke detector.

It also didn't shock me when I pressed my fingernail to the bathroom mirror and saw that my finger and image touched tip to tip, which meant there was a camera in the mirror.

Not ideal, but I've had experience in dodging surveillance and staying in the shadows.

As I crouched in the far corner of the bathroom, pretending to hunt through my things, I frantically searched through the packet of gum, sighing in relief when I found the bugs were intact. Pavel positioned them in the way that he did, probably knowing the thugs would rifle through and clumsily pick the sticks in the middle.

Whatever his method, however, it worked, even if it was pure luck.

Carefully sticking a bug to the end of my finger, I walked as coolly as I could into the room and lounged onto the bed. Stretching overhead, I casually touched the headboard and planted the bug behind it. If anyone was watching, the move was completely normal.

No one broke down the door, so it was safe to assume one bug was planted. Only four more to go.

Pavel said once they were activated, he would be listening in, which is why I began singing to myself. The words were a jumbled mess, a mixture of a few songs thrown together, but the overall message was hopefully understood.

I let it slip I was alone and locked in my room yet to see my baby aka Saint. I also revealed one down, four to go, which I hope he will link to the placement of bugs. As far as this spy stuff goes, I stink, but Pavel is smart. I'm certain he will piece it all together.

Once I was done singing clues, I sat on the edge of the bed, waiting…waiting for what exactly I don't know because I've been sitting here for what feels like years. I'm dog-tired, but I can't sleep. The thought of being vulnerable in this place turns my stomach.

I need to be alert and on my A game because I have no idea what Oscar has in store for me. Leaving me alone in a windowless room is yet another form of torture. I'm bracing for the worst, but I know nothing will prepare me for what's headed my way.

Knowing Saint is under the same roof as I am and not being able to see him is the worst form of punishment. The not knowing where he is, if he is okay, and what Oscar has done to him kills me. Just thinking about him being here and not being able to touch him is more agonizing than any torture methods.

Resting my head in my hands, I slouch low and sigh. My life is barely recognizable anymore. When this entire nightmare started, all I could think about was going home. But now, I don't even know if that's an option.

I can't go back to living a "normal" life because I am not normal—not anymore. Saint once expressed the same sentiment so many nights ago, and now, I understand what he meant. How can I live in the light when so much darkness saturates my soul?

But the thing that terrifies me the most is that I don't fear the darkness any longer. I live for it. It's where I feel alive and where I can be myself and live with all the atrocities I've witnessed and done.

A tear scores my cheek, weeping for the person I once was.

The lock pops free, which has me sitting upright and quickly brushing away my tears. I remain seated with my eyes focused on the door. When it opens, Oscar enters, but he's no longer wearing his robe. Could it be I've missed another sunrise, missed another chance to be reborn?

"How did you sleep?" he asks how he would a friend who stayed the night.

"I didn't," I snap, hoping Pavel is listening in. "I want to see Saint."

Oscar places his hands into his pants pockets. "And I want a unicorn," he mocks, making it clear my demands won't be met that easily. "Come. It's time we spoke."

I don't want to go anywhere with him, but this is my chance to plant the remaining bugs.

Coming to a stand, I casually ensure the gum is hidden in my back pocket. It is. "Fine."

Oscar doesn't waste time and indicates I'm to follow.

My dirty sneakers contrast the soft white carpet as we venture down the long hallway. But I suppose I am more than out of place here in my ripped blue jeans and tattered sweater. Everything is positioned with military precision, which worries me. Where am I going to hide the bugs without detection?

Oscar takes a left and leads me into a dining room. Thankfully, it's not the same one I was in last time I was here. Food is spread across the long table, but I'm not hungry. A maid hurries to the head of the table, pulling out the chair for Oscar.

I look at my surroundings, wondering if this is the main dining room. If it is, this would be an ideal place to plant a bug.

"Sit," he orders, reaching for his crisp white napkin and placing it across his lap.

This will go a lot quicker if I just comply, so I take a seat two chairs away from him as being in his presence sickens me. I watch as he casually fills his plate with an assortment of food. It appears to be breakfast, which means I have been in this place overnight.

"Help yourself," Oscar says, gesturing to the food.

I shake my head in response.

This is all a power play for him, and for the next few minutes, I observe him eat his breakfast, oohing and aahing at how delicious everything is and how I'm missing out. I would rather gouge my eyeballs out with the silver spoon than break bread with him.

He watches me closely over the rim of his white porcelain coffee cup. I'm not sure what he's expecting to see because my infuriated expression hasn't changed since I step foot into this hellhole. Once he's done slurping on his coffee, he places the cup back onto the saucer and carefully dabs at the corners of his mouth with the napkin.

"So I've spoken to Astra," he reveals, still gauging me carefully. "She was most surprised to hear about the latest revelations. However, she doesn't believe you have no clue to Alek's whereabouts. And quite frankly, neither do I."

I remind myself to breathe.

"As it stands, though, you have something we want, and

we…well, *I* have something you want. So it appears we're at a conundrum with what to do. The only reason I have allowed you here is because we need the name of the supplier. Everyone is scared after what happened at Alek's, and in a world where trust is already an issue, now it's impossible to get anyone to talk.

"Alek was the one with the connections, which was stupid on our behalf to not show more interest in that side of the business. But we never thought he'd ever turn into"— he pulls a face as if he's just eaten something rotten—"the pathetic little bitch that he did."

Of course, I'm to blame for this.

"We grew up together. All four of us. Did you know that?"

I nod as Astra mentioned it the night of the masquerade ball.

"We were dirt poor with parents who didn't care if we were alive or dead. Although Astra's parents take the prize for the world's shittiest parents when they sold her for a measly two thousand dollars to a rich pervert. She was smuggled into the country from the Ukraine when she was eight years old."

That explains a lot about her.

There is much debate about psychopaths and nature versus nurture. In Astra's case, it definitely is nurture because I hate to think of the atrocities her young eyes witnessed. She was forced to grow up at a tender age because she really was alone in this world after being abandoned by the people who should have protected her.

A small part of me feels sorry for the eight-year-old Astra. The adult Astra, however, I have no empathy for.

"That rich pervert was Borya's uncle."

Well, I'll be damned.

"Astra and Borya always shared a special connection because they shared the same childhood experiences."

Oscar doesn't need to spell it out. Both children fell prey to the vile ways of adults who should have never been allowed to have kids.

"Alek and I suffered at the hands of weak mothers and abusive stepfathers. But I'm sure you know how Alek's story ended."

Yes, it ended when Alek killed his stepfather.

"Our childhoods have far from a fairy-tale ending, but we owned it. It shaped us into the people we are today. We made a pact, refusing to be like our parents. We were going to be strong and feared, but most of all, we were going to be rich.

"Everything you see, we built with our hands," he says, failing to mention the lives they destroyed to get where they are. "And we were, as they say, living the dream until, well, you came along."

"You seem to be forgetting the fact that I never wanted to be introduced into your world. I had a life before all of this!" I cry, refusing to shoulder any of the blame.

"Don't play the victim," he snaps, slamming his fist onto the table and sending the silverware clattering to the floor. "You had both Alek and Saint wrapped around your little finger. Look what you made them both do!"

I keep my cool, realizing now is the time to plant the bug.

As Oscar takes a moment to compose himself, calling out to the maid in Russian over his shoulder, I subtly dig into my back pocket and find one of the bugs in the gum packet. It's tiny, but the raised surface allows me to slide it off the wrapper and onto my finger.

With one fluid motion, I discreetly stick it under the table. By the time Oscar turns back around, he's none the wiser that Pavel is hopefully listening in.

"I didn't make them do anything," I say, wanting to pick up where we left off. "Alek isn't a coldhearted snake like you. Yes, he has done some disgusting things, but he's also done good." I surprise myself with the outburst because I actually mean it.

Oscar doesn't seem touched by the sentiment.

"I don't know what's so different about you. But there is something...look what you did to Saint."

Guiltily, I lower my eyes, unable to forget his self-sacrifice.

If Zoey and Pavel hadn't intervened, he would be dead because my safety has always been more important than his.

"But you're going to show me."

"What?" I retort, slowly meeting his stare.

Oscar leans back in his chair. "I want to know what about you made two fearless men drop to their knees and surrender everything they have for you."

"There is nothing!" I cry, annoyed at hearing this notion yet again. This is the reason Oscar brought me here weeks ago. He wanted to know what made me so special and how I was able to capture Saint's heart.

But I don't have an answer because I don't know. Love doesn't make sense. Falling in love in the most dire of circumstances shouldn't happen, but it did. I can't explain it because with Saint, it was almost inevitable.

From the moment our lives crossed, something happened. At first, it was cruel and ugly, but now, I need it to breathe. And being away from him is cutting off my air supply, and it won't be long until eventually, I'll stop breathing.

"He cries for you, you know. At night, in his sleep, he whispers your name. Over and over." A wicked grin blooms as he knows what his revelation is doing to me.

"Stop it," I whimper, rage and sadness threatening to drag me under.

It falls on deaf ears. "To absolve him of his pain, I had to give him a little something to help chase away the ghosts that plague his dreams."

"What? What did you give him?" I sit tall, clenching my fists under the table.

"Just a little something to help him sleep. But it seems not even the purest of drugs can rid you from his system."

"You bastard!" I leap from my seat, ready to kill him with my bare hands. "Let him go!"

This is exactly the reaction he wants, but I can't keep calm, knowing what he's done to Saint.

"All in good time. But there are things I want from you. And there are things Astra wants."

"What?" It's all I can stomach to say because here's the catch, the real reason I'm here.

"You killed her beloved, and she must avenge his death."

"Fine. She can have her revenge. Just let Saint go."

Oscar sighs, brushing invisible lint from his sleeve. "I wish it were that simple. But it's not."

And there it is. There are no gray areas. Only black and white. To get Saint back, it simply won't be as easy as handing over the information they want. Yes, they want it, but they want to see me suffer more. And they know I'll do what they say because I'll do anything to set Saint free.

"How can you do this to him?" I spit, unable to mask my hatred for him. "You clearly feel something for him to go to the efforts that you have, yet you punish him and keep him here against his will. And all for what? To see him suffer? Does that give you pleasure?"

Oscar swallows deeply. Have I struck a nerve?

Nevertheless, I'm done playing. "So what are the terms? What do I have to do?"

Oscar skims his fingertips along the table. When he finally speaks, I realize he was only drawing out the inevitable. "It only seems fair you watch your beloved suffer as Astra watched hers. An eye for an eye."

Squeezing my eyelids shut, I lock away my tears because I need to be strong. This place will break me otherwise. "Fine. But I refuse to entertain your sick ways without an end date. There has to be some finality."

Oscar nods. "Yes, okay. I accept those terms. How quickly can Alek's contact meet us?"

"As soon as I call him," I reply, not wanting to get my hopes up.

"Excellent. The doctors think Astra will be strong enough in about two weeks. Does that suit you?"

"Two weeks?" I cry out. Two weeks in this place will amount to two hundred years.

But when Oscar's stern expression doesn't waver, it's evident this isn't up for discussion. "Merely a drop in the ocean compared to the lifetime of pain Astra faces without Borya."

"Fine," I finally agree, but I'm hoping to change his mind in the next few days. Or at the very least, have Pavel come up with another plan before then.

"Wonderful." Oscar claps his hands, celebrating a job well done. "You see, we *can* work together."

"Fuck you," I retort, not appreciating his patronizing tone.

He laughs merrily, my insult bouncing straight off him. Once he's done snickering, he barks an order in Russian. A second later, a man appears holding an old-fashioned phone.

I eye it suspiciously.

"Call him," Oscar says, offering me the handset.

"Call who?" I ask, lost in translation.

"Alek's contact. The man of the hour," he clarifies while I get my head in the game. "To gain your trust, I have used this outdated phone so I'm unable to trace the number. It doesn't even have a redial option."

But I'm not stupid. He is probably tracing the call, which means I'll keep the conversation short. Hopefully, Pavel is listening in, so he will be expecting me.

Reaching for the phone, I ensure our hands don't touch, which, judging by his slanted smirk, Oscar finds quite humorous. Ignoring him, I turn my back and dial the number Pavel gave me. When it rings, my palms begin to sweat.

When it continues to ring without an answer, I begin to panic. Has something gone wrong? Just when I'm about to hang up and dial again, in fear my trembling fingers have dialed the wrong number, Pavel's hoarse voice answers.

He speaks in Russian, which means he knows Oscar is listening.

Putting my game face on, I turn around and lock eyes with Oscar. "It's me. You still want to make money?"

I recite the speech we practiced over and over again. We are going to work the angle that Pavel has only agreed to work with Oscar and Astra because he needs the money and they are trusted confidants of Alek.

"Yes. When?"

I'm about to reply when Oscar gestures he wants the phone. Without a fuss, I pass it to him and hope my nerves don't show.

He never breaks eye contact with me when he begins to speak in Russian. This was one of the possible scenarios Pavel prepared me for, so I stand quietly, refusing to buckle under Oscar's intense stare. They speak for a few moments, which is mainly Oscar asking him questions, I think, because when his eyebrows shoot up toward his hairline, it's evident he's impressed with what he hears.

They finally say their goodbyes, and Oscar hangs up, smiling. "Well, it appears you were telling the truth," he says, pushing back his chair and coming to a stand.

"Of course, I was." I want to know what they discussed, but I don't dare ask.

"I had to make sure," he replies. "Only Alek's contact would know the amount shipped to us two months ago and how much money we paid. I also asked him some questions which were only known by us."

I don't know how Pavel knew, but we have fooled Oscar—for now.

"I will ensure Astra knows a meeting has been set for two weeks from today. She will be most pleased." His comment reveals his desperate need to win his way back into her good books, but I'm unmoved by his happiness.

Folding my arms across my chest, I glare at Oscar, daring him to refuse me. "I held up my end of the bargain. It's now time you do the same. I want to see him."

This is the ultimate standoff because if he denies me, I will throw the silver knife, which is within reach, at his head. He must read my determination because he nods.

"Okay."

I should be happy he agreed, but truth be told, I'm scared. I don't know exactly what I'm walking into, but I know it won't be good.

Oscar doesn't waste any more time and leads me from the dining room down the long corridor. It's eerily quiet; so much so, my footsteps echo off the pristine walls. I have no idea where he's leading me, but the farther we walk, the more ominous things become because something sinister lingers in the air.

When we reach an old wooden door, I wipe my sweaty palms onto my jeans because this seems so out of place in a modern house. Oscar opens it with a big brass key, revealing a steel spiral staircase leading into a dark, dank basement.

He moves aside, hinting I'm to go first. I can't be sure he hasn't brought me here to kill me, but nonetheless, I commence a slow walk down, holding the cool rails so I don't break my neck. A small yelp escapes me when the door slams shut behind me.

However, that soon turns to a surprised gasp because the door closing has triggered a row of lights to illuminate the way down. They are dim, but they are enough for me to see it's not too far down. My feet can barely keep up as I race down the narrow steps, ready to face whatever is down here.

But when I descend the final step, I realize that no, I'm really not because what I see rips the air from my lungs. I come to a violent stop, blinking rapidly to ensure my eyes aren't deceiving me.

They're not.

I can't speak. I'm barely breathing, and I doubt I ever will be able to breathe soundly again because the sight before me will be marred onto my soul forever. I want to go to him, but I can't. My feet refuse to move.

My brain can't process what I'm seeing because it's too horrifying to accept as truth.

"No," I weep, unable to stop my tears, but I will never be able to shed enough to express this guttural hollowness I feel.

A broken man is shackled to a wooden Saint Andrew's Cross. His arms are extended above him, his legs spread. Thick silver chains attach his wrists and ankles to the barbaric device, not allowing him any movement as he is bound tight.

His modesty is covered by a pair of flimsy black underwear.

"No," I repeat, shaking my head, unable to accept this man as being my Saint.

His head hangs low, his chin dropped to his oiled chest.

He barely looks alive. His dirty blond hair covers his face, so a small part of me is in denial, refusing to accept this as him. But when my eyes focus on the tattoo on his flank, the one which inspired mine, the one which reads *SINNER*, I can no longer pretend.

This is my Saint. My warrior. My protector. The man I love with every beat of my heart. But that man…he's gone.

This can't be real. This can't be my life.

Oh, god, I'm going to be sick.

Covering my mouth, I smother my whimpers. I need to be strong. "Wh-what have you done to h-him?" I barely recognize this voice as my own.

"I think the better question is…what *haven't* I done?" is Oscar's sick, smug response. He will pay. Oh yes, he will pay. But for now, I need to make sure Saint is okay.

I frantically scan his body, flinching when I see the healing wound over his chest where Astra's bullet would have killed him. But Oscar has seen he was well looked after because the wound is healing. His tattoos glisten under the dim lighting as it appears his body is slathered in oil.

He has red welts across his muscled chest and legs, and I recognize them well because once upon a time, I had them too. He's been whipped. Fresh slashes trickle red along the inside of his thighs where someone has taken a knife and cut him.

The shallow rise and fall of his chest is the only sign he's alive. When I zero in on the two blood red roses tattooed on his chest and the words *Only God Can Judge Me*, the severity of this clusterfuck hits home and animates me, flipping the switch to survival mode.

I can grieve later because now, I have to act.

I have to save Saint.

A surge pulses through me, and I run forward, gripping his cheeks in my palms and gently coaxing him to look at me. His head is heavy and limp, and his oiled skin leaves him slippery, making it almost impossible to keep his head from dropping back down. He smells of coconuts, and I realize it's whatever oil he's lathered in.

"Saint!" I cry, steadying his cheek with one hand while desperately trying to brush the damp hair from his brow. His long hair flicks forward, shielding his eyes from mine.

A pained moan leaves him as he weakly fights me. "No." He gasps in a winded breath, attempting to shrug from my hold.

But I'm stronger and finally sweep his hair aside so I can see his face. When I do, a fresh set of tears cascade down my cheeks. Those chartreuse eyes, the ones which brought me back to life time and time again, are sealed shut, the deep purple revealing they've been pummeled closed.

His lips are swollen, his bottom one split open and caked with dry blood. His face is a bloodied, broken mess. He barely looks like the man I know.

He moans in pain when I wipe away the blood from his mouth. "Shh, it's okay. I'm here now, and I w-won't let anyone hurt you a-again." I'm trying to be strong, but seeing Saint this way does something that injures me beyond repair.

"No," he groans, the corded veins in his neck popping as he tries to escape my touch. "Don't, don't touch me."

"Saint, it's me. Willow," I coo, unable to stop stroking him, wanting to take away his pain.

"You're not real," he pants, shaking his head, but it lolls to the side as his strength is fading.

For him to be so weak, it's clear Oscar has given him something. This is the only way he could keep him chained up this way.

"I am real," I affirm, stroking his cheeks with my fingertips. "I'm here."

"No!" he cries, his broken body quivering. Even sedated and chained to a cross, his stubbornness doesn't falter. "This is another trick. You're not here."

"Saint, please, believe me. It's me." I tug violently at the restraints around his wrists, but it's useless. They're done up so tight, they've flayed the flesh from his bone.

"You've haunted me every night," he pants, and what he says next shatters me into a million unrepairable pieces. "Haunted me with what I've lost."

"No," I cry, begging he open his eyes and look at me as I softly kiss his cheeks, his nose, his brow. "I'm right here. Open your eyes. You haven't lost me."

His head sags backward, and it's clear he's slipping back into the abyss. But I won't lose him to the darkness. He's been there for far too long.

With my palms cupping his warm cheeks, I lower my lips to his gently and whisper against them the only words I can to make him understand that I'm really here. "запомни, я всегда рядом."

It's what he said to me when he left. So, it seems fitting

because this time, we will never leave one another ever again.

His pained moans soften, and he stills. I hold my breath, praying for a miracle. And when his eyelids flicker open, softly like a butterfly hatching from a cocoon, I get it.

My miracle.

My Saint.

The confusion is clear as he tries to focus. He's fighting to stay awake, so I give him all the time he needs. Caressing over the apple of his cheeks with my thumbs, I lock eyes with the other half of my heart, the half that has been missing until now.

He wets his dry lips, flinching when he tongues over the wound. He examines me closely, and at first, it appears he doesn't recognize me. But when those black orbs spark a vibrant green, the darkness ebbs away.

"Ангел?" he whispers, his disbelief clear as he blinks intermittently. "You're here?"

"Yes, I'm really here," I affirm, brushing back his hair as I sniff back my tears. To hear him utter that name completes me.

"How?" he cries, leaning into my touch. "You should be gone. Back home."

His vulnerability crushes me, but now is not the time to tell him his sacrifice was for nothing because his sister thought she was doing the right thing. I need to get him down. "It doesn't matter. I'm here now, and I'm getting you out of here." I tug at the restraints again, cursing when it's evident they're not coming undone without a key.

He grunts in pain when I touch his wrist, sharply turning

his cheek. And when he does, I see something which changes the course of everything. In the deepest, darkest corner of my mind, I knew this happened, but seeing it…is something else.

Gripping Saint's chin, I turn his cheek so I can take a closer look. I am sickened beyond belief.

I never knew what anger was until this moment. I never thought I was capable of taking another human being's life. But the raised, red bite marks along the column of Saint's neck have me envisioning ways to kill Oscar. And kill him slow.

"Wh-who did this to you?" I stutter over my words, tears of fury burning me raw.

When realization hits Saint, he instantly recoils from my touch. He lowers his head, using his hair as a shield. Something…ugly passes over him.

His detachment confuses me. "Saint—"

But I never get to finish.

"Get her out of here."

"*What?*" I gasp, certain I've had a lapse in hearing. "What are you saying?"

Every part of me is crumbling.

"Leave. I don't want you here," he snarls. "I said go!"

His anger and newfound vitality burn me, and I stagger backward in confusion. "I'm, I'm not going anywhere."

I don't know why he's pushing me away. But when he slowly lifts his chin, I see it…he's ashamed. "Saint—"

But he violently shakes his head, screaming in pain when he violently yanks against the chains. Wrapping my arms around my middle, sporadic sobs spill from me because I don't understand what's happening. "Let me h-help y-you."

Tears are streaming down my cheeks, but he stubbornly won't let me. He says something in Russian. He is breathless, and his body trembles uncontrollably.

Am I causing this reaction? Am I causing him more pain?

Placing a hand over my mouth, I watch on in horror, never anticipating our reunion to pan out this way. We lock eyes, and I see the darkness has won. Saint's demons have triumphed once and for all.

"Come, you heard him. He doesn't want you here." When Oscar grips my bicep, I recoil violently.

How dare he.

Spinning around, I'm primed on killing him. But the gun he holds reveals it's a fight I won't win. But that doesn't stop me as I glare at Oscar even though I'm addressing Saint. "I'm coming back. Whether you want me to or not."

Oscar's lips twist into a sick, victorious smirk. This is what he's always wanted; for Saint to send me away. But I soon wipe his smirk clean.

Standing on tippy toes, I coolly rest my hands on his shoulders and murmur into his ear, "And I'm coming for you too."

Before he has a chance to reprimand me, I walk toward Saint, hand in my back pocket, and press my lips to his cheek, regardless of the fact he withdraws from my touch. When my lips come away with a salty kiss, I avow to make those who hurt him pay.

Stroking his hair one last time, I reach behind him, and whisper, "You're not alone."

He simply hangs his head in defeat.

No matter how badly my heart breaks, I give Saint what he wants and push past Oscar, refusing to show this man weakness because he thrives on the pain. I march up the stairs, adrenaline coursing through me because I meant what I said…Saint is not alone—the bug I planted on the cross he is tied to ensures it.

CHAPTER FIVE

Day 95

I've showered twice, but I still feel filthy. I can still smell the depravity, and I doubt it'll ever leave me.

Leaving Saint down there was the hardest thing I've ever had to do, but as much as it hurts, me being with him was causing him more pain. I'm numb, as seeing the man I love shackled and demeaned that way is something I could never put into words.

The bite marks along his neck reveal Oscar's sick perversion has been put into play. I don't know how far he's taken it, but whatever he's done, he's broken Saint. There is only so much a man can take, and with his fragile mind, I fear he'll be lost to the darkness for good.

I can only hope Pavel hears the agony he's in, prompting him to step up his plan of attack because after seeing Saint, I don't think he'll last two weeks. And neither will I.

A soft knock on the door indicates it's not Oscar, as he

wouldn't knock. When it opens and I see a familiar face, my blood turns cold. The last time I saw Ingrid, she was paraded around like a well-trained poodle. Just as when I saw her then, I feel sorry for her now.

There is something soft, almost naïve about her—qualities a man like Oscar preys on.

With long blonde hair and deep blue eyes, she is absolutely stunning. I can see why Alek succumbed to her charms, which is what, in a roundabout way, started this vendetta between him and Oscar. But the way he spoke about her, and the way she looked at him, it was clear feelings were involved.

She enters the room with a serene grace and softly closes the door.

I wait for her to speak because when my gaze drops to a sheer white garment in her hand, I realize she isn't here for a casual chat.

"I know we've met, but I'm Ingrid," she says in a voice barely above a whisper. Her accent is strong, but I'm not sure where she's from.

"Hi, I'm Willow," I reply, hating that I'm suddenly so standoffish toward her. Until I know if she's friend or foe, I need to keep my walls in place.

"I know." She casts her eyes downward. "Th-thank you for what you did." When I'm silent, unsure what she means, she clarifies, "That night, you asked for clemency for Dominic and me. Thank you."

Something inside me softens, and I instantly warm toward her. We are both prisoners, forced into a world we don't belong.

"You don't have to thank me." I hope Oscar was true to his word. "Do you know if the man downstairs in the basement has been kept there for long?"

"You mean Saint?"

My heart skips a beat. "Yes. Do you know him?"

She nods, using her hair as a veil. "He was kind to me when Alek asked him to take me home."

Alek never went into detail about his affair with Ingrid. Saint mentioned Alek exploited her and discarded her once he was done, but from the way she looked at Alek and the way she just whispered his name, I think he's wrong.

"Is it true? Is it true you don't know where Alek is?" she asks with a quiver to her lip as she raises her chin to look at me.

It's evident she's in pain, but whether I trust her or not, these walls have ears. "Yes, it's true. I got knocked out during the explosion. When I woke up, Alek was gone."

I can't help but feel as if I've just kicked a puppy.

Ingrid's poignant eyes fill with tears. "He must be dead," she says, shaking her head slowly, appearing unable to accept the words as truth.

"Why? Maybe he got out." I attempt to reassure her as I add in the last part softly, hoping it's low enough not to be heard by the surveillance.

But she won't accept it, and when she reveals why that is, I swallow down this constant, lingering lump in my throat when it comes to Alek. "Because he would never leave you. I saw the way he was with you. He cared for you. Deeply. I've never seen him that way with anyone. Even with me."

She quickly slaps a hand over her mouth, appearing regretful for saying too much.

Her comment was supposed to be a compliment, but I don't want to hear it. Alek and I didn't leave on the best of terms. He wasn't even there when I left the orphanage. I wasn't expecting a ticker tape parade, but I expected at least a goodbye.

However, he made his feelings perfectly clear when he walked out of my room.

"You're mistaken," I say with bite. We can't be having this conversation.

Instantly, she submits, bowing her head in apology, and I feel like an ass for snapping.

"Sorry, I'm just worried about Saint. He is very special to me." I don't need to elaborate. She reads me loud and clear.

She lifts her chin, gently brushing the hair from her rosy cheeks. "Yes," she says, replying to my original question. "I believe Oscar has had Saint down there since he arrived weeks ago. Dominic and I have been forbidden to go down there, but late at night, I can"—she licks her lips nervously—"I can hear him scream."

Squeezing my eyes shut, I try to block out the sounds and sight I bore witness to, but nothing can erase them from my mind. They're burned into me forever.

"I have to get him out of there," I whisper, the urgency growing quicker by the minute as I refocus.

Ingrid nods, but she knows it's a lot easier said than done. "Maybe you'll have your chance tonight."

I arch a brow, intrigued.

She only seems to remember the garment in her hand. "I was told to bring you this."

She offers me a sheer sarong which one could be forgiven for mistaking as a curtain.

"Am I supposed to wear that?" I ask, horrified.

She nods.

Her attire isn't any better. Her silky white nightgown doesn't leave much to the imagination either, but this sarong is completely sheer.

"Not going to happen," I say firmly. "What else were you told?"

Ingrid chews her bottom lip. "Once you were dressed, I was to take you to Oscar's bedroom."

Sighing, I wonder when this perversion will end. "Fine, let's go."

Ingrid doesn't press and leaves the sarong on the end of my bed. She opens the door and leads me out into the hallway. I have no idea where Oscar's bedroom is, but I ensure the bugs in my back pocket are within reach so I can plant them when I get a chance.

Ingrid almost floats through the corridor on her bare feet, and I wonder how Oscar could treat someone so angelic the way he does her. What did she do to be here, trapped in this prison?

All thoughts are put on the backburner for now when we climb the elaborate red-carpeted stairs because I know shit is about to get real. This floor is decorated in royal blues and gold hues. Seeing few doorways in this part of the house leads me to believe this is Oscar's private wing, which is usually off-limits.

"Is his office up here?" I ask softly.

Ingrid gestures with her head toward the second door on the left.

Bingo.

Now, I just need to figure out a way inside.

That can wait, though, because when we get to the last room in the hallway, Ingrid knocks on the double doors. Her shoulders rise and her breathing gets heavier, which can only mean we're here. The doors open, and when I see Oscar, donned in silk blue pajamas, I prepare myself for what's about to come.

His arrogant smile soon fades when he sees me in black jeans and a white T-shirt, clothes which were kindly given to me by one of the sisters in the orphanage.

He turns to Ingrid, who cowers under his gaze. "You didn't give her the garment?"

Before she has a chance to reply, I step in. "She did."

"So why aren't you wearing it?" he snaps, his eyes narrowing into slits.

Tapping my chin, I appear to be in mock thought when I reply, "Because see-through isn't really my color."

His jaw clenches.

I'm expecting him to scold me, but he surprises me when he takes a deep breath and then permits us into his bedroom. I go in first, shielding Ingrid because I don't want him to take my insolence out on her.

This room is as obnoxious as Oscar. The domed ceiling has an alcove cut in the center, and a large chandelier hangs from the middle. The ivory furnishings set off the gold color scheme, and the large plush headboard on the king-size bed looks like something fit for royalty.

If the room didn't belong to a psychopath, I would say it was quite beautiful, but where a wall has been cut, replaced with a blue and gold velvet stage curtain, all beauty has long gone. Without a doubt something sinister lurks behind that curtain.

Oscar notices me eyeing it. "Do you like it?"

This man is a narcissistic asshole. "No, I do not like it," I reply blankly. "Why am I here?"

I am done with pretenses and games. I just want to know what's next.

Oscar's patience is wearing thin, but he soon composes himself. "No foreplay then?"

"You really love the sound of your own voice, don't you?" I taunt, unable to hold back.

In response, he laughs. It has the hair on my arms standing on end. "Have it your way then."

I don't know what that means until the curtains part, and my nightmare begins.

Saint is flanked by two men who drag him into the room. His hands are handcuffed behind him. Even though he is stumbling, thanks to the drugs forced into his system, he still struggles against them.

I'm instantly hit with the smell of coconuts, the same fragrance I smelled when down in the basement. He's once again slick with oil, and I can't help but compare his golden skin to that of a basted turkey on Thanksgiving.

Why is Oscar preparing him this way?

His head is downcast, his face shielded by his damp hair, so he doesn't seem to notice me here. But even if he did, after our last encounter, would he want to see me?

The men hold him tightly, stopping a few feet away.

"I have tried, to no avail, to get him to like me, but he just won't submit," Oscar says in a huff before adding, "like you." He peers down at my clothes, curling his lip.

It seems Saint suddenly realizes he's not alone. He slowly lifts his chin, gauging his surroundings. His hair is swept across his eyes, but when they widen, and he blinks once, as if attempting to focus, I know he's seen me.

I want to go to him, but the last time I did that, I seemed to make things worse. So I stand tall, unbending.

Oscar walks toward me, circling me and coming to rest at my back. He runs his hands up and down my arms while I bite the inside of my cheek, tasting the sharp metallic tang of blood. "I think I know why that is. Touch him."

"Excuse me?" I gasp, recoiling from his lips that are way too close to my ear.

"You heard me. It's not my touch he craves. It's yours." But there's a catch. There always is. "What's the matter? You don't want to touch him? Earlier, you couldn't seem to stop."

Saint sways on his feet, but we never break eye contact. He may be dancing with delirium, but he's still semi coherent. He parts his lips, as if attempting to speak, but his mouth hangs open uselessly. It seems he's not in control of his muscles.

This sight is my undoing.

I shrug Oscar away, walking slowly toward Saint. His eyes widen as if he's begging me to stay away. But I can't. However,

I use this opportunity to stumble, breaking my fall by holding the footboard. The move was done on purpose because I have just planted bug number four.

Once I regain my footing, I continue walking toward Saint. The closer I get to him, the harder he fights against his captors to get away from me. I can't help but feel dejected. Regardless, once I'm a few feet away, I stop and curl my hands into fists.

I want nothing more than to touch him, to take away his pain, but it's evident he'd rather I not. When we first met, he shied away from being touched, but we jumped that hurdle, as well as many others. Now, though, this seems so much worse.

"Go on then," Oscar coaxes, thoroughly enjoying the show.

Inhaling, I beg he give me a sign that this is okay. That we will get through this. But when he squeezes his eyes shut and turns his cheek, I know it never will be ever again. Even though he may have given up, I haven't, and I never will.

With a hesitant touch, I slowly place my hands on his cheeks, pleading with him to look at me. He fights me, groaning, but he is no match, thanks to his drugged state.

"Saint, please don't give up," I whisper, sniffing back my tears. "I will get you out of here. I promise."

He merely moans in response.

Brushing back his matted hair, I run my fingers over his full beard and cradle his cheek in my palm. "Where is the stubborn son of a bitch I've come to know? Fight!" My desperation shines. I need him to snap the fuck out of this.

I understand he's broken, but I am too.

"Please, don't leave me." I press my lips to his forehead, to the tip of his nose, and lastly, to his mouth. I kiss him chastely because his lip is still cracked.

A small bubble of hope swells within me when a miracle happens—I feel him kiss me back.

I forget about the two men watching and pretend it's just Saint and me. I gently thread my fingers through the long locks curling at his nape and deepen our connection. He groans softly.

To feel him this way, to have him in my arms is indescribable, and tears stream down my cheeks. When they slip into our parted lips, a pained sigh leaves Saint before he pulls away and rubs his nose against mine, reassuring me.

More tears soon follow.

He may be handcuffed and wounded, both physically and psychologically, but here he is, comforting me. My love for this man knows no bounds, and I will do anything, anything to make sure he leaves here.

Unable to stop myself, I wrap my arms around his nape and hug him tightly, burying my face into the side of his neck. He leans forward, accepting the comfort, accepting my touch. Our hearts beat in unison, finally reunited.

"Trust me, okay?" I whisper into his ear, nuzzling into him and savoring our closeness because I've craved it since the moment I lost him. Even though he doesn't smell like him, my body hums at being pressed up against him this way.

He nods floppily in response. "Okay...ангел."

"Incredible." Oscar's voice ruins the mood. I'd almost forgotten he was here—almost. "That was awfully touching, but I'm still not convinced."

"I don't give a fuck what you think," I spit, spinning quickly over my shoulder to face him. I ensure to keep a hand wrapped around the back of Saint's neck.

Oscar isn't affected in the slightest by my insult. "You will. Ingrid." With a flick of his head, he gestures for her to go to Saint.

I am about to ask what is happening, but when one of the men lets Saint go, only to grab me and drag me over to Oscar, it's apparent that talk time is over.

Oscar wraps his arms around my middle to stop me from turning around and punching him in the face. I wiggle madly, but it's useless. He has a strong hold. The man returns to Saint, who is struggling weakly to break free.

"Let, let her go," he pants, words clearly painful for him to speak.

Oscar doesn't do as he asks. Instead, he reveals why we're really here. "Ingrid, on your knees." When she is about to drop to her knees, facing him, he tsks her. "No, facing Saint."

My stomach drops because I have no idea what's about to happen.

Ingrid does as Oscar asks, not that she has a choice. She awaits further instruction.

"Do you think he is handsome?" Oscar questions her while I fight with all my might to break free.

"Yes, Oscar, very handsome," she replies in a robotic tone, peering up at Saint.

"You have splendid taste. Now it's your turn to touch him."

Ingrid turns over her shoulder to look at Oscar, then at

me. "Haven't I made myself clear enough?" he mocks in a patronizing tone.

Ingrid's lower lip trembles.

"Just in case you've misunderstood, I want you to take Saint's cock and put it into your mouth. He won't come for me, but maybe he'll come for you."

The walls close in on me, and I suddenly can't get enough air.

Saint sways from side to side as he tries to fight his way to freedom, but he's too weak, and so is Ingrid when her eyes express how sorry she is before she turns around. Working on autopilot, she lowers Saint's boxer briefs, revealing his semi erection.

Oscar hisses when he sees Saint naked, a shiver vibrating through him. Bile rises because he makes me sick.

"That's for you," he whispers into my ear while I turn my cheek in disgust.

I now understand why he wanted me to touch Saint. He knew Saint would respond to me, and this sick show can't be complete with a flaccid cock.

"Ingrid."

Her name alone is enough of a command as Ingrid lowers her head and takes Saint into her mouth. At first, I refuse to believe the sight as real, but soon, the sounds of her pleasuring my lover cannot be ignored. She grips the base of him and sucks him deeply while he squirms, grunting against her to break free.

The men hold him tightly, both grinning deviously as they watch Ingrid suck him off.

Every part of me demands I close my eyes to erase this image for good, but I can't because when Saint's frantic eyes meet mine, begging for forgiveness, I need him to know it's okay. I'm here with him.

"Do you want this to stop?" Oscar says, squeezing my middle.

"Yes." I hate that my feeble voice betrays me.

"Tell me where Alek is."

A breath catches in my throat when I realize what this is. I thought I was so smart, certain I had them fooled, but I haven't fooled anyone. They don't believe me, and what better way to test me than by doing…this.

They think by torturing me, I will surrender and give them what they really want, which is Alek. I was fucking stupid not to see this sooner.

But I can't. I tell him, and we're all dead. They will storm the orphanage, killing everyone in their path. Thinking of the sisters who were so kind to me, as well as Mother Superior and all the children, I know I can't risk the lives of so many. I just can't.

"I don't know!" I cry out as his grip on me becomes punishing.

Even though he is only half aware, Saint knows I'm lying, and the wounded look in his eyes affirms this. But if only he knew why I was doing this. I have to trust Pavel because as he said, Alek is our last bargaining chip. But Saint doesn't see it that way.

He sees my words as me choosing Alek's safety over his. But it's not like that. "I'm sorry," I mouth to him, hoping he understands.

He doesn't.

"We'll see," Oscar says, licking my cheek in one long stroke.

The corded veins in Saint's neck are close to popping because it's clear he's trying hard not to respond to her touch. But he's only human. We all are. And soon, I can see him surrender to the torture.

I keep the tears at bay because this is my fault. I deserve this as punishment. If I had given Oscar what he wanted, this would be over for good. Saint's fight soon dwindles, and the noises leaving him turn primeval and angry.

Ingrid takes his cock in deep, gagging when he thrusts into her mouth. He is no longer here. The fire behind his eyes has extinguished, and all that's left is a hollowness which has me choking on my silent tears.

He sees my actions as a betrayal, and he has every right to because I do too.

His body rolls with a sluggish tempo, allowing Ingrid's touch. And even though this shatters me, I understand that after being subjected to nothing but torture, a tender touch heightens everything beyond words.

When you've felt nothing but pain, the pleasure is welcomed. Everything feels so good compared to the suffering. I know this because wasn't I the same way? When Saint spanked me and even when he whipped me, I took the pain and turned it into pleasure, and that's what he's doing right now.

He begins to fight it, but it's no use. His taut body ripples and vibrates before he comes with a strangled, humiliated sob. Ingrid gags but doesn't spill a drop.

The room falls silent while I just want to curl into a ball and die.

My ache is heroin to Oscar. "You see," he mocks. "You aren't that special. He'd come for any whore who dropped to her knees."

But that's not true. This may have been done with intent for me to believe that, but I don't. I know what Oscar wants. He wishes for me to question my relationship with Saint, hoping that I will believe he isn't worth the trouble, and therefore, give Oscar and Astra what they want—Alek.

But it's going to take a lot more than that.

I just hope Saint understands.

Ingrid eventually pulls away, her trembling fingers wiping her mouth. Saint's chest rises and falls, his staggered breathing labored and pained. His head is bowed. I need him to look at me, to assure me that it'll, that *we'll*, be okay.

But he doesn't.

Oscar hums in victory. "You will break. And so will he," he ominously promises, ordering the guards to take Saint away.

The fight in him is gone as he allows them to lead him through the curtain, never turning back.

CHAPTER SIX

Day 96

I returned to my prison cell and cried myself into oblivion. It was peaceful there, a place where I didn't have to face deplorable acts that tainted my very soul. But I couldn't stay there forever because I will not allow this hell to break me.

Once upon a time, Saint was strong for me, and now, I must do the same for him.

Being surrounded by nothing but four walls without a lick of daylight is another form of torture. I feel like I'm going crazy. I've paced this cage countless times, hoping Pavel pulls some Russian spy shit and somersaults through the ceiling with a helicopter in tow.

But no one is here to save me. That wasn't part of the plan. I knew this was going to be tough, but I was not prepared for the things I've seen.

Running a hand through my snarled hair, I wonder how

long Oscar intends to keep me locked in here. Cabin fever has kicked in, and I need out. Not to mention, I can't remember the last time I ate. Unable to stand it any longer, I race to the door and bang on it.

"Hey! Let me out!" I scream, my thumping growing louder.

No surprise, my request is ignored, but I've got nothing but time and anger, so I continue pounding and screaming.

Just when I think I will be forced to do this all day, the lock clicks and the door opens. When I see Oscar, I instantly regret my decision.

"You called?" he sarcastically quips.

"I need to eat."

"Such a demanding little thing, aren't you?"

There is so much wrong with that sentence, but I don't bother to entertain him because I've decided not to speak to him unless necessary. I fold my arms across my chest, arching a brow.

Oscar is highly amused. "All right. Follow me."

We exit in silence, which I'm thankful for.

I'm on high alert, scoping out my surroundings as I have one more bug to plant. I really want to get to Oscar's office, as I can only imagine what goes on in there, but when he leads me into a well-stocked kitchen, my stomach rumbles, and all thoughts of espionage are put on hold.

He walks over to the large silver refrigerator and opens the door. I watch as he retrieves what looks like deli meats, cheese, and a Tupperware container filled with crisp green lettuce. I practically salivate at the sight but keep my hunger hidden because depending on him for survival is just another reason to make him smile.

He places everything on the counter before reaching for two plates. My appetite is suddenly shot because I'd rather starve than share a meal with this man.

"Water?" he casually asks.

My parched throat has me nodding my head. He turns back around and hunts for a bottle of Evian in the fridge. He's being far too civil for my liking, and I can't help but think he's up to something.

"How did you sleep?"

All right, that's it. I'm not here for small talk.

Accepting the bottle of water, I unscrew the lid and drink it dry. Once I'm done, I wipe my lips with the back of my hand. "The little sleep I did have was plagued with nightmares of the man I love getting his dick sucked by your concubine. So what do you think?"

I don't bother masking my feelings for Saint because I am done with pretenses. Oscar can't use it as leverage because it seems we both have one thing in common, and that's Saint.

However, seeing his treatment of him has me wondering if Oscar cares about Saint at all.

My comment has caught him off guard as his mouth opens and closes. I leave him to gape like a fish and lean across the counter to retrieve the food. Tearing open the Tupperware container, I stuff my cheeks full of lettuce.

Still chewing, I rip open the meat packet, uncaring what it is, and cram it into my already full mouth. My gaze remains fixed on Oscar the entire time. I don't fail to notice the lack of silverware, but I don't blame him. Give me a knife or I'd even settle for a spoon, and I would ensure I drove it as deep into Oscar's eyeballs as I could.

"If you weren't so stubborn, this could all be over with. You know what I want."

"Well, I want to paint this room with your entrails, but we can't always get what we want," I say around a mouthful of food.

Oscar launches across the counter, ready to drag me over it. But I stand unmoved, chewing happily. I am slowly becoming desensitized to this world of violence.

"What sort of cheese is this?" I ask calmly, unwrapping it and bringing it to my nose. "I hate blue cheese."

Oscar soon composes himself and takes a step back from the counter, inhaling slowly. He runs a hand down his white shirt, appearing to need a moment to compose himself.

The sight pleases me beyond words, and after ensuring the cheese is free of mold, I break off a chunk with my fingers. Popping it into my mouth, I groan in delight, ruining Oscar's newfound Zen.

"You're only making this harder on yourself. Astra—"

But I'm done talking. "That's some good cheese," I interrupt, chewing loudly and relishing in the sight of Oscar's reddening cheeks. If he and Astra believed I would roll over at the first sign of hardship, then they're in for a surprise.

As I'm tearing into a leafy piece of lettuce, soft voices disturb my eating. I pause my chewing because whoever it is, has Oscar's attention. They're speaking Russian, but when I hear the unmistakable sound of a woman's voice, Oscar's eyes widen before he reaches over the counter and grips my bicep.

"You're going back to your room."

He tries to drag me away, but I plant my feet firmly. Thanks to the counter between us, he doesn't have a strong hold on me, so I rip out from his hold. "Firstly, it's not and will never be my room. And secondly, don't tell me what to do."

He rounds the counter, hands clawed, but soon stops dead in his tracks when the voices grow closer, and finally, they're in the kitchen with us. I turn over my shoulder to see who it is.

One of them is Oscar's men, guiding the couple into the house. But from the flaring of Oscar's nostrils, I dare say they've turned up unannounced. He clears his throat, but his demeanor soon simmers, and he smiles.

He speaks to them in Russian, shaking the tall man's hand. At a guess, I'd say he was in his early thirties. He reeks of authority, and I instantly dislike him. The petite, older woman at his side, however, something about her seems so familiar.

I've never seen her before, of that I'm sure, but I can't deny feeling like we've met. Oscar notices me examining her closely and is clearly worried. He's about to shoo them out of the kitchen, but the woman steps away from the man and extends her hand.

She says hello in Russian, and just as Oscar opens his mouth, no doubt about to tell her I don't speak their language, I reply in Russian. Oscar's opened mouth is now hinged wide.

We shake hands, then she says something else. My Russian is limited, so I stop her from continuing. "Sorry, I only know the basics. Hello. Goodbye. Help me," I add while

Oscar snarls.

She smiles, and again, I can't shake this familiarity I feel around her.

Her steel blue eyes are hardened but not in a cruel way. More so like she's experienced a lot during her lifetime. The designer bag she holds reveals she's now well looked after. But I guess that's because of the man whose arm she holds.

Oscar is getting edgier by the second, which means she could ruin this for him. I need to know why that is. Just as she's about to say something, Oscar cuts her off in Russian, speaking rather quickly. The man nods while the woman looks disappointed she can't stay and chat.

Oscar's goon leaves the room, a hint they're to follow, but I can't let her go without uncovering just who she is. As she goes to turn, I lunge forward and gently stroke her bag. "I love this bag."

"Me too," she says slowly as her English is rather poor. But that's okay because so is my Russian. However, who needs language when you've got Chanel. "I take everywhere with me."

Oscar pushes me away, clearly not impressed with my appreciation of fashion. The man and woman leave the room, but not before she turns over her shoulder to take one last look at me. Once they're gone and out of earshot, Oscar walks toward me, staring me down.

In return, I smile smartly.

It appears he wants to say so many things, but whoever these people are, are evidently more important than reprimanding me.

Another one of Oscar's men appears and no points for guessing why. He's to escort me to my room. So done with the sight of Oscar, I turn to leave but am stopped when his fingers grip my forearm. "You'll learn that doing things my way will be a lot easier for you. And Saint."

If he's trying to scare me, he's shit out of luck. "I never said I wanted easy," I reply, yanking from his hold.

"Have it your way then," Oscar says as I happily leave.

As I walk to my room, chaperone in tow, I can't help but think that yes, I *will* have it my way because attached to the mystery lady's bag is the final bug. I can appreciate fine fashion, but honestly, I'm more of an Old Navy kinda girl.

Thanks to being locked in my cage all day, I had to be inventive to pass the time by. I've created my own circuit which consisted of squats, push-ups, lunges, and whatever else I could think of that would help me stay in shape.

I am dripping with perspiration, but I welcome the burn to my muscles. The more I sweat, the stronger I feel. Engaging in this monotonous activity keeps my mind busy. Every time my thoughts drift to Saint, I push myself harder, the agony the only fuel I need.

I am in the bathroom gulping down handfuls of water when I hear the door open. Quickly drying my hands on the towel, I peek around the doorjamb to see who it is. When our eyes meet, my cheeks blister in rage.

"I'm so sorry, Willow."

I know it's not Ingrid's fault. She didn't have a choice. But images of her down on her knees before Saint with his cock in her mouth have me wanting to kill her. But I rein in my temper.

"Hi," I curtly reply, walking into the bedroom. "What are you doing here? If I'm to be subjected to an encore performance, tell Oscar I would rather stay locked in this room."

She gnaws her bottom lip, wringing her hands in front of her. "I didn't want to—"

But I wave her off, not interested in discussing this further.

Her gaze darts from left to right, which piques my interest. She slowly walks to the corner of the room, gesturing for me to follow. She's here because she doesn't want to be seen by the camera.

I have no idea what is going on until she reaches beneath the collar of her dress and produces a silver necklace. There is a brass key on the end of it, one I've seen before.

"Go see him. Dominic and I will stall Oscar for as long as we can."

I blink once, not sure if we're on the same page.

When she yanks the chain off her neck and shoves it into my hand, I know that we are.

Clenching my fist around the key, I draw it to my heart. "Why are you doing this?" I need to understand why she is risking herself for me.

Shame overcomes her as she bows her head. "This is the only way I can show you how sorry I am."

I instantly regret my hostile reaction toward her because this isn't her fault. It's none of ours.

"Please be quick and keep to the shadows," she whispers, gripping my hand in her cold one.

"Thank you, Ingrid," I say with a quiver to my voice. "I know how dangerous this is for you."

"It's only dangerous if you get caught. Now go." She severs our connection and gestures toward the door. "I will leave the bedroom door open and lock it when you're back, so we don't rouse suspicion."

"Okay." There are a million things I want to say, but there just isn't any time because I'm not planning on coming back here.

Doing as she says, I slink into the camera's blind spot and sneak out the door.

I have no idea where the cameras are, but I have to believe they're currently unmanned, which is why Ingrid was able to sneak into my room undetected. Keeping my back pressed to the wall, I scale down the corridor, hoping my directions aren't off, and I'm going the right way.

Remembering the hideous artwork that resembles green vomit, I turn left and hold my breath when I'm faced with the wooden door. After I quickly ensure I'm not being followed, I slip the key into the lock and sigh in relief when it clicks open.

Without a minute to lose, I quietly close the door behind, which turns on the dim lighting and illuminates my path down to the basement. With my heart in my throat, I quickly descend the stairs, each heavy step cementing the reality of what I'm about to do.

I don't care how, but I am determined to break Saint free tonight. Pavel mentioned a secret passageway in Oscar's bedroom, and I plan on using it. I know where Oscar's bedroom is. No guessing the mysterious curtain is my out. I just have to figure out a way to break Saint free because when I sprint down the last step, it's so much worse than I imagined.

"Saint!" I cry, running toward him, frantically cupping his clammy cheeks. "Can you hear me?" His head is drooped forward, but I lift his face to meet mine.

When I am able to look at him, a pained whimper leaves me. His face is barely recognizable. It's evident he's had the shit beaten out of him.

"Wh-who did this to you?" I gasp, begging he open his eyes.

He moans in response as his head lolls like an overcooked piece of spaghetti.

"I'm getting you out of here," I promise, reaching for his wrists which are bound to the Saint Andrew's Cross.

He shrieks in agonizing pain, which has me jumping back in horror. When I see the cause of his anguish, I can't stop the tears which blind me. His left wrist is bent back at an unnatural angle, and although I'm not a doctor, it's safe to assume it's dislocated.

Saint groans incoherently, shaking his head from side to side. His eyes are still sealed shut, and I wonder if it's easier to face the nightmare this way. But he's not alone.

"Where's the key?" I don't wait for him to reply before I madly search the room. There isn't much down here, just a wooden table which looks like something out of the Middle

Ages. There are a few knives and some shiny devices which make my stomach roil because they're pointy and hard, and most definitely played a part in torturing the man I love.

I toss everything to the ground, screaming in frustration because there is no key.

Running a hand through my hair, I turn in a circle, hoping that by some miracle if I don't find the key, I can use something else to hack through the chains binding Saint's wrists and ankles. When I see the shackles hanging from the wall, bile rises up my throat.

This is a torture chamber in every sense of the word.

"I need you to try to stay awake. Can you do that for me?" I ask, running back over to him and gently caressing his cheek.

He flinches and tries to fight me, as I can only imagine he's only ever felt pain when down here.

"Shh," I coo, brushing the damp hair from his brow tenderly. "It's me. Willow. I need you to open your eyes for me, okay? We're getting out of here."

Pressing my lips to his forehead, I kiss him gently, inhaling his fragrance because I've missed it so much. Even though he still smells of coconut, beneath that sugary scent, his essence still lingers. "I'm so s-sorry he's done this to you." Unable to stop the tears, they cascade down my cheeks and somersault onto his.

He hums, and the sound isn't filled with pain.

"I need you to help me help you. Is there a key down here? Or is there something I can pick the locks with?" I peer up at the manacles around his wrists, wondering if I could use one of the knives to force it open.

There is only one way to find out.

Running over to the mess on the floor, I drop to a squat and hunt for something small enough to wedge into the lock. When I find something that looks like a scalpel, I grab it and sprint back over to Saint.

Working on his non injured wrist, I carefully force the tip of the blade into the lock, wiggling it from side to side. I don't know what I'm doing, but when I feel something give, I continue poking it. Saint's moans seem far away as though he's trapped in a bubble, which somewhat comforts me.

I want to spare him this pain, and if slipping into his happy place allows him even a second of reprieve, then I want him to stay there for as long as he can. I continue working on the lock, perspiration gathering along my brow as I focus on anything giving way.

Deep in concentration, I don't notice that Saint's eyes are open until he speaks. "Go," he pants, attempting to fix his gaze on me.

Adrenaline soars through me, and I desperately brush the hair from his face. His chartreuse eyes simmer dully, but they're open, and that's all that matters. "No, I'm not going anywhere."

He clenches his jaw, his eyes flickering in pain. "Leave… me…here. What I did to you…with Ingrid—"

His words are pained, but so is my heart because his request is one I will not obey. "Shh, save your strength."

When I attempt to work on the lock, he jerks his fist forward, demanding I listen. "It doesn't…matter now."

Blinking back my astonishment at his comment, I

shake my head firmly. "Of course, it matters! I'm not going anywhere."

But it seems by Saint's next assertion, he would rather I was gone. "You know"—he inhales deeply through his nose, catching his breath—"where...Alek is, but you choose to protect...him."

The scalpel trembles in my hand as my lips part in horror.

When I think I can speak, I beg him to believe me. "It's, it's not like that."

But Saint has heard enough. "I-I don't care anymore. Leave me. I deserve this...for what I've done. For what I've done...to you." He squeezes his eyes shut.

"Stop this," I cry, gripping his cheeks and forcing him to look at me. "You don't g-give up, you hear m-me? We are getting out of he-here. You and me." I'm skating so close to the edge. I'm trying to be strong, but seeing him this way, seeing him admit defeat is breaking apart whatever strength I have left.

"You're strong, Saint. Look at what you did. Look what you did to save me." Tears continue to fall because I can't stop this hollowed ache I feel. It's eating a hole straight through me.

But even when shackled and broken beyond repair, his stubbornness still shines. "I didn't save you because if I had... you wouldn't protect him."

And there it is. The reason I hate myself more and more each day.

If only I was stronger, Alek would be dead, and none of this would be happening. But something, something I can't explain, couldn't allow that to happen. I don't know why; I just know that Alek's death feels wrong.

"Why are you here? You were supposed to be gone?" I can understand his confusion. However, I wanted to explain everything when we were finally away from this place. But I owe him an explanation.

"Things didn't go as planned," I confess, biting my lip. "Zoey, she...she was the one who blew up the house."

Saint shakes his head, pained. "So it was all for nothing."

"Don't say that."

He simply lowers his gaze.

"Why are you pushing me away?" I whisper, gently pressing my palm to his cheek. He rips out my heart when he shudders under my hand. Can't he bear my touch? "I...I love you."

I wish the circumstances were different, but I want him to know how I feel because I never got to say it back.

Saint slowly runs his tongue over his split bottom lip, measuring his words. I can understand why that is. "Well, don't."

Staggering backward, I allow the darkness to evade me because his admission has shattered me into a million pieces. Why is he pushing me away?

"I can't stop," I confess with nothing but sadness, wrapping my arms around me. "Even if I tried." My confession has highlighted what a fucking idiot I am; to love someone who wishes you didn't.

Saint's shallow breaths echo the hopelessness, the invisible shackle which holds us down.

"You may have given up, but I haven't," I stubbornly cry.

Saint turns his cheek, pained.

With nothing left to say, I stand on tippy toes and continue working the lock. He may want me to go, but too bad, this isn't his choice. I want to tell Saint about the bug, but I've run out of words. So I work in silence, but the silence speaks volumes.

When the metal budges, a small bubble of hope wells inside me, and I holler in joy, but that's soon replaced with dread when I hear something which jumpstarts my panicky heart.

Saint's head snaps to attention, peering up at the stairs. When he hears the frantic footsteps pound down the steps, his eyes widen.

"Hide!" he cries, begging I listen.

But he should know by now that I don't do what I'm told.

With the scalpel in hand, I quietly run over to the staircase to hide in the shadows. Crouching low, I bide my time, and when I see one of Oscar's men, it seems my time has finally come. He bounces down the last step, not appearing to notice the mess I've made or the fact one of Saint's wrists is unbound.

He slurs something in Russian, hinting he's drunk.

Saint gestures with his eyes that I stay put and not jab the scalpel into this asshole's jugular, but it's too late. Vengeance is a potent drug; I see that now.

He sways to the left, suddenly coming to a slanted stop as he turns his attention to the implements decorating the floor. Before he has a chance to act, I creep up behind him, masking my footsteps and detaching myself from what's right and wrong. The only thing that matters is making this bastard pay.

Without hesitation and with retribution roaring through my veins, I raise my arm upward and stab him swiftly in the side of the throat. Hot, sticky blood coats my fingers before a gurgling sound fills the air. I pull out the scalpel and take a step back, unbelieving I feel no remorse because when the man turns around, clutching his throat with sheer terror in his eyes, I lunge forward and stab him again.

"Ангел, no!" Saint cries, but he doesn't get to decide anymore.

The man drops to his knees, blood spraying from between his fingers thanks to the deep gash in his throat. He attempts to stop the bleeding, but it's too late. He's dying, thanks to my hand. And for the first time ever…I feel nothing.

He lunges for me with a bloodied hand, a final act of defense, but I take a casual step backward, watching him coldly as he bleeds out before my eyes. It doesn't take long before he falls onto his stomach with a thud, his arm stretched out as he tries to reach for his murderer.

His chest wheezes as his lungs are starved of oxygen, and before long, the death rattle stills, announcing his death. The scalpel drops to the ground with a sharp crash. Hell has gained another demon.

Working on autopilot, I drop to a squat and rifle through his pockets. He's still warm to the touch, a thought which suddenly turns my stomach. But I hold back my nausea because it's done. I own this action because I feel no remorse.

Finding a set of keys, I stand quickly, ensuring not to slip in his blood which has stained my sneakers a bright red. Stepping over his body, I walk toward Saint, who shakes his head sadly. "You will always remember your first kill. I'm sorry."

I don't understand what he's apologizing for, but a small voice inside me whispers that what I've done will haunt me for the rest of my life. I tell that voice to shut the fuck up.

My fingers tremble as I try to unlock his cuffs, but I take a deep breath, telling myself to focus. Just as it clicks open, I celebrate prematurely because Saint's screams for me to run hint that nothing will ever be the same again.

I don't know what's happening until I feel a sharp pain in the back of my head. The keys go flying across the room. I tug violently, trying to break free, but someone has their fingers wrapped in my hair. "You fucking bitch! What have you done?"

My head is jarred back roughly, and I desperately try to fight whoever has me by the hair. But when they pull hard enough for tears to leak from my eyes, I realize shit is about to get real.

Saint is still tied by the ankles, but he flails his body wildly, screaming at my assailant to let me go, but my attacker has other ideas. He roars, smashing my face into the wall. I instantly taste blood, but I allow the metallic burn to spur me forward.

I kick backward, connecting with the assailant's shin. He howls and loosens his hold on my hair. On instinct, I turn, and remembering Saint's training, I put everything behind me and punch this bastard straight in the nose.

It squishes like an orange under the impact.

He drops to his knees, cupping his bloody nose, while

I slip and slide in the coagulated blood of the man I killed to dive for the scalpel. I'm about to send another fiend to where he belongs when a voice reminds me that I'm merely a sightseer in this foreign land.

"I'm impressed. I didn't think you had it in you."

With heart in my throat and the blood whooshing through my veins, I spin around and lock eyes with the biggest demon of them all.

Oscar stands just out of reach of Saint with his hands in his pockets. Without thought, a war cry leaves me as I charge forward, scalpel raised, only to be stopped in my tracks when he pulls a gun and trains it on me.

"Drop it." He gestures to the weapon in my hand.

A feral snarl tears from my throat, and I look at Saint who pleads that I stay put and do what he says.

I do.

Tonguing my cheek, I wipe the blood from the gaping wound to my head with the back of my hand, awaiting Oscar's next move.

"You killed one of my men," he says, pointing the gun at the prone man.

When a howl splits the air, he adds, "And you injured another."

Spitting out blood, I shrug untroubled. "An eye for an eye. Isn't that what you said?" I ask, using his words back on him.

Oscar doesn't appreciate my candor. "I should shoot you for what you've done."

"Go on then," I challenge, stepping forward. "I'm sick of your empty threats."

"No!" Saint screams, trying to swing out at Oscar, but he's too far away.

A reptilian smirk spreads across Oscar's lips, a sight which has me recoiling. "I could, but where's the fun in that? We're going to play a little game."

Refusing to show my fear, I stand tall, measuring my breathing.

"Are you still a virgin, sweet Willow?"

Not the question I was expecting, but I fold my arms, unimpressed. "That's none of your business, you perverted creep."

"Ah, on the contrary," he replies, walking toward me and pocketing his gun. Saint squirms against his restraints, but he's not going anywhere. "Thanks to all this commotion, I was interrupted from engaging in a wonderful threesome. But I now see it was all a ruse. How else did you get down here?"

My heart begins to thrash against my rib cage because I don't want to involve Ingrid and Dominic. But I have, which has me realizing the epic clusterfuck I've created. If only I had waited, as Pavel told me to, none of this would have happened.

Ingrid and Dominic wouldn't be in danger, and I wouldn't have…killed a man.

My stomach roils. I think I'm going to be sick.

"So as I see it, you owe me."

"Owe you what?" I spit, suppressing my queasiness.

"A fuck," he casually replies with a flippant wave of his hand.

Saint writhes madly, trying to grab Oscar with his non injured hand, but Oscar steps farther away, laughing. "Judging by your boyfriend's reaction, it seems you were saving yourself for him. How romantic."

"Don't patronize me," I snarl, but regardless of talking big, I'm shaking inside. And Oscar can smell my fear.

"Strip," he demands, eyes cold. "It pleases me to know that I'm the first to taste this forbidden fruit. Even though you're not my flavor, I will thoroughly enjoy it."

He stalks toward me while I back up slowly. I desperately search the room, hoping to find a weapon, anything to protect me. But there's nothing.

"Or maybe Alek beat Saint to the punch."

Saint snarls, screaming in fury as he fruitlessly fights to break free. Oscar has struck a nerve. I dare not add fuel to this raging inferno.

"Come on, then. Don't be shy. Let me see what so many have risked their lives for." He gestures for me to strip, but when I stand rigid, arms wrapped around me in protection, he shows me playtime is over.

I hear the slap before I feel it. My face jars sideways, then a splitting pain shoots up to the gash in my temple. I move my jaw from side to side, shaking the white noise from my brain.

"Don't you fucking touch her!" Saint bellows, his restraints whining under the force as he flails madly. Whether the drugs are slowly evading his system, or he's running on adrenaline, I don't know, but he suddenly seems stronger.

But his pleas only feed Oscar's twisted games.

"I don't think so. I said strip!" He reaches out, and before I have a chance to claw out his eyeballs, he rips my T-shirt down the middle.

Instantly, I cover my breasts, because even though I am wearing a bra, I feel naked under his predatory stare.

He thrives on my innocence. "Oh, I'm going to enjoy this."

He lunges for me, and although I'm fast, he reads my moves and grips my wrist, spinning me around so my back is pressed to his chest. He pins an arm around my waist, prohibiting me from running. In this position, Saint and I are face to face.

The pain echoed in his eyes is reflective to the permanent smudge on my soul. What have we become?

Oscar licks my face as I bat at his arm, trying to break free. "You keep squirming, and I will knock you out cold. I don't need you awake to fuck you, although it'll be more fun if you are."

"No!" I bellow, kicking my feet and clawing at his arm.

"Have it your way then." With one arm wrapped around my middle, he uses the other to press it against my windpipe. I immediately scratch at his arm wildly because I can't breathe. "I'm going to make you watch. Make you watch me defile your sweet ангел."

My fight only has him pressing down on my throat harder as Saint's anguished cries break me in two.

My eyes flicker, threatening to roll into the back of my head because I am on the cusp of passing out. I'm trying to stay awake, but the hold he has on me has cut off my air supply quickly. Saint's pained expression will be the last thing I see before this monster rapes and kills me, and not necessarily in that order.

"Enough!" Saint bellows and the room falls still.

"Give me a better offer then," Oscar replies, trying to subdue me as I will fight until my last breath.

The walls begin closing in on me, and it has nothing to do with the fact I'm seconds away from passing out. "Saint…no." It comes out in a winded plea, but it's too late.

"I won't fight you. You can…you can have me. Just don't hurt her."

I slap at Oscar's arm, desperate to break free because his hold on me wavers. He seems spellbound by Saint's sacrifice. While me, I just want to gouge out this asshole's eyeballs and kill him with my bare hands.

"I will submit to you, Oscar. Isn't that what you've always wanted?"

"Saint." I gasp, eyes wide. "No."

Oscar loosens his hold on me, and I instantly gulp in mouthfuls of air. He doesn't let me go, though.

"Just take her away." Saint nods that it'll be all right, but nothing ever will.

"You don't want her to watch?" Oscar mocks, squeezing me against him. I try to kick him, but his hold on me doesn't allow me to move.

"You can do with me as you please. All I ask is that no harm comes of her."

"You won't fight me?" Oscar questions incredulously.

"No, but only on one condition." I beg he doesn't do this. But it's too late. "Send her back home. To America," he says while I shake my head in horror, every part of me weeping.

Oscar isn't touched. "This is all about trust. If you're lying, I'll be forced to break your other hand."

I snarl at his revelation, attempting to injure him in any way I can, but he simply laughs at my feeble attempts.

"I promise," Saint says with nothing but sincerity. "I won't fight you. But you have to give me your word that she leaves here unharmed. You will grant her safe passage back to America as originally agreed."

Oscar hums in satisfaction. "Very well. You have my word."

"NO!" I roar. Fighting against Oscar, I'm determined to kill this bastard myself. "You can't!" I'm beseeching Saint not to do this again. I refuse to accept my freedom on these terms. It didn't work the first time he bargained with them, and it won't happen this time either.

But his mind is made up. Once again, my well-being is more important to him than his own. "Get her out of here."

"You fucking asshole! Let me go!" I thrash wildly, kicking and clawing, desperate to break free. But Oscar's hold on me never falters.

"I was going to give you this," he says to Saint as I feel him dig around into his pocket, and when he produces a syringe filled with a honey-colored liquid, my rage turns deadly. "But seeing as you'll comply, it seems a shame for it to go to waste."

"You are going to pay, you motherfucker!" The fury inside me is inexplicable. But the harder I fight him, the more amused he becomes.

"Besides, I want you to be awake for what we're about to do," he adds, ignoring my threat.

Saint keeps a brave face, but I can't even imagine how he's feeling right now. What he's offering Oscar is beyond perverse, and if he goes through with it, he will be lost to me forever.

And Oscar knows it.

"This could all be over with," he whispers into my ear. Saint struggles against the restraints. "Just tell me where Alek is. If you'd just done what I asked, I wouldn't be forced to play the bad guy."

"No one is forcing you," I spit, recoiling away from him. "You *are* the bad guy."

"Sticks and stones," he flippantly replies. "Tell me where Alek is, and I will let you both go."

He's spoken loud enough for Saint to hear him, and he's done so with intent. He wants me to hurt Saint yet again by denying I know Alek's whereabouts. Everything is so muddled, but I am certain of one thing...I can't protect him any longer.

I promised Pavel, but if there is a sliver of hope in setting Saint free, I'm going to take it. I have to trust Oscar, which, in light of everything, cements how desperate I am. I know he won't let Saint go, but I have to try. I can't leave here knowing I haven't done all that I could have.

Sighing deeply, I can only hope I'm doing the right thing. "Okay," I confess in a small, defeated voice.

Saint shakes his head fiercely, eyes wide, warning me not to divulge what I know. I don't understand why. Why the sudden change of heart? But I suppose he is aware that by telling Oscar what I know won't make a difference.

Once a snake, always a snake.

Before I have a chance to acknowledge it all, Saint declares, "You've got what you want. Come on then."

Oscar isn't an idiot; he is weighing the truth behind Saint's words. But Saint's promise seals our fate forever.

"I'm yours."

"No!" A guttural cry leaves me, and adrenaline animates me in a way it never has before. I break free from Oscar's hold and run toward Saint, throwing my arms around him. "I won't allow you to do this."

Unable to stop my fears, I sob uncontrollably into his neck, refusing to ever let go. "You'll never be his. Never." I weep, a darkness overshadowing me. "You're mine."

Saint wraps his arm around me, pulling me close as he hugs me with every last ounce of strength he has left. "Always, ангел."

But that doesn't make a difference. Our destinies were fated from the first moment we met. A happily ever after was never in our future as all we have now are memories.

"Please, I-I ca-can't." I'm breaking. Is this what losing a piece of your heart feels like? Because right now, I am incomplete, and I never will be whole ever again.

"You have to be strong. For me. Go now. Go have your butter pecan ice cream."

A raucous sob spills from me because he remembered what I said to him when we were on the island. It seems trivial, but it means so much because he wants me to live. He wants me to be normal and forget he ever existed. "Not w-without you."

"Now isn't our time. But one day, it will be." He kisses over the wound on my temple, but how I wish he could kiss it and make everything better.

"Saint, no." I hold on tight, but he gently coaxes me away.

Even with one arm injured, he is still stronger than me.

We lock eyes—a blue pool of abyss and a splash of warm chartreuse. "I will never stop fighting for you," I promise, reaching around my neck and unclasping my chain. He watches with sadness as I place my necklace around his neck. "I love you."

With a hollow sigh, he caresses the crucifix just as I used to. "I...love you too." His words are filled with nothing but sadness.

But fuck...this. This is not the end.

"Let me help you. Alek is—" I am about to confess it all, but suddenly, my legs grow heavy, and I sway, gripping Saint. I don't know what's happening. I try to fight, but the world tilts, and I tumble to the floor, paralysis taking over.

My eyelids weigh a million pounds, but I force them open and see Oscar standing over me with the empty syringe in hand. "Noooo," I slur, my tongue swollen.

Saint distracted me, knowing I would fight until the bitter end. "I'm sorry." I barely can make out his words, but his expression says it all.

Oscar steps over me, producing a key. I sluggishly watch as Oscar bends down to unlock Saint's ankles. I'm hoping he kills this asshole, giving him everything he deserves, but he doesn't. And that's thanks to me. My freedom is the only thing that matters to him.

Oscar produces a small bottle of liquid, which he squirts onto Saint's chest. Saint stands unmoving. "Coconut is my favorite scent," he says, rubbing the oil into Saint's skin. I didn't understand why he "prepared" him in such a way, but I soon do. "You're going to need a little…lubrication."

"No," I moan. Gathering everything that I have, I try to drag myself toward them, but I don't even move an inch.

Saint never takes his eyes off me. He could fight Oscar because he is stronger and faster, but he knows we wouldn't make it out of this house alive. He is doing this to protect me, and all I can do is lie here, helpless, unable to protect him.

Once Oscar is satisfied with Saint's oiled skin, he threads his hand through his long hair and yanks his head backward. A pained grunt leaves me. That soon turns to an afflicted cry when Oscar plants his lips on Saint's and kisses him.

A single tear slips down my cheek as my entire body is numb. The drugs have won, but more importantly, Oscar has triumphed. He got what he always wanted.

By coming here, I tried to make things better, but I've just made them so much worse. The last thing I see are the dead eyes of the man I killed in front of me. As I embrace the darkness, I realize…I've become the monster I never wanted to be.

CHAPTER SEVEN

Day 20987983038

I'm on fire. I'm sure of it.

Shooting upright, I try to gauge where I am because I'm convinced I swam in a vat of absinthe. My brain isn't just fuzzy, it's filled with cotton, and I can't remember anything. I don't even know how many days have passed because I feel a billion years old.

How did I get here?

Rubbing my aching temple, I blink sluggishly, hoping some memory will resurface soon. However, when my fingers brush over a dry, flaky substance, I wonder if maybe the memories are hidden for a reason.

Although every inch of me demands I crawl back under the covers, I move my weary body and come to a slow, wobbly stand. The room spins in a kaleidoscope of noise, but when that noise transforms into a gargle and then a death rattle, bile rises in my throat, and I'm going to be sick.

With hand over mouth, I ignore the cramping in my muscles as I run into the bathroom and throw up in the sink. I won't make it to the toilet. Though my empty stomach is skinned raw, I clench the porcelain, heaving whatever I have left, but the purge doesn't make me feel any better. This bitterness is ingrained onto my soul, and no matter how hard I try to rid it from my body, nothing will ever eradicate the feeling I have inside me because I…killed a man.

Oh, god. I'm a murderer.

Images, sounds, it all hits me at once, and a violent tremble wracks through me, almost splitting me into two. "No," I whimper, slamming my fist against the porcelain, my head buried in the sink.

But there is no denying it. The reason I can't remember is because my brain has gone into self-preservation mode, attempting to save me from…this. This horrible, empty feeling inside me which will never go away.

"You will always remember your first kill. I'm sorry."

That's what Saint said, but I didn't appreciate his words until now.

A torrent of tears spills from me, and I'm not sure if they'll ever stop. My shaky legs won't hold me up any longer, and I surrender, crumpling to the floor. I drag my knees toward my chest, hugging them tightly as I sob uncontrollably.

I killed someone, and it was all for nothing because Saint still isn't free. If anything, he is more imprisoned now than he ever was. Another memory smashes into me, one so vile, a soundless scream rips from my throat.

It's of Oscar kissing Saint, of him basting him, preparing

him for a meal for one.

I dry heave, the images too sickening to keep locked inside, but I have no right to behave this way because I wasn't the one chained to a torture device, broken and abused.

"Oh, Saint," I cry, covering my face and sobbing into my hands. I don't know what happened, and indisputably, my imagination couldn't even begin to fathom the heinous things done to him.

The perverse things inflicted on his body would have surely broken him because that's what Oscar wanted—to break his mind, body, spirit.

Sitting here crying is doing no one any good, so I sniff back my tears and come to a stand. I don't bother looking at myself in the mirror because I don't need to see my reflection to know I look like utter shit. Stripping out of my clothes, I work on autopilot as I step into the shower. The scalding spray burns my skin, but I hardly feel it. This is what defeat must feel like.

I failed the one person who never failed me. How am I supposed to live with that fact?

Bracing my hands against the tiles, I hang my head and wonder what comes next. Saint sold himself to regain my freedom, but it was all for nothing. How can I go? Leaving him here was never part of the plan.

The water rolls over me, but the warmth does nothing to soothe my anguish. It hurts to breathe. Once I've washed the blood from my hair and body, I switch off the faucets and dry myself. Wrapping the towel around me, I walk into the bedroom and rummage through my bag, not caring what outfit I find.

Once I'm dressed, I peer around the room, desperately needing divine intervention more than ever before. When I fix my gaze on the bed, I decide to do the only thing I can because right now, he is my savior.

Walking over to it, uncaring if anyone is watching or listening in, I sit near the pillows and turn toward the headboard. "Pavel, please come," I whisper. "I failed. I failed epically." He would have heard what happened last night in that basement. "I can't leave him here. I won't. But even if, and that's a big if, we leave here, he's broken. We might leave here physically, but emotionally and psychologically, he will be lost within these walls."

Taking a deep breath, I swallow down my grief. "I'm losing him. The things that have been done to him." I close my eyes, shaking my head slowly. "He won't survive. Oh, God. Please help h-him."

When the lock clicks, and I hear someone, no guessing who, whistling happily, I quickly scrub a hand down my face, not wanting Oscar to know how I'm feeling. He would only thrive on my pain.

His cheerful greeting only validates my theory. "Good morning. I brought you some juice."

The second I see him, the need to vomit arises once again.

There is way too much pep to his step as he saunters toward me, offering me a tall glass of OJ. I eye the glass as though it's a live grenade, and in his hands, it may as well be. If I wasn't so damn thirsty, I'd throw it into his face. It's probably drugged, but I can't feel any worse than I already do.

Reaching for it, I don't say thank you before I gulp it down.

Once I'm done, I place the glass onto the side table, not bothering to engage in small talk. Or any talk for that matter. That doesn't stop Oscar, though.

"I don't know about you, but I slept like a baby."

I grit my teeth together. He's baiting me, but I won't bite.

"You'll be happy to know that in just a few short days, you'll be back home."

"I don't want to go home," I spit, unable to keep up the silent act. "I want what I came here for."

Oscar shakes his head. "That's no longer possible. A deal's a deal."

Shooting up from the mattress, I shove his chest, catching him off guard. "I'll give you the supplier. I'll have him here in an hour."

Oscar combs the sides of his damp hair with his fingers, appearing ruffled by my violence. "A promise is a promise," he says, ignoring my offer and presenting me nothing but clichés. "I'm just getting the papers sorted."

My patience is no longer existent. "Fuck the papers!" I exclaim, clenching my fists by my side to stop from hitting him. "I'll tell you everything."

There is no need for me to elaborate on what that everything entails. Alek is my last bargaining chip, and I am prepared to put all my cards on the table if it'll save Saint.

Oscar sighs deeply. "Oh, lamb, it's too late now. If only you'd been so forthcoming sooner, none of this would have happened."

"What does that mean?"

"It means we had to get creative." When I scrunch up my nose, he explains. "There was always a plan B."

Of course, there was. Didn't we?

Pavel knew this plan wasn't foolproof, but we've just been thrown a curveball because we've been played.

"And what was that?" I humor him, hoping any information I get will help us.

"This was always, always," he says with a firm wave of his hand, "about finding Alek and—"

"And making us pay." I fill in the blanks, but I need clarification.

"Yes, and if we got the name of the supplier, then that was a bonus."

"I can still give you that." Measuring my breathing, I add, "I can still give you both."

"As I said, it's too late now." His eyes are alight as he shares, "I have a business meeting in"—he peers down at his Rolex—"an hour."

I'm a mixed bag of emotions right now. I could tell him where Alek is, but what will that achieve? Our plan B is now void.

"Turn that frown upside down," he mocks while I take a step toward him, ready to slap that smug grin from his cheeks. "You're going home. Isn't that what you always wanted? Of course, if in fact you *do* know where Alek is, then Saint's sacrifice was all for nothing, wasn't it? You're protecting Alek for a reason; therefore, I can't see you leaving for Tinseltown anytime soon."

He's right. Saint handed himself to the devil in vain. If only he hadn't drugged me, things could have been so different. Or would they have been? We underestimated Oscar and Astra, and their need for revenge.

"I have some handymen coming today," he says, indicating this conversation is done. "So don't worry if you hear noise. The gardens are looking a little worse for wear seeing as it's so cold. I'll also have to make some changes to my bedroom."

What he says next is my undoing. "I can't have my lover downstairs, chained up like a dog. However, I thought a nice cage in the corner of the room would be suitable. He is a wild beast after all."

Breathe in.

Breathe out.

But it doesn't help. Nothing will.

"I can see why you like him," he taunts, licking his bottom lip, staring me down. "He split open like a ripened cherry."

I. AM. GOING TO. KILL…HIM.

My body vibrates, and something malevolent overcomes me. Every time I think I know what true fury feels like, this motherfucker has to go and open his mouth. With rage coursing through me, I balance my weight, and just as Saint taught me, I punch this vile animal in the face.

His chin snaps back with a crack, and a winded gasp leaves him as the fact I can pack a punch clearly stuns him. I don't give him time to recover before I strike him again. Saint's drills come back to haunt me.

"Jab to the body! Jab to the head! Then body!"

And I do.

The satisfaction I feel when I see him bleed is like the world's most potent drug, and just when I'm about to take my next hit, my happy high fades. Oscar gathers his bearings and sucker punches me in the stomach. I drop to the floor, gasping for air, but that doesn't stop me because vengeance is the only thing that matters.

I attempt to rise, only for Oscar to knee me in the nose. The carpet breaks my fall as I land on my back. But the blood pouring from my face will not deter me.

Reaching out, I grip his ankle and attempt to yank his feet out from under him. He has the advantage, seeing as he's standing over me, and kicks me in the ribs. Who knew Italian leather could inflict so much pain?

Winded, I clutch my side as I'm certain he's broken a rib, but the pain is nothing compared to the affliction in my heart. He must pay for what he's done to Saint. Limply, I clutch at his pant leg, but he just shakes me off.

Dropping to one knee, he grips me by my collar and yanks me up into a half sitting position. I am floppy like a rag doll. "He belongs to me now," he snarls, inches from my face. It gives me great pleasure to see him bleeding and his eye swelling.

He shakes me when my head lolls to the side, refusing me the grace of slipping into unconsciousness. "Did you hear me, you bitch? That sweet mouth begged for mercy, begged me to stop when I fucked that sweet ass."

My body pulses in a murderous rage. "Saint…doesn't beg." Before he has a chance to spew forth more filth, I spit in his face.

Bloody spittle trickles down his cheek.

He gasps, horrified by my ghastly actions, but there is more where that came from. Without flinching, I brace for impact and headbutt him.

He wavers with a pained oomph, then shoves me back down. I fall into a crumpled heap, seeing stars. Standing quickly, he reaches into his pocket and retrieves a white handkerchief to scrub at his face with. The image has me bursting into maniacal laughter because it's either this, or I will burst into hollow tears.

"Nice hanky," I mock, ignoring the pain in my ribs, in my entire body.

Oscar stares down at me, his cockiness soon being replaced by fear. He's not frightened of me per se; however, he's fearful of what's coming his way because he knows as long as I'm alive, I will never stop hunting him. I will never stop until he's dead.

I brace for another assault, but I don't get one. Instead, he walks from the room and locks the door, leaving me alone with my madness.

Breathing deeply, I use my elbow to drag my body across the floor. Everything hurts, but I welcome it because if what Oscar said is true, then I deserve this pain for what I've done.

With that thought as my lullaby, I collapse in the middle of the room, succumbing to the voices in my head, which scream...*REVENGE.*

"Wake up!"

I am finally lost to the insanity which has been my passenger since day one. I am certain someone is here, but this person, once foe, now friend, can't be here because that would mean…

A potent torrent rushes through me, animating me as I spring up and force my eyes open. My flight or fight takes over as I scan the room frantically. However, who I see crouched down before me has me rubbing my fists into my eye sockets, not believing he is really here.

"Come, we have to be quick." He yanks me up, but my body is limp, and I sag against him. An annoyed grunt gets caught in his throat, but I need a second.

"A-Alek?" My voice sounds like I gargled glass, but he heard me. "You came for me?"

"Of course, I did. Come on. We have to move."

I don't know what's happening. My brain is fried. I wouldn't be surprised if my damaged mind is now concocting scenarios to help me deal with the pain.

But when he brushes the hair from my face, laying a quick kiss to my forehead, and says, "Please," I know this is really happening.

I push past the fog and see that he's dressed in green overalls, ones you would expect to see any gardener wearing. My brain thankfully kickstarts back to life, and I realize this was the ruse to allow him in.

They *were* listening. Oh, thank god.

With my head back in the game, he helps me stand. "Saint."

A name can amount to so much.

Alek nods, wrapping his arm around me to lead me out the door because I am swaying on my feet. "Pavel has got him. But we have to go. Now. The surveillance has been interrupted for only a few minutes."

My questions can wait because right now, the only thing that matters is getting out of here.

I allow him to guide me as it's faster this way. I have no idea where Oscar's men are because it seems the coast is clear. As we are running, well, as I am being dragged down the hallway, I dig in my heels. Alek almost trips over.

"Ingrid and Dominic." I flinch because it hurts to speak. "We can't leave them here."

"We must."

"No!" I stubbornly argue, becoming a dead weight in hopes he stops hauling me like a sack of potatoes. "He will kill them. Please, Alek."

Lifting my chin, I peer into his steel blue eyes and suddenly realize that I am thankful to see him. I can finally accept that I am actually happy to see him. I will deal with that reality later, though.

An exasperated sigh leaves him. "Fine. Where are they?"

I lick my dry lips. "I-I don't know."

Alek shakes his head, his cheeks billowing as he exhales.

We continue hauling ass, and when we reach the staircase

leading to Oscar's bedroom, my adrenaline kicks into overdrive. I shrug out of Alek's arms and take the stairs two at a time. I'm still unsteady and in severe pain, but when I see the door that leads to Oscar's bedroom, I focus on it and nothing else.

Alek is behind me as I burst through the door, crying in relief when I see Pavel because he is holding up a limp Saint. He's wearing a pair of black sweats, and that's all.

"He's out cold," he says in a rushed breath, trying not to do further damage to his injured wrist. "Help me, Alek."

Without hesitation, Alek runs over and loops his arm around Saint's waist, bearing his weight against him. Saint sways backward, mumbling incoherently. The sight breaks my heart, but I don't have time to mourn his battered and bruised body because we need to get him the fuck out of here.

"Let's go!" Pavel yells, turning toward the curtain—our out. He and Alek work in unison, supporting Saint as they drag him through the room.

They are both strong men, but Saint is dead weight, and his bare feet trail along the carpet. I wish I could help, but I would just get in the way.

"What about Ingrid?" We're running out of time, but I have to at least try.

Pavel shakes his head, indicating this is not an option. But when Alek groans, I know that maybe, just maybe there is hope. "Come here, Willow. Help Pavel. I'll go to her room, but if she's not there, we're leaving. Understood?"

Happiness swarms me, and I nod frantically. "Yes."

A newfound strength soars through me, and my injuries

are forgotten as I run to take Alek's place at Saint's side. When the stench of coconuts assaults my sense of smell, I dry retch at first, but then I pull it together.

"Thank you."

Alek nods, cupping my cheek quickly. The gesture is filled with nothing but affection. "I will meet you at the van. Whatever happens, don't stop."

The unspoken lingers as this is dangerous for Alek, but he's doing it...because I asked him to. My demons roar to the surface, but I will deal with them later.

Lifting Saint's arm, I loop it around my shoulder and support his waist; it's not like I haven't done this before. Pavel and I then begin a slow stagger toward the curtain, each step taking us closer to freedom.

Saint mumbles under his breath, and everything about this tears me into two, but I inhale deeply, demanding my breakdown hit the road—for now. Saint leans into me, soft words in Russian tumbling from his lips.

Pavel suddenly hisses before his composure returns. "It's okay, brother. We are getting you out of here." He has understood the muted whispers.

We split the curtain in half and are presented with a winding dark hallway. Pavel has studied the blueprint, so he's able to navigate through the corridor with ease. Our breaths are heavy as we continue staggering, but when Saint leans into me, I sway to the left, bracing the wall to keep from falling.

"It's not much farther," Pavel says, gesturing with his head down the hallway, which is essentially a tunnel.

"It's fine. Let's go." The fact I am dripping with sweat, am splattered in dry blood, and breathing like I have a punctured lung exposes my lie, but we continue, nonetheless.

It feels like forever, but we finally turn a corner and a few feet away are five steps leading up toward a trapdoor. Pavel mentioned this secret passage led into the greenhouse, which is why they were able to get in. By using the ruse of being gardeners, the guards let them in, none the wiser they were being duped.

That doesn't explain how they were able to pull this off without some detection, but when we stumble up the stairs, maneuvering the best way we can with an unconscious Saint in tow, and the trap door opens, things begin to become clear—too clear however. I haven't seen the daylight in so many days, I instantly recoil, hissing like a vampire exposed to the sun.

"Hurry up!" Zoey whispers, frantically peering from left to right. "Sara has the van ready."

My vision is spotted, thanks to the exposure to the natural light, but once it's clear—and I don't mean to sound judgy—I can't help but think she looks like a hooker. Her dress is short, red, and screams honeytrap. I can thank her later.

Pavel mentioned the garage is close by, which gives me hope that maybe, just maybe we will get out of here alive. When we drag Saint up the last step, Zoey's hardness instantly diminishes, and she covers her mouth.

Out here in the daylight, the full extent of Saint's injuries shine. He is covered in purple bruises and inflamed red bite marks. There are fresh wounds which seem to have been inflicted with something sharp all over his chest.

Tears prick her eyes. As they do mine. "Oh, Saint." She soon recovers, though, wiping a stray tear away with the back of her hand.

Turning over my shoulder, I strain my eyes, hoping to see Alek. I know he told me to keep going, but I can't. "Zoey, take him."

I don't wait for her to express her hatred for me because I can see it all over her face. I gently unwrap myself from Saint, where Zoey quickly takes my place. He whimpers when I leave his side.

"Shh," I coo, brushing the hair from his downturned face. "I'll be back."

It seems to appease the demons for now.

We are standing inside the enormous greenhouse, just as Pavel said, so I don't have much time.

"Go!" I demand. Pavel tries to grab my arm, but I shrug from his hold. He doesn't stand a fighting chance because Saint wavers, almost sending both he and Zoey to the ground.

I run down the stairs and navigate through the way we came. My aching ribs demand I stop, but I merely place my hand over them to support them the best way I can. The curved walls of the dark tunnel suddenly close in on me, but I concentrate and call out to Alek.

My voice merely echoes.

Just as I'm about to call for him again, I hear winded breaths and rushed footsteps charging toward me. "I told you not to stop."

I exhale in relief. "You can yell at me later. Let's go." However, when I see we're one person short, I arch a brow.

"Where's Dominic?"

Ingrid is huddled into Alek's side, sobbing. When I look at Alek, he simply shakes his head.

He's not coming because it's safe to assume he's dead. A part of me weeps as he could have been a monster to me, but he wasn't, which I suspect is one of the reasons he's no longer with us. But the main reason is because he was replaced by another pet—Saint. He was no longer needed by Oscar, so he was disposed of, just like trash.

But we don't have time to discuss it. Turning on my heel, I sprint through the tunnel and charge up the stairs. Alek and Ingrid aren't far behind.

"Out through the door and make a left," Alek directs as we haul ass.

Orchids and lilies fill the greenhouse, but regardless of their beauty, they can't erase the horrors within the walls.

Once the cool breeze strokes my heated cheeks, I inhale, gulping in lungfuls of the fresh air. Alek loops his arm through mine, hinting now is not the time to stop and smell the roses. When the garage comes into view, he whistles, and a black van comes tearing out.

The van has Russian writing on the side with a red rose as its centerpiece. It reminds me of the rose tattoos on Saint's chest—his marred chest which reveals the depravities he's endured.

Pavel is driving, while Sara, who is dressed very similar to Zoey, sits in the passenger seat. When the van comes to a screeching stop, kicking up gravel, we run toward it. The side door bursts open, and when Zoey sees Ingrid, she launches from it, shoving Alek in the chest. She catches us both unawares as I have no idea what's gotten into her.

"What is *she* doing here? This wasn't part of the plan."

"Not now," he snarls, smacking her hand away when she tries to push him again.

"You just couldn't help yourself, could you?" Shit, I didn't think this through. Although Zoey claims to be over Alek, seeing Ingrid has obviously opened old wounds. But this isn't Alek's doing.

"It was me!" I yell in a tumble of words. Alek looks at me, appearing surprised I owned up to it.

Her mouth is parted, poised on spewing more anger toward Alek, but when I confess what I did, she turns slowly, glaring something wicked.

"We can do this later, okay? Saint is the only thing that matters now." I raise my hands in surrender, hoping she sees reason. I peer over her shoulder to see him lying prone in the back of the van.

"Zoey, we don't have time!" Pavel revs the engine, but she is a woman hell-bent on fury.

She stalks me, but I stand my ground. This has been inevitable since the moment we met. "We have unfinished business, you and I."

I'm so sick of her. She has been nothing but a thorn in my side since the first moment we met.

Done being civil, I match her pace and stop only inches away. "We do, and once Saint is safe…it's on."

She clenches her jaw before a sinister smirk spreads across her face slowly. All the Bible verses my father read me about going to hell suddenly come to mind because looking into her eyes is akin to gazing at Lucifer himself. "Oh, it's on."

Yes, it is. But right now, I need to be with Saint.

Pushing past her, I jump into the back, instantly dropping to my knees by his side. I gently brush the hair from his face, peering down at him, lost to him because he's finally safe.

Once everyone is in, Pavel kicks the van into drive, and we're off. I can feel Alek watching me as I sit vigil by Saint. He's so cold. I pull the scratchy gray blanket farther up his body so it sits under his chin. When I do, I notice my necklace is gone.

I suppose God couldn't save either of us.

With that thought in mind, I tune everything else out and focus on Saint. I can't stop touching him, and even though Zoey hates me beyond words, she allows me this time with him. I caress his eyebrows, his nose, and down across his lips. Each stroke makes this real.

When we get to the gate, Pavel works his magic, speaking to the guards in Russian. Sara leans over him, her bust on full display as she waves seductively. I now understand why the men weren't on patrol. They were too busy ogling Zoey and Sara. A perfect distraction.

Everyone has done so much to save Saint and me while I…my lower lip trembles.

When the gate opens and Sara blows the guard a kiss, I know we're home free. Pavel waves goodbye. I can taste freedom.

No one says anything as we pull out of the driveway with ease, and that silence continues well into the drive. It seems we were all uncertain if we would make it out alive. But now that we have, the question lingers—what happens now?

Saint moans softly, his head moving from side to side. His eyes flicker. I can only hope his dreams give him a reprieve, if only for a while.

I gently run my fingertips down his cheek, his coarse beard thick and long. He looks so different from when we first met. He was confident and strong, but now, he is broken. Although he was my captor, I was never truly scared. But right now, that's all I am.

I'm scared for what the future holds.

When the listless rhythm of his heart beats under my fingers, a strangled sob tumbles free. Lowering myself toward him, I press my ear over his chest, listening to the cadence. Each slow, hollow beat has me slipping into an abyss, one which doesn't end.

Wrapping my body around his, I close my eyes, giving him my warmth. It's the least I can do, but there is something more, something I will do for the rest of my life. With his heartbeat as my metronome, I surrender.

"I'm sorry." But sorry just isn't good enough.

CHAPTER EIGHT

He looks so small.

So helpless.

Once we broke free from hell, Pavel drove us to the orphanage—our sanctuary. The moment Mother Superior saw Saint, she rushed him into the infirmary and shooed us out the door. I waited for her to emerge, but as minutes turned into hours, I succumbed to exhaustion and fell asleep, my back pressed to the infirmary wall.

When she finally appeared, she told me what I feared— his injuries would heal, but the damage to his mind, well, only time would tell. I asked if I could see him, but she said that I was to give him some time.

So I waited and waited, but when one day became two, I couldn't stand it a second longer. I opened the door, and it's here I've stood for countless moments, unbelieving what I see.

He looks so small.

So helpless.

I've always known Saint to be unbreakable. Throughout this entire ordeal, he's been my rock, my savior. But seeing him tucked tight into this single bed with a blanket drawn to his chin, he looks foreign, almost like he wears Saint's face, but it's not him.

One of the sisters sits by his side, reading from the Bible. When she sees me by the door, she smiles. "He will be okay," she reassures me. "He's just sleeping."

"I know Mother Superior told me to stay away, but can I sit with him? Just for a few minutes?" My voice barely sounds like my own. It seems we're all strangers in our skin.

The sister closes her Bible and places it onto the small side table. "Of course. He's been drifting in and out of sleep, so don't be alarmed if he doesn't respond to you. We've given him a mild sedative to help him sleep. He needs to heal."

Nodding quickly, I can't tear my eyes away from the bed.

Saint's chest rises and falls, the shallow rhythm almost hypnotic. Unlike the drug-induced state he was once in, this time, these drugs are to help him.

The sister walks past me, gently placing her hand to my shoulder. "He'll be all right. He just needs time."

And there is that word again. Time.

They are just being polite, though, because what they're really trying to say is that he needs time away from me. She leaves me alone, not taking my silence personally.

It's just Saint and me, what I've wanted for so long, but now that my wish has been granted, I don't know what to do.

I want to say so many things, but where do I start?

Taking a small breath, I woman the fuck up and go to him.

Standing by his bedside, I peer down at him, wringing my hands out in front of me. The purple on his face has faded, making way to a pale green. He's healing, but it's the wounds I cannot see that worry me the most.

Pulling up the chair, I take a seat as close as I can to the bed. I want to touch him, but I don't want to rouse him because for the first time in a long time, he doesn't look in pain. I'm so thankful I can no longer smell coconuts. All that lingers is him.

"I'm sorry," I whisper, lowering my chin sadly. "I should have done more. There is so much I wish I could take back, but I can't. I will never forgive myself for letting you down because you never once did for me."

Unable to stop myself, I gently rub over his arm through the blanket. I need this contact. I need him. However, when a pained whimper escapes him, I quickly draw my hand back.

"I will give you all the time you need," I promise, sniffing back my tears. "But I promise you, he will never get away with what he's done."

I won't speak his name in this house of God, but that doesn't mean I won't continue to plan my revenge.

"Rest now and get better. I'll be here once you wake up." I want more than anything to kiss him, to seal my promise this way, but I don't.

When the sister re-enters the room, I know my time is up. "Thank you."

She nods with a small smile.

Taking one last look at Saint, I stand, ignoring the pain in my ribs and body because that can wait. However, the sister notices me flinch. "Are you hurt?"

Earlier, I visited the bathroom and wiped some of the blood off my face, but the smudges of red still linger. She's been polite not to stare, but it seems she can't help but be merciful, even to a sinner like me.

"I'll be fine," I reassure, hobbling past her. I don't wait for her reply and make my way into the hallway.

Now that I've seen Saint, I decide to shower and burn these clothes. Once I'm done exorcising the demons, I will find Pavel and Alek and ask what happens now. The joyous voices of the children chip away at the darkness pervading my soul. I turn the corner and walk past Alek's room, noticing Ingrid is with him.

She sits on Alek's small bed, crying softly while he comforts her with his arm wrapped around her shoulders. I can't hear what he's saying, but whatever it is, it seems to soothe her. She's huddled into his side, and swathed in his sweater, she finally looks unafraid.

The vision is one of protection, one which I instigated, seeing as I insisted we save her, so why do I suddenly feel off balance? Seeing Alek and Ingrid together incites something inside me, something I can't explain.

I will never see Alek as the "good guy," but seeing him console Ingrid has me wondering if maybe someone like him is really capable of turning over a new leaf. A small, irksome voice whispers that if that were true, maybe Alek's feelings for me are genuine.

Remembering the masquerade ball before all of this turned to utter shit, I recall Alek's speech.

"I wanted to celebrate her existence with all of you because she means…so much to me."

I didn't know what to make of it, and I still don't, but seeing him show compassion has me wondering if he really meant it? I want to scoff at such a thought, but if he did mean it, how does that make me feel? He is the reason I'm here and why I've done what I've had to, to survive. I've come to terms with the fact that I don't hate him, so the question is, why don't I?

He presses his lips to the top of Ingrid's head, cooing softly.

Feeling like I'm encroaching on a private moment, I silently scamper to my room. Once inside, I hunt through my drawers, thankful when I see the sisters have restocked them. I literally left Oscar's with only the clothes on my back, so being offered the luxury of clean garments reminds me of how fortunate I am to be here.

Grabbing a pair of jeans, a wool sweater, a pair of socks, and sneakers, I make my way to the bathroom, where I wash away the filth clinging to my skin. I will never be able to fully rid myself of it, though, because the majority of it blemishes my soul.

The things I've seen and the things I've done will forever haunt me, but I deserve the affliction. With that thought in mind, I turn the faucet to cold and stand under the freezing cold spray. Only when my teeth chatter and my entire body is covered in goose bumps do I turn the water off.

I dry off and dress, not bothering with makeup or using any product in my hair. Once my laces are tied, I march out into the corridor, intent on finding Pavel. Alek is probably still with Ingrid, so I decide to go solo.

The playrooms are filled with children sitting at the long tables. Every color of paint and crayon are at their disposal. One of the sisters sits in a large rocking chair in the corner of the room surrounded by a circle of eager kids as she reads them a story.

Something so mundane warms me because I've missed this simplicity. Once upon a time, I took all of this for granted, but now, I wonder if I'll be ordinary ever again. When one of the little girls with blonde pigtails notices me looking in, she waves, flashing a toothless smile.

I wave back, melancholy overtaking me because another thought hits me—will that ordinary life provide me children? I never gave much thought to being a mother, but now that the possibility seems so out of reach, I crave nothing more.

But what sort of mom will I be? When my child asks me about my past, what will I say? Your mom lied, cheated, and killed? Because that's what I've done.

"Hey. I'm glad I found you."

When I hear Pavel address me, I quickly brush away the tears I didn't even realize had fallen with the back of my hand. "Hey."

He looks into the window I am standing outside of, no doubt wondering what caused the nostalgia.

"We need to talk," I firmly state, ignoring my emotion.

When he nods, I'm thankful he didn't ask what's wrong.

He leads me down the hallway, and I keep eyes aimed forward as I can't afford any further distractions. We enter the library, which is filled to the ceiling with books thanks to Alek, but I quash down the sentiment and focus on the task at hand.

We take a seat at a table. "How's Saint?" he asks, bringing forward his chair.

I shrug, not seeing the point in being evasive. "You heard everything, didn't you?"

He nods firmly.

"Well then, you can guess how he is." I don't mean to be rude, but every time I think about what was done to him, I can't shake this cloud of guilt looming over me. "Thank you for coming for us, but we could have done this from the beginning."

Pavel pulls in his lips. "No, we couldn't have. We were only able to pull it off because of the inside intel. We only knew of Oscar's coming and goings because of the bugs."

I wish that fact could ease this heaviness pushing against my chest, but it doesn't.

"You were smart, Willow."

I scoff in response. "I was far from smart. If I was, Saint wouldn't have gotten hurt."

"We always knew this plan wasn't perfect," he argues. "But what matters is that we got Saint back."

"But in what state? You know the things that were done to him." He lowers his eyes. "When he wakes, I don't think he'll have wanted us to save him."

And there it is—the truth that has been staring me in the face this entire time.

Pavel simply stays silent, not bothering to argue. I don't know if that's because he's run out of fight, or if it's because he agrees.

However, there *is* someone who doesn't agree, but no surprise there. "You underestimate my brother." Zoey pulls up a seat at our table, ensuring she sits as far away from me as possible.

If looks could kill, I would be a smoldering pile of ashes. She and I have a date with destiny, but it will have to wait. For now.

"Saint endured a lot." I wish I could emphasize just how much. But if Pavel heard what happened down in the dungeon, then odds are, she did too. No wonder she hates me more than she already does. "I know he is strong, but you can't come back from certain things."

She rolls her eyes as she leans back in her seat. "Well, maybe if you did what you were supposed to do, then we wouldn't be having this conversation."

Lunging forward, I slam my fist onto the table. "You don't think I know that? I wish I could take his place. Every single day, that was all I wanted! But don't you dare come here on your high horse without accepting culpability. You're just as guilty as I am!"

Just as Zoey is about to claw my eyes out from across the table, Pavel uses his arms as a barricade to stop this from turning ugly. "Ladies, enough."

Zoey's eyes are locked with mine, but I won't back down.

If she wants a fight, then I'm ready. However, when Sister Margaret walks past, pushing her library book trolley, I'm ashamed for losing my temper.

The mood settles for now.

"You're both on the same side," Pavel says while Zoey and I snort at his ridiculous claim. "So you need to put your differences aside and focus on what's ahead."

With great difficulty, I sit back in my seat. But I don't take my eyes off Zoey. "What's the plan?"

"As I said, you were smart to plant those bugs where you did. Remember that lady who visited the house?" I don't need him to clarify as I know who he is talking about. "Why did you want us to know of her comings and goings?"

I shrug, still confused as to why I felt compelled to plant the bug on her purse. "I honestly don't know. She just seemed…familiar. Was I wrong to do that?"

When Pavel shakes his head, I sigh in relief. "No, you weren't. By doing so, we were able to gather so much information."

"What information? And who was that woman?"

Pavel is about to reply, but it seems it isn't his place to because what I hear slip past Alek's lips changes everything. "That woman is my mother."

I open but soon close my mouth, not even sure what I want to say. Alek takes a seat beside me while Ingrid opts to stand by his side, a move not missed by a glaring Zoey.

Alek waits for me to process what he just shared, but he'll be waiting a while because what in the ever-living fuck? *His mom?* I don't even know what to do with this piece of information. I knew she looked familiar, but I never thought that was because her son was the person who kidnapped me.

I need a minute.

"What Alek says is true," Pavel says, filling in the silence. "That woman is Zoya. And the man she was with, that is Serg."

When Alek shifts in his seat, it's clear this is only the tip of the iceberg.

"Who is Serg?" I dare to ask, unsure what the answer will be.

Pavel is about to reply, but this is personal, too personal for Alek. "My brother."

I blink once, stunned. *"Brother?"* He never mentioned any siblings.

Alek's stern nod reveals I wasn't hearing things. "Your mom is…is…" I'm searching for the right word, but Alek soon fills in the blanks for me.

"Is working with my brother? Is that what you're asking?"

"I suppose I am," I reply, unable to close my gaping mouth.

Alek clenches the arms of the chair. He's barely keeping it together. "Yes. Serg is my half-brother."

This is too much.

Thinking back to the time when Alek mentioned his father, it was clear he was fond of his dad. There was never any love lost between him and his mom because he mentioned when his father died, she was too busy spending her husband's money to look after her kids. At the time, I didn't give much thought to his siblings because I didn't care to know, but now that I know his history, there is no guessing who Serg's father is.

"Boris Ivanov was Serg's father, wasn't he?" The man Alek killed when he was thirteen years old.

The mere mention of Alek's stepfather has him growling low as he twirls his pinkie ring—the one he took from Boris's finger. "Yes."

Holy shit.

Serg would have been a baby when Alek killed his father, so I can only guess what his relationship with Alek is like. He never knew his father, thanks to Alek. Nothing good can come from this.

"So what role do they play in this?" I ask, preparing myself for every outcome.

"Remember Chow?"

"How could I forget?" I counter quickly, shuddering at the painful memory.

Alek frowns, deep in thought. "I shot him because why?"

"Because you're a narcissistic psychopath?" I offer, meaning every word.

Alek flinches, which instantly has me regretting my choice of words, but if he has a point, I wish he'd make it. I'm not here to play twenty questions. "Because he was selling to my rival," Alek explains in case I've forgotten. "And that person was Serg."

I almost fall off my chair.

No wonder it was personal for him. By killing Chow, Alek was sending a message to not only the underground he ruled, but to his brother as well.

"It seems crime runs in the family," Zoey says, folding her arms across her chest.

"Serg thinks that by talking big, you've got pull in this city. But that's not how it works. I needed to show him not to fuck with me and not to fuck with my empire, which I built from the ground up. And as expected, when he heard of Chow's death by my hand, he went into hiding like the little momma's boy that he is." There is nothing but contempt toward Serg. It seems their hatred runs both ways.

"Only when he presumed I was dead did he have the balls to show his face again, and thanks to my mother interfering, he was able to get in touch with Astra and Oscar."

Something clicks into place, and I remember the night of the poker game when Astra was able to convince Alek to play by using her necklace as a wager. That necklace belonged to his mother, and at the time, I wondered why Astra had it.

It seems she had it because it was given to her by Alek's mom, something which angered Alek enough to throw good sense to the wind.

"What do you mean Zoya interfered?" I ask, needing to fill the holes in the story.

Alek's nostrils flare as he exhales heavily. Ingrid gently touches his shoulder in support. "It means my mother is still a pathetic weakling. When I killed her husband, I made sure she knew never to contact me again. But over the years, she and Astra kept in touch. My mother always had a soft spot for her as she was the daughter she never had. Their contact didn't bother me as long as Astra never mentioned her to me. But now, I'm bothered.

"My mom failed one son, so it seems she wants to make amends with her second. Without her, Serg wouldn't have been able to contact Astra or Oscar because they never knew he existed. I ensured that little bastard was never linked to my name."

Well, I did not see that coming.

"But now they do. And they trust him because my mom is vouching for him."

"That's why you wanted that necklace back?" I ask, not needing to explain which one. "Your mom gave that to Astra as a message, didn't she? She wanted you to know that she was still in your life, one way or another."

Alek's jaw clenches. "Yes. That necklace was my grandmother's, my father's mother, and by giving that to Astra, she was giving me a clear fuck you. She never forgave me for killing Boris. And now it seems history is repeating itself because just as she tried to fill my father's shoes with Boris, she is trying to fill my shoes with Serg."

"So she has no idea you're still alive?" I ask, my head reeling.

"No, I don't think so. From what we've heard from that meeting Oscar had with Serg and her, they believe I'm dead. Oscar, though, he isn't convinced, and he knows that by doing business with them, it will bring me out of hiding."

"Why?"

"Because I will never allow that little shit to take my place. He will never be me!" Alek shouts, slamming his palms onto the table.

This is personal for Alek, and I can understand his need for vengeance. His issues with his mother shaped him into the person he is today. By allowing this to happen, does he feel like he is letting his father down somehow?

"Serg knows some low-level dealers but not big enough to fulfill the demand. Serg found Chow because he was indiscreet, which is why things ended for him the way that they did." His flippant explanation is wrong, so wrong. "Serg says he has a new supplier, but Adam isn't stupid. From what I can tell, he's lying low. So it's got to be someone else. But who? They have a meeting in two weeks."

"So Oscar and Astra are trusting him on word alone?" I question, arching a brow.

"If manipulation was an Olympic sport, my mother would be the world champion," Alek replies with a scowl.

"I don't understand why she's helping him. Wouldn't she want a better life for her son?" I realize what I've said, but it's too late. Alek frowns, taking my words to heart because she didn't care enough to save him.

"To someone who loves money first, second, and last, she doesn't care. She saw how I built my enterprise, and now, she wants in."

I didn't get that impression from her, though. Serg, I instantly took a dislike to. But Zoya seemed…nice. But what do I know?

"So what's the plan?"

Pavel cracks his neck from side to side, which is never a good sign.

Alek looks around, clearly not wanting Sister Margaret to overhear. "We let this so-called meeting take place and watch and learn. We learn who the main players are, and then we bring down the empire, brick by brick. We can't act until we know every single player who's involved."

"Why can't we just go to the police?" I question. Alek's plan sounds like it'll end messy and bloody.

Zoey shakes her head, appearing amused by my comment. "And tell them what exactly? Ingrid and I are ex-sex slaves? Pavel is responsible for countless bombings around Russia? Alek used to be Russia's number one bad guy? Most unsolved mafia murders were done by Saint? And you were kidnapped and sold? Is that what you want to tell them?"

When phrased like that, I can see the reason behind her amusement. But this plan just sounds like another suicide mission.

"Zoey is right," Alek says while she gloats. "The police are corrupt. They will side with whoever has the biggest dollar signs and influence attached to their names. I have tried to reach out to my former contacts, but no one wants to help. I am an outsider now. No one trusts me after all that's happened."

What he really means is when he showed a softer side with me. Leaders can't be weak. And that's what everyone thinks of Alek now.

Running a hand down my face, I realize this is really happening. "Okay, so we watch and learn? And then what?"

Alek takes a moment, evening his breaths. "Then we annihilate everyone involved, and I take back what's mine."

"You're not serious?" I spit, unbelieving what I'm hearing. "You intend on going back to your life before, before…"

"You?" Zoey sarcastically says, filling in the blanks. But I ignore her.

"What do you expect?" Alek replies softly. When he

reaches for my hand, I pull it away and place it under the table.

"I expected you to learn from your mistakes. I thought you had!" I can't keep the annoyance from my tone.

He tries to reason with me, but all I hear is a cop-out. "This is my life, дорогой. I don't know any other way. Once I'm back in power, I will be able to organize safe passage for you to return home. For you and Saint. This is what he wanted for you from the very beginning."

He is serving my dream on a silver platter, but that doesn't make this right. He is going to take out anyone who stands in his way, only to take their place? When will this end? I thought he had changed, but he hasn't.

Money, power, greed; that's all that matters to Alek.

"Now, I can't offer you anything. But if I do this, it will mean I can finally do right by you."

"Oh, bullshit!" I kick back my chair as I stand. "Don't you dare use me as an excuse. This plan is no different than when you paid a quarter of a million for me!"

Zoey blinks once, clearly stunned by my revelation.

"All this is, is a play for power. You're prepared to kill god knows how many so you're once again respected and feared. You're no better than them. Actually, you're worse," I spit, curling my lip, sickened.

Alek sighs, closing his eyes in defeat.

"Pavel, how can you allow this to happen?" I shout, eyeing him angrily. "You said it was time things ended. How can you help him after everything he's done?"

Those words are my undoing because when Zoey comes to a slow stand, it appears like our time has finally come. "How can *you*?" she questions with a sneer. "How can you have feelings for him after everything *he's done to you?* So don't you dare think you're any better than us…because you're not."

Something about Alek's demeanor changes. He slowly raises his chin to look at me, something akin to hope sparking in his eyes. Zoey just said I had feelings for him, for this monster. It's the first time it's been spoken aloud, and I don't know what to do.

I've not known what this something is I feel for Alek, but could Zoey be right? Do I have…*feelings* for this man? Not feelings of love, but feelings of…like?

No.

My body retaliates violently at the thought, and just when Zoey opens her mouth, no doubt about to spew forth more venom, I decide to shut it for good. Without thought, I coolly round the table, and before she has a chance to ask what the hell I'm doing, I slap her across the cheek.

The sting in my hand is instant gratification and so is witnessing her cupping her reddening cheek.

"That's for getting me kidnapped," I spit, suddenly realizing how big a role she's played in all of this. "My husband may have sold me to Alek, but Saint kidnapped me because he was trying to win back your freedom, which you didn't even want! So as I see it, everything started with you."

A shriek erupts from her as she violently charges forward and shoves me in the chest. I stumble back a few feet as she packs a punch, but I soon find my footing and charge for her as she charges for me. There isn't hair-pulling or catty scratching, which I actually respect her for. She strikes out and connects with my jaw.

My head snaps back, the sting shooting all through my body. "Lucky shot," I snarl, wiping my bleeding lip with the back of my hand. My sore ribs are protesting for me not to do this, but it's too late.

We stalk each other, fists raised as we keep on our toes, never taking our eyes off the other. Alek and Pavel attempt to intervene, but nothing will stop us. Zoey shoves Pavel, which gives me the opportunity to connect with her face.

She grunts as my fist collides with her cheek.

"Your brother has sacrificed so much for you." We circle the other on the defense. "And *now* you want to appreciate everything he's done. If you'd have left years ago, when he begged you to, none of this would have happened."

"Shut your mouth!" she yells, but her arrogance soon returns. "Besides, you're worse than I am. At least *I* can admit I loved Alek. I *never* loved two men…unlike you."

What in the actual fuck? *Love?* I do *not* love Aleksei Popov.

Her lies are the fuel inciting this inferno, and uncaring I've let my guard down, I charge toward her, primed on killing her with my bare hands. She attempts to punch me in the ribs, but I jump back and focus on nothing but maiming her. I remember Saint's training and deliver a combination of punches to her body and her face.

Winded breaths leave her as she tries to fend me off, but I am so fucking angry that nothing can pry me away. She falls onto her back from the unexpected assault, which has me diving on top of her and delivering punch after punch to her face.

She flails madly, but I'm straddling her. She's pinned with nowhere to go. "Get off me!" she bellows, but I can't stop. Even when her flesh squishes under my blows and my stomach roils in disgust, I continue hitting her.

I barely feel Alek and Pavel loop their arms around me and attempt to drag me off her because with a strength comparable to being possessed by the devil, I shove them off and jump back on top of her. "You know nothing! Nothing!" I scream, slapping her cheek.

Her head lolls to the side as she's on the cusp of passing out, but even that sight doesn't have me showing mercy. I grip her hair and slam her head onto the carpet, the vibration pulsating through me.

I know what I'm doing is wrong, and that I should stop, but I can't. She deserves to suffer for what she's done. "This is all your fault!" I cry over and over as I continue slapping and punching her, needing to punish her.

Rage animates me, and the room spins violently. I can't gulp in air fast enough. Zoey isn't moving, but I won't be satisfied until she's dead. Just as I'm about to strike her once again, I hear a voice; my tether to this plane calls to me, dragging me from this darkness pervading my soul.

"Ангел, enough. She's had enough."

But I shake my head, refusing to fall victim to the deceits because I am done being weak. I should have done more; I should have saved him because that's all he's ever done for me.

"Shh, come now, stop." When I feel his familiar warmth cradle me tightly, and his signature fragrance lull the noise, I have no other choice but to surrender. He was my master, and even though I never listened, sooner or later, I eventually submitted—just as I do now.

A relief swarms me when he pulls me from her body because I don't think I would have stopped. He brushes the hair from my cheeks, sweeping the tears from my eyes as he silently assures me it'll be okay.

My mind is clouded, but when I lock eyes with a chartreuse embrace, I sob uncontrollably. "I'm...s-sorry," I manage to choke out between winded breaths, but Saint shakes his head as he wraps me into his arms.

I go willingly as he drags me onto his lap, never letting him go. I bury my face into the crook of his neck, weeping for everything we've become. "Forgive m-me," I stutter, choking on my tears.

Saint rubs my back but doesn't speak.

I'm seeking absolution for so much that sorry just doesn't even begin to cover it. I need to find another word or, better yet, invent one to express this regret inside me. But for now, I allow this moment of kindness because I don't know when I will be shown one again.

CHAPTER NINE

The silence is deafening. I suppose that's because, sooner or later, I will be surrounded with nothing but noise.

As Pavel and Max carefully carried an unconscious Zoey to the infirmary, what I had done hit me, and I was violently ill. Sister Margaret helped me to the bathroom, but I didn't deserve her kindness. I had disrespected her and her place of worship.

I promised to scrub the blood and vomit from the carpet and begged for her forgiveness, but she said she wasn't the one I should be apologizing to.

And she's right.

With that as food for thought, I went back to my room, head hanging in shame.

I am horrified by my actions. If Saint hadn't intervened…

Thinking of him has me rubbing my arms because he

hasn't come to see me. It's been hours since he pulled me, foaming at the mouth, off his sister. I know he's probably comforting her, but I thought he'd be here.

I can't blame him for staying away, though, because I'd want to stay away from me too. I don't know what I've become. From the person I once was to the person I am now; I have died a thousand deaths and been reborn into...this. This malevolent person who only seems to do wrong.

There are many reasons I wanted to kill her, but the main one which drove my need for violence is because of what she said. I don't...love Alek. The sentiment is almost comical.

Yes, I've always struggled with what *this* is with Alek, but love? I can't accept that as truth. He is the reason I'm here, why I was able to beat Zoey with my bare hands without remorse. If I feel anything other than hatred toward him, what does that say about me?

Anyone looking in would tell me I'm a fucking weakling, a pathetic idiot, and they're right.

I am.

Drawing my legs toward my chest, I hug them tightly and rest my cheek on my knees, unsure what tomorrow holds. I am so broken, and I don't know if I'll ever be able to be put back together again.

"Can we talk?"

I didn't even hear him enter.

His voice is filled with hurt, anger, but most of all, uncertainty. It seems we're both lost souls.

Pulling it together, I slowly raise my cheek and meet Saint's eyes. He is clutching his side as he's clearly still wounded. The bruises are fading, but what's plaguing him internally is, no doubt, still raw. The thought has a newfound sadness sinking low.

Saint drags the wooden chair from the corner of the room and places it a few feet away from me. I'm sitting on the floor with my back pressed to the bed and have no intention of getting up. He winces as he takes a seat.

I wait for him because I don't know what to say. Even when he kidnapped me, there was never this silence between us. I opted not to speak to him, yes, but I had a million things I wanted to say. But now, there is nothing.

"How are you?"

I merely shrug in response.

He shifts slightly, cradling his bandaged hand. Images of it bent back at a grotesque angle assault me, and I squeeze my eyes shut.

"Look at me." When I refuse, he adds a pained, "Please."

I slowly comply.

We are both so badly wounded, both physically and emotionally. Our relationship, which was once a constant, is now unknown.

"I don't know what to say," he confesses, shaking his head. "I don't know how to make this right anymore."

"There is no right," I whisper, tears clinging to my lashes. "There never was."

Saint sighs, beyond exhausted. "I wish I had never met you." My heart constricts, but I know what he means because I feel it too. "I wish you could have lived a normal life away from this."

"Well, I can't," I reply. "It's too late. What has been done can never be undone."

He casts his eyes toward the floor.

"On the island, you said to me your hands have done some unspeakable things. Do you remember?"

He nods slowly, his hair shrouding his downturned face.

"Well now, so have mine." I turn my hands over and over, and although they are now clean of blood, there was a time they weren't. "But I don't have any regrets. I would do it all again. I am so sick of feeling scared all the time. It's easier if I don't feel."

Saint's chin snaps up. "Don't say that. Don't switch off your humanity."

"I don't want to feel," I repeat, suppressing the vacant screams of the men and women I've wounded and killed.

"Ангел." Saint wearily rises from the chair and lowers himself to the floor. I want to touch him, but I don't. "I'm sorry for everything. I—"

I cut him off, shaking my head fiercely. "Don't you dare apologize to me. I'm the one who's sorry. For everything. Back at Oscar's—"

Saint's Adam's apple bobs as he swallows deeply.

"I never chose Alek over you. I need you to know that. But when I was about to tell Oscar everything, why did you stop me?"

"Because I had to trust there was a reason you protected him."

"There was!" I exclaim, beseeching he believe me. "Pavel said he was our ace in the hole. But I shouldn't have allowed it to get that far."

"You didn't allow anything," he counters sharply. "Besides, revealing Alek's whereabouts wouldn't have made a difference. We were just pawns to them."

He's right, but that doesn't alleviate this guilt.

"You shouldn't have come for me," he says with regret. "You should have left me."

"Never," I affirm, shaking my head. "I protect the things I love."

I've said this to him once before in reference to Harriet Pot Pie. Back then, I never, in a million years, thought I'd be referencing it to him.

He appears saddened by the fact. I don't understand why that is until he speaks. "What happened with Ingrid—"

The memory crashes into me, and I swallow down the putrid bile. "Please don't. I don't want to talk about it."

But Saint won't let matters lie. "I'm weak. I shouldn't have...I didn't mean..." It seems he can't find the right words. Taking a breath, he continues. "I'm sorry you had to see that. I can't imagine how that made you feel."

"It's okay."

"No, it's not fucking okay!" he bellows, slamming his fist onto the floor.

"Saint." I reach out to touch him, but he recoils so violently, I am left stunned.

What the hell?

My mouth parts, unsure what to make of his retreat. This is how he was when we first met—he didn't like to be touched—but I brought down those walls. However, it seems,

I have managed to erect them once again, brick by brick.

I try not to let my anguish show, but I'm hurt. And confused.

"Will Zoey be all right?" I need to change the subject.

Saint seems relieved that I have. "She'll live. It seems you do listen every now and again," he says, referring to his training.

The mood lightens for a moment, and I attempt a smile. It's gone a second later. "I didn't mean to hurt her that badly." I imagine he'd be angry with me for hurting his sister. But something about him has changed. He seems…detached.

"It's done," he replies coldly. I soon find out the reason behind his disconnection. "I heard what she said. About Alek. And I saw how you responded."

I lick my sudden dry lips. "She doesn't know what she's talking about." My reply is feeble, but I need him to know that I don't feel that for Alek.

But it seems he's made his own conclusions. "It's okay. I don't blame you."

"Don't blame me for what?" I question, my voice swathed in horror. When he doesn't reply, I decide to press. "Back at Alek's, the reason you let him live was because of me. You were going to leave me with him because—"

Saint appears defeated as he exhales steadily.

"Did you mean it?" There is no need for me to elaborate. He knows what I'm asking.

The seconds suddenly feel like hours because the longer he takes to respond, the harder I'll fall.

"Yes. And I know you have feelings for him."

"Saint, no," I cry, wanting nothing more than to reach out and touch him. But I don't because I can't stand the rejection. "I don't."

"It's all right."

But it's really not. None of this is. "No. It's not all right. I don't have feelings for him how you think I do." And I mean it. But I can see why he would recognize it another way.

Saint wants Alek dead, but I am woman enough to admit that I don't.

I still don't understand what I feel toward Alek, and I doubt I ever will. But being here with Saint, regardless of this distance between us, I know my feelings for him are real, so real they rob the very air I breathe. There is no mistaking what this is, and that's love. I love him. So much. Which is the reason I know I don't love Alek.

I don't feel this undeniable pull toward Alek. And the thought of being without him doesn't leave me with a gaping hole in my chest. But when I think about losing Saint, my entire world crumbles, giving way to perpetual darkness.

But he doesn't seem convinced.

"Don't shut me out. We'll work this out together."

His shoulders depress as he hangs his head low. "Don't try to fix me, Willow. I was broken a long time ago."

His admission has me weeping silent tears. "Don't say that. What you did, what you sacrificed at Oscar's—" My words fade into the abyss because it's apparent those wounds are still raw when he clenches his jaw.

"I don't want to talk about it." His animated eyes are a sure sign that if I push too hard, he will retreat further away, and if

I'm not careful, he will be lost to me for good.

"Okay. But eventually, you'll have to." I let it go—for now. "So what happens now?"

Saint runs a hand over his beard, nothing but exhaustion riddling him. "We leave. Being here puts too many people in danger."

I always knew this place was temporary. And although leaving saddens me, he's right. I can imagine no stone will remain unturned until we're found.

"We'll go to the mountains. Where Zoey was," he reveals, catching me off guard.

"And Pavel is okay with this plan? Isn't us going there putting his mom in danger?" Zoey told me she was healed thanks to the woman she affectionately referred to as grandmother.

"He knows what has to be done."

"And what's that?" I fearfully ask.

Saint's nostrils flare. "We end this. Once and for all."

"So that means you give Alek what he wants?" I can't believe he'd be on board with this. "How can Pavel agree to this? After everything Alek has done to him, why is Pavel, why are you helping him?"

"Pavel knows the terms are different now. His mother will be well looked after and so will his children. This will ensure his family's safety for generations to come."

Children? This is news to me.

"This is wrong." I run my fingers through my hair, tugging at the strands.

Saint watches me closely, but he places his clenched fist

against his thigh, suppressing the need to comfort me. "I don't care anymore. Zoey told me what she did. She shouldn't have. She should have just let me take care of it."

This robotic version of Saint confirms what I feared—he is broken beyond repair.

"There is only one person I want to kill, and he'll be my last. I'm done with this life." His entire demeanor transforms into something bleak, and it frightens me.

"So we're back to the beginning? With Alek holding our future in the palm of his hands?"

Saint nods with regret. "We need him."

"For what?" I can't keep the disbelief from my voice. But what he says next rips the air from my lungs.

"To go back home."

I open, then close my mouth because I was not expecting that response. Does he mean that we will go back to America together? The prospect is too overwhelming to process.

"For once, Alek is the one we can trust."

"And if he doesn't stick to his word?" I ask, unsure why the sudden faith in Alek.

"He will. And I believe him."

And there it is in a nutshell. The truth staring us in the face since the beginning. We need Alek to go home.

"Russia will always be home to villains, but in this case, it's better the devil you know. Pavel doesn't want the job, so that leaves Alek. We will work together, learning all we can. Pavel has some connections, ones who will hopefully become Alek's allies. This isn't going to be easy, and it's going to take time. We can't go in with our guns blazing. We have to be smart."

I understand what he means. Been there, done that, and look what that achieved.

"At the moment, Astra and"—he swallows deeply—"Oscar are the top dogs. We need them to believe that nothing is amiss. We have the element of surprise, thanks to you."

I blink once, confused. "To me?"

Saint nods. "They're unaware we know of their dealings with Serg, and that's because you were smart enough to plant the bug where you did."

I pale, unsure how he will respond. "You know about them?"

"Yes, Pavel told me." That means he probably knows I planted more. "As long as Zoya has that bag, we have ears on the inside."

She did tell me she took that bag with her everywhere. My hope soon returns.

"We let the deal with Serg go down because we need to know every person involved."

I know the answer, but I ask anyway. "And then what?"

Saint narrows his eyes, fire burning behind them as he responds with venom and without pause. "And then…we kill them all."

This was always a tale embroiled in blood, deceit, and revenge. And it seems there is no way out without people dying. I may not like it, and I will *never* accept it, but this is what I must do if I want to go home.

This is personal for Saint, and it's clear he will kill anyone who stands in his way of retribution. I understand his reasons, but I'm afraid of what his need for vengeance will do to him.

"And what happens when this is over, Saint?" Even though he is mere feet away, the gap between us is miles apart. "You said we need Alek to go home. Does that include you going home?"

Coming to a slow stand, he sighs heavily. He matches my stare, his perfect poker face in play. "Don't ask things you know the answer to."

He's said this once before. And just as I did then, I feel utterly powerless, imprisoned to the noise as I reply, "I'll never stop asking that, regardless if I know the answer."

Saint arches a brow, understanding the significance. I didn't give up then, and I don't intend on starting now. He leaves me alone as there is nothing left to say. Drawing my knees toward my chest, I hug them tight, a feeling of helplessness swarming me.

I thought by setting Saint free, everything would be okay.

How naïve I was.

CHAPTER

TEN

Saying goodbye to Mother Superior and the sisters was harder than I thought. They became my family, people I could trust. The children were sound asleep, oblivious to our departure, which is exactly how I wanted it. They too became familiar faces, ones who helped me have hope.

But now, as we leave behind my sanctuary, all I'll have are memories because I know I will never see them again. We've been on the road for what seems likes hours, but I suppose being squashed into the back of a van with the woman you almost beat to death, her brother, and an ex-concubine who sucked off your boyfriend while you watched makes everything feel like forever.

Pavel is driving, and Alek is riding shotgun. Sara and Max are following in a black SUV. Lucky them.

I've hardly said a word because what is there to say?

Saint can barely stand the sight of me, Ingrid would rather be anywhere but between us, and Zoey is, well, Zoey. She resembles a mummy as she's covered in bandages. I'm not proud of the fact I'm to blame.

All in all, this idea of camping out together while we devise a plan spells disaster. If Oscar and Astra don't kill us first, odds are one of us will be dead come the end of the week from either giving into our murderous urges or dying by plummeting to our death, thanks to Pavel's driving.

I hold the ceiling for support as the roads are small and winding. There are no windows back here, so I lean forward to peer out the windshield. Seeing no streetlights or passing cars, I know we truly are in the middle of nowhere.

When Saint said the mountains, he wasn't kidding because we're high up. The rugged terrain is covered by thick foliage. If one didn't know where to look, they would get lost. I doubt any GPS could track these roads. And as for cell coverage, I don't think they even use landlines.

But that's the point. We're here to remain incognito and untraceable. Yet all I see is another prison. The thought has me bowing my head and rubbing the back of my neck as I take three calming breaths.

A small part of me hopes Saint will ask if I'm okay, but he doesn't. I understand why he feels resentment toward me. If it wasn't for me, he wouldn't have suffered at the hands of Oscar, and all for what? He bargained for my freedom, but here I am, still a prisoner in this fucking country.

But I don't know where we stand. Earlier, he couldn't bear me to touch him. And now, he can't even look at me.

"How much farther?" I ask Pavel. I need to get out of this

van.

"Not far," he replies, but that doesn't really help.

Alek peers over his shoulder, and when he sees me crouched over, practicing my yoga breathing, he reaches across to rub my shoulder. It's a friendly gesture, one I don't even think twice about, but when I feel three sets of eyes burn a hole straight through me, I realize I'll have to change my attitude. I gently shrug out of his hold.

When the tires crunch over gravel and Pavel slows, I exhale in relief because we're here. Before he has a chance to kill the engine, Saint slides open the door, appearing just as desperate to get out as I am. I quickly follow, thankful when the arctic breeze cools my heated cheeks.

Rubbing my hands together, I blow on them, hoping not to get hypothermia because it's so damn cold. Looking around, I see what can only be described as a modest-sized log cabin ahead. A plume of smoke wafts from the chimney, which my shivering body is thankful for.

A wooden barn sits behind the cabin, and to the left is what appears to be a garage. Apart from that, it's only tall trees as far as the eye can see. This seclusion has me wondering if I should call shotgun on the barn as the thought of freezing to death is preferable to having to sleep under the same roof as Zoey.

The front door opens and out hobbles an elderly lady in black with an army of cats and dogs following. She is clearly the alpha. Pavel speaks fondly to her in Russian as she waits on the porch for him to gather his things. With the door open, I can see over her shoulders, and thankfully, the place looks bigger than I thought.

"бабушка!" There is no mistaking the happiness in Zoey's tone. I've not heard it before. It sounds almost foreign.

She limps over to her, taking the steps carefully because she's still unsteady on her feet. When Pavel's mother sees Zoey's battered and bruised appearance, she grips her cheeks, and a flurry of Russian spills from her furrowed lips.

Zoey shakes her head, placing a hand over Pavel's mom's, clearly trying to soothe her worries. However, when her wise old eyes glare at Alek, it's clear she believes he's the cause of her injuries. I'm about to step forward and tell her it was me, but Alek is at my side, gently cupping my elbow to stop my advance.

"She hates me anyway," he whispers, saving me the wrath. I appreciate the sentiment and nod my thanks.

"I'll sleep out in the barn," Saint says, which has me quickly severing our connection. I can't seem to do anything right.

Pavel's mom stubbornly shakes her head. But Saint won't have it any other way. "Are you sure?" Pavel asks, the cloud of smoke drifting from his lips highlighting how cold it is. "It'll be tight inside, but we can make it work."

"It's fine." Saint waves at Pavel's mom and turns into the direction of the barn.

But there is no way I am letting him off that easily.

"I'll stay there too." I'm hardly in appropriate clothing to be sleeping outdoors, but it's not snowing—yet.

Saint shakes his head firmly. "No, you won't. You're staying inside."

His bossiness only adds to my determination because even though he's reprimanding me, at least he's speaking to me. "No."

"No?" he questions, arching a surprised brow. I think he was expecting more of an argument, but no is no. There is no need for further elaboration.

I walk toward the barn, but Saint reaches out and grips my forearm. A gasp leaves me because it's the first time he's touched me without shuddering. The connection between us is electric, and all thoughts of freezing to death are soon replaced with a searing heat about to consume me whole.

"It'll get to below minus temperatures," he says, trying to scare me. But I don't scare easy. He should know this by now.

"I'll manage," I taunt, my cheeks reddening with the excitement of sparring with him this way. My numb toes demand I listen to him, but I'll happily lose an appendage if it means I get some alone time with him.

His grip on me tightens, which only enflames me further. I match him, stare for stare, daring him to do his best.

"Don't push me," he warns, but the threat is music to my ears, and I smirk, challenging him.

When the warm amber to his eye's swirls to life, I smother my moan. He is coming to life in front of me, and how I've missed that fire, that burn which has set me alight time and time again.

Disobeying Saint is what I do best, and if defying him every chance I get will bring him back to me, then call me a sinner. All hail the saints and sinners because it appears I have to be both to save my man from himself.

He slowly pulls me toward him, his towering frame leaving me breathless. I peer up at him from under my lashes. The background fades into nothingness, and it's only us. "And what are you going to do about it?" I quip, licking my lower lip.

I am burned alive by the amber flash as he eagerly follows the movement. The tension is suffocating, but I bathe in it because this closeness with Saint thrums an electrical pulse straight through me. Images of him taking me over his knee as he spanked me for my insolence flood me, and I can't suppress the whimper which slips free.

This is the ultimate standoff, one which I will happily lose. He can read my perversion, and when a slanted grin tugs at his supple lips, I see it—the first sign of hope. Who knew defying him would eventually work in my favor?

As much as I want to climb him like a tree, I don't because this is going to take time. He is broken, but I will help him heal. I don't care how long it takes or how hard he pushes me away; I'm here to stay.

With that as my mantra, I pry his fingers off me. I need to keep my cool. I've tried to be kind, but I should know by now, like me, Saint doesn't want nice—he wants pain.

"Thought so," I goad, referring to him standing around, dick in hand as I turn on my heel and make my way to the barn.

A victory walk has never felt more satisfying. That victory is short-lived, however, when I open the door and see that I'll be sharing my lodgings with sheep, chickens, and a cow. But I suck it up. I've made my bed, or rather, I've made my hay bale, so it's time I laid in it.

The door slamming behind me has me humming under my breath calmly. He is watching me test out a few bales of hay as one would if shopping for a new mattress. They all feel the same, but I toss my backpack onto the farthest one away from him.

"Comfortable?"

"Very," I reply, happily perching on the edge of my new bed and crossing my ankles as I look at him. "This one has my name on it." I bounce up and down to prove my point. The coarse straw pokes me in the ass, but I smile, nonetheless.

Saint doesn't appreciate my humor as he folds his arms across his broad chest. "What are you doing?"

"Making my bed," I counter blankly, intending the double meaning behind the phrase.

He inhales slowly. I'm clearly testing his patience. "You know what I mean."

"No, actually, I don't." I come to a stand, using this opportunity to my advantage. "You won't talk to me. I don't know what you're thinking. So if sleeping in cow manure gets you talking, then so be it."

He shakes his head angrily. "You're doing this to prove a point?"

"No," I exclaim, leaving crescent dents in my palms from digging my fingernails in deep to keep from reaching out and touching him. "I'm doing this because I love you!"

He hisses and takes a step back, but I won't allow his retreat to stop me this time.

"I don't care if you, if you don't love me anymore"—I

swallow down the emptiness that statement holds while he averts his gaze—"but I'm staying. I won't ask you what happened."

Saint interlaces his hands behind his neck as he lifts his chin to the ceiling. "You already know," he says with a measured pace.

There is so much pain behind his reply that I don't bother correcting him because I can only guess. For him to heal, he needs to talk about his pain; otherwise, it will fester, and Oscar will have won.

"I can only imagine, and I'm sorry, I really am, but please don't shut me out." Sorry seems like such a cop-out because it can never encompass what I'm trying to say.

I want to say so much more, but Saint's walls are watertight. He won't let me in, and that's okay. I'll give him time, but he needs to know I'm not going anywhere.

"I'm going to sleep." I turn my back to him so he can't see my tears.

The bales of hay provide no comfort, but I try my best to arrange them so they surround me and block out the cold. I yank out a few handfuls of hay and toss them onto the ground. Not the most luxurious mattress lining, but I doubt I'll be able to sleep anyway.

Digging around in my backpack, I find another sweater and put it on. I decide to use a spare T-shirt as a pillow. With everything set, I lower my stiff body to the ground, ignoring the pins and needles shooting straight through me thanks to the subzero temperature. There wasn't any wood to light a fire, so here's hoping I don't freeze to death.

The T-shirt is a pathetic substitute for a pillow, but I fold it and position it under my head. I may as well be using a pancake, but I've slept in worse conditions. With that thought in mind, I curl myself into a ball and squeeze my eyes shut.

Thanks to the howling wind, the entire barn rattles, and images of being stuck in Oz come to mind. They say counting sheep when one can't sleep helps with insomnia, and I wonder if literally counting them, seeing as I'm surrounded by them, works the same way.

My teeth chatter because no matter how hard I try to keep warm, a constant chill envelops me. I shuffle closer toward the bales, hoping they'll provide some warmth, but the only thing that will do that is a blanket or…the warmth of another body.

And when that is presented to me, I can't stop the contented sigh which slips past my lips.

I am incased in his warmth, his smell, and everything that is Saint. He lies behind me, ensuring not to touch, but he's close enough that I can feel his breath on the back of my neck. Instantly, the chill thaws, and I melt into our almost union because it's progress.

Memories of when we lay this way on the yacht before we were shipwrecked assault me, reminding me that no matter what we've been through, we've always drifted to the surface. I can only hope it's the same this time.

His steady breathing lulls me into a tranquil bubble, and I allow sleep to invade me. As I'm hanging onto the last thread of my consciousness, I hear something which breaks and mends my heart all in the same inhale.

"Don't give up on me," Saint whispers, shuffling closer so

we're pressed back to front.

He should know by now that surrendering isn't in my nature, and when it comes to him…I will never give up.

On him.

Or on us.

Although my body is screaming at me, I wake after what feels like a few solid hours of sleep. The warmth which sang me into oblivion has gone, hinting Saint has already risen.

Opening my eyes, I rub them and slowly come to a sit. The daylight streaming in from the cracks in the wooden walls hint that another day has passed. I've lost count of how many days I've been here, but honestly, it feels like years.

I stand and stretch my arms over my head. The beautiful cow with the shiny black coat moos at me.

"Hello to you too." I smile because being here reminds me of growing up on the farm. Memories of my father have me wishing he was here. On instinct, I reach up to touch the cross around my neck, but it's gone. I have no idea where it is, seeing as Saint doesn't seem to have it either.

Just another thing lost to this fucking country.

Deciding to find the bathroom, I shoulder my backpack, give the cow a pat on her nose, and make my way outside. The moment I step out, a ferocious gust of wind almost knocks me over. Folding my arms around myself, I make a run for the house.

Unsure if I'm welcome inside, I knock on the door and bounce from foot to foot to keep warm. I really need to invest in some thicker clothes. Pavel opens the door, pursing his lips in confusion.

"Can I come in?" I ask, clarifying why I'm standing outside, freezing my ass off.

He opens the door wider, permitting me entry, and when I smell the freshly brewed coffee wafting through the air, I lick my lips hungrily.

Once inside, the crackling open fire is like a beacon to my frozen appendages, and I make a beeline for it, warming my hands in front of it. Taking a moment, I peer around at my surroundings and see that the living area is quite homey.

The interior is wooden with some brickwork to help keep out the cold. The furnishings are rustic and well-loved but complement the cabin nicely.

"Can I use the bathroom?" I ask Pavel, my teeth still chattering.

"Of course. You don't have to stay in the barn," he says with a sigh. "There is enough room in here."

"I don't mind."

He thankfully doesn't persist. "Once you're done, we're going to sit down and talk about what happens next."

I nod, but Pavel can tell something is on my mind.

"I know you're wondering how could I help him." Pavel doesn't engage in small talk, which is another thing I like about him. "Firstly, the money is a big factor. Alek says it'll be different this time, and I believe him because he is running short of allies. He needs me because I am the one with the power."

That makes sense. Alek has no one on his side and needs Pavel's contacts to regain control.

"Secondly, I don't know any other life, Willow," he confesses with a hint of sadness. "I wouldn't know what to do with my freedom. Alek promises he will look after my family, and that's all that matters to me. I know you may not be able to understand my reasons, but Alek is the lesser of two evils."

Although I understand, it doesn't make me feel any better. Once Alek regains his throne, it'll be like nothing happened, and all of this will have been for nothing. We've come full circle, but we haven't progressed or grown. We're merely making the same mistakes twice.

I decide to leave this discussion for later. "Okay. I won't be long."

He exhales in defeat, but points at the second doorway down the corridor. "Bathroom's that way. My mom found some warmer clothes for you girls to wear, but I don't know if they'll fit."

But I wave him off, thankful she went to the effort. "What's your mom's name?"

"Larisa," he replies with a small smile, showing his affection toward her.

Relieved to be warmer, I make my way down the short hallway. I knock softly on the bathroom door, and when the coast is clear, I open it. The toilet has my full bladder rejoicing, and I waddle over to it.

Once I'm done, I see a pile of clothes in the corner of the room. The puffy army green jacket with fur around the hood is calling my name. I also see some thick pants and snow boots. I don't want to hog everything, so I will only grab the essentials.

Stripping down, I wait for the warm water to fire up, eager to thaw out the remaining chill to my bones. The moment I step under the spray, a moan escapes me because the hot water feels amazing. I hope it's okay to help myself to the toiletries, and I shampoo and condition my hair. I use the shower gel next.

Once I'm clean, I turn off the water as I don't want to waste it in case others still need to shower. I dry off and wrap the towel around me. Hunting through the clothes, I grab a pair of thick wool trousers, a long-sleeved sweater, and the jacket.

I have a clean pair of underwear in my bag which I slip into after I've applied deodorant and then dress in the warmer clothes. They're a little big, but they'll do. The black boots are lined with white faux fur and fit perfectly. I run my fingers through my hair which has grown in length. The scruffy style is edgy, giving me a hard look. I like it as it matches how I feel.

Once I brush my teeth, I clean up after myself and gather the wet towel and jacket. I don't know where anyone else is, but I hope Larisa won't mind if I grab a cup of coffee. As I step out into the hallway, I notice three doors, which I'm assuming lead into bedrooms.

We have a full house with nine of us in total, so it goes without saying, there will be a lot of sharing happening. I'm suddenly thankful to be sleeping in the barn.

I find the kitchen and see Larisa inside. She is standing

over a stove, cooking eggs. When she hears me enter, she turns over her shoulder and nods. There is no bullshit about this woman, and I remember Zoey once said there was nothing grandmotherly about her. I now can see why.

I hold up the wet towel, wondering if she speaks English. "Thank you for letting me use your bathroom. And for the clothes. Where should I put this?"

She gestures with her head toward a door behind her which I'm assuming leads outside.

I walk past, ensuring not to disturb her because I won't lie, Larisa scares me. I open the door and see a small, undercover laundry area. I toss the towel into the hamper and quickly close the door, not wanting to let the cold in.

"Can I help?" It's the least I can do, seeing as she's letting me stay here.

However, she points her spoon toward the table, hinting I'm to sit. The steaming pot of coffee has me happily complying.

"Coffee?" I ask her, raising a mug in case she doesn't understand me. She shakes her head.

Pouring myself a cup, I can't shake the feeling Larisa hates my guts. Even though she hasn't spoken a single word to me, her body language has pretty much flipped me off since the moment we met. I know it's because of what I did to Zoey.

She turned up black and blue, and no doubt, she told Larisa the reason. She has every right to be mad at me because it's clear she's fond of her. Here, I am the outsider, but haven't I always been?

I sip my coffee in silence, but the peace doesn't bother me. It's actually quite nice to sit and gather my thoughts. That is soon shattered when Zoey ruins the calm.

She speaks to Larisa in Russian but ignores me, of course. I'm surprised she doesn't throw the hot coffee in my face after she pours herself a cup. Her bruises are hideous, and I avert my gaze, ashamed I lost my temper.

She may be a lying, insensitive asshole, but I shouldn't have attacked her the way that I did. I stooped to her level by behaving that way.

Alek and Ingrid enter together, and I don't miss Zoey's glower. Alek addresses Larisa, who barks a response. Maybe she just hates everyone.

When Alek sees me at the table, he smiles, and I hate that it seems genuine when I'm still angry with him. Ingrid stands behind Alek, which only enrages Zoey all the more. All in all, the tension can be cut with a knife and seeing as there are many pointy implements within reach, it wouldn't surprise me if someone took that metaphor literally.

Sara and Max are next to enter and seeing Sara has me standing, wanting to give my friend a hug. "Hi," I say as we embrace warmly. We haven't had a chance to talk.

Once we break apart, I decide to stay standing as the room is suddenly crowded.

Pavel enters through the back door with a basket full of eggs. Sharing breakfast with everyone is as ridiculous as it sounds, and if I wasn't so hungry, I would skip it altogether and stick with coffee. But having no idea what the day holds, I decide to face it with a full stomach.

Pavel kisses his mom on the cheek as he places the eggs on the counter. The sight warms me because I never had this affection with my mom. Although I don't agree with him working with Alek, I understand it because it's clear his family is very important to him.

Larisa says something in Russian that has everyone grabbing a plate. When Sara notices that I'm lost in translation, she clarifies, "She said breakfast is ready."

"Thanks, Sara," I say, accepting the plate she offers me. "I haven't had a chance to speak to you since we've been back. I'm sorry."

She shakes her head. "It's okay. I understand. How's Saint?"

Instantly, I cast my eyes downward.

"He'll be okay." I know she's trying to make me feel better, but honestly, no one knows that. The fact he won't speak to me about anything has me wondering if maybe he blames me for everything. I *am* the reason he was tortured and abused. He has every right to hate me. I hate me too.

Sighing, my appetite soon disappears as the thought of eating anything turns my stomach.

I'm about to leave everyone to their breakfast as the chewing and slurping are already grating at my raw nerves, but when the back door opens and in jogs a sweaty, breathless Saint, I forget everything. He eclipses the sun, the moon, the entire fucking planet.

His damp hair is tied back, but a few stray strands have escaped, framing his hard, chiseled face. He's in sweats and a tight white T-shirt that clings to his hardened body. It's apparent he's just gone for a run. When he locks eyes with me, I smile, unapologetic he caught me staring.

His lips twitch into a half smile in response. It's progress.

He ignores everyone and helps himself to a glass of water. After gulping it down, he refills the glass and has another drink. His back is turned as he is clearly not interested in playing happy family. Someone who does, however, is Zoey.

She sheepishly walks over to where he stands. "Hey, Saint." She touches his arm but pulls it away quickly when he hisses and recoils about three feet.

He doesn't like to be touched, and I don't blame him. After everything he endured, I can only imagine what memories the touch of another evokes.

He inhales sharply before his composure returns. "Hey," he finally replies, finishing his water.

I watch closely, unsure what is about to transpire.

"How are you?" She is testing the waters as she too doesn't know how to handle her brother.

"Fine," he replies curtly.

Everyone stops eating and watches the exchange between siblings.

"You don't look fine," she presses, and I'll give it to her, she has bigger balls than me because I know when not to poke the bear.

"Well, I am." Saint rinses his glass and places it in the dishrack, hinting this conversation is done with. But Zoey doesn't know when to quit.

"Don't be angry with me. I was the one who rescued you."

Oh, shit. I'm about to witness World War III erupt.

"You shouldn't have," Saint snarls, turning to face her. "If you'd minded your own business, then they'd all be dead."

"And so would you!" she yells, shoving him in the chest. "I won't apologize for saving your life."

One thing we agree on.

"So, it's okay for you, but when I tried over and over again to save you, I was the bastard?" he exclaims, spreading his arms out wide.

Her regret is clear because he's right. All of this has happened because of her, and now that she's finally seen the light, she wants a pat on the back? Fuck her.

I can't keep my mouth shut and advance, but Saint's head snaps my way, his wide eyes demanding I stay put. It's obvious he doesn't trust me near his sister, and I wonder whose side he would choose if we were to fight again.

My body is itching that I move, but I obey his silent request.

The crackle over a speaker breaks the tension and is thankfully the distraction we all need. When Alek pauses chewing, my guess is that the woman's voice we hear is his mom's. Pavel quickly increases the volume on his phone, which seems to be how he's been listening to the bugs.

A man speaks to her in Russian.

When Alek grips his coffee cup, appearing to want to strangle it, I assume the man is his brother. I have no idea what they're saying, but I'm hoping it's good news for us. I may not know what is being said, but I do understand Alek's name, which is being dropped quite a few times.

Sighing, I lean against the counter, sipping my coffee quietly and waiting patiently for someone to fill me in. I can feel Saint's eyes on me, and it takes all my willpower not to look, but when he walks over and stands beside me, I can't help but shuffle closer.

He leans down, close to my ear, and his warmth wraps me tight, refusing to let go. "It's Alek's mom and his brother," Saint explains while I inhale slowly. "The meeting has been moved forward a week."

"Why?"

"Because of our escape."

"Oh."

Saint's breath glides down the column of my neck as he leans in closer. "They're all paranoid. No one trusts anyone. Serg is worried."

I'm trying my absolute hardest to listen and not to buckle under him. "Worried about what?"

"He was certain Alek had died in the explosion, but now, he's not sure. He wants to move things along quickly, in case they get cold feet."

I don't fail to notice how he refuses to use Oscar's name. The thought of that bastard has me clenching my fists. "Do we know where they're meeting? Or who the new supplier is?"

Saint turns his ear, continuing to listen to the voices over the speaker. When he nods firmly, I wonder why the room just dropped ten thousand degrees. A snarl rumbles from Alek's chest before he stands abruptly, toppling the chair over with the force.

I watch in confusion as he tears out the back door. Ingrid rises quickly and chases after him. Zoey looks seconds away from tripping her. What the fuck just happened?

"Yes. The drop-off will be at Alek's," Saint says while I arch a brow.

"At Alek's what?"

"House," he replies, but that does nothing to answer my question.

"House? He doesn't have a house."

"No, you're right. But what's left standing is where they've decided to meet. It's merely rubble, but they just need a discreet location, one which will smoke Alek out. No pun intended," he adds, referring to what happened to Alek's once lavish home.

"Why would they do that?" I am so lost in translation.

Saint exhales, his warm breath wrapping me tight, but I focus on his words and not what being this close to him is doing to my body. "His reaction is why. They've not done this to be sentimental and reminisce about the good ole days. They're doing this knowing that if Alek is alive, he'll be at that meeting."

My mouth pops open.

"And the supplier is Raul…Chow's son."

"Holy shit." I gasp, not believing this is really happening. "Raul has taken over for his father, it seems. No wonder Serg has this hookup." Alek mentioned Chow was dealing to Serg as well as him, which is the reason he killed him.

I doubt Serg had a hard time convincing Raul to deal to him since they both want the same thing—Alek's head on a platter—and this partnership is a definite way to draw him out of hiding.

"Their corruption really knows no bounds," I reply, understanding why Alek stormed out.

"No, they're smart. They want revenge on all of us. And they know Alek is the weakest link."

Pavel nods, clearly agreeing with Saint. "He's right." He switches off the feed, running a hand over his head. "We can't risk him going. This is a trap."

"I know." Saint slowly pulls away from me, and I mourn the loss. "What do you suggest?"

"How about we tie *him* up? See how *he* likes it," Zoey suggests, eyes narrowed.

"Not a bad idea," Pavel replies, but we all know that won't work. "They're on to us. Oscar and Astra will have an army of men waiting for us. If they're wrong and Alek doesn't show, then no loss, no foul. But if he is alive, they know there is no way he would allow his brother to take his place."

"Alek's pride will fuck us over then?" I say, mouthing a sorry to Larisa as I feel guilty for swearing in front of her. She shrugs in response.

"This isn't good." Pavel sighs in annoyance. "This changes everything. It was supposed to be simple, and we'd have time to prepare. But Alek won't stand for this. His pride won't allow it. Them doing this on his home turf is a major fuck you."

Larisa doesn't bat an eyelash. She is clearly accustomed to profanity.

Saint purses his lips, appearing deep in thought. "They are merely working on a hunch. They still don't know we have the upper hand. We listen closely to their movements, their plans, and we find their vulnerabilities. And then, we exploit them."

"We have one week, brother." Pavel holds up a finger in

case Saint is lost in translation.

He's not. "Then we better not waste any time. We stick to the original plan, but we just speed things up."

Pavel laughs, but it's not a humored sound. "This takes time. Trust isn't earned in a week. Not to mention, how are we going to remain hidden? The house is in ruins. We will be ambushed the moment we step foot onto that land."

"Then what do you suggest?" Saint asks, all ears.

Zoey answers. "Here's a thought, how about we just let Alek go?"

The room falls silent as we mull over her suggestion. She uses this to further her discussion.

"He will get us killed. There is no doubt this will be a bloodbath. I don't fancy getting myself killed in the name of some family vendetta."

Saint clenches his jaw because I know there is more at stake than just Alek's revenge. He won't rest until Oscar is dead, and he won't settle for anyone else killing him. He has to be the one. But now, this changes everything.

"We need him, Zoey," Saint says, which has me sighing a silent breath of relief.

"What for?" She screws up her nose, confused and horrified he has suggested such a thing.

"We need him to get the fuck out of here."

Her mouth shapes into an O of understanding. This is the reason Saint left me in Alek's care.

"I don't have any ID. Or a passport. Do you?"

"No," she replies sheepishly, her bravado dying as quickly as it arose. "So you want to go back to America?"

A breath gets trapped in my throat as I inhale sharply. I too want to know the answer to this question.

Saint's silence is all the answer she needs.

"You're doing this for *her*. Aren't you?" When he averts his gaze, she shakes her head, furious. "Un-fucking-believable. You'd risk us all so she can go back home to her *husband*? Is that it? You're more pussy-whipped than I thought."

Saint advances, as does Zoey, and neither sibling backs down. But I can't let them fight. Not over this. Not over me. It's time I chose a side because there is no happy medium. No Switzerland. For this to end, I know what I have to do.

"Stop!" My feet slip and slid over the flooring as I rush to wedge my way between Zoey and Saint. I stop them from colliding by keeping them at arm's length. My hands are pressed over Saint's chest and Zoey's. Their frantic hearts beat the same wild rhythm.

"Don't touch me!" Zoey cries, gripping my wrist in an attempt to pry me off her, but I stand my ground.

"Enough! I won't have you fighting over this."

"Too late," she snarls, digging her fingernails into me.

Peering up at Saint from under my lashes, I end this once and for all. "I won't have you fighting over this because Zoey, I agree with you."

"What?" both Zoey and Saint gasp at the same time.

When I think it's safe, I slowly lower my arms, but stay rooted between them. "Pavel, is there any way you could get us some passports?"

Saint is stunned by my actions.

"Yes, I know a guy. I think I could manage it," he replies

calmly. I was stupid not to think of this sooner. But there's a reason for it.

My eyes never leave Saint's. "Good. Can you call him? We'll need them before this meeting takes place because I don't trust Alek. If he gets wind of the fact we don't need him anymore, he will have no qualms about feeding us to the sharks."

"What are you doing?" Saint asks, his cheeks turning a deep crimson.

"Making a better plan," I retort without pause. "You said we need Alek to get the fuck out of Russia. Well now, we don't."

"For once, I agree with her." Zoey's camaraderie means nothing to me because I only want the approval of one person.

"It's not that simple," Saint states heatedly.

"Why not?" I challenge because this darkness he has, it will ruin him. But I'll die fighting before that happens.

"You know why." His nostrils flare as he breathes steadily.

"I know, but is it worth dying over? Because that's what'll happen. If we go to that drop-off, we will die. Is that what you want?"

I am walking a very dangerous line, but when haven't I?

"Not for you, I don't."

I turn my cheek because his honesty has slapped me. "So all of this was for nothing? Is that what you're telling me?"

Silence. And the silence enrages me.

"I once told you, you were a coward; do you remember?" This is going to go one of two ways—bad or fucking diabolical.

Welcome to the madness.

Saint's chest rises and falls slowly. A sure sign he is going to explode. It's not a deterrent, however.

"I said do...you...remember?" My pause grates him raw. He clenches his jaw, eyes ablaze.

"What are you doing?" he asks once again, dangerously calm.

"I'm asking you a question," I smugly reply, folding my arms across my chest as I turn slowly to face him and only him.

He takes a menacing step forward, but instead of cowering in fear, I cock my head, daring him to do his worst because I am suddenly struck with an idea. I'm baiting him on purpose, and it's working.

Oh, how it's worked.

"Come with me...ангел."

Praise all the saints above...

The world spins as he grips my bicep so hard, a whimper escapes me, but that sound isn't because he's hurting me; it's because it feels so fucking good. He drags me through the kitchen as he shoulders open the back door.

He continues hauling me through the yard, and I don't fight him because this is what I wanted... I wanted him to feel. I've tried to be understanding and kind, but that hasn't worked, so now I'm going to play dirty, just as he did when he fucked that woman and made me watch.

I wouldn't speak to him, just as he hasn't spoken to me, so he found my weak spot, just as I found his. Saint can't stand not being in control, and that's exactly what happened with Oscar. I need him to see that this wasn't his fault. He needs to rid himself of these demons before they overshadow him forever.

He kicks open the barn door and hurls me inside. His back faces me as the lock clicks into place. The steady rise and fall of his shoulders is almost hypnotic, but when he reaches around and unfastens his hair, I know there will be nothing soothing about the next few minutes.

His head is lowered as he deliberately places his splayed hands against the wood and utters a simple yet powerful word which brings me to my knees—literally.

"Kneel."

For once, I do what he says.

Lowering myself to the ground, I cast my eyes downward, awaiting further command. His exhalations are heavy, and it's remarkable how I can sense so much from his breathing alone. He's barely holding on. My disobedience is testing him, just as it did when we first met.

"Why do you constantly defy me?"

I'm not sure if he's thinking aloud, so I remain quiet. His heavy footsteps alert me to his movement. My heart is in my throat as he circles me slowly.

"Answer me."

I wet my dry lips before speaking. "Because I can."

A cracking hints that my reply has him clenching his fist.

"Why are you doing this?" There is genuine curiosity behind his question.

"Doing what?" I embrace my courage and gradually lift my eyes. When we lock gazes, the warm amber sends a shiver straight through me. "Making you feel?"

"What are you talking about?" he spits, but he knows.

"Since we've been back, you've shut yourself off from everything. From me. And it scares me. I don't know what I can do to help you. Making you angry is the only response I can get from you. So if this makes you feel…something, if punishing me for everything that has happened to you will bring you back to me, then do it.

"Punish me…мастер."

He hisses and takes a step back.

"Do it," I encourage with nothing but determination. "I will happily submit if it takes your pain away."

Saint is barely holding on. His fist is clenched, and his long, wild hair sharpens his feral features.

His hesitation spurs me on because I can see it…piece by piece, the violence is bringing him back to me. "I deserve it…I killed a m-man. I have blood on my hands now too, but I don't regret it. I would do it again in a heartbeat if it meant saving you."

"Stop it!" he screams, charging forward. Once upon a time, I would beg for clemency, but now, I dance with the bloodshed.

"No," I challenge, not cowering as I peer up at him. "I won't stop. I will never give up on you. Even if you've given up on me."

Something detonates inside Saint, something he has tried so hard to forget. There is no proper way to behave after everything he's been through. I want him to feel everything—anger, pain, sorrow, regret, shame, love, hate…I want it all because I…want him.

"You want control after it was taken away from you, so

take it. Take it back."

He is struggling with what's right and wrong, so I make the decision for him.

"On that yacht, when you spanked me, when you whipped me, I liked it." It's the first time I've admitted my sins. "And I know you liked it too. Just as I know you liked it when you were inside me." He tongues his upper lip slowly, which has everything of mine clenching. "Do you remember what you said? You said we're one and the same. The pain is our heroin, reminding us that we're human."

His eyes flicker to black.

"But maybe you've gone soft? Maybe you don't have the balls?"

Game.

Set.

Match.

He tips his face to the heavens and inhales slowly. "Strip." He ends his command on an exhale.

Catching pneumonia is very possible, but I don't care. Coming to a slow stand, I fix my gaze firmly on Saint as I take off my boots and socks. Next to go are my pants. There is no hesitation as I take off the long-sleeved sweater.

Saint cocks his head and folds his arms, hinting I'm not done.

Reaching behind me, I unhook my bra, my nipples instantly pebbling when the cool air caresses them like a lover's touch. I drop it onto the pile of clothes next to me.

Saint runs two fingers down the center of his lips—the sight is too much for words.

We stand still with our eyes locked as the room is sparking with an electrical pulse that leaves me trembling. But I started this, and now, it's time I finished it. Hooking my thumbs into the waistband of my underwear, I slide out of them and kick them aside.

When I stand upright, I don't cover my modesty. Instead, I allow him to see me; all of me. His gaze zeros in on my side, and a winded gasp leaves him. I know what's stirred this response from him. He's seen my tattoo. He couldn't see it before because of the angle I was standing. But now, he can.

He takes a small step back.

Violence is what bonded us together, and in a fucked-up way, I hope it can do so again. Saint likes pain; the thrill of it makes him feel alive. Until I met him, I didn't understand, but now, I do. So without faltering, I drop to my knees, welcoming the pain because I want it. I want him.

Though he remains motionless, the fire burning behind those eyes reveals he is anything but silent inside. I know Saint, and he is wrestling with his emotions. He's never wanted to hurt me, but now, I believe he doesn't trust himself because I don't think he'll be able to stop.

He's burdened by the atrocities he's endured, and now that he's in control, he is blinded by its potency. But I trust him. I always have, which is why I utter, "Do it."

This is what he's always wanted—the docile lamb. So it doesn't surprise me when he bends down and picks up his belt. It hangs from his fingers innocently, but I know there is nothing harmless about it. But I won't go back on my word.

Saint's breathing is heavy as he stalks forward, his cheeks

bellowing as he inhales and exhales steadily. But I don't shy away. Or whimper. I take it like a…man? *Fuck that*. I decide then and there to make my own motto, one for the sisterhood all over the world.

I am woman, hear me roar, and I will take it like the fucking fierce woman that I am. This isn't a man's world; this is *my* world. With that as my newfound mantra, I brace for anything because I can take it. When Saint comes to a stop at my back, I am nothing but calm.

I await the brutal lash of his belt, the one I've felt before because once I feel the sting, we can salvage his soul. But as the time ticks on, I realize something is wrong. Saint doesn't hesitate. He never has.

I thought this would work. I thought this is what he wanted. Was I wrong? Then a horrible thought smashes into me. "Do you not love me anymore? Is that it?"

Saint once told me he fears love, but loves fear. It was his way of telling me that he loved me. Is it because I'm not afraid of him that he doesn't love me anymore?

"You can't do it because you don't care? Is that why? I know how fucked up that is, but I know you need pain to survive."

Suddenly, I feel anything but fierce. I feel fucking stupid.

Lowering my chin to my chest, I wonder if maybe this is it this time. Maybe there is no coming back from everything we've gone through. The thought shatters my heart because I have failed him. How could I have been so blind?

I'm about to stand, about to run and hide, but something that can only be comparable to a miracle happens before me. I blink once, unsure if I'm seeing and hearing things. But I'm not.

"I once did, but now"—I witness Saint dropping to his knees in front of me and lifting my downturned chin with a finger—"the only thing I need…is you."

"Wh-what?" I stumble over a simple word because this is too much.

The chartreuse swirls flash to life, robbing me of breath. When he glides his thumb along my jaw, I can't stop the tears because this is the first time he's touched me so tenderly. And I never thought I'd experience it again.

"You still love m-me?" My tremble reveals my inner turmoil.

Saint fixes his penetrating stare onto me, setting me on fire. "Always, ангел. And I'll never stop. I will love you with my last intake of breath, and when my heart stops beating, know that it only beat for you."

I allow him to touch me and refamiliarize himself with me. He traces over my lips, and they part as a gasp escapes me. He works the tip of his finger into my mouth, hissing when he feels the wetness along my inner bottom lip.

He slowly removes his finger, and before I have a chance to miss his touch, he slips it into his mouth, his eyes flickering when sampling my taste. The sight leaves me a quivering mess.

"I don't understand. Why did you push me away?"

Once Saint is done, he removes his finger. I am frightened he will get up and leave, but he doesn't. He does something which he's never done before—he surrenders…to me.

On his knees before me, he peels back those layers and allows me to see something beautiful—him. "I am…

humiliated," he reveals, painfully slow. "And I failed you. My grand plan to save you has just fucked everything up."

But that can wait. I want to discuss something else first.

I arch a brow. "Humiliated?"

He nods, his hair shrouding his face. "How can you…love me after everything you saw?"

"Oh, Saint," I whimper. "It's because of everything I saw that I love you."

But he won't accept my reply. "What I did with Ingrid…."

"Shh."

But he doesn't want me to coo him. He needs to accept culpability to move on. "Since the moment I met you, I've done nothing but hurt you. I don't deserve your love. I never have. And if I were a stronger man, I would have done the right thing and never given in to this…hunger, this possession I feel for you.

"But I'm not. I'm weak, which is why—" The cause of his sudden pause has waves of anger crashing into me. "Which is why…O…Oscar did what he did…to me."

"What, what did he do?"

For the shadows to be gone, he needs to exorcise his demons. I know it's hard, but if he doesn't, he will never heal, and Oscar will have won. He strokes over his bandaged hand, which is no longer dislocated thanks to the sisters, appearing to be lost in the past.

"What didn't he do." He doesn't need to spell it out. Oscar all but told me he raped Saint and did so without regret.

I understand why he's ashamed, but this isn't his fault. Just as it wasn't mine when Kenny forced himself onto me. "For you to be free, you take back your life. He may have broken your body, but your heart, your soul, that is mine. And I promise you, that bastard will pay for what he did."

Saint licks his bottom lip, averting his gaze. "You aren't... disgusted by me?"

"Of course not. None of this is your fault. The feelings of shame, disgust, embarrassment, I understand. I carried them with me for so many years. But that all ended the day you saved me and killed my demons. You did what I couldn't, and you never judged me for it, so why would I judge you?"

I hope he understands that none of this is on him. He was abused, and if my situation can show parallels and help him see that we both fell prey, then losing a piece of my innocence wasn't in vain. "Were you disgusted by me? When I told you what happened with Kenny?"

His chin snaps up as he shakes his head violently. "No, absolutely not."

"Then we are one and the same," I declare as both of our situations were out of our hands.

Something shifts, it's small, but I see it—the darkness ebbs away, giving way to light. By confessing his sins, he will absolve and forgive himself. "I can still"—he swallows deeply as though he's tasted something rotten—"feel his touch. Taste his lips. Smell coconuts."

With the slowest of movements, I place my hand to his cheek. "Replace his touch, his smell, his body with mine."

He leans into my palm, tears welling as he confesses something which shatters him. "I don't deserve it. He made it...he made it feel...good."

And there it is—the real reason he's so ashamed. He sees his pleasure as a betrayal to me and to himself. But I understand because just as I have questioned my empathy toward Alek, Sara explained why we find pleasure in pain.

"Because when you have so little, something small means so much, and in our case, that something small is kindness. Like a starving dog, waiting under the table to get thrown a scrap, we are thankful when we are shown any kind of mercy."

And that is why Saint was able to find pleasure.

Oscar tortured him, broke him, and the small scrap of compassion was the only thing Saint could hold onto to stop himself from succumbing to the darkness for good.

"It's okay," I assure him, running my fingertips over his soft beard. "There is nothing for you to be ashamed of."

Saint sighs, riddled with so much emotion. "I wanted to fight him, but I didn't." And I know why that is. He made a deal with Oscar to be submissive on the proviso that I was safe. "But in the end, he drugged me anyway. I was too… uptight, he said."

I close my eyes, sickened.

"He spoke of you, and when he removed this"—I watch in awe as he reaches into his back pocket and produces my necklace—"something happened. He held it out to me, and all I could smell, all I could feel was you. I recalled our meeting, not knowing how you would change my world forever. I remembered how you fought every chance you got, regardless of the consequences. And I realized I didn't remember when I fell in love with you because I feel like I've loved you my whole life."

My heart constricts because how can I not be touched by his words.

"Before I knew what was happening, I was…responding because I was thinking of you." He shrinks from my touch, ashamed.

"You were drugged and manipulated, Saint. You can't be blamed for your actions."

"Stop making excuses for me!" he cries, allowing angry tears to sear down his cheeks. "I should have been stronger. You deserve someone better than me; someone who isn't weak. Someone who didn't fucking kidnap you!"

He attempts to stand, but I refuse to allow Oscar's depravities to win. I latch onto his wrist, and before he has a chance to speak, I place his hand over my tattoo. "I don't want anyone else. I want you."

The warmth from his touch sends my body into overdrive, and everything clenches and prickles in awareness.

"It's always been you," I confess, squeezing his hand over my flank.

Saint hisses as he gently removes our hands from my side so he's able to take a closer look at my tattoo. When he sees his name inked onto my skin, he blossoms before my eyes. But his self-hatred won't let go without a fight. "Why? Why would you taint yourself with my name?"

My beautifully wounded man, how he underestimates his worth. It's time he sees it. It's time he realizes that he is all I want. Now and forever.

Pressing us chest to chest, I wrap my hand around the back of his neck and confess, "I love you for the man that you are. Not the man you think you should be."

His lips part, but I am done talking. I smash my mouth to his, claiming it, claiming *him* as mine. I'm frightened he will push me away, but he doesn't. He kisses me back without apology as we both hungrily paw at one another, unable to keep up with the frantic rhythm. His long hair feels like heaven under my fingers as I thread my hands through it and pull hard.

A grunt leaves him, but the pain spurs him on. We need this. We need to feel this heartfelt promise after being surrounded by nothing but deceit.

He wraps his large hand around my waist, drawing me even closer to him as he devours my mouth with an insatiable appetite. I can barely keep up with the intensity because his actions are unapologetic and full of desperate yearning.

Our tongues duel, fighting for control, but in the end, he wins. Kissing suddenly isn't enough, and he flips me onto my back, his heavy weight crushing me with absolute perfection. I am engulfed in his smell, his heat, but I want more. So much more.

I tug at the hem of his T-shirt, demanding I want it off, and Saint complies as he reaches over his head and tears it off from the back of his collar. We separate for a nanosecond before he's back, kissing the ever-living fuck out of me.

His bare chest pressed to mine is a heady aphrodisiac, and the sting of his barbell only heightens the longing pulsating through me. His delicious hard-on pushes into me, and I smother my moan by biting his tongue.

He grunts, rolling his hips, and the friction of his pants has me seeing stars. "Take them off," I half beg between his kisses.

My plea has him slowing.

He presses his forehead to mine, inhaling deeply, as he caresses my nose with his. "Are you sure?"

I never really had many expectations to what my first time would be like. But being here now, with Saint, I know that regardless of any scenario I could have imagined, nothing would ever compare to this. There are no words to express the emotions running through me because giving myself to him is the most natural thing in the world. He is as much a part of me as I am of myself.

He mistakes my silence as uncertainty. "We don't have—"

But I cut him off. No more don'ts.

"Yes."

He inhales sharply, licking his delicious lips. "I don't want to hurt you."

"You won't," I reply, brushing the hair from his brow. However, I suddenly realize that I am the one who should be assuring him. "If this is too much for you, though, we can—"

But he won't hear a word of it as he avidly confesses, "No, I want it to be your touch I remember. Your kisses I taste. And your body I feel underneath me."

I nod slowly.

Oscar took a part of Saint that he will never get back. So I want to give Saint a piece of myself to help him heal, the piece that was always destined to be his. "I love you."

He inhales in triumph, and for the first time in a long time, he smiles. "And I you."

His admission is everything and so much more.

Looping my hand around the back of his neck, I coax him back to my mouth where we kiss with a sluggish cadence. This is new ground for us both, and it seems we're happy to take it slow. His tongue circles mine, the action evoking erotic images of him moving in a similar way between my thighs.

The coarse hay is rough beneath me, but the sting only seems to add to my heightened state. Even so, Saint's kisses slow down. He reaches overhead, over the bales of hay and produces a gray blanket. I'm not sure where he got it, but I'm thankful when he lays it down beside us. With one last kiss, he rolls off me and sits, taking off his shoes.

I shuffle onto the blanket, watching breathlessly. When he attempts to join me, I place a hand to his chest. "You forgot to take off your pants."

A dimpled smirk smacks me in the solar plexus as its radiance challenges the sun. "All in good time, ангел."

Just the name alone turns me to mush, and I fall back onto the blanket as Saint sits back on his heels at my feet. He peers down at me with such hunger, I feel myself turning red all over. He takes his time combing over every inch of me as I do him.

His long hair is wild, his chest is rippling, and his tattoos come to life before me. The delicate feathers that sweep across his taut biceps leave me breathless. *He* is truly the angel. The scars across his body only have me loving him all the more.

With a gentle touch, he sweeps his fingertips across my tattoo. My skin instantly breaks out into goose bumps. He traces each letter, appearing mesmerized by the sight. Who knew five letters could evoke such an awakening within me because by the time he crosses the T, my body is a quivering mess.

My breathing is uneven, hinting to my needs.

Once he's done spelling out his name, he slides his fingers upward and cups my right breast. Instantly, I arch my back, whimpering. He flicks my pearled nipple with his thumb, licking his lips when I cry out softly.

Unable to help myself, I rub my thighs together, the friction alleviating some of the pressure building, but nothing, bar Saint, will soothe that burn. "Open your legs."

Once upon a time, I would have shied away at such a demand but not anymore. Although I am still a little nervous, I slowly comply. When I do, a hiss escapes Saint. He focuses on my sex with his chartreuse swirls, sparking a dangerous mix of pleasure and pain.

Who needs foreplay when you have this stifling anticipation?

"When we were on the island," I say, my cheeks reddening at the memory, "I saw you…I saw you jerking off."

His lips lift into a slanted, wicked grin.

"I liked it," I confess. "I shouldn't have, but I did. I couldn't see properly, though, because it was dark. Will you, will you show me?"

My request has caught him off guard.

The reason I asked this is because yes, hell to the fuck yes, do I want to see him pleasure himself, but I also want to ensure he is okay with this. I don't want him to freak out, especially after everything he's been through.

His impressive bulge has me unable to tear my eyes away from the front of his pants because I know what that bulge feels and tastes like.

"Fuck, ангел. If you don't mask your thoughts, I'm going to come like a pubescent teen."

No surprise, he can read my mind, but I can't filter those erotic visions.

"Please," I beg, uncaring I sound like a wanton fiend.

He takes a moment, maybe to center himself or draw out the torture, but I don't know or care because when he lowers his sweats and his dick springs to life, I forget everything and focus on his big, beautiful cock. His left hand is still bandaged, but he takes his shaft into his right and begins touching himself slowly.

I lean up on my elbows, needing a closer look because this is something else. His movements are unhurried as he strokes up and down sluggishly. His eyes are locked with mine, making what I'm witnessing all the more depraved.

He begins to pump faster, his defined abs quivering under the force. His delicious V pops as he tenses his muscles and his strokes become more and more wild. Images of him inside me flood my brain, and I bite my lip to smother a moan.

The action doesn't go unnoticed by Saint.

He continues to pleasure himself as hot, sated groans slither past his parted lips. I am hot all over, and if I don't douse these flames, I am sure to combust. So without pause, I slip my hand between my legs and begin to touch myself too.

I lift my head so I'm able to see him, and what I witness is a true vision. His body ripples and quivers, and his cock is so impossibly large, I moan at the realization of what we're about to do. I wanted to make sure he was okay with us being intimate, and I think that he is.

"I can't take it," he growls hastily.

I have no idea what he's talking about until he swoops down and replaces my fingers with his hot, needy mouth. He isn't slow or cautious, which is exactly what I want. He spreads my legs open and buries himself in my sex, tonguing me fiercely.

I bow off the ground, clutching at the blanket beneath me because holy fuck, I am so turned on I feel as if I'm going to shatter into a million pieces. Saint squeezes my thighs, coaxing me to open wider. When I do, I scream in sheer ecstasy.

He devours my sex, licking and sampling me until I am begging for a release. His coarse beard adds to the friction, and I know it won't be long until I'm crying out his name. With a firm squeeze, he touches my tattoo, and even though he hasn't said it, I know he likes having his name inked on my flesh.

He once told me he wanted to mark me like a caveman, and now he has—forever.

I thread my hands through his mussed hair, tugging hard as I need something to hold. He eats me with love, with passion, with need, and I don't stand a chance. A tremor robs me of air, but before I have a chance to chase a release, Saint pulls away.

A strangled groan escapes me.

Before I can even ask what he's doing, he slides up my body and kisses me madly. I don't care that I can taste myself on his lips because it adds to this primeval act. He fucks my mouth with his tongue in the same way he did my sex.

I am panting and sweaty, and every part of me tingles. But when Saint walks his fingers down my body, I know this is only the beginning. He rubs my outer sex, humming into my mouth when he glides over my ripe flesh.

He inserts a finger, and we both hiss at the connection. But it's not enough. Reaching down, I beg he add another digit. It doesn't take much persuasion because he gives in the moment I arch my back, welcoming him home.

He stretches me wide while I die a small death.

"Ангел, this is going to hurt a little. But once this part is over, I promise it'll feel good. Okay?" he pledges against my lips.

"O-kay," I manage to pant.

With eyes locked, he kisses me softly, attempting to distract me because he begins to stretch me wider as he turns his fingers. He sinks deeper, so deep I feel like I can't breathe. I whimper because the pain is different from anything I've felt before.

"Breathe," he whispers, breaking our kiss, only to trail his lips down my neck. He sucks over my racing pulse, biting softly.

I do as he says. But unexpectedly, it's too much.

"Saint!" I cry out, clutching his shoulders when he curls his fingers, and suddenly, something pops—my thin veil of virginity is no more.

"Are you okay?" he asks breathlessly, hovering over me, watching me closely.

I nod quickly.

I don't know why, but tears suddenly spring to life,

contradicting my claims.

"I've hurt you," he says with regret.

Placing a trembling hand to his cheek, I say, "No, you haven't. I'm just...happy." He arches a brow, confused. "Something which has ruled my life is now gone, and that just makes me...ordinary."

My virginity was part of the reason I was thrown into the deep end without a life vest, but now that it's gone, I am just like everyone else. There is nothing special about me.

But when Saint shakes his head, stroking over my eyebrows, the slope of my nose, and lastly, my lips, I realize that's not entirely true, and for once, I don't shy away from the fact.

"Oh, ангел, you'll never be ordinary."

My heart swells as he presses his lips to mine.

We kiss deliriously slow, my body quivering with what's to come. I've never wanted anything more than I do this. He adjusts himself between my legs, never breaking the rhythm of our kisses. When I feel him hot, hard, and ready, I brace myself for him to enter me.

He doesn't.

He teases me instead, kissing down my neck and then taking my nipple into his mouth. I run my fingernails down his muscled back, gasping as each lash of his tongue sends me closer to the edge. My breast pops free from his mouth as he detours to my scar. He gently kisses over it.

I know he still feels guilty for shooting me, but every scar has just made us both tougher. It shows the world that we were stronger than whatever tried to beat us. Saint is covered in wounds, and each one is an affirmation that he will always be my bad Saint.

"I love you," I whisper although that doesn't quite sum up how I feel.

But when he smiles and looks at me like I am the most precious thing in the world, I know that it's enough.

"Ты мое сердце. Моя жизнь. Я обещаю защищать тебя до конца моей жизни. Когда-то ты была моя пленница, но теперь я твой. Я люблю тебя."

My brain turns to mush because whenever he speaks Russian, I am held captive. He softly bites my jaw while I arch backward, opening myself up to him. "Wh-what did you say?"

"I said…" he utters against my lips, "you are my heart."

He doesn't give me a chance to reply because he shifts, placing his blunt head against my sex. My eyes widen, and with an intake of breath, he enters me slowly. I clutch his shoulders, my mouth parting with voiceless pleas.

"My life," he continues, driving into me gradually, inch by glorious inch.

I am lost to his voice, his body, and grow lax, allowing this magnificent man to claim what is and has always been his.

"I promise to protect you for the rest of my life."

Oh…my god. I am being split into two.

When he's imbedded halfway into me, he pauses and places a gentle kiss to my brow. "You were once my captive, but now…" He allows my muscles to adjust to his size before he exhales and sinks into me all the way to the hilt.

I gasp because now, we are one, and what he says next cements this union evermore. "I'm yours. I love you." And with that, he begins to move inside me.

The feel of him being rooted so deep takes my breath away, and my eyes flicker under the intensity of being joined this way. It hurts, but underneath that pain, Saint is able to draw the pleasure to the forefront. I focus on the way our bodies fit together, and after a while, there is nothing but…this.

He pulls out, then sinks all the way back in. He does it over and over again. I am lost in him, in this ecstasy, and when he increases the rhythm, I cry out, on the verge of tears. "Put your arms above your head, ангел."

I do as he says, and he grips my wrists in one hand, shackling me. The imagery reminds me of when he bound me on the yacht, and it heightens my already aroused state.

"Faster," I whimper, bowing my back, desperate to feel him everywhere because no matter how close we are, we're not close enough, and we never will be.

Saint complies with my pleas, increasing his speed, a primeval grunt escaping him.

The slapping of our ripe, slick flesh combined with the sensation of being connected in this way has me losing myself to the bliss. I never thought it would feel this good, but wherever Saint touches, I come alive. He is deep, so incredibly deep, and the momentum of his strokes has my entire body moving upward with the force.

"Fuck," he curses, peering down at where we are joined. "You okay?"

His breathless question leaves me aching because he will always ensure my needs are met before his. "Yes, more than okay. I never…" I lick my lips and arch my neck backward. "I never thought it could be this way."

"Me either," he confesses, which surprises me. He lowers his head and suckles my breast. His large hand cups it whole. "Move with me, ангел."

He releases me so I'm able to wrap my arms around his neck and mold my body around his. Each time he pushes, I pull, the perfect yin and yang. The pain begins to subside and gives way to this euphoria that has me clenching tight.

A string of Russian leaves him.

He continues moving inside me, and I meet him thrust for thrust. I am clumsy and out of sync at times, but he makes me feel nothing but beautiful as he whispers sweet nothings into my ear. The friction of our bodies colliding into one another has the fire inside me smoldering bright. A coil begins to unravel within, and a sheen of perspiration dampens my skin.

My release is close—I can taste it—but I don't want this feeling to end. I claw at Saint's back, groaning and mumbling incoherently. He pistons his hips, humming each time he goes in deep. A heat crackles from my core and rumbles straight through me.

"Oh, god," I cry, holding him tightly.

He takes my leg and wraps it around his tapered waist, deepening the angle of his thrusts. I am like an overcooked piece of spaghetti and lose all control of my body. Saint's hair flicks forward as he lowers his face to mine, kissing me with fire.

He rolls his hips, rubbing over my clit, and I whimper into his mouth. He does this over and over, stimulating every part of me. I like that he's not gentle. I like that he's not in control and lost to the emotion. It shows me that he's feeling everything I'm feeling too.

Lacing my fingers through his hair, I bow off the ground, a vibration cheating me of air. "Holy shit," I pant, every part of me pulsating.

I am hot, so hot, and when Saint slams into me, once, twice, fingering over my tattoo, growling, "Only us, only this…forever, ангел," I explode in a beautiful, quivering mess.

My orgasm tackles me hard, and I doubt I'll come back from this high anytime soon. He continues pumping into me, speaking words in Russian that sound filthy and depraved. It only has me screaming louder as I squeeze my eyes shut.

He pinches my nipple before gripping my waist tight. I open my eyes and witness a sight which has a reckless longing stirring once again. The corded veins in his neck are strained as he tosses his head back, fucking me senseless.

But this is more than that. This is professing to the world that I belong to him, and he belongs to me. This is possession. And obsession. This is love.

I run my trembling fingers over his tattoo; my sinner, my saint.

A rumble erupts from his formidable chest as he attempts to pull out, but I clutch my leg around him, holding him prisoner. He doesn't stand a chance as he comes inside me with an impassioned moan. His cries are beautiful—they are vulnerable, and they reveal we've both been reborn.

Collapsing on top of me, he's breathless, sticky, and spent. I cradle him to my chest, kissing his damp skin. We stay entwined this way for seconds, minutes, hours. I honestly don't know because for the first time in my life, I have finally found where I belong.

"Are you okay?" he hoarsely asks into the crook of my neck.

I nod shakily, stroking his hair.

When he meets my satisfied gaze, I gasp because I have never seen his eyes so lucid before. The green almost burns me with their clarity. He reaches over my head, and before I have a chance to ask what he's doing, he fastens my necklace around me.

The familiar weight comforts me beyond words. But when I remember what he told me, about Oscar using it against him, I wonder if wearing it may be a bad idea. I reach behind me, about to take it off, but he stops me.

"I don't have to wear it," I explain, looking up at him as he's still lying on top of me.

"I know how much it means to you," he replies, running his thumb across the apple of my cheek.

"You mean more," I counter without missing a beat.

Saint's smile is heavy with happiness but also exhaustion. "And that makes me the luckiest son of a bitch alive." He rolls off me, and before I have a chance to miss his warmth, he drags me into his arms. He gathers the ends of the blanket and wraps us up tight.

"What happens tomorrow?" I whisper, gently toying with the dark strands of hair on his chest. To be able to be with him this way, without fear of getting caught, is foreign, but it's something I can get used to fast.

He hums, resting his chin atop my head. "We will deal

with it tomorrow. Now, we sleep."

"You're so bossy," I quip, grinning.

"Don't make me spank you," he sleepily says. I nestle against him, the heat of his body and blanket soon lulling me into a drowsy bubble. Saint's gentle breathing reveals he's sound asleep.

My mind fights to stay awake, but eventually, I succumb to the silence. However, I know it won't be long until my nightmares find me, promising that tomorrow, there is no middle ground. Tomorrow, we throw Alek to the wolves.

God, save my soul.

CHAPTER ELEVEN

The delicious scent of coffee rouses me. But when that fragrance is combined with a far more intoxicating smell, I appreciate the fact that Saint will always be far more potent than any drug. Stretching like a lioness lazing in the sun, I slowly open my eyes against the blinding morning light.

However, when I see Saint sitting beside me topless, his beauty rivals the daylight. "Mornin." His husky voice evokes images of us being entwined last night.

My cheeks instantly blister.

He offers me a steaming cup of coffee with a smirk. Clutching the blanket to my very naked chest, I sit upright and accept it. Once I take a sip, the fog from my brain clears, and I wonder what the right protocol is for having the morning-after talk.

But honestly, I don't know if I want to discuss anything.

It happened, and I have no regrets. But when Saint clears his throat and rubs the back of his neck, I pale. Does he regret it?

"So, about last night…"

Lord, have mercy on me. If he tells me it shouldn't have happened, I will curl into a ball and cry.

"I was careless. I'm sorry."

Okay, not the response I was expecting. I scrunch up my nose in confusion. I have no idea what he's talking about.

When he reads my confusion, he clarifies, "Do we need to go to a pharmacy?"

"Pharmacy? I feel fine. A little sore, yes, but…oh. Oh." When I realize what he means, I quickly shake my head. "No, it's okay. All good." I don't want to go into detail that I have an IUD, and thankfully, he gets it.

"I should have been more responsible," he berates himself. But he didn't twist my arm. We both wanted it. Besides, I wasn't expecting him to whip out a condom. We are in the middle of nowhere, wearing borrowed clothes.

"Don't," I coo, placing my palm to his cheek. He leans into my touch. "It was perfect."

"I was rough. Are you okay?" His expression turns poignant. But I won't allow him to think something that isn't true.

"More than okay," I reply without pause.

"I just…" His tongue darts out to lick his top lip. "I just lose control with you."

"And is that such a bad thing?" I tease with a small smile.

My humor has the desired effect. "Thank you."

"I should be the one thanking you," I counter.

Saint laughs, which abates all tension between us, and he drags me onto his lap. The blanket pools around me as I press my naked chest to his. Wrapping my arms around his neck, I can't help but drown in those eyes.

"Thank you for pushing me. I don't know where I would be if you hadn't. I'm sorry if I ever made you feel like I didn't love you. I just needed time to process...everything. But I don't think I ever will."

And I don't blame him. He was tortured and violated—mind, body, and soul—and no one would be expected to return the same.

"I understand, but I'm here for you. Always," I promise, toying with the strands of hair curling at his nape.

"Being with you makes it better," he professes, which warms my heart, but we can't ignore the inevitable any longer.

"What are we going to do now?"

Saint sighs. "Do you think I want to work with him? He is the lesser of two evils," he explains, but I know. There is no need for him to explain. "But...seeing the way he looks at you, I don't think I can. Do you, do you feel anything for him?"

I swallow down the ball of nerves because this is the first time he's asked this outright. I don't want to lie to him, but I also don't want to hurt his feelings. So I answer the only way I can. "I don't hate him. I know that I should, but I don't. I don't know what that means, but it's the truth."

Saint nods, exhaling deeply. I understand that's most likely not the response he wanted, but I can't lie. "It means that you're a good person. You want to see the good in everyone."

He strokes over the cross at my throat, smiling.

"I love you," I say aloud for the both of us.

"And I love you."

Nothing else is said about my "feelings" for Alek because I don't understand them, and I probably never will.

"Let's get this over with."

I don't know what that means because Saint hasn't given me an answer to what he proposes we do. His vengeance for Oscar is warranted, but if we follow Alek, we will die. There is no doubt about it. I have tried so hard to save Alek, but this time, I can't.

His pride and honor won't let sleeping dogs lie. He will go to that meeting knowing the consequences, and there isn't a damn thing I can do about it. But I don't want that same fate for Saint. Or me.

Unsure what the next few minutes hold, I give Saint's lips a quick peck before standing and dressing quickly. Now that I don't have his warm body wrapped around mine, the cold takes my breath away.

"We can sleep inside from now on," he says, slipping into a long-sleeved T-shirt.

"No, I'm okay out here. It reminds me of the island."

Saint pauses from slipping into a black jacket. "And you associate fond memories with that place?"

His question catches me off guard, so I take my time zipping up my coat. When I think I can reply without my quivering voice betraying me, I nod. "It's where I met Harriet Pot Pie," I tease before falling serious. "Regardless of everything, I've never regretted a moment spent with you. Yes, I wish we could have met under entirely different circumstances, but in the end, it led to this."

And by this, I mean being in love with Saint. And by growing into this person I am today.

Saint finishes dressing, then walks over to me. I stand still as he examines me closely as if he's looking at a precious jewel. "Your ability to always find a positive in…everything, astounds me."

I don't have a chance to thank him because he presses his lips to mine, stealing my breath. The kiss is chaste compared to last night, but I've come to appreciate our kisses come in many different forms. And this soft, slow kiss is exactly what I need.

He breaks away, rubbing his nose against mine. "Let's go."

The weather has turned bitter, so we make a mad dash toward the house. No doubt snow will soon fall. When Saint leads me inside, the warmth of the fire is a welcomed embrace. When I see Zoey, however, that welcome is short-lived.

She's still pissed off at her brother after yesterday's altercation, but Saint doesn't seem bothered. "Where is Alek?"

She gestures with her head toward the kitchen. It seems they're not on speaking terms.

We make our way into the kitchen, and when I see Alek at the table, something inside me wilts. I don't know what Saint has decided to do. Are we going with him? Or will we bow out? Both options have me averting my gaze when Alek gives us his attention.

Pavel sits beside him, scrolling through his phone, pen in hand. Ingrid barely touches her eggs. All in all, the mood is somber.

Saint doesn't drag this out. "What have you decided to

do?"

"With what?" Alek says, leaning back in his seat.

"Are you going to the meeting?"

Alek is taken aback. "Of course, I'm going. That isn't even a question."

When Saint releases my hand, I watch with bated breath. "Then we're out."

I blink once, absolutely stunned.

The silence can be cut with a knife.

"I see." Alek finally speaks.

"If you're set on going, then I can't change your mind. But you know this is a suicide mission. If you go to that meeting, you will die."

Even though Saint is right, I honestly didn't believe he would do this. I thought his need for retribution would blind him to reason, but I thought wrong. I can't hide my relief that he chose this way.

"How about you, Pavel?"

Zoey chooses this moment to join the discussion. I wonder where her loyalties lie.

Pavel sighs heavily, which is all the answer Alek needs. He too knows that going into this unprepared will result in our deaths.

"Holy shit, so this is it? Will you at least allow me to use your contacts?"

Pavel nods, but it's clear that regardless of how many allies Alek can get on his side, it won't be enough.

"If you choose to wait, if we can devise a smarter plan, then I will fight with you. If not, you're on your own."

Saint is so matter of fact, it scares me. Although he's doing the smart thing, it doesn't mean it's the right way. By doing this, Oscar will never pay for what he did, and that doesn't sit right with me. I can only imagine how it makes Saint feel.

Alek is also on the same page. "I didn't think you'd give up and roll over like a dog."

Saint's fists curl as his body begins to tremble in rage. When he takes a step forward, I instantly clutch his fist, rubbing my thumb along his knuckles. Fighting won't solve anything. Alek's astute eyes drop to our connection. He knows why Saint is doing this. It's for me.

"I'm not giving up. I just know when the odds aren't in my favor. You should too."

Alek straightens in his seat, his hard exterior refusing to budge. "Very well then. I will send Oscar your regards."

That *bastard*. How dare he. He is baiting Saint. I can only hope he doesn't take it.

When he gently severs our hold and takes a confident step toward Alek, I brace for anything. I am stumbling through this without any idea of how it will end. "As I see it, you owe me. I did spare your miserable life. You kill that motherfucker for me, then our debt is settled."

Well, I clearly didn't expect that.

What in the ever-living fuck? Saint has asked Alek to kill Oscar when his hands should spill that monster's blood.

Guilt swarms me. He's doing this for me. Giving up his chance of revenge so we can escape together. How is that fair to him? I guess there is no fair in this scenario, so that is a small comfort.

Alek purses his lips as he was not expecting this outcome. Zoey hasn't spoken up and neither has Ingrid. He's on his own.

"Okay, I accept. I do this, and we're even. Once I regain my place, you will leave me alone? You won't seek revenge for the past?"

Saint nods once, but it's in vain. There is no way Alek will get out of this unscathed. There are no winners in this situation. Only losers. Alek comes to a slow stand, eyes locked on me. Another wave of guilt drags me under, and I look away.

But this is what I should have done from the very beginning. No matter how wrong it feels.

"Pavel, will you write out a list of everyone you think I should contact? It seems there isn't a moment to waste."

Pavel nods, and anyone can see he too feels guilty for leaving Alek to the wolves.

"Thank you, old friend. I will ensure you get everything promised to you."

Pavel seems surprised that Alek would still deliver on his promise to take care of him and his family, regardless of the fact he has turned his back on him. And that's the reason I can't hate Alek.

"If you'll excuse me, I need some fresh air." When Ingrid stands, Alek gently places a hand on her shoulder, sitting her back down. "Stay here, возлюбленная. It's cold out."

She does as she's told.

Alek is expressionless as he exits through the back door.

Once he's gone, I exhale slowly because I can't help but feel remorseful. He has a choice to wait, but his pride and honor won't allow it.

Saint isn't touched by sentiments. "Can you still organize those passports for us, Pavel?"

Pavel shakes his head to clear the fog from his brain. It seems we're all, bar Saint, stunned by what just happened. "Yes. It'll take some time, but my guy can organize everything you need."

I know this was my idea, but I can't help but ask, "So going to the consulate is a definite no?"

I am so sick of the lies. I just want things to go back to normal. But we're way past that.

"And say what?" Saint asks without any judgment. "What story do we give?"

He's right. I knew this was the case, but why does everything have to be so difficult all the time?

"I'm a fugitive," he says without pause. "No matter how I got here, and what I was forced to do, I won't leave this country. I'll be tried and punished for what I've done."

"He's right." Pavel supports Saint's claims. "For you to leave here, Saint and Willow have to die. You'll have new identities. We'll work out a story in case any questions are asked. I'll make sure my contacts ensure the story checks out. It won't be cheap however."

"No problem. I've got money." Yes, he does. Twenty million, to be precise. I know this because he was prepared to use it to save my life.

When Saint notices me gnawing on my lip, he gently releases it, jerking me into the now. This is really happening. "On record, you're technically dead anyway. It'll be okay. There is nothing to worry about."

And that's thanks to my darling husband.

"Let's make the call, Pavel." Saint clearly wants this done as soon as possible.

Pavel nods and stands.

"Is there room for me?"

And my day just got worse.

I forgot Zoey was even here, which was my error, as she's just muscled in on our plan. I shouldn't expect her to stay here, but I wish she would. I don't even know what's ahead for Saint and me, so with Zoey in tow, I can't see it being good.

Saint turns over his shoulder to look at her. He too is surprised. "You want to go back home?"

Zoey shrugs, but it's written all over her face. She does.

Saint looks down at me as we haven't discussed this far ahead. We were happy to get through a day without being killed, but now, talks of the future are daunting. I want to be with him, and I think he wants to be with me, but we haven't discussed the logistics—like where we would live or if his she-devil sister was coming with us.

This entire situation turns my stomach.

"It can be arranged." Pavel cuts through the silence.

"Thank you. If that's what you want, Zoey, then I can't stop you." That is not a welcoming invitation, but it isn't a no either.

Half a smile spreads across Zoey's lips.

Saint kisses my cheek, leaving me with my mouth gaping as he leaves the room with Pavel to discuss our escape plan. When I meet Zoey's eyes and she grins, the urge to slap her overcomes me. But I resist the urge, seeing as we may be roomies come next week.

"I'm going to take a shower." Showering is the least of my concerns, but I need to get out of here.

Since my things are out in the barn, it gives me an excuse to walk out the back door with the intent of never coming back. The wind howls around me, but I continue walking as the fresh air simmers my raging nerves.

I can't believe she is coming with us. If she was so eager to go back to America, why the fuck didn't she leave when Saint begged her to? My hatred for this woman knows no bounds, and the need to hit something increases.

I'm beyond irate when I yank open the barn door, so when I see Alek sitting on a bale of hay, I give into my primeval need to scream. "What are you doing in here?" I shout, slamming the door shut behind me.

He merely crosses an ankle over the other, not appreciating my hysteria. "I just want to talk."

"Then talk," I snap, staying far away from him.

"So you're okay with this plan?"

"When did I ever have a say in what I was okay with?"

Alek is startled by my response. "I'm sorry about that. I'm sorry for everything."

Now I'm the one caught off guard as this is the first time he's apologized to me. "It's too late for apologies."

"Be that as it may, I still want you to know how sorry I am."

"Why?" I fold my arms across my chest.

"I need your forgiveness in case things turn dire."

My mouth opens, but I close it quickly as I was not

expecting that response.

"I have no backup, so I don't need to go into detail how this will most likely end."

"You can wait," I say when I finally find my voice.

"Wait for what? For those bastards to shame me more. I will not."

"Your pride will get you killed," I snap, shaking my head at his stubbornness. But what he says next has me realizing what a hypocrite I am.

"Didn't yours nearly get you killed? You knew there was a risk defying Saint, and me, but that didn't stop you. So surely you can understand why I must do this."

He's right. Goddamn him.

"And if you succeed? If, by some miracle, you defeat them all, what happens then?" I question, refusing to see the parallels between us. "Another girl takes over from where we left? You get another Zoey? Another Sara? Is that it?"

Alek seems offended I would ever think that of him. "Things will be different."

But I just don't believe him. "Will they? You say that now, but money, power it does things. I've seen it. I thought you'd learned by now."

Alek stands abruptly, marching over to where I am. "What did you think? I would go back to America with you and Saint, where we could reminisce about the good ole days?"

I scoff, refusing to be belittled. "Of course not."

"Then what? Maybe I could buy a nice little cottage somewhere, find a wife, and pop out a few rug rats?"

"Don't patronize me," I spit, not appreciating his sarcasm.

"There is no other way for me. Just as there isn't for Saint."

I take a step back, eyes narrowed. "You don't know what you're talking about."

But that doesn't stop Alek. "You've neutered him. Taken away what is rightfully his."

"I have done nothing of the sort." But a small part of me is nodding her head because she agrees with Alek. That part can go to hell.

"If you wanted me dead, you should have just killed me on that yacht."

"*What?*" There is no point masking my surprise because it seems Alek was privy to everything this entire time.

He takes his time, strolling toward me. "You think I didn't know that you loved him, and he loved you? Or when you asked me to move into his room, you believed I didn't know it was because his room had no cameras?"

I am rooted to the spot, stunned.

"I allowed this because my feelings for you…they're real."

"Why didn't you punish me?" I manage to push out in a whisper.

Alek stops a few feet away from me with his hands in his pockets, and he sighs. "Because I'm not the monster you believe me to be. I thought you'd see that and maybe feel something for me too."

Nothing I say could ever reflect how I'm feeling right now because I believe him. I'm allowing a man to be slaughtered. So tell me, who's the monster?

"Do you think I want to feel this way for you? I hate it. You destroyed my life." With a hesitant touch, he runs two fingers down my cheek.

I should recoil. But I don't.

"It doesn't matter. He won. A virgin's blush no more."

His words are the wake-up call I needed. "This was never a game." I turn my cheek, breaking our connection.

"You're right. It never was. But I will always wonder, why did you choose him when you could have had me?"

I'm about to call him out for the arrogant asshole he is, but I'm left astounded yet again.

"We are the same, Saint and me. He has killed as well as I have. He isn't the good guy. And neither am I."

"You are worlds apart," I exclaim, but the walls begin closing in on me.

"I may have bought you, but he kidnapped you. I like bloodshed and so does he. So you're wrong, sweet ангел. We aren't so different after all."

It's not true. Alek and Saint are nothing alike. So why does everything he just said grate me raw?

"I know you feel something for me."

I want to deny it, but what would be the point? I've admitted it to Saint. I've admitted it to myself. "Whatever I feel for you, I am disgusted by it." I tell him the God's honest truth.

He winces because my admission is hardly gracious.

"I don't want you dead. I know that." And suddenly, I find the perfect analogy to how I feel. It was once said to me, and now, I understand it. Perfectly. "But don't mistake my kindness for weakness. You have a choice, where I didn't. If you do this, this is all on you.

"So the answer to your question is, regardless of everything he's done, I will choose him, always, because he's always chosen me. Good guy, bad guy, I don't care because in the end, he's *my* guy, and I accept him for what he is. Just as he does me."

And suddenly, an epiphany hits.

I was so angry with myself for feeling something other than hate for Alek. But now…I get it. I would be inhuman if I didn't feel something for someone who loves me. I will never, *never* love him the same way, but the fact he can love someone other than himself proves he isn't a loveless monster. *I* would be the monster if I didn't show compassion when he has done so with me.

"Everything all right?" Saint enters the barn hesitantly, looking back and forth between Alek and me.

"Yes," I reply with a small smile because for the first time, in a long time, it really is.

Alek, however, doesn't agree. "How can you allow him to live after everything he did to you?"

Saint's nostrils flare as he takes a steadying breath. "Some things are more important than vengeance."

My heart swells with love because I know he's talking about me. But Alek is right. I know a small piece of Saint will always be lost in that basement. He says he doesn't need revenge, but I don't believe him. And neither does Alek.

"Where is your pride? Your honor?"

"You're seriously questioning *my* honor after all you've done?" Saint snarls, spine rigid.

"You're hardly a saint," Alek says, sardonically. "You were never one to walk away from a fight. Especially one that was personal."

I want to jump in, but I don't. This has been a long time coming. Just like Zoey and me.

Saint is close to exploding—I can see it—but he keeps his calm for now. "Some battles are not worth fighting, especially ones you're bound to lose. You can go in there, armed to the teeth, and you'll still lose, Aleksei. Surely, you can see that."

Alek is a stubborn son of a bitch, and he shrugs nonchalantly. "At least I will go down fighting. Unlike you. Running away like a scared little mouse."

"I'm not scared," Saint snarls, eyes narrowed.

But Alek's slanted grin challenges his claims. "Suit yourself. Go back to America and live a boring, normal life. But we both know, sooner or later, it won't be enough. The bloodlust will come calling late at night. And when it does, just remember what you gave up."

I lower my eyes, saddened by Alek's words because he's right. After all we've endured, are we fooling ourselves? Is "normal" on the agenda for us? Can I really go back home and start again? The darkness has become a part of me now because secretly, the darkness is where I can dance with demons and not be ashamed.

I never "fit in" with the norm. I was always different. I never knew why that was until I met Saint. I am far stronger than I believed myself to be, and going back to reality scares me more than living this wicked life.

Just who have I become?

"Leave." One simple word encompasses so much because it's a warning. Saint has given Alek one chance to leave this barn unscathed.

Alek sighs heavily and goes to turn, but not before he signs his own death warrant. "Suit yourself, friend, but it seems she's made a fool of us both. She's brought two powerful men to their knees, but at least you got something for all the trouble she's put us through."

I don't even have time to open my mouth, amped on telling Alek to go to hell, because Saint beats me to the punch—literally. Without hesitation, Saint propels forward and punches Alek in the jaw. The crack is so loud, it vibrates all the way to my toes.

Alek stumbles back a few feet, shaking his head, but when a cocky grin spreads across his lips, I know it's game on. They charge at one another, a war cry leaving them both. Saint ducks as Alek delivers an uppercut and jabs Alek in the side.

A pained oomph leaves Alek as the sharp sound indicates Saint has broken some ribs. It doesn't stop him, though. It only seems to spur him on. He punches Alek in quick succession—in the face, to the body—while Alek attempts to lay a punch. But Saint is too fast.

Alek doesn't stand a chance as Saint kicks his shin. He buckles under the pressure, crumpling to his knees. "Now it's your turn to kneel," Saint spits, delivering a blow to his jaw.

Alek's head snaps back, which has me covering my mouth in horror. I have no doubt he will kill him, but this isn't my fight. So I stay on the sidelines, watching on with wide eyes.

Saint knees him under the chin, resulting in Alek falling onto his back. Saint dives on top of him, yanking him up by his collar. "For years, I was forced to do your dirty work, but no more. I owe you nothing," he snarls, nose to nose. "Don't you *ever* speak about her again."

Alek is floppy as Saint shakes him furiously, but it doesn't deter him. "You should thank me. If it wasn't for me, you'd have never met her."

"And that shows the difference between us. I would have rather never met her and saved her from this reality. I would give anything for her to forget all of this and to live a normal life. But she can't. None of us can because of you." Saint shoves Alek back down, standing dangerously slow.

This time, Alek knows when to stay down as this is one fight he will never win. He knows what Saint is capable of because he is the one who made him after all. Leaning up on his elbows, he wipes his bloody lip with the back of her hand. "It's always easy to blame someone else."

"And that's because you *are* to blame," I spit, all compassion for him gone.

"If that makes you sleep better at night, дорогой, then so be it. But I know a small part of you likes the pain."

My pale cheeks give away my guilt because he's right.

Just as he opens his mouth, Saint shuts it for good as he drops to one knee and punches Alek out cold. He hovers over Alek's body, his shoulders raised. Absolute rage pours off him. I don't know if I should intervene, but when Saint inhales before coming to a stand, it's clear he's done.

He doesn't have a scratch on him. He was too fast, too feral for Alek. He turns slowly, those poignant eyes sparking to life when they lock onto me. "I'm going to shower."

And just like that, we ignore the violence that has

become as much a part of our lives as breathing. We are both desensitized to it. But before he leaves, I need to ask. "What happens when we go back to America? I can't see Zoey becoming my BFF anytime soon."

Even though this is not really the time to discuss such trivial things, I need to know what comes next. I refuse to allow this violence to be all I know.

Saint looks beyond exhausted. He looks plagued. "What do you want to happen?"

There are so many things, but only one which stands out, which reveals what a wicked creature I really am. "There is one thing that seems inevitable."

Saint arches a brow, indicating he's listening.

"And that's to pay a visit to my darling husband."

"That's a given," he replies with a strained smile. "We can work everything out once we get the fuck out of here. Okay?"

"Okay." There is no point in pressing the issue because he's right. We still have so many hurdles in front of us. But it's nice knowing we're on the same page when it comes to Drew.

"Are you sure you want to do this?" I know it's wrong to ask this of him, to not press that he fights and get his revenge, but I'm selfish. I want my HEA with him without a cliffhanger in sight.

What he replies with warms me deeply. "I want you." But he still doesn't answer my question.

"Thank you for doing this…for me. It's a big ask, asking you not to fight, but I can't lose you again."

He appears to want to say something else, but then he changes his mind at the last minute. He grabs his stuff and walks out the door.

I can't shake the feeling that something other than the entire shitstorm that just went down is wrong, and when I peer down at an unconscious Alek, I realize what that is. Once this is done with, I will be able to get my revenge on Drew. But Saint won't get the vengeance he deserves.

How do I feel about that? How would I feel if someone told me I couldn't inflict the same amount of pain on Drew as he had on me?

Gulping, I clutch at the cross at my throat, knowing that in this situation, two wrongs just may make a right.

CHAPTER TWELVE

The next few days passed by relatively slowly, but I suppose that's because my life has been stuck on fast-forward for so long. Saint and I have been listening in on the bugs I planted, but we haven't learned anything new.

Oscar confirms what we already know—by conducting business with Serg, at the location they've chosen, they're hoping to draw Alek out of hiding. Two birds, one stone. They have an army—and that isn't an exaggeration—of men willing to protect Astra, their new leader.

From what we can tell, Oscar is merely a lackey, tagging along for the ride. Astra is intent on revenge while Oscar just wants to wreak havoc wherever he can.

Two nights ago, Astra finally emerged from hiding. Oscar mentioned she was tending to her wounds as she was hurt quite badly in the explosion. Too bad the explosion couldn't ravage her personality because when she waltzed into Oscar's house, demanding bloodshed and violence, it seems she hasn't changed.

We didn't overhear too much as they were out of range, but we heard enough. Alek is what Astra really wants. The drugs are a bonus.

Finally coming to terms with my "feelings" for Alek has been a small weight lifted from my shoulders. He hasn't spoken to me since Saint beat him to a bloody pulp, but that's okay. I've come to realize that I can't save everyone.

He knows the risks, but he is still intent on going. All I can do now is focus on my future.

Saint and I are sitting around the fireplace because the snow has overthrown the cold. Now, it's not just cold, it's fucking freezing. Saint reads the newspaper while I'm flicking through a fashion magazine from the early 90s. It seems Larisa is a hoarder.

Pavel enters, thankfully interrupting my perusal of claw clips and denim overalls. "It's done," he states, which has both Saint and I peering up in question.

He reaches into his jacket pocket, producing two passports. "Tomorrow, you can go home."

Those words are so foreign because I never thought I'd hear them again. But as Pavel holds our ticket out of here, I quickly catch up to speed. "Tomorrow?" I ask in case I had a lapse in hearing.

Saint lowers the newspaper, his interest piqued.

"Yes, it's all been taken care of." Pavel tosses my passport into my lap as I'm sitting cross-legged on the floor. I dare not open it as I catch it. It feels like dynamite in my hands.

Saint reaches for his. "What's the plan?"

"Well, it goes without saying that you can't just catch a flight out of here. I've organized a private charter plane to fly you out of Moscow tomorrow evening to London. The flight isn't long. Roughly three and a half hours. From Heathrow, you will catch an international flight just like your average seasoned traveler. You land in Los Angeles after eleven or so hours."

I blink once, stunned because this is a plan, and it could work.

"Don't ask questions when you get on that charter plane. The less you know, the better. The pilot owes me a favor but don't mistake him for a friend. It wasn't cheap," Pavel reveals, but Saint shrugs untroubled as he opens the passport.

I watch closely as he stares at the document. "William Daniels," Saint reads, arching a brow. "That's an easy one to remember."

And just like that, Saint goes by a new name.

My fingers tremble as I open the crisp passport. I can't believe how real it looks. The photo which Pavel took a couple of days ago stares back at me, as does the name Emma Miller. The details claim my birthday is February first.

"When you get to America, someone will meet you at the gate, where you will bypass customs and immigration. Believe me, that wasn't easy to arrange, but it's done. Once you're through, you're on your own. If anyone asks any questions, let the person who meets you take care of it. Keep a low profile, all right? If you fuck up, I can't help you."

"We won't," Saint replies, snapping the passport shut.

"I have Zoey's passport also."

His comment has me lifting my gaze. So it appears she's coming too. Saint notices I clam up, but he doesn't say anything.

"Congratulations, *Will*," Pavel says, slapping Saint on the shoulder. "You've just gotten your ticket out of here."

Those words are a cause to celebrate, so why does it feel like we're both mourning the death of a friend? When I peer back down at the passport, I realize the reason is because to leave this country, I have to leave Willow Shaw behind.

I know it's just a name, but what it represents leaves a gaping hole in my chest. If I were to be honest, I'm leaving more than a name behind. I'm leaving behind who I am and starting a brand-new life, and that's frightening.

"I also have driver's licenses and social security cards. You're pretty much all set." This plan sounds foolproof, but I know there is no such thing.

You'd think given what we hold in our hands, Saint and I would be celebrating, but a somber mood stirs between us. Everything is so different now, and if I'm honest, going back to reality terrifies me.

The front door opens, and the howling wind blows in behind Larisa as she lugs two large suitcases. Pavel quickly helps her as she shakes the flecks of snow from her graying hair. She has really stuck her neck out for us. I wish there was a way I could thank her.

When my stomach grumbles, I realize a way that I can. "Let's celebrate," I announce, wanting to break this stagnant feeling lingering in the air.

Saint and Pavel look at me with interest.

"Seeing as this is our last night here, how about I cook dinner?"

"A last supper?" Pavel questions, which seems to be quite an appropriate thing to say.

"I suppose you could say that," I reply. Ironically, Alek will be facing his foes tomorrow. We all know he won't leave there alive, which is why Pavel's comment is fitting.

The thought of him going in there, knowing he will die, still saddens me, but this is his call. He knows how we all feel. But there is no changing his mind.

"Besides, it's the least I can do to thank Larisa for her hospitality." I smile at her.

She grunts in response, hinting she isn't doing this for me.

Sara enters, giggling as Max trails behind her. She freezes, surprised to see us. When she sheepishly meets my eyes, I can't believe I haven't noticed this earlier. She likes Max. And from the way Max hovers close to her, I dare say he reciprocates.

Once upon a time, Max had a thing for Zoey, but it seems he's moved on to bigger and better things. I still don't like him, but he's proven to be loyal. Besides, anyone who can make Sara blush that way can't be half bad.

Coming to a stand, I pocket my passport. "I was thinking of cooking dinner tonight for everyone," I explain to Sara.

"Oh, that sounds like a lovely idea. Maybe I could help?" she offers, wringing her hands in front of her.

Although trivial, the prospect of doing something normal with my friend ebbs away at this heaviness weighing me down.

"I'd love that." However, I realize I should confirm it's okay with Larisa as it is her kitchen. "Would it be all right if we cooked dinner?"

By the way Pavel looks down at his mom, smiling, it's evident he loves her dearly. I wonder if he misses his kids. But I suppose now that he isn't enslaved to Alek, he can see them more. He too can start over again. It's a fresh start for us all. But no matter how hard I try to rationalize Alek's death, I still feel like a horrible human being.

Larisa says something in Russian, which has Saint and Pavel bursting into husky chuckles. I have no idea what she just said, but she clarifies a moment later.

"Suit yourself," she says with a thick Russian accent, which startles me because I just assumed she didn't speak any English. "But no burgers for dinner." I open but soon close my mouth as I have no idea what to say. "I watch *Man Versus Food*."

"I, um, okay. No, of course not, ma'am," I finally settle on because her light tone reveals she just made a joke.

"That's a little stereotypical, Мама." Pavel wraps his arm around Larisa's shoulders, still laughing. She leans into her son's side, grinning.

And just like that, something gives, and the tension lessens.

"If you need anything, let me know. But the kitchen is well stocked," Pavel says to me. He kisses his mother's brow before reaching for the suitcases. "Saint asked my mom to buy a few essentials for you three because you can't check in empty luggage."

Sara blinks quickly because this is news to her. I will fill her in once we're alone.

Saint rises from the tattered recliner, hinting they're going to look over their loot. It seems he's thought of everything.

"Unless you need me, I'm going to pack."

Pack for our new life. I gulp at the thought.

"I've got it," I reply, nodding. "Go ahead. I'll pack after dinner."

I want to suggest he take a nap before dinner because he looks exhausted, but I don't. His fatigue won't be cured with a simple siesta. His soul will forever be weary because of what I've asked him to do. Or rather, not to do, and that's fight with Alek.

Saint walks over and grips the back of my neck, drawing us nose to nose. His exhale seems to be heavy with relief. "You're going home."

"*We're* going home," I correct, cupping his cheeks.

He nods slowly, but I'm not convinced.

Now isn't the time to address it, and honestly, I just want to focus on something mundane like cooking dinner. The doom and gloom will always be waiting in the wings for me. We break apart, and I watch as he takes the handle of one suitcase and ambles down the hallway with it.

Pavel follows.

Once they're gone, I meet Larisa's stare. Her astute eyes reveal she's seen it all. She knows why Saint is defeated. She also knows it's because of me.

"Shall we get started?" Sara is also privy to the tension, but like the angel she is, she saves me from having to explain myself to Larisa. Not that she cares, but needing to justify myself suddenly seems important.

Max makes himself scarce while Larisa sinks into the recliner and reaches for the newspaper Saint was reading.

Sara loops her arm through mine, leading me into the kitchen. I'm thankful we're alone because I need a moment to catch my breath.

"So, you're leaving?" Sara asks, turning around to face me.

"Yes, tomorrow."

"To-tomorrow?" she stutters, eyes wide. "Wow, that's fast. Well, not really, but you know what I mean."

And I do. This has been a long time coming; the reason I fought so hard. But now that it's here, it doesn't feel real.

"I know. I'm finding it hard to wrap my head around it, to be honest. But it's happening." I reach into my pocket and hand over my passport.

Sara opens it, eyebrows shooting up into her hairline. "It looks so real."

"Good," I reply. Biting my thumbnail, I'm suddenly nervous.

She closes the passport and passes it back to me. "Is Zoey coming too?"

Sighing, I nod. "Yes, apparently."

Her face turns sympathetic. "Well, this is wonderful news. I'm so happy for you. Will you go back home? To LA?"

With a shrug, I answer, "I don't know what happens after we arrive in America. Saint and I haven't discussed that far ahead. I don't think we believed it would ever happen. But it has."

Sara narrows her eyes, watching me closely. "Why do you sound like this is a bad thing?"

Sara and I have shared so much. In a short amount of time, she has become a close friend, and one who can read me quite well, it appears. Slumping onto a chair, I run my fingers through my hair, exhaling in defeat. "It's not. It's just—"

But I don't even know what I'm trying to say.

"You're scared?" she offers as a plausible explanation, which is, in part, true.

"Yes. So scared," I confess. "This has all happened so fast, and I'm terrified that if I get my hopes up, something else will foil our escape. I've been held captive for…" I pause, needing to think, but I've lost count of how many months have passed.

"I don't even know how long, and the prospect of freedom terrifies me."

Sara doesn't judge. She simply pulls up a seat and sits down beside me. "When I was younger, we had a pet bird," she reveals. I nod, happy to discuss her bird if it means we don't have to dissect my feelings. But I soon realize there is a moral to the story.

"He was a little yellow canary. Although caged, he used to sing the most beautiful songs. I often wondered how something imprisoned could sing all day long. Late one night, after my father came home stumbling drunk, he saw me talking to Pepsi. The bird," she clarifies. I smile, remembering I once had a bird or, rather, a chicken of my own.

"He scolded me, calling me stupid for making friends with a bird. He said I was stupid like my mother." A tear trickles down her cheek, but she quickly wipes it away. "He threatened that one day, when I wasn't looking, he would feed Pepsi to the barn cats."

It seems her father was always a bastard.

"I couldn't let that happen," she continues. "Early the next morning, I opened Pepsi's cage to grant him freedom, and it broke my heart as he was the only friend I had. My mother had run off with our neighbor, and I was an only child. I had no one. Only Pepsi. I thought he would be happy. I thought he would spread his wings and fly."

She has my undivided attention as I need to know where she is going with this.

"But he didn't. Even with the door open, he stayed perched on his swing, singing his song. I didn't understand it. Why wasn't he flying to safety? I tried to coax him out by placing his cage outside. But it didn't work. He simply was happy living his life in a cage.

"For three days, I tried everything, but Pepsi wasn't interested. He ate his food, drank his water, and sang his happy song. It was a hot summer's day; I remember it like it was yesterday as a new family moved across the road from us. They had a little girl, same age as me. She asked if I wanted to come over and play.

"My father wasn't home, and I knew he wouldn't be back for hours, so I said yes. Her name was Emile. Her mother was Nancy." She recounts their names with love, and it's clear she holds them close to her heart.

"We played tag, and she even let me ride her bike. It was one of the best days of my life. But when the sun began to set, I knew it was time to go home. My father would be back soon. I waved goodbye, and I remember how happy I felt. I felt like my cage, just like Pepsi's, had been opened. But going back home, I couldn't help but feel like I was going back to my prison.

"I prepared dinner and waited for my father. While waiting, I decided to check on Pepsi." She swallows while I am on the edge of my seat, lost in her tale. "But he wasn't there. I checked everywhere, but he was gone. I was sad that he was gone, but I was also happy because he was free.

"Every so often, I heard Pepsi's sweet song, but it had changed. It was louder and more vibrant, and I now know that's because he was free. Although it took him a while, he left his cage when he was ready because the unknown is far more terrifying than being held captive. It was what he knew. But in the end, Pepsi left and followed his instincts. He was meant to be free. He was supposed to fly high and not look back.

"Birds aren't meant to be kept in cages. And neither are you."

She reaches forward and wipes a tear from my cheek.

"The door is open for you now, and just like Pepsi, you're afraid, and that's okay. This is what you've come to know. But once you spread your wings, Willow, I know you won't look back."

That analogy touches me in a way I can't explain because I am that bird. I'm afraid because the door to my cage has been closed for so long, and I don't know what's on the other side. But I'm not a quitter. Pepsi had far more challenges than I do, yet he found the courage, and so shall I.

Gripping Sara's hand in mine, I whisper, "Thank you."

We sit in silence for a moment, needing the time to reflect on everything that's happened to us.

"Where will you go?" I ask because her future is also uncertain.

When her cheeks soften to a light pink, I know what the answer is. "Max has offered to help me start over. I wouldn't know where to start."

I nod slowly, but she misinterprets my silence.

"I hope you're not angry with me. I know he wasn't very nice to you. But—"

I soon cut her off. "Hey, no judgment here. Zero." And it's true. Falling in love with my kidnapper and feeling something other than hate for the man who orchestrated it all doesn't really warrant any judgment on my behalf.

"We're just friends. After Hans…" Her quivering pause speaks volumes. "Maybe one day, but right now, I'm just looking forward to starting a new life."

"You deserve all the happiness. We both do," I say, meaning every word.

She smiles, and it's a sight I will never forget. People like Sara helped me to survive, and I will never forget that.

Sara wipes her red-rimmed eyes. "Okay, let's get started on dinner. Any ideas on what to cook?"

Brushing away my tears, I smile, the first genuine smile in a long time. "No clue. But burgers are definitely off the menu. Who knew Larisa had cable?"

Sara bursts into magical laughter.

Sara and I have prepared a feast without a burger in sight. Larisa's kitchen is well stocked, allowing us to entertain our inner *MasterChefs*.

We are going all out as Sara has decided she will leave tomorrow also. She said with me gone, she doesn't have any reason to stay, which just cemented the fact that I'll miss her so much when we part ways.

I promised to keep in touch if I could, but I'm not sure just how low-key my life will have to be. She joked that one day, she would come visit. She doesn't realize how badly I want for that to be true.

An abundance of food covers the table, and the sight warms a small part of me because this will indeed be the last time I share a meal with the people I've come to trust. Once tomorrow comes, there will be no looking back. Even though the thought frightens me, knowing Saint will be by my side soothes my nerves.

Sadly, my nerves are soon provoked once more when Zoey bounces into the kitchen, sniffing the air. "Something smells—" Her sentence dies a quick death when she realizes she was about to compliment my cooking.

She's been MIA for the most part as she and Saint are still not on good terms. As for she and I, I doubt we ever will be on any term other than wanting to kill one another.

"I hope you're hungry," Sara says, filling in the awkward silence. She places the chicken casserole on the table, reminding me the garlic bread is still in the oven. I go about dishing it up as it gives me something to do.

Max enters a moment later, hands filled with freshly cut wood for the fire. He gives Sara a discreet smile, but it's not subtle enough because Zoey blinks once, stunned that she's missed this. I never uncovered if anything actually happened between her and Max, but it's too late. It's clear he only has eyes for Sara.

Sara's cheeks turn a sweet pink as she quickly busies herself.

No matter our past, if Max makes her happy, then he's okay in my book. And besides, Saint trusted me in his care, so he can't be all bad.

Ingrid and Pavel follow soon after, chatting in Russian. It's nice to see Ingrid relaxed. I haven't asked her about Dominic, but I have no doubt that Oscar disposed of him once he no longer served a purpose. I don't realize my hands are burning in the scalding water I have filled the sink with until someone stands beside me and switches off the taps.

Shaking my head to clear the fog, I meet those familiar chartreuse swirls that kickstart my heart. Nothing but concern is reflected in Saint's eyes, so I smile wearily, not wanting to worry him. He doesn't buy it, though. "What are you thinking about?"

"A lot of things," I reply honestly.

He reaches into the water and gently removes my hands. Reaching for a dishcloth, he dries them carefully. His touch and the kind gesture instantly send my body into overdrive, and a flush spreads from head to toe.

"Good or bad?" he questions, arching a dark brow.

My hands are dried, but I don't fail to notice he continues to hold them in his.

"A little of both," I reply, licking my dry lips because being this close to him sets me on fire.

He tilts his head to the side, watching me closely.

"Did you pack?" The hitch to my voice reveals what his proximity is doing to me.

His breathing is unhurried, which only seems to accelerate mine. "Yes, all set. I've left your things in the bathroom."

"Thanks."

The slow rhythm of his finger over the top of my knuckles has me soon forgetting we're talking. Peering up at him from under my lashes, I wonder if we can skip dinner altogether and head straight for dessert. When a lopsided smirk splays across Saint's bowed lips, I know he's on the same page as I am.

Maybe things will be okay, after all.

However, when the backdoor opens and Alek enters, all the warm and fuzzies disappear. He stops in his tracks and looks at the table. "We're celebrating?"

Saint turns around and leans against the counter, ensuring my hand remains locked in his. A tangible tension bounces between them as I believe Alek is sincerely stunned that Saint said no to fighting.

Zoey, of course, is the one to deliver the good or bad news, depending on which way you look at it. "Didn't you hear? We're going back home."

Alek is visibly shocked by her supposed good news. "When?"

"Tomorrow," she replies, twisting the knife in deeper.

The small twitch beneath his left eye betrays him. I've learned to read him just as well as he can read me. All hope is now lost. A small part of him believed we would help him fight a battle he *will* lose on his own. But now, he's realized that he's really on his own.

It appears this really is the last supper for each of us but for entirely different reasons.

"Oh." Alek clears his throat and smiles. "Well, this is definitely cause for a celebration then. I'm pleased for you all."

A blind man could see he's lying through his teeth. But I've made my choice. And so has he.

"If all goes well, maybe you could come visit us?" Zoey says with nothing but sarcasm. "Although, I don't know how much traveling around you could do? New York to LA might be pushing it if you want to remain incognito."

Is she implying what I think she is?

After everything Saint and I have been through, does she think we're going to have a long-distance relationship? When she directs a smug smirk my way, I know that yes, she does. I don't know what to say, but I don't need to say a word.

"He can just visit you in New York then."

Zoey's grin is soon replaced with a frown. "You're not going back home?"

Saint shrugs coolly. "Ангел has to take care of a few things in LA." *Mainly my husband.* "And where she goes, I go."

Well, god damn.

Uncaring that we're in a room full of people, I press my lips to his and kiss him softly. "Ditto," I whisper against his mouth.

The kiss is chaste, but the promise behind it is anything but modest. My worries soon ebb away. Zoey's irritated huff has me smiling because maybe, just maybe, things will work out just fine. And when Larisa enters, whistling in approval of the food laid out before her, I'm hopeful that my luck will finally change.

Dinner was a complete success.

After three servings of mac and cheese, I was convinced Larisa had come over to the dark side. It was nice to see her smile and joke with Pavel. The mood was relatively relaxed, but the unspoken lingered.

Once we finished our meal, we had to deal with what tomorrow would bring. All of us would be embarking on personal journeys that would change our lives forever. Alek excused himself after dessert. I guessed this sense of normalcy was too much for him to handle.

Although my future is uncertain, at least I know I'll have one. Alek, however, will not.

Sara insisted on doing the dishes so I could shower and pack. I didn't argue because I could use some time to myself. Once I sorted through my clothes and zipped up my suitcase, a sense of finality overcame me. This was really it.

I've showered and changed into the polka dot pajamas Larissa bought for me. Fingering the frilly lace collar, I can't help but admire something so small because I look out of place. Yes, back at Alek's house, I had every lavish garment at my disposal, but something so ordinary as pajamas reminds me of the simple life I am about to return to.

I have forgotten what it feels like to be normal. I'm sure, in time, I will adjust, but as I look at my makeup-free face in the mirror, I wonder if I want to. Will the simple life, after everything I've seen and done, be enough?

Sighing, I rinse the toothpaste from my mouth, dispelling such thoughts. I slip into my boots and jacket, ready to tackle the run from the house to the barn. Just as I grab my suitcase, the door opens, but who I see on the other side has me pausing in my tracks.

"Oh, sorry. I thought it was unoccupied." Just as Alek is about to close the door, I reach out and grip the handle, stopping him. I've caught him, and also myself, off guard. He peers down at my hand, confused.

He waits for me to explain, but honestly, I don't know what to say.

"What time are you leaving tomorrow?" he asks, breaking the silence.

"I'm not sure of the time. But Pavel did say at night." This is to ensure we don't rouse any suspicion.

Alek nods once.

Regardless of everything we've been through, I have always had something to say. Whether it was to hurl abuse at him or pretend to like him, I was never speechless until now. The inevitability of what he's doing hits home, and my stomach fills with dread.

This is his decision, but I need him to know how I feel. I don't know why it's important, it just is. "How can you go into this knowing you'll die?"

I've never been one for pretenses, and I don't plan on starting now.

Alek sighs, and for the first time ever, he appears defeated. "Didn't you?"

His question wasn't the response I was expecting.

"Although our circumstances were different, you knew your choices would most likely get you killed or, at the very least, hurt. So do you really need to ask me that?"

He's right. I never gave up fighting because I would have rather...died than surrendered. I lower my eyes, swarmed with guilt.

As my hands once were, Alek's hands are now tied. He would rather die in a blaze of glory than live cowering in fear, and I respect him for that. Throughout this all, I can say without shame that Aleksei Popov is one badass motherfucker. But that doesn't help chip away at the lump in my throat.

"Hey." With the gentlest of touches, he places two fingers under my chin. I go willingly, allowing such a gesture because it'll be the last time. The thought has a tear falling. "Don't waste your tears on me."

He sweeps it away with his thumb.

"I am so sorry for everything. I know it'll never be enough, but I need you to know it anyway. I don't expect your forgiveness; I don't deserve it. But you were the most pleasant surprise, Willow Shaw. And I meant every single word that I've said. But so have you."

His comment has me sniffing back my tears.

"You promised me that you'd never beg, and you were right. You haven't."

This was said when he was certain he would take my virginity and win my love, but those words were spoken in what seems like a lifetime ago.

My heart begins to quicken because something monumental lingers on his tongue. I don't want him to say it because it'll awaken so much if he does.

He strokes over the apple of my cheek, leveling me with nothing but sincerity. "Even now, when you know all you'd have to do is…beg me not to do this, you still won't."

And there it is. The reason for my guilt.

It seems I can save him by uttering a single word, but what will I destroy by doing so?

Placing my hand over his, I squeeze it gently. It's the first time I've touched him openly. Something sparks behind his steel blue eyes, something I haven't seen. Hope. He is hopeful I have the magical potion to make all of this go away.

But I don't. I never did.

Stepping forward, I close the distance between us. "When you had me kidnapped, gagged, and held captive against my will, I never had a choice. But you do. I did what I had to, to survive because I was forced to. My choices were taken away from me because of you. So if you think I am going to beg you not to do this, then you'll be sorely disappointed. Yet again.

Goodbye, Aleksei."

Before he has a chance to reply, I press my lips to his and seal this finale with a kiss—a goodbye kiss because this is what it is. There is no tomorrow for Alek, but there is for me. I let go of my guilt and surrender to the light because I fucking deserve it.

After everything I've endured, I deserve my happily ever after.

There is no affection, no fireworks; it's simply a gesture to bid farewell to who I was and embrace who I will become. And Alek finally knows this because regardless of everything, I've won. And he has no one to blame but himself.

With nothing but pride, I pull away, staring my kidnapper in the eye for the final time. There are no encores this time. With that and my luggage in tow, I push past him, ignoring a surprised Zoey as she witnessed it all, and focus on my future waiting for me in that barn.

The harsh weather is no deterrent for me as I leave my suitcase by the front door and charge outside into the falling snow. Tipping my face to the heavens, I smile and laugh like a madwoman because I was once a captive, but now, I'm free. Just like Pepsi, I've found my wings, and it's time to fly.

Without a moment to waste, I run toward the barn, finally unafraid of what tomorrow holds. The blaring wind almost rips the door from the hinges, but once inside, I close it softly because what I see warms every part of me from head to toe.

Saint sleeps soundly by the crackling fire.

The fur throw sits low on his waist, the warm amber from the flames setting his skin alight. The raised scars scattered across his broad chest are the most beautiful things I've ever seen as they represent his strength. No matter what tried to beat him, he won.

I am the luckiest woman alive to have this man's affection, and I promise here, now, that I will do everything in my power to make him happy for the rest of my life. And it seems the rest of my life starts now because when a small whimper escapes Saint, I run to his aid.

"No," he cries, his face contorting in pain. "Don't."

"Shh," I coo, dropping to my knees and brushing the sweaty hair from his brow.

The moment I touch him, he bolts upright, cupping my throat. I allow him to manhandle me as I raise my hands in surrender. "It's me. Shh, it's me."

His eyes are consumed by a bottomless black while his chest rises and falls rapidly. He looks ready to kill, but I don't cower. I simply allow him to come back to me when he's ready. His grip on my throat tightens as he gauges his surroundings.

The pain shoots straight through me, resulting in an ache between my legs. "It's okay. You're safe."

His breathing begins to slow, and piece by piece, he returns to the now. "Ангел?"

When I nod slowly, he instantly removes his hand, hissing in anger when he realizes what he did. He opens his mouth, ready to apologize, but I don't want his apologies. I want something else.

I swoop forward, smashing our lips together, humming when I taste him—warm and sweet.

He's taken aback by my aggression, but it doesn't take

long for him to catch up to speed. He drags me onto his lap, yanking at the buttons on my jacket before he almost shreds it in half as he tears it off my shoulders. My pajama top is next to go as we only separate long enough to toss it across the barn before we're back to kissing madly.

He cups my breasts, growling when I cry out as he tugs on my nipple. I arch my back, an invitation he accepts when he lowers his head and takes my right breast into his mouth. He suckles deeply, biting sharply when I thread my fingers through his long, wild hair and pull.

We are animated, crazed, pawing at one another because the desperation to be one consumes every action. I find him hot, hard, and ready beneath the throw when I grip his shaft. He hisses into my mouth, pumping into my hand as I begin to stroke him.

"Naked. Now," he orders, fumbling with the drawstring on my bottoms. Just as I am about to pull off my boots, he pushes me onto my back.

Leaning up on my elbows, I watch in fascination as he takes one boot in his hand and slowly slides it off. Then he does the same with the other boot. His eyes rival the crackling fire when he reaches forward and strips me bare. He tosses my pajama bottoms to the side before leaning back on his heels.

My attention is instantly riveted to the straining hard-on protruding from him, and when he takes my ankle and draws my foot toward his lips, I almost want to skip the foreplay and feel him imbedded deep within me. However, when he bites over the arch of my foot, I soon enjoy the feeling of being consumed, quite literally, from head to toe.

The coarseness of his beard combined with the softness of his lips is an unexpected headrush of endorphins, and I cry out, gripping the fur throw beneath me. On the yacht, he brushed over my anklet, and although it is long gone, lost to the sea, I can't help but compare that moment to now.

I will always be his captive because although I'm no longer bound, the invisible manacles around my heart will bind me to him always. From the first moment we met, there was always a tangible electrical pulse between us, and now, I know what that is.

At first, it was fear, but now, it's nothing but irrevocable love. And I cannot wait to spend the rest of my life loving Saint Hennessy.

"Tell me what you're thinking," Saint huskily demands, trailing a line of hot kisses up my leg.

Falling onto my back, I surrender to the feeling of being eaten alive because it's utterly addictive. "I was thinking about tomorrow."

"Mmmhmm," he mumbles from around my flesh.

"What you said to Zoey, about where I go, you go? I feel the same way." I bite my lip to smother a moan when he tongues up toward my knee.

He leans forward and licks a slow, deliberate path across my inner thigh. "I'll need some time to…adapt to humanity," he confesses with a pause. "And learn how to be normal again."

His scorching breath against my skin has my eyes rolling to the back of my head.

"It's going to be hard not to stab someone in the jugular for pissing me off."

The visions of the violence he's inflicted on others, mainly because of me, have my sex pulsing. I can't deny his bad-boy persona is a fucking turn-on because he doesn't even have to try.

"I never thought I'd say this." I gasp when he inches toward my sex. "But I miss the island. It was simple there. The only person you had to worry about pissing you off was me. Oh, holy fuck!" I curse when he tongues over my sex in one quick lick.

I bow my hips, but his amused chuckles reveal he's in the mood to make me beg.

"And piss me off you did," he counters, moving onto my other leg sluggishly. "But you challenged me, and I like a challenge, ангел. Turn over."

I turn to mush at his command and quickly comply. My breaths are heavy as I await further instruction.

I am covered in goose bumps when he runs two fingers down the length of my spine. When he gets to the top of my ass, he caresses over my cheeks softly. "I shouldn't have liked spanking you so much. But I did. Do you want to know why?"

"Because you're a sick, perverted bastard?" I quip, chewing the inside of my cheek when he skims a finger down the pleat of my ass.

His husky laugh heightens my already aroused state, but I bide my time because the reward will be oh, so sweet. "Besides that," he mocks, moving toward my sex. "I knew you liked it. Even before you told me, I knew how it made you feel. I also knew you could handle anything I gave you. You never cowered. Even when things were fucking dismal, you stood strong. My defiant goddess.

"However, you infuriated me…so much."

"If you're expecting an apology, then you'll be waiting a long time." I arch my back, hoping he will douse the fire between my legs, but of course, he doesn't.

"I don't want an apology," he says in a dangerously low voice.

"Well, what do you want?" It's a double-edged sword. I wait with bated breath for his reply.

"Oh, ангел, you should know the answer to that." Just as I'm about to ask what he means, he does something which confirms that no matter where we go or what we do, he will always be my мастер.

He spanks me.

Hard.

And I like it.

I see stars, the kind of stars that are so bright they blind you, but you accept the repercussion because the consequence is so worth the risk.

"And that's to infuriate *you*."

I don't have time to bait him because he brings his hand down again, the force stinging my ass. The impact radiates all the way to my center, and I whimper, desperate for more.

"You do that every day," I defy, hoping my bravado masks the internal struggle not to flip over and beg him to put me out of my misery.

"That smart mouth of yours doesn't know when to quit. On all fours." His command is hot and full of promise, and without wasting a moment, I get on my hands and knees.

We haven't had sex since he took my virginity, which was partly my doing because I was sore. But now, all I can focus on is feeling him inside me once again. He kneels behind me and caresses between my shoulder blades, and then across to my side. His fingertips dance over my flank, stroking over my tattoo.

I am a live wire, anticipating everything and anything because I don't know what he has planned for me, but with my ass in the air, I know it's going to be good. With a torturous slow rhythm, he glides his fingers down my body, coming to a stop at my ass. He cups one cheek, then he spanks me once again with a heavy exhale.

My body recoils forward with the force, but I bounce back into position, wanting more. He does it again and again. My flesh is on fire as it flickers from the pleasure and pain. I hang my head between my shoulders, quivering in need when he lowers his lips to my ass and follows the sting with a kiss.

Every part of me clenches in need.

"Get down on your elbows and spread your legs."

Biting my lip, I stifle my moan and comply. This position leaves nothing to the imagination, which is exactly what Saint wants because when he spreads my ass cheeks and lowers his mouth to my sex, there is nothing between us but this unadulterated bliss.

He scoops an arm under my belly, coaxing me to lift my hips higher and ride his face as he eats me out. I buck backward, moaning in pleasure as he works his tongue into me. The fur throw rubs against my nipples as my breasts sway back and forth. Everything is heightened, and I can't stop the screams that escape me.

Saint squeezes my ass cheek before spanking me again. His mouth and tongue never break tempo as he continues to consume me with an urgent demand. I propel forward from the force of his hand, but when he rubs my tender flesh and suckles my clit quickly, I'm unable to stop myself from bouncing on his face, desperate for a release. But he is teasing me, prolonging my orgasm and staying true to his word.

He is beyond infuriating because this is torture.

I angle my hips to increase the friction, but he drives his tongue in deep, inches from my sweet spot. "Fuck," I groan, clenching my body in frustration.

A warm, victorious chuckle vibrates all through me as Saint continues. His mouth is wet and supple, and his beard is coarse, adding to this conflicting sensation of pleasure and pain. He is fierce and wild, and when he licks upward, circling my puckered entrance with his tongue, I concede because I am going to fucking explode.

"Please, Saint. I want—"

However, I can no longer speak because he robs me of breath when he bites my ass cheek, then aligns our bodies and sinks into me with an impassioned moan. My eyes bulge from my head. I'm filled full to the brim, but when he grips my hips and begins to move, I want more.

He drives into me with long, deep strokes, pulling out and then plunging back in. I take everything he gives, and even though this is only my second time, I learn the dance quick enough because our bodies work in unison.

His breaths are hot and heavy, and the slapping of our

slick flesh adds to the sensation of being joined this way. I can feel every hard inch of him entering me without apology as he imbeds himself deep. This position intensifies the pleasure because each stroke seems to rub over my swollen clit.

I bounce back onto his cock, whimpering loudly because the faster we move, the more heightened my senses become. He controls the speed and tempo, fucking me with feral hunger. His grip on my waist is punishing, but I like it.

He reaches for my right swaying breast, squeezing passionately and thumbing over my pearled nipple. He circles my areola, humming when I cry out in delight.

I can feel him everywhere, on every single inch of me, and when he reaches down and rubs my center, I don't stand a chance and detonate in a loud, desperate cry. My body uncoils, and I suddenly feel like I'm floating.

But Saint isn't done. He continues sinking into me, and when he curses in Russian, it only reignites my fire.

Once the last tremor rocks my body, I clench my muscles, relishing in Saint's guttural groan. I have no idea what I'm doing, but work on instinct and move my hips forward. Before he has a chance to question what I'm doing, I spin around and push him onto his back.

He falls willingly, watching with ravenous eyes as I climb onto his lap. Positioning myself over him, I grip his cock and slowly sink onto it. A string of Russian leaves him as he arches his head backward, his Adam's apple bobbing as he swallows deeply.

Whenever he speaks Russian, something comes over me, and now is no exception. I rock my hips, hissing in disbelief at how deep he is. I feel awkward as I have no idea if I'm doing this right, but it feels fucking incredible, nonetheless.

I place my hands against his slick chest, running my finger over his barbell as I continue rocking. Spread out before me, I look down at the beast and admire how truly epic he is. He is rough and wild, and when we lock eyes, I am lost to this feeling of being joined as one.

He watches me closely, running his hands up and down my thighs as I find my rhythm. "You're fucking beautiful," he says as I move my hips back and forth.

"Does this feel okay?" I breathlessly ask, biting my lip when he jerks inside me.

"More than just okay. I will never get enough of you. Of this," he pants, wrapping his large hand around my flank, over my tattoo. "это навсегда. я обещаю."

"Oh, god," I cry out, bowing backward. He suddenly rears up and suckles my breast. His tongue flicks over my nipple while I squeeze my eyes shut. "What, what did you say?"

"I said—" He suddenly coaxes me to change my rhythm as he lies back down. Instead of rocking, he locks his hands around my waist and lifts me, then slams me onto him, impaling me on his cock.

"Holy Mother of God!" I scream, shuddering uncontrollably.

A smirk tugs at his bowed lips. "Feel good?"

My head is like a spring as I nod quickly.

Once he knows I'm okay with this change in pace, he encourages me to bounce on him, which has us both moaning each time he hits me deep. I catch on soon enough and begin to bounce. Up and down. Up and down.

"I said," he continues, the corded veins in his thick neck straining as he allows me free rein of his body. "This is forever. I promise."

His pledge is more than I could ever ask for and spurs me to move faster. "I love you," I whimper, peering downward at where we're connected. The sight is beyond words.

He reaches between us and begins to play with my clit. The visual, combined with the action and mixed with me bobbing wildly on his cock, has the bundle of nerves inside me coming undone. This is sensory overload because I don't know what to focus on. It all feels so good.

"And I you," he replies, reaching up and cupping the back of my neck. He drags me toward his lips where he kisses the ever-living fuck out of me.

Our tongues battle to be the alpha, but when he pulls, I push, and because of this, we both dominate the other. He suckles my bottom lip, moaning when I bite his.

He pistons his hips, stroking over every inch of me while I surrender to this carnality. Our breaths are heavy, laden with absolute obsession for the other. We would die to protect the other because without each other, we don't exist.

He is my heart. My soul. "I can't wait to spend forever with you," I whisper against his lips.

"Me too, ангел."

The promise is too much, and something savage possesses me. I move with frantic swiftness, clenching my muscles and riding him wildly. I arch backward, the angle deepening the penetration as I rest my hand against his thigh for balance.

He fondles my breasts, then slides his hand up to cup the base of my throat. He squeezes softly, coaxing me to tip my head back farther.

I ride him hard and fast while he holds my throat, and the imagery sends me over the edge. He isn't choking me, by any means, but the fact I am breathless and my heart is thrashing wildly have me gulping in air before I pass out.

When he tightens his hold, I trust him completely and continue to ride him without pause. Truth be told, when I gasp for air, something shatters inside me, and I feel like I'm going to come. He instantly releases his grip and strokes along the column of my neck to make sure he didn't hurt me.

But he didn't.

This kinky play is hot and dominant which seems fitting as we both take and give. We're on an equal playing field because no one is master or submissive. This is about our mutual gratification.

I spring back forward, biting my lip when I watch him beneath me, cheeks flushed, hair unruly, and a look of feral possession owning him. I want to eat him alive. Unable to help myself, I touch his scar, the one inflicted by Astra's bullet.

He flinches slightly, but when I attempt to pull away, he grips my wrist. He wants me to touch it so I no longer look at it with regret. He wants me to know it wasn't my fault. "I can't believe I almost lost you," I whisper, thinking of the many hardships we've faced.

"I'm here now." And he is.

This is all that matters because we've survived. And I plan on living every day of my life to the fullest.

Saint's mounting breaths hint he's almost reached the pinnacle, but so have I because this is suddenly too much. My body writhes and shudders. I am spent. But I want to see him come first.

Pain gets us both off, so I tug at his nipple piercing and bite down over his thrashing pulse as I milk his dick. An unruly moan pushes past his parted lips, and his body tightens before he comes with a fucking sexy deep grunt.

Feeling him constrict and twine around my body is all that it takes, and with one last pump of my hips, I follow him into the abyss. My body shudders, and I am sweltering from head to toe, but I ride the wave, unable to stop the elated moans that burst from me.

It feels like minutes, but once I come down, I collapse onto Saint's chest, smiling when I feel his heart beating frantically under mine. I am sticky and spent, but this is absolute perfection because I have never felt more at peace than I do right now.

Saint wraps the fur throw around us, running his fingers up and down my back while he kisses my temple. We bask in the afterglow because that wasn't making love or merely having sex. That was ownership and possession of the other because our love runs on an almost infatuated level.

I can't live without him, and it seems he can't live without me.

Nothing makes sense without Saint, but his promise assures me I'll never have to be without him again. With that as my final thought, I close my eyes and sleep soundly as this is the first day in our forever.

CHAPTER

THIRTEEN

It's still dark out when I wake, but that's okay because I can't deal with the harsh light of day just yet. Saint is sleeping soundly beside me with his arm draped over my chest. Even when asleep, he can't help but protect me.

I take a moment to look at him as the hue from the crackling fire paints his body in warm tones of orange and yellow. Today is the day which changes everything. Yes, each moment that led to this day has been unpredictable, but this is the first time I am truly clueless to what comes next.

It's hard to believe it's as simple as boarding a plane and going back home, but it is. We've all made our decisions about what happens from here on out, Alek included. I wonder if anything feels different with him, knowing what he does.

I wonder if his morning cup of coffee tastes any sweeter? Or if the first light of day will appear brighter? Everything that was once taken for granted now seems like the most precious thing in the world because it's the last time he will ever experience them again.

There is no point being naïve in this situation—come nightfall, when I board that plane, Alek will be dead.

With a sigh, I gently lift Saint's arm off me as I don't want to wake him and quietly dress. I leave him sleeping peacefully as I walk to the house, in desperate need of coffee.

Heavy snow has fallen overnight, and regardless of my circumstances, I can't help but marvel at how beautiful the simplicity is. Underneath it all lies an entirely different landscape, but the whiteness conceals the horrors and gives one a sense that everything is pure.

If only that were true.

I let myself in through the back door, relishing in the warmth from the fireplace and the aroma of coffee. No one is in the kitchen, but someone is up. I help myself to the freshly brewed coffee, inhaling deeply when I draw the mug to lips.

I'm not hungry, so I decide to get ready once I'm done with my coffee. I've packed but want to look over everything again and familiarize myself with my belongings. Pavel said everything is taken care of, but I don't want to be caught off guard if asked my birthdate and have a mind freeze.

Truth be told, I'm nervous, and I need a distraction for so many reasons. When I hear gentle footsteps enter the kitchen, it appears my distraction has come in the form of Ingrid. I'm about to ask how she slept, but when I notice her red-rimmed eyes, I don't bother.

"What's the matter?" I ask her, placing my mug onto the

counter.

She runs a hand down her face, shaking her head. "He's gone."

"Who's gone?" I ask. However, when fresh tears fill her eyes, I know who.

I take a moment to process what she's just revealed. Even though I never expected a heartfelt farewell, I at least thought I'd have a chance to say goodbye. Alek, it seems, had other ideas and preferred to slip away undetected.

"Maybe he went for a walk?" I suggest even though I'm certain that's not the case.

Ingrid nods in hope, but when Zoey enters, she shatters any scenario and presents the truth. "He didn't go for a walk. He's gone."

I want to question what makes her so sure, but the pink tinge to her cheeks is all the answer I need. "I drank too much last night and ended up in his room," Zoey explains. "I... kissed him. He kissed me back. But it was filled with finality... and longing for someone else." I avert my eyes. "So I left. I was going to apologize this morning for my unwanted advances, but all of his stuff was gone."

Well, it seems she wasn't as over him as she thought she was. But we all know firsthand the potency of Alekesi.

I clear my throat, suddenly uncomfortable.

Ingrid lowers her eyes, wounded. I don't know what went on between her and Alek, but it's no secret she loved him. I don't doubt his feelings for her—I saw it—but we will never know for certain because he's gone.

For him to slip away into the dark of night is so...

anticlimactic, but it's also very Alek.

He doesn't care about anyone other than himself. He didn't think of others who may want to say goodbye, like Ingrid or maybe even me. I don't know why it's important, but saying goodbye to him once and for all was like closing this chapter for good. But now, I'll always be left with this unresolved feeling within.

"Did he leave a note?" Ingrid asks, clinging onto a small shred of hope.

When Zoey looks at her like she's fucking insane, that's all the answer she needs.

"If you'll excuse me." Ingrid doesn't wait for either of us to say a word. She hurries back to her room where, I assume, she'll mourn the death of someone she loved.

Her departure leaves me alone with Zoey, who, for the first time, looks sheepish. But I'm not here to judge her. Her decisions are hers alone to make.

"Coffee?"

Her eyebrows shoot up into her hairline. It's clear she wasn't expecting me to behave so civilly toward her. But she nods.

Turning around, I reach for a mug in the cupboard and pour her a cup. When I offer it to her, she looks at it like I've slipped in some poison, and I can't blame her. It's not like I haven't done it before. She finally accepts.

This isn't at all awkward.

We sip our coffees in silence because although there is much to discuss, it seems neither of us have the energy to engage in small talk. We're both surprised by Alek's decision to leave unannounced, but while Zoey is saddened by his decision, I am enraged that it was that easy for him to walk away.

Yes, last night, we said informal goodbyes, but he owes me, he owes Saint more than this. I can't help but think that he took the coward's way out. He'd rather slip away than be forced to look Saint in the eyes and accept defeat. I feel cheated.

"I thought you'd be happy he's gone," Zoey says, in tune to my thinking.

"I am," I reply, meeting her eyes. "But him leaving that way is…gutless."

"Maybe he's not one for goodbyes," she quips, but I don't buy it. "Besides, you said your *goodbyes* last night."

The clenching of her jaw reveals she's speaking about what she saw. But if she thinks that "kiss" was filled with affection, she's blind. If it was anything more, then Alek wouldn't have gone, and she knows it. But her jealousy distorts the truth.

However, that's her problem, not mine.

"Hey." Saint's hoarse voice has Zoey and me focusing our attention on the back door. He looks back and forth between us, sensing something is amiss.

"Coffee?" It seems to be the answer at the moment.

Saint nods, and I pass him my mug because I suddenly feel queasy.

Alek leaving the way he did, has really pissed me off. He's the first one to talk about honor, so where was his when he decided to run away with his tail tucked between his legs?

"What's the matter?" Saint grips my elbow, coaxing me to tell him what's on my mind.

"Alek is gone," I reply, unable to keep the bitterness from my tone. "He didn't even have the balls to say goodbye."

Saint shrugs, but there is no missing the tic under his eye. "It doesn't matter. Saying goodbye doesn't change the outcome of our decisions."

Like hell it doesn't. "You're missing the point."

This ending is like reading the last book in a trilogy, anticipating a big climactic twist only to be disappointed to uncover the hero and heroine go riding off into the sunset and live happily ever after. Where's the fun in that?

"He owes you more," I press, shaking my head. But there is something else, something I can't quite put my finger on. "I can't help but feel he got off scot-free."

"Scot-free?" Zoey admonishes. "He's willingly walking into his death. I hardly call that *scot-free*."

Saint arches a brow, wondering why she's defending him. When she casts her eyes downward, he reads between the lines. He seems disappointed she submitted this one final time.

Slipping into a positive mindset, I try to see the good in him leaving this way. Good riddance to him. But when Larisa hobbles into the kitchen, I can't help but think Alek will never get to her age because in just a few short hours, he'll be dead. And that means we'll have to live with this unresolved bullshit ending for the rest of our lives.

"Ангел, leave it," Saint warns because he can read my dissatisfaction. But I can't.

"Saint—"

"I said leave it." Saint's caution is filled with warning. "We are leaving here. Tonight. That's all I care about."

But he can't be satisfied with this outcome. It feels like the bad guys have won. With that thought comes another, and I gulp down my guilt because that is, in part, because of me. I asked Saint not to fight, fearing he would get hurt, but us leaving suddenly feels reflective of what Alek has done.

The smart thing to do would be to get on that plane and not look back because this can finally be over with. But it feels like such a cop-out.

"Stop it." Saint cups my cheek in his warm palm, leveling me with those eyes. "Let go of whatever you're thinking. It's done. Besides, what would we say? Thanks for the memories? Knowing what he's walking into is satisfaction enough."

Is it, though?

However, his stubborn stance on the topic reveals this isn't up for discussion. I could press, but Saint's mind is made up. This, it appears, *is* our ending.

Pavel enters with a green duffle bag thrown over his shoulder. When he sees us standing around, he pauses. "Everything all right?"

Saint's sigh is heavy as I suspect he is waiting for me to argue that everything is far from all right. But I don't. No matter how I feel, if Saint is happy with leaving this way, then I will bite my tongue.

"What's in the bag?" I ask, changing the subject.

"Ah…just clothes."

His hesitation raises red flags, and when Larisa stops hunting through the refrigerator to give him a confused look, I know he's lying. But I bite my tongue yet again.

"I have some paperwork you'll have to give to the pilot." I'm not sure if this is code for Pavel wanting to speak to Saint in private.

"Okay." Saint kisses my forehead.

All this secrecy is adding to my already frayed nerves.

Saint and Pavel exit the kitchen, leaving me alone with Larisa and Zoey who also seem to sense the concealment.

Needing some time alone, I grab a coffee and make my way into the living room. The fireplace has been my best friend during my time here, and I take a seat in front of it, staring into the bright orange flames.

This entire situation leaves me restless and leaving can't come soon enough.

"Hey." Sara sits down beside me, drawing her knees toward her chest. "Are you okay?"

Shrugging, I take a sip of coffee.

"Did something happen?"

"Alek is gone," I reply blankly.

"Oh." Her response reveals her surprise. "Are you upset he's gone?" She is trying to work out why I am so irritated because Alek being gone means we can all move on.

"I'm annoyed," I answer, turning to look at her. "He just left."

"Were you expecting more?" she asks curiously.

I mull over her question because I don't know why this bugs me so much. "Yes, I was. He owes you an apology for everything he's done to you. He also should have given Saint the respect he deserves and looked him in the eye and ended this between them—once and for all. Not to mention, he didn't even say goodbye to Ingrid. She deserved that."

Sara nods. "I understand. But apologizing to me wouldn't bring Hans back. Nor would it make what he did to Saint okay. Alek may have changed, but his past actions can never be forgiven. Him leaving this way doesn't change anything. We only worked with one another because there was no other way. We wanted the same thing, and to achieve that, we had to work together."

"I disagree," I argue. "We don't even know what he has planned. How do we know he's even going to do what he says? Can we trust him not to double-cross us?"

"Why does it matter?"

And that's the catch. I don't have the answer.

"I don't know. It just does," I reply honestly.

Sara seems to ponder over my response. "It's okay to be worried about him. You wouldn't be human if you didn't."

But that's not it. "I'm not. I just, something feels unresolved by us leaving this way."

"Will you ever really get closure?" she questions gently. "What's happened to us will leave us forever questioning why. Why us? What did we do to deserve this? And regardless of the answers we're given, it'll never be enough.

"Sometimes, you have to accept that life just…is. And not dwell on the past. We have to learn from the past and ensure we don't make the same mistakes in the future."

She's right, but that still doesn't make this heavy feeling in the pit of my stomach go away. There is something I need to do; I just don't know what that is—yet.

"I'm really going to miss you." This, however, is something

I don't need clarification on.

"Me too." Sara smiles, but it's heavy with sadness. "I'm so happy to have met you. I hope when we're both settled and things aren't so crazy, we will see one another again."

I swallow down the lump in my throat because Sara and I have bonded over the most atrocious acts. One doesn't forget such a connection because experiences such as ours fortify true friendship forever. "I hope so too. Where are you and Max headed?"

"He has made arrangements for us to go to France."

"Back home?" I question with surprise as I know her relationship with her father is volatile. He was the reason she was imprisoned in the first place.

"Not at first," she replies in a faraway voice, her eyes focused on the fire. "But maybe one day."

I admire her so much. Although docile, she is far braver and stronger than I am.

"I was thinking of visiting my neighbors," she reveals with a small smile. A part of me wishes Pepsi was included in the reunion.

"That all sounds really wonderful. I can't wait to hear all about it."

Sara nods while I sip my coffee. We're deep in thought because our futures, something which was uncertain for us both, are within grasp. This is our goodbye because come nightfall, we will go our separate ways.

Some goodbyes are better than others. But this isn't goodbye—it's so long, for now.

It's amazing the things you'll miss when knowing you'll never see them again. This barn is one of those things.

Standing in the middle of the room, I look around and commit to memory the time spent here. Nothing will ever compare to this place because my life changed forever here. My gaze drifts to the spot where Saint and I consummated our love, and an unexpected nostalgia swells.

Regardless of our dire circumstances, we have survived. No matter the obstacles, we're here, together, and that thought gives me some comfort because all of it wasn't for nothing.

Before all of this, I was held prisoner to the past, but now, those shackles are free, and I am reborn. I don't know what'll happen when we get to America, but for the first time, I don't mind. I have been through hell and back, and here I stand, ready for the next chapter in my life.

I'm no longer scared. I'm calm. Alek has been on my mind, but this is one battle I've lost, so I must accept defeat. It pains me to know that soon, Alek will be dead, and Oscar and Astra will be free. Such a disappointing ending. I hate it.

But sometimes, you have to sacrifice a plot twist to get your happily ever after, and when Saint walks into the barn, I know he was worth it all.

"Ready?" he asks.

He's been awfully quiet all day, but we all have. We've all

been in our own heads, lost to what comes next.

"Yes," I reply, taking everything in one last time. Walking over to the stall, I pat the cow on the nose, wishing her well. These humble lodgings have been my sanctuary, and I'll never forget them for as long as I live.

"Are you okay?"

With a sigh, I nod. "I am."

Saint allows me all the time I need. But I'm ready. It's finally time. My suitcase is already in the van, so with nothing left inside here for me, I walk toward Saint and link my fingers through his. I lock eyes with him, our gaze saying so much.

I never thought it would come to this. I never believed he would be the one to baptize me into this new world, but he did. He has opened my eyes and heart, and I will never forget everything we've been through.

Without a word, we leave this world, intent on embarking upon something new. The snow is thick, so we shield our faces and march our way through. Larisa stands in the doorway, watching Pavel pack everything into the black van.

Sara and Max are placing their belongings in the back seat of their SUV.

Zoey emerges from the house, stopping by Larisa. I can't hear what they're saying, but when Zoey hugs her, it isn't hard to guess their farewell is heartfelt. Larisa hugs her tightly, rubbing her back gently.

Seeing Zoey this way gives me hope that she isn't completely dead inside. I doubt we'll ever be friends, but for Saint's sake, I'll try. Sara walks over to us, blowing on her hands. "Max and I are going the same way as you are. We'll be behind you for most of the journey. Well, happy travels," she says with a smile.

"You too, Sara. Stay safe."

Saint gives my hand a reassuring squeeze before hugging Sara gently. "All the best, Sara. I hope you find happiness."

Tears suddenly well in her eyes, which instantly have my own threatening to break free. "You too, Saint," she replies, nuzzling into his neck as she stands on her tippy toes.

They too have shared so much heartache; it's nice to see their farewell is different.

"I'll never forget you," she whispers, closing her eyes. "Thank you for everything you did for Hans. He respected you so much."

"Shh," he coos, rubbing her back. "Let's not speak of the past. Only the future."

When a single tear falls down her cheek, I chew my lip to stop mine from spilling. Max walks over, appearing rather sheepish. We haven't exactly been friends, but we've been on the same side. And that's enough.

"Good luck with everything," he says, extending a hand. I accept it because regardless of our past, he's been good to my friend, and that's all that matters.

Once Sara finishes saying farewell to Saint, she gives me a tight hug and kisses my cheek. There isn't anything further to say because no matter how many times we say goodbye, it'll never make this any easier. Max wraps his arm around her shuddering shoulders and leads her toward the SUV.

Pavel starts the engine, hinting it's time to go.

Zoey wipes her eyes as she walks down the stairs. She

slides open the door, but suddenly stops dead in her tracks.

"Fuck." Saint curses under his breath. His boots sink into the deep snow as he marches toward her. I follow in hot pursuit, wondering what's going on.

When I see Ingrid crouched in the back of the van, I have my answer.

"Why is she here?" Zoey snarls, burning Ingrid alive with her death glares.

"Because I'm dropping her off at a friend's," Pavel replies from the front seat. Ingrid's hollowed expression has me wondering where exactly Pavel is taking her.

She is broken; this beautiful angelic being is broken beyond repair. I can only hope she'll finally find peace where she's going.

Zoey opens her mouth, primed on arguing as Ingrid is still public enemy number one, but Saint grips her arm and shakes his head. "Just get in the van, Zoey."

She could argue, but she knows when a battle is lost, and this is one of them. With an unhappy grumble, she complies.

Larisa has provided us with a haven, and even though she hasn't liked me, I still want to thank her for taking me in. I walk up the stairs and offer my hand. "Спасибо."

When she shakes it firmly, I'm relieved she's accepted my gratitude.

I don't know what else to say because someone like Larisa doesn't dabble in bullshit. She's a straight shooter, and I don't want to insult her by delivering her a clichéd line.

I am about to turn around and leave, but she pulls me toward her, robbing me of air as she delivers a line of her own.

"Never compromise what you think is right. Doesn't matter the risk. The risk to your heart is more," she affirms in broken English, her astute eyes boring into me.

My mouth parts in surprise because I have no fucking idea what she just said. Is this some Russian proverb? I'm about to ask her what she means, but she nods once, as if that's the answer I need.

Saint approaches seconds later, but he didn't see our exchange because she has released my hand. He gives her a tight hug, speaking to her in Russian. I am too dumbfounded to even process what is going on. Saint casually reaches for my hand and leads me down the stairs.

I quickly turn over my shoulder, desperate to ask Larisa what she meant, but she doesn't look back, and it appears she believes neither should I. By closing the door, she's forcing me to figure this out on my own.

"You want to ride shotgun?" Saint asks me, rubbing my arms to create heat because I'm shivering. But it has nothing to do with the cold.

Peering up at him from under my lashes, I take in the man who he is and subconsciously know Larisa's words are connected to him. Even though it's cold as hell, I'm suddenly burning up.

"Ангел?" he questions, sensing my sudden clam up.

"Never compromise what you think is right. Doesn't matter the risk. The risk to your heart is more."

My heart is Saint, and Larisa knows it. So what is she trying to say?

Sadly, I've run out of time to figure it out. "We have to

leave now; otherwise, you will miss your flight." Pavel's voice alerts me to the fact that we're cutting it close, so irrespective that every bone in my body is in protest, I peck Saint on the lips and get into the back of the van.

He watches me closely with his hand poised on the door as if he wants to say something. Something invisible lingers, but it appears neither of us knows what it is. Just like déjà vu, when you sense you should know something—like you've already experienced a situation or a feeling—but you just can't pinpoint what it is. This is what it feels like.

I'm hoping he is about to solve the mystery, but when he closes the door, the air deflates out of me like a balloon. I sag into my seat, defeated.

When Saint jumps into the passenger seat and fastens his seat belt, Pavel puts the van into drive, and just like that, we're gone. The seat belt cuts off my air supply, so I place my hand under the belt and pull it away from my body.

It's stifling hot in here, thanks to the heater cranking, and you'd think, thanks to the subzero temperature, that I'd be basking in the heat. But I'm not. I'm on fire.

Pavel and Saint speak softly, but I don't hear a word. I peer out the windshield and watch my freedom unfurl before me. The punishing terrain is twisted in white sleet. Pavel navigates the roads with care, but I grip the seat beneath me, clawing the leather to shreds.

Zoey catches wind of my meltdown and nudges me with her knee. "What's wrong with you?" Her question is laced with interest rather than concern.

"Nothing," I reply breathlessly. I don't want to talk in fear of throwing up.

Saint turns over his shoulder to look at me, but I give him a weak smile, not wanting to worry him.

"These winding roads are making me queasy. That's all." Holy shit, as far as excuses go, that is fucking lame, *LAME*, seeing as I was stuck on a yacht for days, but it's the best I can do.

"I'll slow down," Pavel says, and I'm thankful at least one person believes me.

Closing my eyes, I inhale and exhale slowly, shutting out what Larisa said, but the harder I try to ignore it, the louder and more persistent it becomes.

Larisa has said all of five words to me since I arrived at her home and then decides to drop this philosophical bombshell on me the moment I leave. Now she expects me to understand what the hell she was trying to say.

With eyes closed, I'm able to shut out the white noise and focus on her words because there is a meaning behind them. What I think is right—that ship has sailed long ago. There is nothing right about this entire shitshow.

From the first moment to this very end, everything has revolved around surviving, regardless if it was right or not. So what changes now?

Ingrid is left broken and alone, headed to god knows where to heal her wounds—where is the right in that? Sara is left without Hans, without a family—where is the right in that? We're headed toward an airstrip where we will board a plane and are supposed to forget the atrocities that occurred to us—where in the ever-living fuck…

Fuck.

Fuck.

Zoey once called Larisa a witch doctor. I now see why.

"Stop the van," I whisper so softly, I'm unsure if I spoke it aloud or just in my head. "Stop it."

When the van continues driving, the need to flee suffocates me. I need to get out. I'm going to vomit. "Stop the van!"

Saint frantically turns over his shoulder. "Ангел?"

Pavel stops talking, peering at me in the rearview mirror. I thought I'd see surprise reflected back at me, but I don't. He pulls over to the side of the road, and before he has a chance to stop, I rip open the door and fly outside.

My boots skid along the icy road, but I grip the guardrail and take three deep breaths. I feel slightly better, but when Saint grips me by the elbow and spins me around, the nausea returns.

"What's wrong?"

Holy shit, I think the better question here is what's right? Larisa allowed me to see this, allowed me to see what I knew was there all along. Back at her house, there was something I needed to do. I didn't know what that was until now.

God save me from the mess I'm about to make.

"We have to go back," I say, watching in utter fear as Saint steps back, stunned. But this is nothing compared to what's coming.

"*What?*"

"We, we can't leave him," I reply, licking my sudden dry lips. "If we do, we're no better than them."

Saint shakes his head furiously. "Let me get this straight,

you want to go back to *him*? To Aleksei?"

A single word can bring down a nation, just as I have. "Yes."

"Willow…why?" Saint is barely reining in the rage as his fists clench and unclench dangerously slow.

"Because it's the right thing to do." Larisa's words only confirm my truth. "No matter what's been done, we can't let him die."

"*We* will die," Saint snarls, eyeing me like I'm the enemy.

"Only He knows that." The cross around my neck tingles, a confirmation I'm doing the right thing.

"Do you know what you're asking me to do?"

I nod, wishing I could take away his pain. But I can't.

"You're ripping out my fucking heart!" he utters with so much passion. "Why do you see the good in everyone?"

"Because I'll never give up hope," I reply, hoping he understands. He doesn't.

"You're doing this for *him*?"

Disgust coats his venomous words, but he's misunderstood. The reason I'm doing this runs far deeper than what he thinks.

"The risk to your heart is more."

Stepping forward with palms raised in surrender, I hope he appreciates why I'm doing this when I whisper, "No, I'm doing this for you."

A plume of smoke slips past Saint's lips as he gasps.

"Look me in the eye and tell me you're okay with letting that vile…monster live? Are you really okay with leaving and not making him pay for what he did?"

There is no need to establish who I am speaking about.

Saint may think Alek is the reason I want to go back, and yes, he is in part. He's a pawn in this game, we all are, and we all have a part to play. And Saint's turn is now.

"I'm doing what you asked me to!" he cries, arms spread out wide. He is frustrated and confused.

"I know, and I was wrong to ask that of you. I'm sorry."

"Don't be sorry, it's done. I'll learn to live with my choice."

But he isn't fooling anyone because that's a life half lived.

I ensure to keep my distance because Saint is a live wire. And he has every right to be. "No matter how much we have, it'll never be enough. Life will always be lacking something. A certain flavor, a particular pitch, nothing will ever be good enough because you will never be satisfied. You will never be whole."

Saint closes his eyes and tips his chin to the heavens. "Why are you doing this?"

Taking small, measured steps toward him, I reveal, "I asked you for something I had no right to. This is your fight, and I took it away from you. I can't ask you to sacrifice this because if you were to ask me the same with Drew, I would lose a small part of myself too."

Hoping that he sees reason, I give him the time he needs.

"He left like a coward, and I refuse to accept that ending. We have unresolved business, and we would be cowards too if we didn't end this for good. No more looking over our shoulders. We need closure…whatever that may be.

"I thought I was doing the right thing by saving you, but something Larisa said opened my eyes."

Saint's chest rises and falls deliberately as he is measuring his breathing. I know I should have done this sooner, but I thought I was doing the right thing.

"What did she say?" I'm surprised to hear Zoey's voice. She remains in the van, but she's heard everything.

"She said I was to never compromise what I think is right. Doesn't matter the risk. The risk to my heart is more," I recite. Spoken aloud, I'm even more confident I'm doing the right thing.

Zoey seems to ponder on what I've just told her. "And how do you interpret that? It could mean a million things."

She's right. But to me, it's the difference between living in the darkness and light.

"What I think is right is that bastard, Oscar, deserves to pay for what he's done. As does Astra. I thought I was doing the right thing by leaving, but it feels as though we're running away."

Saint's eyes spark an electric green as he focuses them my way.

"The risk if we do go is that we may die. But I'm willing to sacrifice that because the risk to my heart, the risk to *you*, Saint," I clarify so he knows that my heart is him, "is worth it because you will always live in the shadows if you don't kill that motherfucker."

His voice is hoarse as he questions, "And saving Alek is the right thing to do?"

And once again, I'm stuck at a moral crossroads.

"After everything he's done, saving him doesn't seem like the right thing to do, but neither is letting him die," I explain. "Yes, he's the bad guy, but I would be too if I let him die. Doing this doesn't make me weak…"

"It makes you strong."

I can't hide my surprise when Zoey speaks.

"And you're okay with this plan?" Saint asks Zoey, looking at us as though we've both gone mad.

"He doesn't deserve my compassion, but he has it."

"Why? He abused you!" Saint shouts, enraged. "Treated you like dirt."

"I abused myself," she argues calmly. "I could have left at any time, but I didn't because I loved him. I always will, and like Willow, I can't stand back and watch him die."

"I don't understand this!" Saint's statement is filled with hate and confusion, and I can relate because I feel it too.

"I don't either, but maybe one day, I will. I just know we have to go. Now. But the choice is yours."

Saint looks at me with nothing but fire as he mulls over everything he's just heard. None of this makes sense, but it never has. Falling in love with Saint shouldn't have happened, but it did. Nor was becoming a fierce fighter because of what I've endured. But everything has happened for a reason.

Meeting Alek resulted in many deaths, one of which was my stepfather. If I hadn't met him, Kenny would still be alive, and a small part of me would still be cowering in fear. Everything has happened for a reason, and I suppose for every action there is a consequence.

Oscar's despicable actions have resulted in the consequences he's about to face. If he doesn't, it almost feels as if his actions will go unpunished, and I can't live with that. As for Alek, his actions have led to him losing a kingdom, and those actions were falling in love with me.

Nothing will ever, *ever* excuse what he did, but letting him die will be a permanent smudge on my soul. It will eat away at me forever. My father may be gone, but I know what he'd want me to do. And for Saint, the consequence of letting Oscar live will be his self-hate, which will eventually lose him to the darkness for good.

The bad guys can't win. And if we walk away now, that's what'll happen.

"Count me in." Zoey and I may be at war with one another, but it seems we can fight together when it means saving something we believe in.

"Me too," Ingrid says with a firm nod from behind Zoey.

Max and Sara have parked their car behind our van, watching with interest. Pavel exits the driver's side and walks toward Max. He winds down the window, and I can only guess that Pavel's explained what's going on. Sara's eyes widen as I know this is crazy, but when she nods once, hinting she too is with me, I realize this is something we all have to do.

Pavel walks over to us, blowing on his cold hands as it's begun to snow once again. He doesn't say anything. He simply stands off to the side, awaiting Saint's response.

Flecks of snow have stuck to his lashes as he stands unbending, stewing over everything I've said. I wish we had more time, but we've never had that—only fleeting moments to make life-changing decisions.

"We could have lived a happy, normal life. You could have had your happily ever after."

I smile, but it's bittersweet. "I will. As long as we're

together, I will get my fairy-tale ending."

"And if we're not?" he questions, walking toward me slowly.

"Then I will enjoy whatever ending is destined for us." He flinches at such dire thoughts. "No one knows their fate, but this is us taking it by the balls and making it ours."

I wait with bated breath as he gently places a warm palm on my cheek. His touch instantly thaws my chill. "I was ruined from the first moment I met you. You were never my prisoner…I was yours. I still am."

I nestle into him, the connection exactly what I need.

"If we do this, I can't promise you forever." He runs his thumb along the apple of my cheek, eyes boring into me, stressing the direness of our decision. There are no guarantees we will survive this unscathed.

Placing my hand over his, I squeeze softly. "Well then, I'll settle for now because I'd rather have all of you than half of you, which is what you will be if you let him live."

"Is that the same for you if you let him die?" he counters, referring to Alek rather than Oscar, but the sentiment is the same.

I ponder his question because it isn't as clear-cut as that. "In some ways, I suppose that it is."

The decision is now up to Saint. He knows how I feel. Whatever choice he makes, he has to make it soon. I hope he makes the right one.

With snow falling around us, setting a somewhat magical backdrop, Saint lowers his lips to mine and kisses me softly. I melt into his mouth, into him because he completes me.

Just as quickly as he kisses me, though, he pulls away, and I instantly miss his touch. But what he says next has another fire stoking within.

"There are explosives in that bag, aren't there?"

My attention rivets to Pavel who has stood quietly throughout this. When he grins, that soon changes. "You know me well, brother."

My mouth parts in understanding because I was right to be suspicious of the bag I saw Pavel carrying back at the house. There aren't clothes in there, as he claimed there to be, but instead something which will give us half a chance.

"Just in case?" Saint asks with a smirk.

"Just in case," Pavel confirms with a nod. "But if we're doing this, we'll have to move. From what I can pick up from the bugs, things haven't started to get messy. Yet."

This must mean Alek's mom is there. Or they have moved to Oscar's lair.

"Why are you helping him?" Saint asks Pavel.

But what Pavel says next confirms his loyalty will always be with his friend. "I'm not helping him. I'm helping you. Just as you've helped all of us. That bastard deserves everything we're about to inflict, and inflict slowly."

Max and Sara have joined our circle, and I can't help but wonder why they would risk their lives for us as well. But being thrown together with a bunch of strangers and enduring the most gruesome acts have created a band of misfits who formed a bond that cannot be broken.

We are loyal. We are strong. But most importantly, we are a family…a family who fights together.

Saint peers around at each of us with something I haven't seen reflected in those depths for a very long time—hope. Even though the future is uncertain, we want this future. When Saint's gaze lands on me, everything falls quiet.

Whatever happens, I am thankful for it all because a life half lived with Saint is better than living a long lie.

"If we get out of this alive, you're in so much trouble." Saint tongues his upper lip. The delicious promise has my heart skipping a beat.

With that as my incentive, I smirk, a winner's grin because regardless of my ending, that's what I am. "Let the trouble begin."

CHAPTER

FOURTEEN

ronic, isn't it? Driving toward danger feels more like freedom than when I was headed for the airstrip. I thought I was doing the right thing, but I was wrong. Yes, I wish I'd realized this days ago, but I didn't even know what I wanted until Larisa spoke her words of wisdom. I just needed a push.

And push she gave.

We're all in agreement about what has to happen—Oscar and Astra must die. Anyone who stands in our way will meet the same fate.

Max, Zoey, and Sara are following us. Ingrid, Saint, Pavel, and I are in the van, mulling over our plans. The last we heard, Serg told Zoya to stay in the car. Ten minutes later, gunshots were heard. Pavel was convinced it was Alek because one of Pavel's contacts who needed the money was able to amass a small arsenal for him.

That was thirty minutes ago.

Zoya's transmission is dead. We don't know what that means other than the fact we no longer have tabs on the place. We don't know what we're walking into, but that isn't anything new.

Google Maps hasn't updated Alek's newly blown to smithereens house, so we're working off the original blueprint. There really is no way to know where the perimeter of men will start, so we're going off logistics.

Alek let it slip to Pavel that he'll be attacking from the east of where his house once stood because there is no longer any road access. He doubts Astra would fancy trekking through the dense woodlands surrounding the property, so she'll take the main road, which is still standing.

She will require her band of men to protect her, so Alek's thoughts were that the area wouldn't be saturated with guards. We can only hope.

I don't know how many men he could take down before being disarmed, but when we reach my former prison site, it won't be long until I find out. The headlights have been turned off, so we're relying on the moonlight to guide us through.

"Stop here," Saint commands, looking from left to right to ensure the coast is clear. "Not too close. We will have to walk the rest of the way."

I can't see much of anything out here because all that surrounds us is a thick blackness, contrasted with a casing of white snow. I wasn't nervous—until now.

"Remember, go slow. Be quiet," Pavel instructs, reaching for his revolver from the glove compartment.

The duffle bag sitting by my feet is our holy grail. It's filled with the guns, the knives, and our gold mine, the explosives. The plan is simple—arm up and don't die.

Saint, who is sitting in the back with me, opens up the bag and hunts through it. I can't see very well, but it's evident from his rummaging that he's looking for something specific. I find out what that is a moment later.

"Put this on." I'm about to ask what it is, when he places something heavy over my head and chest. I don't have time to argue before he's fastening the straps into place.

"A bulletproof vest. That's a great idea." When he retrieves another one and hands it to Ingrid in the passenger seat, I strain my eyes to see where his is.

When it's clear Pavel only packed two, I attempt to unfasten the strap, but Saint stops me. "Where is yours?" I ask in vain.

"I don't need one."

I can't help my eye roll. "This is completely sexist. Why do the women get one and the men don't?"

Pavel beats his chest with a hollowed echo, proving me wrong. Who knew a bulletproof vest was his go-to like a sweater would be for most?

"So everyone needs one but you? Is that right? I didn't realize you were bulletproof." I can't keep the bite from my tone because the last time he tried this martyr bullshit, he almost exploded.

This isn't negotiable.

"I don't need one because I have this." When he pulls out what I can only describe as a mini rocket launcher, I almost surrender. Almost.

"That will eventually run out of…" I want to say bullets, but I have no idea what that thing fires. Pavel needs a new hobby. "Ammo," I settle for. "And what happens then?"

Saint strokes over my trembling lips. "By the time that happens, they'll all be dead."

His cockiness should be reassuring, but it only has me further on edge. "We don't even know what we're walking into."

"This will be no different than any other fight I've been in. It'll be okay, ангел," he reassures me, his eyes glowing out here in the darkness. "Besides, you've got my back."

When the heavy metal of two guns are settled within my palms, I realize things are about to get real.

I am armed to the teeth and feel incredibly selfish because I hope there is enough weaponry to go around. Who knew those words would become my life.

When Pavel's cell vibrates, he quickly conceals it under his hand to read the text message. "Max is ready when we are." It seems Max is also a gun enthusiast because he has his own supply on hand. I wonder if he came prepared with a bulletproof vest, though.

The thought of Sara going out there scares me. Zoey can handle herself, but I don't know if Sara can. It was decided that no one would stay behind because it was far too dangerous. Safety in numbers, Pavel said, and Saint agreed.

But now that we're out here in the darkness, about to face the unknown, I don't know if that's such a good idea. I would be a hypocrite to ask Sara to stay, though.

"You don't have to do this," Saint says, placing a gun into the waistband of his black jeans. I think, by some miracle, he's hoping I change my mind. "You can stay here and just shoot anything that moves."

I love that he's trying to protect me even when he knows what my answer will be. "Let's go."

Ingrid's thick jacket hides her bulletproof vest, as will mine when I slip it on. With shaky fingers, I fasten each button, fumbling with the last one. Saint's fingers envelop mine, steadying me. He secures the button for me. His breath brushes the hair from my cheeks. "You follow my command. Don't be a hero. Stay behind me at all times."

I'd salute if this wasn't scary as all hell.

"No matter what happens, you stay with me, all right?"

Pressing my palm to his cheek, I run my fingers through his beard. "I'll never leave you," and I mean that in every possible way there is.

I know things are about to get messy, but I am here for the thick of it.

Gripping the back of my head, he presses his forehead to mine. After inhaling heavily, he kisses me with nothing but fierce need. Our tongues contest, fighting for domination, but this kiss is about taking and giving. We both need to survive this.

I thread my fingers through his long hair, wanting nothing more than to climb him and forget the troubles we face. But the fire soon simmers as it's time. Our kisses grow languid, but I promise myself this is just a sample of what my future holds once the night is done.

"Once we're outside, no talking. Mask any noise as best you can."

Saint rubs his nose against mine, holding my nape tightly. The quiver to his touch is only because he fears for my safety, not his. I know Saint, and all he'll worry about is keeping me safe.

With a deep sigh, he releases me. But when those bright chartreuse orbs spark to life, a surge of adrenaline overcomes me. I'm as ready as I'll ever be.

Pavel nods, and with the slowest and quietest of movements, he opens the driver's door. Saint ensures I'm armed before he does the same. Ingrid follows. Once Pavel is outside, Saint passes him the duffle that holds the explosives.

From what I saw, it looks like Pavel has made a bomb, but I can't be too sure. Whatever it is, it eases some of my nerves because I've seen the damage his bombs can do. Max, Sara, and Zoey creep over to where we are.

Saint offers me his hand as he steps from the van. I accept, ensuring to be light-footed as I step onto the snow. Thankfully, Pavel's hand gestures are easy enough to read. He lowers his hand, telling us to stay low before signaling it's time to move.

Pavel, Max, and Saint are in front while Sara and I are behind them. Ingrid and Zoey are behind us, keeping their eyes peeled for any threat lurking in the shadows. Our paces are measured and in sync so as not to draw attention to our presence.

I don't know how far away we are because nothing is distinguishable. There are barren trees, their branches twisted into distorted angles, while the ground is covered in thick snow. Our boots sink into the snow, masking the sound of our footsteps.

We skulk in the shadows on high alert, anticipating an ambush, but we don't encounter one. I don't know whether to be relieved or terrified. Saint turns over his shoulder to look at me, and I nod that I'm okay.

We continue this formation for minutes with the same results. We don't hear anything, nor do we see anyone. Maybe they've moved to another location? If they were still here, surely, we'd have seen something or, at the very least, heard something. But we haven't experienced either.

Pavel remains on high alert, peering from left to right the farther we walk. I can't shake the feeling that this feels too calm, too quiet. It feels like a setup. Pavel holds up his fist, hinting we're to stop. We're crouched low, awaiting his command.

"What do you think?" he whispers to Saint, who shrugs.

"I don't like how quiet it is. Something doesn't feel right. We have no idea of their location, so they could be anywhere."

And that's the problem. We've walked into this plan literally blind. We don't know where they are, who we're facing, and as far as plans go, this is fucking absurd. But it was now or never.

"We split up," Zoey suggests, which is shut down before she can continue.

"Absolutely not," Saint barks in a whisper.

My teeth begin to chatter because it's freezing out here in the open, and my pants are wet from the snow. If we don't make any progress soon, odds are we'll freeze to death out here. "I think she's right."

Saint glares at me as though I've gone mad. I don't fail to see that no matter how much Zoey and I hate one another, we always seem to be on the same page when it comes to devising a plan.

"We can't cover enough ground this way," I argue. "At this rate, we'll freeze to death."

Saint pinches the bridge of his nose, clearly annoyed.

"I don't like this any more than you do, but she's right," Pavel says. "Something is wrong. We should have heard an echo at the very least. Or seen a light. If they're out here, they can't be in the dark. Something isn't right."

And there's that word again. Right. I have to listen to my gut. If I'd listened to my gut earlier, we wouldn't be here in the dark, freezing our asses off.

Saint sighs heavily. "Fine. Willow, Ingrid, Zoey with me. Pavel, you go with Max and Sara."

Relief swarms me, knowing Sara is safe with Max and Pavel. But shame on me—I should know by now that nothing is that easy.

In a split second, I experience all my senses at once. I hear the gunshots. I see the night come alight with fire. I smell the gunpowder. I touch the cold snow as I fall onto my stomach. And lastly, I taste blood. But the question is whose?

I don't have time to find the answers because the air is being siphoned from me when Saint throws himself over me to shield me from gunfire. The gunshots zip around us, and I watch with eyes that aren't mine as shards of snow somersault up into the air as the bullets lodge deep into the ground.

I can't see anyone else around me.

"Saint!" I scream to be heard over the ringing of gunfire. "Where's Sara? We have to find her. She doesn't have a vest!"

He only cocoons his body around me tighter.

We are ambushed, and judging by the bullets whizzing around us, an army awaits to bring us down.

This is my fault. I'm to blame. It was my idea to come here. They had a choice not to come, but they'd never leave us to deal with this alone. Saint draws the gun from his jeans and begins to fire it around us. The noise isn't just deafening; it rumbles all the way to my core.

I can hear Saint yelling, but I can't make out what he's saying. He continues to fire his gun, but I'm still blinded to anything around us.

With great difficulty, I reach into the small of my back, fumbling for the gun. When I'm able to reach it, I aim it out in front of me. I'm squashed onto my belly with limited room, but having the gun allows me to defend myself if I need to.

My hand trembles as I wave the barrel from left to right. I'm on high alert, sharpening my eyes to see in the dark.

Saint continues shooting into the darkness, and when his gun clicks, hinting he's out of bullets, I frantically offer him mine. He accepts and continues to shoot. I don't know where the rocket launcher is, but it makes sense for Saint to be able to actually see his attacker before firing that thing.

Just as quickly as the madness begun, it suddenly ends.

My ears ring from the damaging sound, but now that it's deadly quiet, I suddenly prefer the noise.

"Are you all right?" Saint asks in a panic.

"Yes," I reply. "What's happening?"

Pavel's voice echoes from our left. He says something in Russian.

"We're okay," Saint yells. "I have Willow. Zoey?"

"I'm here," Zoey answers from what seems like miles away.

"I'm with Sara," Max shouts.

I feel Saint's chest shudder in relief with an exhale.

"Why did they stop?" Zoey asks.

"I don't know," Saint replies.

Now that I'm not cowering in fear for my life, I realize we are one man down. "Ingrid?" I call out.

There is no reply.

"Ingrid?" Pavel repeats, but we're greeted with more silence.

"Fuck," Saint curses, slowly unwrapping himself from me.

He comes to a quick stand, then offers me his hand. The moment we connect, I sigh, thankful he's okay.

"Where is Ingrid?" I ask, looking around for any sign of her.

Saint kisses my forehead and frantically runs his hands down my face, appearing to want to ensure I'm really okay. I grip his wrists, stopping him.

"Where is Ingrid?" I repeat.

His astute eyes scan our surroundings, but he doesn't need to tell me he doesn't know; I can see the hopelessness reflected in them.

Pavel, Max, Sara, and Zoey come running toward us. "Has anyone seen Ingrid?" Saint asks them.

They all shake their heads.

My skin prickles—something wicked is coming.

A succession of lights flickers on, one by one, illuminating the night sky. The snow comes to life; the whiteness so crisp, I have to shield my eyes. Once I've adjusted as best as I can, I slowly peer around me. Now that my environment is lit up like a Christmas tree on crack, I can see through the gaps in the tall trees. The winter has stripped them bare, adding to the creepy scene before me.

What I witness, though, is far eerier than anything I could have imagined.

Saint reads me like a book and grips my bicep. "Let me go!" I shout, shaking him off. But he makes it clear he won't do anything of the sort when he tightens his hold. "What are you doing?"

"Ангел, stay."

"Are you mad?" I shriek, still fighting him. "No. I won't."

"We will do her more harm if we don't!" he growls, a warning that has me yielding. Time stands still as I watch something I don't understand, but like a voyeur, I can't look away.

A string of Russian leaves Pavel as he drops to his knees, crazily hunting through the open duffel bag. Now that we've got light, we can all see that something else is missing—the bomb. It doesn't take us long to piece together what's going on when a discarded bulletproof vest lays haphazardly in the snow.

All of us turn to watch the scene before us.

The gunshots came from the hundred or so men who

stand beyond the trees. The lights are thanks to the headlights of the cars lined up like regimented soldiers. I don't know what to process first. There is so much going on.

The reason the gunfire stopped is thanks to Ingrid, who floats through the snow, arms raised in surrender, not appearing concerned that she's about to face the devil or, rather, *devils*. Oscar and Astra stand feet away from her. He looks regal in his furs and shit-eating grin. Astra, however, looks different. She is sporting a cane, an eyepatch, and has a blue silk scarf wrapped around her head.

Regardless of her new look, she still reeks of power. And the reason for their supremacy kneels in front of them with his hands tied behind his back—a beaten and bloody Alek.

Honestly, I'm surprised he's still alive.

A low growl erupts from Saint as he focuses his attention on Oscar. This is going to get messy.

I have no idea why Oscar and Astra's goons have yet to haul our asses away. They clearly know we're here. I suppose we're all waiting for what comes next because as Ingrid approaches Oscar and drops to her knees, it seems anything is possible.

Serg is standing off to the side, eyeballing Alek. I wonder if he played a part in inflicting those wounds.

"You've been a bad, bad girl," Oscar chides Ingrid who bows her head. "What are you doing here?"

"I came to ask for your forgiveness," she replies softly, which is a load of shit. She wouldn't have a bomb hidden under her jacket if that were true. "I want to come home."

Oscar peers down at her, eyes narrowed. He doesn't buy

it. "You betrayed me. Why would I give you another chance?"

"I know, and I'm sorry. I was scared. After what happened to Dominic, I thought I was next."

"Dominic wasn't of value to me any longer. He served his purpose. Out with the old and in with the new," he says arrogantly, staring into the distance. He does this with intent to piss Saint off because he knows we're here.

Saint advances, but I grip his bicep, shaking my head. It's time he listened to his own advice. We don't know what's about to happen. What we do know, though, if we traipse into the madness, we won't be leaving in one piece.

We have to be smart about this because Ingrid is there, with a bomb, for a reason. We need to figure out what her game plan is. And we need to uncover why the gunfire stopped.

"I was wrong. I beg for your forgiveness," she pleads, linking her hands together.

Oscar appears to mull over her request. "Why should I forgive you?"

"Because I'm not here alone."

"What the fuck is she doing?" Zoey hisses, crouching low to get a better look at the scene yards away.

We're all wondering the same thing.

Oscar looks at Astra whose interest is definitely piqued. "We know you aren't, sweetie," she says with a patronizing smile. "So if there is a point, make it."

"Saint didn't blow up Alek's home." Astra's fists clench as this blast was the reason she looks like the wicked witch she is. "Pavel and Zoey did. And they are planning on doing the same thing now."

Astra's ruby lips part while Oscar tugs at the fur on his jacket collar. This is a curveball they did not see coming. But neither have we because she's the one who's packing, not us.

"What's going on?" Sara whispers, eyes the size of saucers. Max rubs her back.

I wish I could shed light on our current situation because I have no idea what she's doing. Pavel, however, does.

"She's bait."

"What?" I question, not liking the sound of that. He doesn't have time to answer me.

"Seize them," Astra commands with a wave of her hand. She's ready for her revenge.

Just as I'm about to reach for my other gun, Oscar reaches into his jacket and produces a gun of his own. He presses it to Ingrid's temple with a grin.

"Come out, come out, wherever you are," he mocks, hinting he has the upper hand.

"Motherfucker," I curse, hating how vulnerable we'll be going out there. "What the hell is going on?"

Saint grips my elbow and leads me forward as it's evident he rather we walk into this nightmare than be dragged. Armed men emerge from the shadows, eager to appease their queen, but Saint shrugs them off when they attempt to touch him.

When one beefy goon seizes my wrist and tugs me toward him, Saint launches forward, and with the swiftness of a cheetah, he headbutts him. Other men don't fancy getting knocked out cold like the chump at my feet, so they gesture with their heads that we're to move.

Max, Sara, and Zoey don't get the same treatment and are hauled forward. They don't fight because they too have no idea what's going on. The men seem to know better than to touch Pavel. He bends down and picks up the duffel.

We walk toward our doom, dodging and winding past the trees, unsure what our fate will bring. When we break past the safety of the woods and are exposed in the clearing, I see the starkness of our reality up close.

We are surrounded, and no matter how much ammo we have, it would never be enough. They have more manpower, and without a doubt, we were destined to lose this fight. I can't shake the guilt I feel because even though I knew we would be outnumbered, I thought we'd at least have a fighting chance.

But we don't.

We are outnumbered about twenty to one.

When I stumble forward, thanks to one of the men shoving me in the back, I lock eyes with Alek. He gasps when he sees me, but I'm not sure if it's in shock or relief. Up close, he looks worse than I thought. When he flinches, it's apparent he's broken something.

Seeing *him* kneeling and bound should give me satisfaction. It doesn't.

"What are you doing here?" He focuses beyond me, his mouth agape. "What are you all doing here?"

Saint is by my side in an instant, but there is no doubt his focus is divided. When Oscar smirks that reptilian grin, I almost leap forward and smack it from his face.

"It seems trouble follows wherever you go." Astra directs her comment at me, and I can't help but smile in response.

The distance did her justice because now that I'm up close, holy shit, she looks like Frankenstein's bride. Oscar mentioned she was wounded in the explosion, but he failed to mention she's missing an eye. I doubt the black eyepatch she wears is in the support of pirates worldwide.

Small red scars slash her face, probably from the shrapnel, thanks to Pavel's bombs. No wonder she played nice with Ingrid. She isn't keen on reliving the past.

"And it seems someone will need to follow wherever you go in case you bump into a tree. Wow. Can you see me?" I wave my hands in front of me. Saint snickers.

She doesn't appreciate my dig and makes that clear when she nods to one of her men who comes up behind me. Before I have a chance to smack his hands away, he frisks me, removing the gun from the small of my back. Thankfully, he doesn't feel the bulletproof vest.

The rest of the puppets do the same to Max, Sara, Pavel, Zoey, and Saint. Ingrid looks at me, her eyes pleading. But pleading for what? She's the one who threw us under the bus, and I can only hope there's a good reason for it.

Once we're disarmed, Astra hobbles forward. I pray she falls on her ass as her heeled boots and cane aren't exactly snow-appropriate attire.

I yawn, looking down at my imaginary watch, hinting Astra's walk is more like a stroll. A sloth's stroll. "Holy shit, bitch likes to make an entrance. Hurry up already before I die from hypothermia."

My words are her fuel and all it takes is a simple nod before I'm gasping for air as one of her men strikes me in the stomach with the butt of his rifle. Saint elbows the man in the nose swiftly, ready to gouge out his eyeballs.

But when Zoey yelps, his rage soon simmers.

I'm bent in half, winded, but manage to look up to see Zoey's neck tilted back at a grotesque angle. A man has his fingers threaded through her hair, arching her head backward. She slaps at his hand, but he replies by pressing a serrated knife to her throat.

Astra smiles when she witnesses my panic.

"Let her go," Saint snarls, his fists clenched. It's taking every ounce of willpower he has not to charge over and kill the man who dares to touch his sister with his bare hands.

"Oh, please, things have only just begun," Oscar says before blowing him a kiss. "I've missed you. My bed is awfully cold without you."

A fury unleashes from Saint as he propels forward, fists curled into claws, but he soon stops dead in his tracks when I scream out in pain. I didn't mean to, but the bastard who just kidney punched me caught me unawares. I drop to my knees, gasping in air.

For good measure, he knees me in the nose.

I tumble onto my back, the world spinning around me. I try to sit up but am put back down when someone pistol whips me. Blood clouds my vision. "Motherfucker," I slur, watching the white snow turn a deep shade of crimson with my blood.

"Saint, don't." Pavel's warning alerts me that something is happening. Saint, of course, ignores Pavel and races to my aid.

When a man stands in his way, Saint almost knocks his

head off as he delivers an uppercut that has the man dropping to the snow. No one dares to stand in his way as he drops to his knees and gently helps me sit up.

He applies pressure to the wound to my temple, but I lethargically swat at his hand. "I'm fine."

His apprehensive eyes scan over every inch of me, telling me how sorry he is.

"Aww, isn't that sweet," Astra mocks. "I used to have someone who tended to me too. That was before you killed him."

"Fuck Borya," Saint spits, glaring at her. "He was weak. And pathetic. Good riddance to him. One less asshole I have to kill."

Astra's calm composure is no more, and a war cry leaves her as she staggers forward slowly, primed on killing Saint. He kisses my forehead, then rises to a commanding stance. She doesn't stand a chance. He's not afraid of her, of anyone. The only thing he's afraid of is me getting hurt.

And Oscar knows it. He's seen it firsthand.

"Astra, darling, stop, you're embarrassing yourself." He's right. I'll give the woman credit, though, that regardless of her injuries, she doesn't back down.

"Don't tell me what to do," she snaps but eventually comes to a stop.

Now that my vision has cleared, I see the shitshow for what it is. Pavel is still holding the duffel, but he wouldn't get it unzipped in time as a hundred eyes are on him. Max and Sara are held at gunpoint. As for Zoey, she's still squirming against the knife at her throat.

All in all, we're fucked.

Alek appears guilt-ridden as he lowers his eyes, focusing on the bloodied snow. Ingrid is as solid as stone.

"They want you to get angry, but they don't realize we are in control."

"Do you even think before you open your big, stupid mouth?" I snort in laughter as I come to a shaky stand. Oscar tilts his head in confusion. "As if we could forget. We're unarmed and outnumbered. I'm pretty sure we know who's in control."

Not the appropriate time to be making jokes, but if I'm going to die, at least I can do so by having the last laugh.

"Why did you come here?" Oscar asks, unamused by my outburst. "Not that I'm disappointed to see you. We were hoping you'd come. It makes this all the more fun with everyone here. We would have settled for Alek, but now, the opportunities are limitless."

I swallow in dread.

"You could have left here and been free. Isn't that why you did all this? To regain your freedom? But it seems every chance you get, you're back here, poking your nose in business that isn't your concern."

Alek peers up, appearing interested in my response.

"All of you are here, risking your lives, for what?" When there is silence, Oscar offers, "To save the man who tortured all of you in one way or another? You should be thanking me."

"Thanking you?" I question, staring Oscar down. "We're here because regardless of his crimes, Alek doesn't deserve this. We'd be no better than you two if we walk away and let this happen."

I know how that makes me sound.

I wish I was the hero of this story, but I'm not. I'm weak. I'm flawed. If you were in my shoes, you'd probably make a million different choices. But you're not. This is my story, my shoes, ones I have to walk in for the rest of my life, so I'll live with the repercussions. I've made peace with that fact.

"I think it's because you love him," Oscar says, looking at Saint and arching a brow. He's trying to start shit.

"I don't give a fuck what you think," I snap, refusing to fall victim to these mind games.

Astra's face twists in pleasure. "If you don't love him, then you won't care if I shoot him where he kneels."

She reaches into her fur jacket and produces a small handgun.

"You are clearly not listening." I sigh, but the sight of her packing makes me nervous. She had no qualms about shooting Saint. If she shoots Alek, then all of this would have been for nothing.

"Oh, but I am listening. Loud and clear. You may think you don't love Aleksei, but for you to be here, you have to feel something for him. You've risked the lives of everyone."

I flinch, her comment wounding me.

"But I'm feeling rather charitable."

I highly doubt that.

We watch as she hobbles over to Alek, unsure where this show is headed. When she finally reaches him, she strokes his hair. One could mistake her actions as tender, but we know better. "Seeing as I lost the love of my life, I think it's only fair you do too."

Alek wets his puffy lips. "What?"

"Well, you were the one who announced to the world how much you were changed, thanks to her. So an eye for an eye." She means that literally and figuratively, I'm guessing. "It only seems right. Or maybe you didn't love her as much as you claimed you did, after all. Who will you save? Yourself? Or her?"

Saint shields me with his body. There is no way he is letting that happen.

"All because I loved someone more than you...is that why you're punishing me?" Alek asks softly. "You could never stand being anyone's inferior; you had to have the undivided love of everyone."

When her lower lip quivers, it's apparent he's struck a nerve.

Her shitty childhood does support his claims. As does the fact that she's a narcissistic bitch. He doesn't mean love in the romantic sense, but Astra wants everyone's love to make up for the fact she got none as a child.

"If anyone deserves punishment, then it's me."

"Where's the fun in that?" Astra replies, caressing Alek's cheek.

The touch of death.

She turns and aims her gun my way. Saint is guarding me, but when two men yank me out from his protection, it's clear Astra won't allow anything to stand in her way.

Saint breaks one of their noses before breaking the other's leg. But where two fall, another two appear. We both attempt to fight them off, but Astra snaps her fingers, summoning more men.

"You can't fight them all," she cockily says.

"I'll die trying," Saint bellows, placing me behind him. We're back to back, moving in a circle, kicking, punching, defending one another. We're able to defend ourselves, but soon, we're flooded and pulled apart.

I fight like a wildcat, not caring that two men are tearing me in half as they tug at my arms. Saint rushes forward but is pistol whipped, again and again.

"No!" I scream frantically, trying to break free.

He drops to the snow and is kicked repeatedly. He tries to defend himself, but there are so many of them. There is no point in begging for his clemency because these monsters thrive on pain. And I'm about to see how much so.

"Enough!" Astra commands, raising her fist in the air. With one last kick, the men stop.

Saint wheezes but comes to a half sitting position, clutching his side. My attempts to break free are useless.

"You really shouldn't have come, Saint, because you're still more useful to us alive than you are dead."

"I'm sorry," I cry, struggling against the men. "This is my fault."

"Shh, ангел. No, it's not." He shakes his head, eyes desperate to comfort me even when I don't deserve it.

"What do you want?" he asks, wiping the blood from his chin with the back of his hand. He looks feral, and regardless of the fact he's beaten and bloody, he's still in control.

Astra purses her lips. "I want you to choose. Alek can't, so you will make the choice for him."

Saint's Adam's apple bobs as he swallows. "Choose what?"

The world is his oyster because god knows what these assholes are proposing.

"Who will you save? Her?" She points the gun my way before swaying it toward Zoey. "Or her? Borya's death must be avenged. And this is a good start."

Zoey struggles against her captor, but he only presses the serrated knife deeper into her neck.

"Someone has to die. And someone has to live. Those are the rules."

"No." Saint comes to a slow stand. "I won't choose. If anyone has to die, then it'll be me."

"No!" I bellow. Not again.

"Those aren't the options," Astra tsks. "If only you'd come with us when the offer was there, then all of this could have turned out differently. So I want you to choose who to save. And who to kill."

Zoey begins to sob, and the sound is so foreign to me because even though she is a bitch, she is a hard-nosed bitch who doesn't cry. Until now.

"Zoey, don't cry," Saint coos, his face twisted in pain. "It'll be all right. I won't let anything happen to you."

She sniffs shakily, nodding. "I deserve it. This is my f-fault. I was just trying to h-help." She is referring to blowing up Alek's home. "I'm so s-sorry for everything, Saint."

Funny, it's the first time I remember it was here it once stood. In the distance, I can see some twisted rubble. A roof? Maybe even a wall? Everything is so different now.

"I know," he assures her kindly.

"Ticktock," Astra says, now the one to look down at her imaginary watch. Fuck her.

And here we are, stuck at a crossroads. Will Saint save his sister, the person responsible for all of this? Or me? The person who is also responsible for all of this.

I suddenly realize Zoey and I despise the other because we are the same. We're stubborn, don't take no for an answer, and we fight for what's right. No matter how much I hate her, I admire her just as much. Which is why I make the decision for Saint.

"Kill me."

Saint takes a staggered step backward.

"Kill me, Saint. I will make the choice for you. They're going to kill me anyway." I look at Astra who doesn't deny my claims.

Saint turns a ghastly shade of white. "No," he cries, shaking his head firmly. "I will not."

"Then you'll have to kill your sister because there aren't any other options."

Saint looks like he's about to be sick as he places a fist to his lips to hold down his vomit. He knows we don't have the luxury of bargaining with these assholes. Been there, done that.

Zoey gasps, appearing surprised by my self-sacrifice. Yes, it's honorable, but I wouldn't be this calm if I wasn't wearing a bulletproof vest. She has a knife to her throat, but me, if I can sway them into shooting me in the chest, then maybe we have a fighting shot.

I attempt to play visual charades with Saint, hoping he reads between the lines. But just for good measure, I say, "It's okay, but make sure you aim for my heart; it's broken without you anyway."

His eyebrows shoot up into his hairline, a sign that he's clued in to my plan. I don't know what good it'll do, but here's to hoping once Astra witnesses my death, her need for vengeance will be quenched. It's no secret she blames me for her kingdom crumbling, so if my "death" can settle the score, then line me up.

"While you're deciding, how about you pass me that bag, Pavel? Ingrid mentioned there were explosives." Oscar gestures with two fingers that Pavel is to hand the duffel over.

Shit.

This is not good. Once Oscar opens that bag and sees there is, in fact, no bomb, he will ask questions, and questions lead to uncovering the fact I'm wearing a bulletproof vest. We're running out of time.

"Do it!" I cry, spreading my arms out wide. "Now."

Saint's body begins to tremble, and I imagine the snow splitting down the middle with the force. He too knows there is no time to waste.

"I can't!" he cries. We both know if he cedes too quickly, it'll rouse suspicion. He was about to sacrifice himself for me, so giving in to Astra's ultimatum doesn't seem plausible.

However, when a man rips the duffel from Pavel, I need to think on my feet. "You can. Astra is right. I do…I-love Aleksei. That's why I'm here."

A growl so deep rumbles from Saint, I take a small step

backward.

"I'm sorry. I never meant for this to happen."

Astra gestures to the man who has the duffle to stop as the bag can wait. Watching me rip out Saint's heart is far more interesting.

"How could you do this? After everything he's done." Saint shakes his head, sickened.

The line suddenly blurs between reality and fiction.

Alek looks hopeful, that maybe what I say is true. I don't hate him, but my feelings for him will never be anything more than accepting this truth. However, deep down, I know Saint doesn't fully believe me. Whether it's jealousy or insecurity, I don't know, which is why our little exchange is believable.

"I know. I'm not strong like you are, which is why I deserve to die by your hand. I'm sorry for everything." My sincerity is real because I truly am sorry. Hating Alek and leaving him to the wolves would have been far easier than the predicament we've found ourselves in by coming here.

But I would be lying to not only myself but to Saint as well. And besides, we have unfinished business with the man who looks at Saint with nothing but desire. This needs to finish. And now.

"Take Zoey and start over. That's why this all started. Let it end with my death."

"No!" I'm surprised when I hear Alek's voice. "Don't you touch her! Kill me, kill me instead."

I gasp, stunned by his self-sacrifice because he actually means it.

Saint turns his chin slowly, scowling at Alek. "That won't

be a problem."

Astra grins, thoroughly enjoying the drama she's caused. "It seems everyone is more than willing to sacrifice themselves for someone else. How...tragic." She doesn't seem touched. "Borya never had that opportunity because you killed him. You all did."

From the corner of my eye, I notice Pavel gesturing for Ingrid to move. Everyone has seemed to have forgotten about her, too engrossed in the tragedy unfolding before them. Ingrid rises slowly and begins a slow walk toward one of the cars.

I need to keep the attention on me because whatever Ingrid and Pavel have planned, it'll hopefully get us out of the shit I brought them into.

"You're right, Astra."

I've caught her off guard. "Right about what?"

"About Borya. I'm sorry he's dead. No matter what he did, you still loved him. We don't choose the people we fall in love with."

Her mouth parts as I've rendered her speechless. "Don't patronize me."

"I'm not." And I mean it. "No one understands the love you feel for another. I'm not claiming to. But I respect you for it because, deep down under this bitch façade, you are capable of loving someone other than yourself. Which is why Alek doesn't deserve to die. Which is why I'm here. He was capable of loving me."

I lock eyes with Alek, wanting him to know this. This could have turned out a million other ways because our relationship has been volatile, but to see him on his knees, bloodied and begging for my life, makes me believe things have come full circle.

This isn't an ideal ending, but it's an ending, and it's one I can accept. I needed to hear Alek's pleas to save me because it confirms that what I've done, what I intend to do is right.

Astra holds her head high, but I can see what my words have done. If I were in her shoes and someone killed Saint, I too would want revenge on those who ended his life. But all is not fair in love and war since we're on opposing sides.

I watch Ingrid creep closer and closer to an unmanned black car. She seems to be gauging the distance between it and Oscar.

Serg decides this touchy-feely crap isn't going to stick and grips Alek's hair, jarring his neck backward. "Where was the love for my father when you killed him?" he snarls, peering down at him with nothing but contempt.

Alek bursts into a humored cackle. "Get over it, already, *brother*."

Serg responds by kneeing him in the chin. It doesn't seem he will be getting over it anytime soon.

We are all here for our own reasons, but at the very core, we're driven by love. Our actions are fueled by it. Though Oscar may be the exception to that rule. He may think he loves Saint, but he only loves how Saint makes him feel.

"This is all very Oprah worthy, but I'm bored." He reaches into his pocket and produces a gun, aiming it at me. "If you can't do it, Saint, then I will."

Saint instantly dives in front of me, prepared to take the

bullet. We haven't fooled anyone.

"Fine, then." Oscar quickly shifts his mark to Zoey.

Saint is torn, knowing he will aim for her head. A fatal shot.

"Okay! Enough." He bends down and picks up the gun he kicked from one of our attackers' hand. He is trembling when he swivels to face me.

I stand motionless and raise my hands in surrender. I trust him.

Pavel is creeping toward Zoey, his eyes still peeled on Ingrid. Something lingers on the horizon. Since Ingrid has the bomb strapped under her jacket, what does she plan on doing with it?

Alek wrestles to break free, but Serg grips the back of his neck, grinning. "Now it's your turn to watch the one you love die."

"Saint, don't you dare do this! She doesn't deserve this."

Saint inhales sharply, tipping his face to the heavens.

"I'm so sorry, Willow," Alek cries, wriggling against Serg's hold. "I never meant this for you. That's why I left without saying goodbye. I didn't want this for you."

"Too late now," Oscar singsongs.

Astra is awfully quiet, and I can only hope that's because she's had a change of heart. When she strolls forward, I hold my breath. "I don't want to kill you, Alek. Zoya has been like a mother to me." I recognize the necklace she's wearing, the one Zoya gave her. "But you must understand, I can't allow Borya's death to go unpunished. Someone needs to pay."

"I know that," he pleads, looking at her with remorse.

"But not Willow. She is innocent in all of this."

Oscar scoffs, his finger poised on the trigger.

"What can I do? To save her?" He is bargaining for my life.

Astra runs a hand down her ruined face, appearing to be in thought. "Nothing, Alek. She's a dead woman walking."

"моя любовь, please. Anything. Whatever you want, I will give you." I recognize the phrase he just used. He called her my love.

Something changes in her. I can see it. She was once loved, her beauty unrivaled, just as the queen was in *Snow White*. But now, she's shown her true form of the haggard old witch which lay hidden behind her charm.

"You were the one who blew up Alek's home?" she addresses Zoey. Pavel stops dead in his tracks.

Zoey's eyes are wide as she fights against the knife at her throat. "Yes," she replies without remorse.

Astra mulls over her response. "So you and Pavel were really the ones who killed Borya then?"

Shit.

This isn't going according to plan.

Zoey doesn't back down and isn't intimated in the slightest. "I suppose we are."

"Maybe we can come to a compromise then?" Astra says to Alek.

"What is it?"

"I need a king, seeing as mine was taken away."

When Oscar pales, we realize this has run off its course.

Astra hobbles closer toward Alek, coming to a stop before

him. "Who will want me now? I'm ruined." She turns her cheek, shielding her face behind the large hood of her jacket.

"No, you are still just as beautiful," Alek says, peering up at her. He is so playing her. But it works.

"Let him go," Astra commands Serg, who shakes his head, angered she would suggest such a thing. "I said let him go!"

I lick my lips, horrified by what I'm witnessing.

Serg finally surrenders, but only after he makes his distaste clear.

"Stand," Astra orders Alek. With a pained grunt, he does. "Kiss me."

Without delay, Alek gently cups her cheek and presses his lips to hers. She moans into his mouth, standing on tippy toes to reach his full height. The kiss is hardly chaste, and my cheeks redden from not only the cold. I wonder if maybe their past included being romantically involved at one point?

Once they're done, Astra pulls away, wiping her lips with two fingers. She hums in delight. "Okay, I will let your pet live." My relief is short-lived when she inhales before commanding, "On your knees."

I have no idea what she means until she turns around and directs her attention to Zoey and Pavel. "You're the reason Borya is dead, so as I see it, you should both pay."

"No!" I cry out, running toward them. But when a man wraps his arm around my middle to stop me, it's evident I'm not going anywhere. A hollowed scream tears from Saint as he tries to protect me, but he is knocked to the snow and kicked repeatedly.

"I said on your knees!" she screams, clutching the top

of her cane. "Unless you have a problem with them dying, Aleksei?"

"Alek, say something!" I plead, begging he save their lives. He doesn't know I have a bulletproof vest, but regardless, he shouldn't roll over this way. He needs to fight for not only my life, but for the lives of Zoey and Pavel who risked theirs to save his.

But he doesn't. He simply shakes his head, condemning them to death. "I'm sorry." His apology is heartfelt, but it's not good enough. "Please forgive me, Zoey, Pavel, for the wrong I've done."

When both Pavel and Zoey refuse to obey, four men beat them into submission. Zoey doesn't stand a chance and falls with a thud, sobbing when she eventually complies. Pavel puts up a fight, but ultimately, he too is forced to kneel. Men bend his arms backward, threatening to break them if he moves.

A brawny man with cold, black eyes cocks his gun and places it to Zoey's temple. Fat tears trickle down her cheeks as she locks gazes with Saint. "It's okay, Saint. It'll be o-okay. I love y-you. I'm s-sorry I didn't tell you that more often. Tell Mom and Dad I'm so s-sorry. Thank you for never giving up on me. It's now my turn...to save you."

"No!" he cries, clawing at the snow. He attempts to rise but continues getting beaten down.

Zoey's eyes meet mine. "For what it's worth, Willow...I love and hate you all in the same breath. Look after my brother."

"Don't you dare give up! Fight!" I shout at her, kicking and clawing at my captor, but his grip is tight. There is no way

I'm escaping. Ingrid is about ten feet away from a car, and when she looks at me with a nod, I know what she's going to do. How didn't I see it sooner?

Ingrid took that bomb with the intent to save us by blowing herself up. That explains why she discarded the vest. She never had any intention of coming out of this alive. She had to time it perfectly not to turn any heads when she snuck into a car and used the gas as extra ammo to kill as many of these motherfuckers as she could.

Why didn't she just detonate it when she was within reach? It's because she knows this is our fight, this is the reason we're here. For Oscar and Astra to pay for what they did and pay by Saint's hand. If she were to detonate when at Oscar's feet, this would have been for nothing.

She has sacrificed everything for us because this has given us half a chance. She knew if we went in, guns blazing, we'd die, but this bomb is a distraction. But this plan will result in her death. And I can't allow that to happen.

"Oh my god, no!" I shriek to her, to Astra, to everyone. "Alek, don't let them kill her!" I'm not just speaking about Zoey. "Please!"

"I'm sorry, дорогая. But I won't allow you to die."

My pleas are useless. He sees this sacrifice as saving me, but I don't want to be saved. Not like this. We need an out, and we need one now. I can't allow Ingrid to do this. With adrenaline and fire burning through my veins, I strike my head backward and connect with my attacker's nose.

I don't have time to celebrate in the noise. I scramble for the gun he dropped, my cold fingers clenching the cool metal of the grip, and I aim for the man with the gun pointed at Zoey. Saint manages to fight free and dives for Zoey.

All I register is a guttural scream and an earsplitting boom before I feel a pain tear at my chest.

The air whooshes from my lungs as I'm propelled backward, thanks to the bullet to my chest. For a split second, I believe I'm dead, but the bullet has just lodged in my bulletproof vest. I'm sure of it. I want to pat myself down to be sure, but I have the upper hand as they think I'm dead.

"I've wanted to do that for weeks!" Oscar's snide comment alerts me that he was the one who shot me.

But that's okay. This is the distraction we need to stop Ingrid from doing something stupid.

Everything is going to be okay.

Or so I thought.

I don't understand what I'm hearing because it doesn't make any sense. "Zoey…c'mon, wake up. Please, wake up."

Wake up?

I hear these words followed by a bloodcurdling scream. Why is Saint shouting? Zoey is okay.

Isn't she?

I don't have time to question it because all I hear is a thunderous, "Run!" before the world explodes around me. It's like I'm reliving the past twice as the heat from the explosion almost burns me raw.

Pandemonium erupts, and I know playing dead is no longer an option because if I don't get the fuck up, I won't be playing. I spring to my feet, ignoring the fact the world is currently tilted, and keep low as the gunshots begin to ring out around me. The battlefield is gruesome, littered with dead bodies and scattered body parts.

The roaring fire crackles cruelly, and I shield my eyes, hoping to see through the flames. Saint is nowhere to be seen. Seeing a discarded gun in front of me, I pick it up and keep low as I attempt to find him.

Pained screams fill the night air, alerting me that many of our attackers lay wounded and close to death. The flaming ball of fire, which was once a car, burns like the flames of hell. Pavel's bomb was effective once again, but knowing Ingrid's death was the reason for the explosion brings tears to my eyes.

Pavel said she was bait. I now know what he meant.

"No!" I cry out, allowing the tears to fall. I tried to save her, but in the end, she saved me. She saved us all.

Her death will not be in vain.

"Saint!" I scream to be heard over the commotion. I can't see three feet in front of me through the thick black smoke. "Pavel!"

But I'm on my own.

I'm on high alert as I snap my head from left to right, scoping out my surroundings as best I can. When I hear rushed footsteps, followed by a war cry, I duck low and aim my gun into the distance. My hand trembles as I await my attacker, and when I see him, I scream for him to stop.

But he doesn't.

He charges for me, his own gun raised, intent on blowing a hole straight through me. Nothing about him indicates he plans to stop, so it's either him or me—survival of the fittest.

"Please, stop! I'll shoot you. I swear I w-will!" My warning falls on deaf ears as he snarls, picking up pace.

So without hesitation, I train my gun on him, inhale, and fire.

He tumbles to the ground in a twisted heap, and I blink once, unsure if I actually pulled the trigger. However, when he doesn't move, I know that I did. I've killed another man. I try not to focus on that fact as I continue to look for Saint. I did what I had to.

The smoke makes it impossible to breathe, so I raise the collar of my sweater and place it over my nose. I trip over fallen bodies as I blindly continue to search for anyone who isn't the enemy.

Men grip onto my legs with burned or missing fingers, but I shake them off, ignoring their pleas for help. They made their choice, and I will live with mine. I was far enough away to be spared the wrath of the explosion, but what about everyone else?

Ingrid chose the car farthest away from us, but there is no guarantee everyone else was as lucky as me. With that as my motivation, I continue looking for my friends. But the dense smoke and the crackle of the world exploding around me make my search impossible.

My ears are ringing, and I have double vision, but giving up isn't in the cards. "Saint!" My anxious voice echoes around me. I need to find him.

I don't know how long I blindly search for him, but it feels like hours. All I can hear is his bloodcurdling scream on repeat. Shaking my head, I focus on my surroundings with my gun aimed out in front of me. Someone emerges from the smoke, and when I see who it is, I exhale in utter relief.

"Pavel! Are you all right?" He is covered in soot and blood, but this is another day in the office for him.

"Yes, you?"

I nod quickly. "Have you seen Saint?"

"No, the last I saw, he was dragging Zoey to safety."

"Zoey…c'mon, wake up. Please, wake up."

Those were the last words I heard before all of this went to hell. Does that mean Zoey was shot? If Saint was dragging her to safety, then it's safe to assume she can't do so herself.

"We need to find the others!" I shout while Pavel nods.

"Stick together."

I wasn't planning on doing anything else.

We hunt through the battleground, the smoke slowly clearing to make way to the most heinous sight. Men lay in distorted shapes, unrecognizable. I swallow down my vomit and continue stepping over them like they are nothing but trash. The snow will forever be tarnished a blood red.

Pavel is close by, his guns trained on anything that moves.

A bloodied man comes charging at us, gun raised, but Pavel shoots him without remorse. He flops to the ground, twitching as the life drains from him.

This ghastly scene is my doing. I created this hell on earth. By coming here, I seemed to have made things so much worse. I wanted Saint to get his revenge, but did I do the wrong thing? Have I sentenced us all to death?

"You knew Ingrid was going to blow herself up, didn't you?" I question Pavel, needing to ensure my thinking is right.

"Yes," he replies with a sharp nod. He clucks his tongue

when he sees my regret. "There are causalities in war."

I close my eyes, sickened.

He grips my arm, coaxing me to move. I can mourn the lives lost after this is over with.

We continue our search, and each body I step over isn't someone I know. I'm a sinner when I feel nothing but relief for that fact. Pavel fights off men who are out for revenge, and so do I, but when I hear a loud bang and feel a searing pain in my thigh, it's evident I won't be fighting for much longer.

I drop to the snow, clutching my leg as hot, sticky blood coats my fingers. I've been shot.

"Willow!" Pavel shouts, attempting to run to my aid, but he's suddenly swarmed by five angry men. They latch onto him like lions, stalking their next meal.

I watch from the ground as he tries to fight them off, but when one swings a baton and connects with Pavel's temple, he's out cold.

"No!" I shout, attempting to crawl to him, but the pain in my leg is unbearable. The men turn their attention to me, their lips twisting into menacing grins.

As they run for me, I desperately drag my body along the snow, ignoring the excruciating agony ricocheting throughout my body. They holler in excitement, the hunter finding their prey. I've barely moved three feet, but I continue pulling myself along, refusing to surrender.

When it's evident I won't outrun them, I stop, and half sitting, I aim my gun and fire. One of the bullets lodges in the shoulder of a man, but it only seems to anger him further. He continues running at me, fueled by pain and anger.

When the chamber of my gun clicks empty, I throw it at them with a roar. It's too late, though, because they're feet away. Instead of fleeing, I sit upright and face my attackers. I refuse to cower.

One of them launches for me, and I brace to be tackled to my death, but a flash comes out of nowhere and takes the man down. My brain can't comprehend what is going on because the men suddenly dig in their heels, flecks of snow kicking up in protest.

I'm about to sag in relief, but when I see who my rescuer is, I wish they'd killed me.

I don't have time to fight because Oscar is on top of me, his arm pressed over my windpipe as he chokes me. Regardless of the pain, I kick out my legs and claw at his forearm. But the harder I fight, the harder he presses.

My head sinks into the soft snow, forcing Oscar to press down more firmly.

I gasp for air, smacking his arm and twisting with all my might, but his wide, animated eyes reveal he isn't letting me get away this time. The pressure behind my eyeballs threatens to pop them from my head.

"Die, you bitch!" he screams, spittle coating my face.

The pain in my leg is suddenly nothing compared to being suffocated to death. I can't breathe, and my grip on this plane is wavering. In and out, I float, unsure where reality and fiction meet.

I begin to envision a different life, one where I'm not surrounded by death and gore. I'm back in LA in the constant sunshine and not a hint of snow can be found. I am modeling the newest trend, strutting my shit without a care in the world.

Yes, that life was mine, and I want it back. I want to forget the past few months and go back to living a normal, boring life. A voice screams at me that that existence was only half lived, but I don't care. It would mean I didn't jeopardize the lives of so many others. It would mean I didn't have blood on my hands.

That truth is the reason I stop fighting and finally surrender. I lost. My eyes flicker as I embrace the darkness for good. It's quiet here, and I don't feel any pain. I can heal.

But I should know by now that hell is empty, and all the sinners are here.

A swirling of color followed by an influx of air assaults my senses, and I spring up, coughing desperately as I inhale sharply. It's too much, too fast, but I don't care. My oxygen-starved lungs sing in rejoice. Rubbing over my throat, I peer around me, and when I see the reason I'm not dead, a sob slips free.

A wild Saint has Oscar pinned to the ground, his knees either side of him, holding *him* prisoner this time. He pummels his face while Oscar's in a frenzy trying to defend himself. But Saint only hits him harder. Watching this scene unfold is like being stuck in a dream because I have only imagined what this moment would look like. But actually seeing it is unlike anything I could have dreamed.

The brutality I bear witness to has a warmth spreading over me, and it has nothing to do with the gaping gunshot wound to my leg. I am internally cheering Saint on as one would at a football match because I want our team to win, and the only win I will accept is when Oscar lays dead, dead by Saint's hand.

Specks of blood flick up into the air, revealing Saint has busted open Oscar's nose, lip, face. After a while, Oscar stops struggling, but that's too gracious a death for him. Saint stops hitting him and yanks him up by the collar.

His head is floppy as Saint presses them nose to nose. "Wake up, you son of a bitch!" He shakes him violently.

A pained moan escapes Oscar. His face is slathered in crimson, but when his icy eyes flicker open, it's game on. "There are so many ways I want to hurt you," Saint purrs with dangerous fury. "But there will never be enough time, never enough violence to make you suffer for what you did to me. To Willow."

Oscar opens his mouth, but Saint strikes forward and headbutts him. Oscar's head cracks back with a nauseating thud.

"This should give me satisfaction," Saint spits, tightening his fingers around Oscar's collar. "But it doesn't. I could kill you a thousand times in a thousand different ways, and it still wouldn't be enough."

The crack in Saint's voice reveals these scars will never heal.

"Please, don't. I love…you." Oscar's pleas only incite the inferno.

Saint snickers, absolute malice painting his forbidding features. "You don't know how to love. But, and that's a big but, if you are capable of loving someone other than yourself, then killing you is poetic justice."

Blood slips through my fingers as I apply pressure on my wound. It doesn't hurt anymore. It's beyond pain. But I can deal with my injuries later. This is what I came here for. I watch with quietude as Saint reaches into the small of his back and retrieves a large knife.

He stands slowly, leaving Oscar on his knees as he thumbs over the sharp tip of the blade. Oscar peers up at him, eyes pleading he has mercy on him. But he is way past salvation.

I brace for revenge, for this to be finally over with…but all I get is another fucking curveball as the universe throws one last surprise my way.

"Drop it."

I have no idea what is going on until I feel someone yank me up by my hair. On instinct, I try to twist free, but it's too late. I'm held fucking prisoner yet again. Astra stands behind me with a gun pressed into my lower back.

Saint's head snaps my way, his eyes closing in defeat.

But this is not happening again. "Don't you dare," I command Saint. "Do it. End this. Now."

He shakes his head, knowing what I'm asking, but I won't let this happen again. They can't win. Everyone has made sacrifices, and this is mine.

Astra cocks the gun, a sign she isn't bluffing. But I am tired. So fucking tired. I want it to end. With Oscar's death and Saint's redemption.

I lock gazes with the man who changed my world forever, and nod in a silent plea for him to end this. But he won't… which means I will.

"I love you. So much." My voice trembles while Saint

stands transfixed on what I just said. "You once said my demons dance with yours. And you're right. They always have. Our love wasn't perfect, but it was ours. And it was worth every single imperfect moment. You are worthy of life, Saint…live it."

Before Saint can stop me, I jab my elbow back, connecting with Astra's stomach. Although it throws her off balance, there is no doubt what she will do once she steadies. She will end my life. And I welcome it.

Saint's screams are laden with every emotion under this darkened sky, but I shut them out and await my fate. A bullet slices the air, and I gasp, certain it's my kiss of death, but when something heavy falls against me, and I'm still standing, I realize I'm not certain of anything at all.

Hobbling quickly, I swivel to see Astra's body lying in a bloody, contorted heap. Her eyes glass over, thanks to the bullet wound in the middle of her forehead. I stand motionless, staring down at the woman who held so much power, but now, she's nothing because she's fucking dead… dead, thanks to the gun Alek holds.

He shot her.

He blinks slowly, cradling the gun in what appears to be disbelief. Something so small can shift the world in mere seconds. Realization overcomes him, and he drops the gun, dumbfounded. Although she was pure evil, she was his friend.

Everything moves in slow motion as we all stare at the fallen queen, which is a rookie move. Oscar lunges for the gun and aims…but that's the last thing he'll ever do because a slash of red paints the snow, before a low gurgling pierces the still air.

A puff of smoke bubbles to life as I gasp. What I see is horrifying as well as beautiful. Saint's downturned chin, his heaving chest, and his rigid shoulders all point to one thing.

This was always going to end with violence, and Oscar has finally gotten what he deserved. Saint stands above him, the knife he holds dripping ruby droplets onto the white sleet. The imagery is actually quite striking—vivid blood coating the white snow red.

Oscar clutches his bleeding throat with one hand, his eyes wide, while he tugs at Saint's pants with the other. Unmoved, Saint stares into his eyes, watching the life drain from him. Oscar tries to speak, but it appears the knife wound to his neck has severed his vocal cords.

This isn't a satisfactory ending because it seems easy compared to what Saint endured, but when Oscar tumbles to his stomach, wheezing a death rattle, a small piece of Saint returns.

Before long, Oscar's twitches still, and the underworld gains another monster.

We're surrounded by an eerie silence as we take in the bedlam around us. There is so much destruction, so much death. Now that the smoke has cleared, I can see what we created—this is hell on earth. Men are strewn throughout the land, either dead or crawling for help.

Pavel lies feet away, unmoving.

The sight has me scanning frantically until it halts on something I don't understand.

Max cradles a limp body, drawing her toward his chest as

he cries. My mind goes into self-preservation mode because that is the only way I can process this.

"No!" he howls, cradling the person he holds like she is the most precious thing in the world.

Her familiar long dark hair stabs a hole straight through me, and I clutch my middle, afraid the earth is about to swallow me whole.

Saint doesn't comfort me. Instead, I watch as he staggers over to a large barren tree where a body lays underneath. He drops to his knees with his head bowed as he surrenders in defeat.

My brain is telling me that the bodies belong to people I knew, people I was supposed to protect. But the fact they are deathly motionless alerts me to my failure.

"No," I whimper, unsteady on my feet as I attempt to stop the world from tipping on its axis. But it doesn't stop. It never will.

Zoey, Ingrid, and Sara are…dead because of me. I failed them. They knew this was dangerous, but if it wasn't for me, for my inexplicable urge to see Alek and to avenge Saint, then they would still be alive. Saint reaches out and brushes over Zoey's hair, a broken sob leaving him.

"I just, I just wanted to make it better," I whisper aloud, shaking my head at the carnage in front of me. But I haven't.

Something burns inside me, and the harder I try to escape it, the hotter it burns. I don't know what it is, but something threatens to choke me.

Astra and Oscar are dead, but I'm not relieved. I thought I would be, but I can't help but feel like the final piece of this puzzle is missing. My attention bounces sluggishly among the people around me, but I always seem to come back to one person.

Aleksei Popov.

I didn't understand why it was so important to come back here. Why the heavy feeling in the pit of my stomach wouldn't go away. There was something I needed to do by coming here. I didn't know what that was...but now...I do.

I'm to blame for all of this, but so is Alek. Our culpability is shared. If only he had spoken up and stopped Astra, Zoey would be alive. And Saint wouldn't be burdened with this tragic grief forever. I never understood why I didn't hate Alek when I should have, and it's all because of this moment.

Every single action has led to this.

My weary body cries in defeat as I lean forward and grab a lone gun. Alek walks over, tattered and torn, but smiles. "You don't need that. We won," he gloats, which flicks my switch to drive.

There are no winners here.

With the heavy metal in my steady hand, it's an extension of my body as I aim. Utter confusion swarms Alek, but he continues walking toward me.

He's always so smug and so presumptuous. It's time I showed him who I really am. It's time I showed myself too.

"Get on your knees." My voice cuts through the static, setting the stage for things to come.

Alek continues to stroll until I cock the gun slowly. He suddenly pauses, tilting his head in confusion.

"I said...get on your knees," I repeat, dangerously slow.

Alek deliberately raises his hands in surrender when he realizes I'm serious. "дорогая, what are you doing?"

"What was always destined," I reply calmly.

"I'm sorry they're dead. I truly am," he says, hands still raised, but it's too late for apologies. They won't bring back Zoey, Ingrid, or Sara. "I'm sorry your life means more to me than theirs. I'm selfish, but I don't make apologies for the decisions I've made."

Flinching at his candidness, I get my head in the game. "This entire time, I never understood what I…felt"—I swallow down my admission—"for you. I should have hated you. Despised you for what you did. But I didn't. I could never work out why that was."

A wave of relief washes over Alek. It's short-lived.

"But now I realize hating you would be hypocritical because I always knew what I had to do. I thought by coming here, I was saving you, but in reality, I was saving me. I'm broken," I confess, shaking the heartache away. "And the only way to heal…is by making you pay. So, once again, I ask you, get down on your *fucking* knees."

A slight tremble wracks Alek's body, but he slowly complies as he kneels feet away.

Inhaling, I ignore the pang of guilt I feel because this is why I had to come back. This is my closure. This is the only way I can leave this country and start my life over again. I couldn't let anyone else kill Alek because they didn't deserve the privilege, but I do.

He kidnapped me, humiliated me, and he did so all because he could. Even though his feelings for me are real, I can't ignore everything he's done. Every action comes with a consequence, and this is Alek's. It's time he paid his dues.

With staggered steps, I hobble toward him, dragging my foot through the snow. Before I met him, I never thought I was capable of the strength I've displayed. But the violence I've come to learn to survive courses through me now, and I'm afraid it has overthrown the good.

Coming to a stop a few feet away, I rest my armed hand by my side. "I can't let you live; you know that."

Alek gradually peers up at me, his gaze never wavering. Kudos to him. But he knew it would always end like this. "I know, which is, in part, the reason I left without saying goodbye. I deserve it. What I did to you, to so many, I can never take back. But I'm a coward. I thought I could run away from the mess I've made, but I should have always known you would be the executioner.

"I need you to know that I'm sorry. My feelings for you were always real. And if you can accept that, then I will happily die by your hand. I...love you."

My heart breaks because at this moment, I realize that in my own fucked-up way...I love him too.

This man was once upon a time the most feared and powerful man in all of Russia. But now, beaten and bruised, he just looks like a victim, like the victims who suffered by his hand.

I'll allow him this repentance because just as my father offered his flock, I will absolve Alek of his sins. He will go wherever he is destined with some of his soul intact.

"Do you forgive me?" he asks, eyes pleading.

After all I've witnessed, I will never be okay, but I will try. I can't carry this bitterness any longer. Otherwise, all of this would have been for nothing.

With a steady breath, I raise my gun and aim the muzzle at the center of Alek's forehead. "I forgive you. But I will never forgive myself for all that I've done."

He nods, lowering his head and accepting his fate.

Everything happens for a reason; I need to believe that because once I pull this trigger, the reason Alek is dead will be because of me.

Thinking of every single moment which led me here, I inhale and am about to squeeze the trigger without regret. But the darkness is soon consumed by the light when Saint unhurriedly pushes the barrel of the gun away and stands in front of Alek. I instantly pull back as a blanket of guilt envelops me.

"Don't do this, ангел."

I blink once, bewildered by his request. "What?"

When he deliberately raises his hands in surrender, my heart breaks in two. "If you do this, you'll be lost to yourself for good. Believe me, I know. With each life you take, it takes a piece of yourself also. And before long, you're left with an emptiness that is so deep, you'll wish you were dead too."

My eyes fill with tears, but I don't allow them to fall. "Saint, move," I snarl, gesturing with the gun for him to step away. But he doesn't.

"Killing him doesn't achieve anything, and I see that now," he confesses, his face a twisted, heartbreaking mess. "I thought killing him would make me feel better, but it won't.

Killing him won't bring back the people we've lost. Zoey is...
dead because Alek decided to save you. I can't hate him for
that."

His words break me all over again.

"It will help avenge them," I argue, not understanding
why he would protect Alek. Killing him was the only thing
driving him for so long, so I don't understand why he is doing
this.

With nothing but guilt, he reveals why a second later.
"We're both guilty of destroying your life."

"No," I rebuke, shaking my head fiercely.

"Yes, and if he deserves this punishment, then so do I."

"But I love you," I say with a cracked promise. I need him
to see that this is different.

"And I love you," Saint replies sadly. "But Alek loves you
too. You can't blame him for doing the things he's done to
protect you because haven't you done the same thing for the
people you love?"

Check and mate.

He's right.

I want to say that it's different, that we're the good guys in
this story, but we stopped being the good guys long ago. We're
all sinners in one way or another.

"I can't let you kill him because killing him will kill you
too, ангел. You may think it'll help appease the demons, but it
won't. It'll only feed them, and they're never satisfied. They'll
always want more."

A hollowed sadness evades every part of me as I finally
permit my tears to fall.

What Saint says touches me deeply because he's right. Even though I love him more than I could ever express, he will always be my kidnapper. If we were to go back to the "real world," what would we tell others? We met because he was hired to kidnap me and hand me over to a sadistic drug lord, who fell in love with me?

There is no normal for us. And even though I don't care, I know that Saint does because eventually, I will too.

"In this world"—he gestures with his finger around us— "we make sense. We work. But out there, we don't. I will be a reminder of something ugly with tiny glimmers of beauty."

"That's enough for me!" I cry, but my desperation reveals the morsels of doubt I suddenly feel.

This entire time, I was so worried about what would happen once we escaped, but I never really thought about what a future with Saint would be like. It wouldn't matter where we lived or what we did; our past would always be with us.

"My sister is dead," he reveals with a hitch to his words. "I can't go back to living like she never existed. Like this never happened. We both need time."

"Time for what?" I whisper, the gun in my hand now nothing but a joke.

"Time to stop hating ourselves. And time to heal," he replies, lowering his hands.

"You don't want to be with m-me?" I whisper, my lower lip quivering.

Saint sighs, before gently reaching out to brush the hair from my brow. "It's because I want that, that I… have to let you go. Every time I try to save you, it backfires and makes things so much worse. So now, I am giving you something you've never been given since this entire ordeal began. I am giving you a choice.

"Walk away and start over. Forget about me."

"I can never forget," I reply, inconsolable. "And I don't want to!"

Saint cups my cheeks, nothing but solemn regret plaguing him. "But I want you to. I want you to go back to America and forget this world exists."

"I ca-can't," I cry, wishing I could hold it together. "I won't go. I'm staying with y-you."

"I know you feel that now, but please understand, I need time to heal too. I came here to protect my sister, but life never turns out how you expect because I failed. I never anticipated meeting you and falling so deeply in love that my entire world would shift and you would become my sun and the moon."

He wipes away my tears with his thumbs, his chartreuse orbs sparking to life in the dark as they once did all those nights ago when this nightmare began. "I'm broken, so fucking broken. I am shrouded by nothing but darkness. I don't know how to make it go away," he confesses sadly.

"If not for the darkness…we'd never see the stars," I whisper, everything tumbling around me.

He smiles, but it's so bittersweet. "It'll be our time, whether in this lifetime or the one after that. I promise."

A hollowed sob escapes me as the gun falls to the snow, and I wrap my arms around my middle. "I don't understand this. I thought l-love was enough."

Saint lowers his lips to my cheek and tenderly kisses away my tears. "It's because of love that I'm doing this. I want to be the best man I can for you, and at the moment, I need to find out who that man is."

"I-I can't do this without you," I whimper, closing my eyes as he washes away my sadness.

"Yes, you can. And you will. I want you to be happy, Willow. Please, for me, live." And what he says next is the reason I'll walk away. "And please...let me. Promise me."

Nothing has ever been harder than this exact moment in time. "Okay...I pr-promise."

I can't take it any longer and throw my arms around him, sobbing into his neck. I don't know if my tears will ever stop because no matter how wrong this feels, how this is going against everything I want, I know that Saint is right.

We came together in the most heinous of circumstances, and we found strength and love in something littered with ugliness. But now that that ugliness is gone and we have an opportunity to start afresh, we both need to find who we are again and whether we fit together.

I know for Saint that time may not heal all wounds because he has lost so much. He needs to find himself, and he needs to do that alone because the saying rings true—how can you make someone else happy if you're not happy with yourself?

Our love for each other isn't the problem; it's that we both need to love ourselves again.

I can't look myself in the mirror and be happy with the person who stares back. And neither can Saint. We have to heal our souls.

Saint rubs my back, pressing his lips over my temple. "Take the keys to the van and drive. You keep on driving until you reach that airstrip."

"This doesn't make any sense," I say, a mixed bag of emotion. "All of this was for nothing."

Saint shakes his head. "No, this was for *everything*. The future awaits us now because of this moment."

A low moan is a silver lining because Pavel isn't dead. "Go, Willow," he says, sitting up with a pained grunt. "I will make the call. You'll be safe."

"And what about you?" I ask, referring to them all.

"We'll be okay."

Leaving Saint doesn't make sense, and I know that. But in some stories, the princess doesn't always get her happily ever after. However, when I gently pull out of Saint's arms and affix my eyes to his, I know that this is my happily ever after…for now.

There are no words to express how to say goodbye to the man you love. But this time, our goodbye was written in the stars. Loving Saint was like wishing upon a shooting star—a fast-moving commotion that burned out before it hit the ground.

Saint steps aside, allowing me to look at Alek, who is still on his knees. The moonlight catches his tears.

"I know that your feelings for me are real." Alek's eyes widen at my admission. "Thank you…for protecting me. I'll forgive you, only if you forgive me."

"There is nothing to forgive," he says with sincerity. "I

will never forget you. You broke my heart, but by the same token…you made me whole. Thank you."

My heart breaks at his admission. "Goodbye, Aleksei."

"Goodbye, дорогая." And with this goodbye, he finally lets me go.

I don't know what his future holds, but he has one, so let's hope he's learned from the error of his ways. I don't know where his mom or brother are, but none of that is my concern anymore. I've been given my way out, and that's all I ever wanted. And I intend to take it.

My attention focuses on Max, who still holds Sara, brushing back her hair. I remember what she told me.

"But once you spread your wings, Willow, I know you won't look back."

I can only hope Sara, as well as Ingrid, have spread their wings and are finally free.

Max nods once, a mutual respect passing between us. I know he will ensure Sara gets the burial she deserves. "She died fighting. She died a hero," I whisper, holding back my tears. "I love you, Sara. Be free."

Zoey's body lies where Saint left her under the tree, and even though we never saw eye to eye, she deserves the respect of me saying goodbye. So with a stagger, I make my way to where she is. Her long hair sits neatly around her face as if Saint brushed it and ensured she was as beautiful in death as she was alive. She merely looks asleep. The gunshot wound to the back of her head hides the true horror.

Coming to a painful squat near her side, I stare at the woman who was nothing but brave. Bending down, I lay a gentle kiss to her cold cheek. "For what it's worth…I love and hate you all in the same breath too. Thank you."

There are so many things I want to thank her for, but most of all, I want to thank her for finally putting Saint first.

Saint is behind me. I can sense his presence, just like always, and I bask in the feeling because these moments are destined to become a distant memory.

Once I'm done mourning Zoey's and Sara's deaths, I stand slowly, but I don't turn around. I don't think I can leave him if I do. He wraps his arms around me, drawing my back to his chest. "Someone will look at your leg once you arrive at the airstrip."

The wound on my leg pales in comparison to the one on my heart.

He slips what I'm guessing are the van keys into my pocket. I know this is supposed to be my freedom, but I can't help but feel so imprisoned inside.

"Will I ever see you again?"

Silence.

It's all the answer I need.

Leaning into him, I memorize the contour of his body, the shallow of his breaths. I remember his scent, but most of all, I will remember what it felt like to be loved by him. And that is the only thing that will get me through each day without him.

With eyes closed, I savor this moment because it's to be our last. And in a bloodstained field, in a foreign land, a former captive said to her captor, "Thank you for being my best and worst memory."

And in return, he smiled because she was finally free.

EPILOGUE

One Year Later

"Oh, Pookie, you shouldn't spoil me like this!" shrieks the irksome blonde, twirling her wrist so the light can catch her diamond bracelet.

"Only the best for my girl."

There is only one suitable response for such a puke-worthy reply—an eye roll. But I quash down my need to vomit and wait in the shadows because this is all about timing.

Time.

The only thing that has been my constant companion for the past year.

They say time heals all wounds, but they're wrong. Yes, time moves on, allowing distance to pass from the one event that changed your world forever, but that doesn't help lessen the suffocating feeling whenever I think of...him.

A year ago, I was granted my freedom, and although every bone in my body rebelled at the thought of leaving, I took it, nonetheless. I took the keys Saint gave me, punched in the address to the airstrip, and I drove.

The entire time, all I wanted to do was turn the van around and go back, but I didn't. I kept the tears away because I had cried enough. Once I arrived at the airstrip, I was seen by Pavel's friend who was a doctor. He stitched me up, as it was only a flesh wound, and gave me the okay to fly.

The pilot didn't ask questions as neither of us were in the mood for small talk. The moment I stepped foot onto the small plane and buckled up, I felt like I could breathe for the first time in a long time. The entire flight, I peered out the window, wondering how the world below could have caused me so much pain. It appeared so small, so insignificant, but it changed me forever.

When the pilot, who didn't bother to give me his name, landed in London, he wished me luck. I was on my own, but that suited me just fine because I knew from then on out, I would only have myself to rely on. I changed clothes on the plane, so I didn't resemble a mess, but I was certain the moment I stepped into the real world, I would be spotted for the imposter that I was.

Before leaving the plane, I gave the pilot Saint's things, as he had left his passport and belongings in the van. He nodded, but of course gave me no hint as to whether he would see Saint or not. With nothing holding me back, I grabbed my suitcase and re-entered the world.

At first, it was too much, too fast, and before I even

reached the terminal, I hid in the bathroom three separate times. There were too many people, and a bout of anxiety tackled me from nowhere. I felt suffocated among the crowd, and I needed some time to gather my bearings before I boarded the plane.

I hadn't been around new people in a long time, and it was difficult not knowing who to trust. Back in Russia, I had to be on my A game, but here, I was just another passenger going home. When I finally had the guts to emerge from the restroom, I checked in and was surprised to see that I was seated in first class.

I was welcomed onto the plane like royalty, but if they knew what I'd done, their opinion of me would have surely been tarnished for good. I gripped the chair beneath me, certain my ruse would be up at any moment, and I would be hauled off the plane and punished for my crimes.

But that never happened.

I was offered a glass of champagne and satin pajamas instead.

When the pilot announced it was time for departure, I held my breath, but when the plane took to the skies, I realized it was really over.

I was free.

I was beyond exhausted, but I was too afraid to sleep. I didn't trust anyone, a bad habit I'd picked up, thanks to being subjected to events that shaped me into this paranoid, defensive person. I wanted to lower my guard, but when the flight attendant asked if I wanted chicken or beef for dinner, I eyed her like she had slipped poison into my meal.

I was too paranoid to eat or drink, so I simply sat silently, on high alert, awaiting the next threat. My strange behavior didn't go unnoticed by my fellow passengers. But it was a taste of what I was to face when I finally arrived home.

When the plane's wheels touched down in LAX, I let out a silent sob. I had made it. It felt like a dream as I disembarked and stepped foot onto home soil. I had envisioned this day for so long, but now that it had arrived, the feeling was bittersweet.

I was home, but my heart was still in Russia, or god knew where.

A man held a sign with my name, my new name, that is, as I stepped into the airport. Just like the pilot from the charter plane, he didn't talk much. He walked me through customs, and then we drove and drove until we reached a small city in California. We were nowhere near LA, but that suited me just fine.

As we drove into this town, the welcome sign stated the population was just over seven thousand. I was to make that number a plus one. The driver gave me a credit card and a cell phone, as well as some cash. When I asked who organized all this, he said W. Daniels aka Saint.

My heart grew heavy as I knew all of this was possible thanks to Saint and Pavel. I owed them my life.

Only when I locked the door and turned on all the lights in my new home—as I was afraid of the dark—did I allow myself to grieve. I held it together until this moment. I slid down the door and peered around at my beautiful belongings, sobbing into my hands. I was happy, but my happiness had come with a price.

This was supposed to be the ending where I spent the rest of my life with Saint. But as the days turned into weeks and the weeks into months, I realized this ending was the one that set us both free. But it hurt to be without him, and even when the nightmares faded, that pain was always there.

I stopped being a hermit about three months later, but I still kept to myself. The thought of socializing with anyone sent me into a panic as I was afraid they'd uncover what I did. I didn't drive. Instead, I rode around the slow-moving town on a bike.

The freedom of coming and going was difficult at first, but I eventually got used to it once again. Every week, two thousand dollars was deposited into my bank account. I knew who it was. When I asked the bank tellers if they could trace where the deposits came from, they said it was from an offshore account.

I didn't want to press, afraid of drawing attention to myself. I didn't need all that money, but Saint ensured I was well looked after. But it wasn't his money I wanted. I wanted him. But I understood why he did what he did. We were both broken and needed time to heal.

But not a day went by that I didn't think of him, and after months and months of pining for him, I decided to try to find him. But I didn't know where to start. I called every Hennessy in Syracuse, New York, pretending to be a telemarketer, conducting a current population survey in hopes of finding out any information I could.

I came up empty. Turns out no one wanted to talk to strangers. That included me.

I toyed with the idea of hiring a private investigator, but who could I trust to be discreet? I made Google my best friend and investigated what I could on my own. I wondered if maybe there were any records of Zoey's death and burial. There wasn't. I couldn't find anything on Sara either.

What I did find, however, was something that made me smile—the first smile in months.

The orphanage in Russia had been given a facelift. A reported million-plus dollars went into the rebuild, but there was no word on where the money had come from. The newspaper article showed Mother Superior standing on the newly constructed front steps surrounded by her children. They all looked so happy with their new home.

In the background, naked to the untrained eye, I saw something or, rather, *someone*. It was Alek.

Although he looked completely different with a longer hairstyle and full beard, I knew it was him. But something was different about him. He looked happy.

He had his arms around two small children who leaned into him, their toothless smiles revealing their genuine happiness at him being there.

I wondered if he had returned to crime to be able to afford the rebuild, as I guessed he was the one responsible for the funds. I didn't know what was left of the world we burned to the ground, but I didn't think someone like Alek could stay away from that lifestyle for too long.

Although every bone in my body told me not to, I called the orphanage. Mother Superior was happy to hear from me, cheerfully detailing all the changes the orphanage had undergone. I asked how Alek was, and she said safe, which was code for she respected his privacy and wouldn't tell me anything else.

She did share with me that she hadn't seen or spoken to Saint. She clearly knew I left Russia without him. When she asked me if I wanted to pass a message onto Alek, I said no. I had nothing I wanted to say. Maybe one day I will.

Besides, I have a feeling Aleksei's story has only just begun.

I wished her well, and that was the last we spoke.

It seemed Saint had disappeared off the face of the earth, which is what he wanted. He knew where I was, and if he wanted me to know where he was, he could contact me at any time. But he didn't. I read between the lines and respected his wishes even though it hacked at my heart with a fucking chainsaw.

After a while, I grew angry with him. It seemed so easy for him to stay away. Maybe he didn't really care after all. Which is why I didn't want his money and decided to get a job. I had to relearn how to mix with society and not seek out a weapon the moment someone stepped within three feet of me.

I became a farmhand, finding the animals easier to deal with than people. They didn't ask questions. They couldn't see the pain I hid behind every single day. My favorite chore was collecting the eggs early in the morning. It reminded me of Harriet Pot Pie.

So my life consisted of working long days, then coming home, eating dinner, and reading before bed. It was a simple existence, but it was mine.

No one bothered me, which is how I liked it, and for a little while, life was good. Well, as good as life can be for someone who was totally alone.

One day, however, everything changed, and that came when I was flicking through an article online about self-made entrepreneurs. When Drew's face assaulted my screen, I actually had to run to the bathroom because I got sick.

He never strayed far from my thoughts, but I was no longer intent on vengeance because I had lost the will to fight. I was living under a constant shadow, and I had no energy to live, let alone hatch a plan of revenge. But that changed when I saw that Drew was getting married—again.

The peppy blonde had stars in her eyes, reminding me of the person I once was. She was an up-and-coming model. Drew seemed to have a pattern.

Drew didn't mourn my death. He was living life as though I didn't exist, and here I was, feeling sorry for myself. It was the wake-up call I needed.

Anger I haven't felt in so long rattled me to the core, and before I knew what I was doing, I was making appointments with the beauty salons across town. I had my hair cut and styled. I also got some much-needed waxing. If I was going to do this, I would ensure to do it looking nothing less than fucking fabulous.

I didn't want to resemble the living dead even though that was exactly what I would be when I turned up on Drew's doorstep and yelled surprise, bitch!

I waited for the perfect moment because as I've come to learn, everything is about timing. Each moment in time is lived for the next. And although I missed Saint more than I thought humanly possible, it was time I let him go.

He never left my heart, but I allowed myself to live. He had asked this of me, and I intended to honor him, hoping he was doing the same thing. I had promised to let him go so he could live. So he could do some soul searching. I only agreed because his happiness means more to me than my own.

As much as it pained me, I forced myself to socialize. The local church was my go-to because I felt the safest there. I wasn't a social butterfly, but I wasn't a recluse anymore either, and after a while, I learned how to be human again. What I did, the lives I took, I repented for every day.

I was given a second chance, and it was time I took it, which is why I am standing in the hallway of my ex-husband's home.

I peer around the doorjamb, gagging when I witness Drew kissing his new squeeze passionately. She giggles before pulling away. "I'll see you after yoga."

Drew spanks her ass, grinning like a pig in shit.

She grabs her backpack and bounces out the room, unbeknownst that I wait in the shadows, ready to strike. When the front door closes, I bide my time, wanting to give Drew a false sense of security. He loosens his tie before stepping onto the balcony.

The backdrop of when the last time I saw him isn't missed, which is what sets my plan into motion.

I am barefoot, wearing a simple white cotton summer dress. It's what I wore the last time he saw me, saw me being kidnapped all because he sucked at poker.

I creep into the bedroom, the soft carpet muting my steps. Drew takes a drag off a joint, leaning against the railings, oblivious to what's coming. When I'm a few feet away, I stop in the balcony doorway and smile. Finally, I am happy because this is me, taking back my life.

What do you say to your ex-husband who only married you to settle a debt and now thinks you're dead? There only seems to be one word that's fitting.

Inhaling, I fill my lungs with victory. Let the shitshow start. "Boo!"

Drew jumps so high his joint slips from his fingers and tumbles over the railing. He swivels quickly, and the horrified look on his face has me rejoicing.

"Wil-Wil-Willow?" he finally manages to spit out.

I wave in response.

"What the fuck?" He grinds his fists into his eyeballs, hoping the weed is messing with him.

When he removes his hands and sees that I'm still standing, he yelps. "Are you a ghost?"

I would feel sorry for Drew if not for the fact he sold me to a Russian drug lord. And a ghost? Really? How did I ever find this dipshit attractive?

When I take a step toward him, he backs up against the railing, eyes wide. His fear spurs me on. I don't speak, which seems to freak him out more than he already is. When I'm standing in front of him, I come to a stop and smile. It's not a happy smile, however; it's more along the lines of I'm here to steal your soul.

Drew looks down at me, wetting his lips. When I don't

speak, something shifts, and his fear is replaced with humor. "Holy shit," he gasps, hand over his heart. "I will have to tell Keno that whatever he put in that weed I want more of."

He actually believes I'm a hallucination. This just gets better by the minute.

He reaches out to poke me, which is when I shoot out my hand, grip his finger, and snap it in half.

Three…two…one.

"What the fuck!" Drew's howls are music to my depraved soul because even though I have repented and made peace with who I am, that doesn't mean I can't be a little wicked every now and again.

He cradles his finger, hollering in pain, while I admire my freshly painted nails, bored with his melodramatics. "Oh, grow a pair. It's just a broken finger."

When I speak, his wails transform into a terrified shriek.

"This isn't possible," he splutters, shaking his head.

"Aw, Pookie, what's the matter? Not happy to see your *wife*?"

Drew tries to run, but he has nowhere to go. Unless he fancies taking a swan dive over the railing. But that would be far too easy.

"So how did you dig your way out of debt? I'm assuming you've burned through the money Alek *paid* you for me."

"How do you know about that?"

"Because you married the wrong girl," I counter smartly, tsking him.

He opens his mouth, but I am done listening.

"How much was the life insurance policy you took out

on me?"

When his mouth opens and closes like a useless fish, I knee him in the groin. He turns a lovely shade of pink before toppling forward. I hold him up by the shoulder, shuddering at the touch.

"There was no policy," he wheezes.

"Drew, this will be a lot easier on you if you stop lying."

"Get out of my house, you psycho bitch." He coughs as he attempts to breathe. "How did you even get in?"

"I picked the lock," I reply as if it's a no-brainer.

"Who are you?" He gasps, eyes wide, stunned by my revelation.

When I push him back, he comes to a wobbly stand. "I'm the woman who you thought would roll over and die. Well, surprise, I didn't. So now, it's your turn to…die."

He turns a ghastly shade of white. "You don't mean that."

"Oh, but I do," I counter, standing on tippy toes and leveling him with nothing but sincerity. "As much as I would take great pleasure in seeing that, it doesn't seem like enough. I want you to disappear. For good."

"What?"

"You will pack up your shit and disappear. Today. Drew Gibbs is a name of the past," I explain as simply as I can.

But we don't seem to be on the same page.

"I'm not going anywhere. I built a name for myself."
Insert eye roll.

"You built a name for yourself by lying and cheating. You were broke, which is the reason you married me. You sold me to pay off your debt. You're no entrepreneur. You're a dick. A dick whose karma train is coming. Choo-choo."

Drew finally realizes I'm not playing and narrows his eyes into slits. "Why would I go?"

"Because if you don't, I will go to the police and tell them everything. Not only will you be charged for insurance fraud, but you'll also be facing time for human trafficking. Throw in money laundering and you'll be looking at some serious time."

Drew's color transforms from red to white back to red. "You can't do this to me."

"I can, and I am," I reply confidently, brushing invisible lint from his shirt.

"Where am I supposed to go?"

"Not my problem."

"Babe," he reasons, trying to turn on the charm. He reaches out to stroke my cheek. I stop him by breaking his nose.

"Motherfucker!" he screeches, cupping his bleeding nose. I would be lying if I said seeing him bleed doesn't give me great satisfaction.

"Don't patronize me. You have one hour to pack your shit."

Drew is beyond furious. "No one will believe you. Who's going to believe I sold you to a Russian mobster in a game of poker to pay off a quarter-million debt I owed?"

When I'm silent, he gloats, thinking he's won.

"The insurance policy was one million dollars, by the way, so your sweet ass was worth a lot of money. And I would do it again. Given half the chance, I would sell you or any other bitch to get what I wanted. And do you think money laundering is something new? Please. How do you think I got to where I am in the first place? Hard work?"

A twitch under my eye gives away my anger. "So you never loved me?" I know the answer, but I need to hear it.

"You stupid hillbilly." He snickers, removing his hand from his nose. He wears his blood with pride. "No, I never loved you. All it was, was a game to get what I want. I'll give you points for trying to play with the big boys, but you lost. I won. I won the moment I sold you to clear my debt. And the cherry on top is when my crocodile tears convinced the insurance company that you were lost at sea."

He gives me a repeat performance when his eyes fill with tears.

At this moment, I wonder if maybe I could rethink my plan and strangle him with his Armani tie. But remember… it's all about timing.

"Not so smart now, are you?"

Oh, how his words just continue digging his grave.

He looks at me like he expects me to break down into hysterical tears, but I don't. Instead, I commence a slow clap.

Drew cocks his head, utterly confused.

I decide to clarify because I'm sick of looking at his face.

I won. I won the moment I sold you to clear my debt. And the cherry on top is when my crocodile tears convinced the insurance company that you were lost at sea.

"Oopsie." I giggle, opening my mouth in mock horror. "It seems this hillbilly isn't so stupid after all."

What Drew hears is a playback recording of our entire

conversation. He didn't think I came here unprepared, did he? I pressed record on my phone the moment I walked into his room. Everything we just said has been recorded. Every damning word.

"If I go to the police with this, as well as the insurance company…" There is no need for me to fill in the blanks.

"You set me up."

"Not so smart now, are you?" I repeat his words back to him, smiling smugly. "I'm giving you a chance. Unlike you did to me. If you're not gone in an hour, this recording will go to every tabloid around the world. I'm sure *Forbes Magazine* will be pleased to know their up-and-coming star is really a cheat and liar."

"This will ruin me," he says, acting like I'm supposed to give a shit.

"Only if you stick around," I correct. "I know a nice remote villa in the Greek Islands you could always use as your new home." The smile I beam exposes all my teeth because I am grinning so hard.

Drew can see it. He's lost.

There is no gray. Only black and white.

If he stays, I leak the tape everywhere, ruining him. I will also go to the police and insurance company, which will ensure he does time. A pretty boy like him will not fare well in jail. However, if he leaves and drops off the face of this earth, then he has a chance to live. Something I was never given.

As I see it, I'm being awfully generous.

To Drew, a narcissist who loves praise and winning, this is the worst form of punishment I could deliver. He'll be left all alone.

"I'll be watching you. If I so much as see your name anywhere, I will ruin you…just as you did to me. Now it's your turn to die."

I don't mean that literally, but for Drew to survive this, he will have to be someone else, just like me. From this moment forward, Drew Gibbs is dead. Just as Willow Shaw is.

If he had any balls, he would end my life, but he knows those baby soft, small hands don't stand a chance against me. Hence, me manhandling him a little. But that term is so fucking sexist. Drew Gibbs got *womanhandled* by me.

Boom!

"This isn't the last you've seen of me. You'll be hearing from my lawyer." He pushes past me, frantically hunting through his walk-in closet for a bag, but I know he's all smoke and mirrors because Drew only cares about one person, and that's himself.

I'm sure he'll lay low for a while in hopes I will get over this, but I will ensure he doesn't do this to any other women. I have nothing but time on my hands, and I need a hobby. It seems I just found one.

He rushes around the room, throwing the essentials into his bag. My job here is done. This is what I came for. However, when I walk past the bed and see his cell light up with a picture message of someone who isn't his fiancée, who also isn't wearing much or, rather, *anything*, I realize there is one more thing I have to do.

"Hey, Drew," I say sweetly.

He spins, opening his mouth to no doubt call me every

name under the sun, but I don't give him the chance before I sucker punch him in the jaw. He falls onto his back with a thud. He's out cold.

My hand feels broken, but it's worth the pain.

Grabbing his cell, I find his fiancée's number and forward the picture message to her. As well as a dozen other texts from different women. Do I feel guilty for shattering her bubble? Not really, no. As I see it, I'm saving her from future heartache.

Namaste.

Now his disappearance won't rouse any suspicion because his fiancée will tell the world what a lying, cheating asshole he truly is. And instead of facing the music, everyone will believe he has gone into hiding. This really is the icing on the cake.

I leave my ex-husband unconscious on the floor as I slip on my tennis shoes which I left by the door and strut my shit. I walk from this home with no intention of ever returning. I can't deny this is the best I've felt in, well, forever. I leave the front door open as I descend the winding driveway. Here's hoping he gets robbed. Or I'd even settle for a bear taking a giant shit on his Persian rug.

I caught an Uber here, but I decide to walk as I can't seem to get enough of being outdoors. Being a prisoner does that. With no real destination in mind, I walk the streets for hours, each step alleviating some of this emptiness within.

I feel accomplished for playing Drew at his own game, but the one person I want to celebrate this with is a million miles away. That thought brings back the hollowness and the anger, but I suck it up and decide to get ice cream. Ice cream makes everything better.

Dot's is my most favorite ice cream place in all of LA, and after the miles I just walked, I decide to double up on my scoops. The bell above the door chimes, announcing my arrival, but no one is waiting for me inside.

Ignoring the pang to my heart, I make my way to the long glass counter, scanning the endless flavors. I don't know if I want gelato or ice cream. But my decision is made when my eyes land on the homemade butter pecan.

It's my favorite for obvious reasons, but it's not the taste which has tears springing to life. It reminds me of the island, of when I told Saint about Dot's. He was out cold, but when he came to, he replied with what his favorite flavor was—rocky road.

I chew the inside of my cheek to stop myself from crying. But the harder I try, the more impossible it becomes because a simple thing like getting ice cream is something we will never do because he is gone, and it hurts. So much.

I've tried to be strong, but I miss him...every single moment of every single day. I understand his decisions, but I will never heal entirely because a piece of me is missing, and that piece is him. But I'm angry with him as well.

I'm split down the middle, bordering on love and hate.

Wiping away my tears with my thumbs, I pull it together because someone stands next to me in line. I'm about to tell them to order before me because I know I look like a lunatic crying over ice cream, but I don't have a chance to speak, or move...or breathe.

"You should get the rocky road."

Time doesn't stand still. Not like it does in the movies.

It fucking explodes. I was half living until this moment, and everything is suddenly brighter, sweeter because the sun has finally risen. I was cast in the shadows, but now, I slowly lift my chin and lock eyes with a sunrise—a chartreuse dawn.

I blink once, twice, three times to be sure, but each time I open my eyes, I see the same thing.

The only thing that matters.

Saint.

It's sensory overload, and I need a moment to compose anything remotely coherent. My vision however doesn't need a moment. It eats him up from head to toe.

He's in ripped black jeans and a dark navy V-neck tee that clings to him like a second skin. His angel wings which stop mid forearm glisten under the light, and I claw my palms to stop myself from reaching out and touching them.

His dirty blond hair is long, tied back, with wisps slipping free, framing his chiseled face. He has some light scruff, which only seems to emphasize the pinkness of his full lips. My memory has clearly done a poor job of remembering him because damn…wow. I have no words.

He shuffles his combat boots, which alerts me to the fact I am gaping at him like a creeper. I quickly focus my attention upward, which doesn't help because I am held prisoner under his piercing green eyes.

I want to say so many things, but I don't know where to start. Now that he's here, I can't help but wonder what he wants and how long he's staying. I can't say goodbye to him, not again. I wouldn't survive it a second time.

My sunrise is suddenly eclipsed, and I can't mask my

fears. "Where have you been?" I ask, unable to keep the hurt from my tone.

As usual, he is aloof, and I can't read what he's thinking. But if he was expecting a happy reunion, he's shit out of luck. My fears soon transform into anger. He turns up looking composed and fucking gorgeous while I generally have to check if I'm wearing pants most days.

"You're not happy to see me?" Has his voice always been this smooth?

However, I don't let that distract me. I had made peace with the fact I wouldn't see him again, so this has thrown everything off balance. "Honestly, I don't know how I feel. You can't just show up here. I have a life, you know."

I omit the fact my life is relatively boring because that's beside the point.

Saint rubs the back of his neck. "I know. I'm sorry."

"Sorry for what exactly?" He has a lot to be sorry for, like ghosting me this past year.

When someone clears their throat, I realize there is a line behind us. Ice-cream enthusiasts just want their fix, and Saint and I are delaying their gratification by airing our dirty laundry. When he appears to be mulling over what to say, I huff an exasperated sigh and push past him, ignoring the way my body responds to him even after all this time.

The bell dings, announcing my departure, but I honestly don't know if I'm coming or going when it comes to Saint. Half of me wants to throw my arms around him and never let him go, and the other half, the stubborn, mad as hell half, wants to slap him.

Pacing briskly down the sidewalk, I decide the best option would be to put some space between us. I need time to digest this before I do something I regret. But when a warm palm wraps around my bicep and spins me around, all rationale floats to the California wind.

I act on instinct as the mad as hell half wins and slap Saint's cheek. He grunts under the force, and so do I because holy shit, I think I just broke my hand—again.

Immediately I clutch it to my chest, wincing in pain. Saint reaches out to touch me, but I shrink back, not needing his hands on me right now to cloud my judgment.

He reads between the lines and keeps his hands to himself. "What happened?" He nods toward my cradled fist.

"I hurt it when I connected with my ex-husband's face."

His lips twitch. "Are you all right?"

The only suitable response is a maniacal laugh.

An unexpected madness overcomes me, and I begin to cackle uncontrollably. I don't bother fighting it because after a year of utter despair, it feels good to laugh. But those tears of happiness soon switch to sadness, and my laughter is weighed down with wretched sobs.

I'm so embarrassed, but I can't stop. It flows out of me like a wild rapid, and I'm suddenly crying a year's worth of tears. "Wh-where have you b-been?" I stutter, my vision blurred with tears.

Saint clenches his fists by his sides, and I know he's suppressing the urge to reach out and console me. "I'm sorry it took me so long," he says with nothing but sincerity.

"You could have called," I offer, wiping away my tears

angrily.

"I could have," he replies with a nod. "And I wanted to. So many times."

"Then why didn't you?"

Saint tongues his bottom lip, sighing. "I made a promise to you, that I would be the best man that I could. It's taken… time."

I don't sense any deception in his admission.

Now that I've had my meltdown, I pull myself together. "And how did you go with that?"

Saint takes his time replying. "It's a work in progress."

I appreciate his honesty.

Someone brushes past us, reminding me that we're standing in the middle of the sidewalk. The sensible thing would be to invite him back to my house and talk. But when I catch him watching me closely, his eyes consumed with wanton blackness, I know that's a bad idea.

"So your husband finally got what he deserved?"

"Ex," I clarify. "And yes, he did. I told him not to show his face again. It's his turn to disappear."

A smirk graces his lips.

I have so much I want to say, but I don't know what. This is the first time this uncomfortable silence has lingered. "Are you planning to stick around?"

He kicks the pavement and shoves his hands deep into his pockets. "That all depends."

I gulp. "On what?"

"On whether you're going to hit me again."

This time, I can't hide my smile. "Well, that all depends

on what you say."

This banter is our go-to, and it settles my nerves somewhat. But regardless, I need to go home and clear my head. Now that he's back, I need to figure out what I want. It seems weird for us just to go back to the way things were because they were filled with violence and bloodshed.

Images I haven't visited in a very long time float to the surface, and a chill overcomes me. Saint instantly recognizes the goose bumps aren't of the good kind.

"I should go home. I need to think."

Saint nods, appearing to respect my wishes. "Okay. Did you want me to hail a cab?"

"No, it's okay. I got it."

The tangible electricity between us leaves me gasping for air, and if I don't get out of here now, I will throw good sense to the wind.

"Well, see ya," I say with a wave. I bet I look as ridiculous as I feel.

Saint nods again.

When I don't move, however, he peers at me with a slanted grin. Leaving him feels all kinds of wrong, but I eventually turn in the direction I came from and begin to walk. I will call an Uber when I get to the end of the street because I need to put some distance between us.

I quicken my steps, cursing each one because they take me farther away from Saint. I'm almost winded at the thought because that really happened—Saint is really here, and here I am...walking away. What is wrong with this picture?

But I reason with myself that this is the right thing to do.

So why does it feel so wrong?

Yes, I am hurt, angry, annoyed, frustrated, and every other adjective associated with a breakup, but walking away won't rectify those feelings. If anything, it makes me feel worse. But the old Saint I knew would never allow me to walk away.

He would throw me up against a wall, snarl in my face that I'm being nothing but stubborn, and demand I behave. But maybe that Saint is truly dead and gone. He said he needed time to find a better version of himself. But this lukewarm, passive version is not who I want.

I want the passionate, the domineering, the arrogant man who robbed me of air whenever he walked into a room. I want him to cuff me, to spank me, to call me his ангел because that's when I felt most alive. If I eliminate the circumstances, the violence, the unsavory characters and pull back the layers, underneath it all, there is something beautiful…and that's us.

Our relationship isn't conventional, I know that, but we survived the ultimate relationship test. Nothing tore us down because our love was unstoppable. This entire time…*that's* what dictated our narrative.

Our crazy, unconventional, undying love is the reason for this all…and if I walk away from it, this truly would have been for nothing. Time doesn't heal wounds—it makes you see what a fucking idiot you are.

Just as I'm about to spin around, I'm calmly snatched off the street and dragged into an alley. God knows I should be scared, but I'm done with being afraid. I thought He had forsaken me. But I was wrong because as Saint slams me up against a brick wall and cages me with his arms, I know that

He was with me this entire time.

He sent me Saint.

My chest heaves thanks to the adrenaline coursing through me when I lock eyes with Saint. He is inches away, his hands on either side of my head, but I don't flinch.

"See ya?" he questions, his hot breath blowing the hair from my face.

"Yes, it's how civilized people say goodbye," I taunt, lamely attempting to break free. He only pushes me against the wall harder.

"I missed that smart mouth," he counters, focusing on the subject in question. "You know what happens when you misbehave."

Oh yes, I do.

"You don't get to walk away."

"Why not? You did," I reply, my anger shining.

"I know, but that's because I'm weak. But you, you were always strong." He threads his large hand through my hair while I smother a moan. "I thought I needed time, but the longer I was away, it just made me realize how wrong I was."

"And it took you a year to realize this?" I question with fire.

He licks his lips. "I stayed away because I wanted you to have a normal life...away from me. Away from the memories I evoke. But staying away from you is like fighting nature. You were in everything. Every sunrise, it was your glow warming my deadened heart. Every sweet smell, it was your skin I inhaled to make me feel whole."

My eyes flicker when he lowers his nose to the side of my

neck and inhales.

"I left Russia and sailed the seas alone. I couldn't bear to fit in with society because I came to learn quickly, I don't like people."

I can't help but chuckle.

"I never stopped thinking about you, but I told myself you needed time to heal, as did I. What we went through, no one will understand." His warm breath bathes the column of my neck, sending shivers all the way to my toes.

"But as the days turned into months, I came to realize that our story would be a tragedy only if we let it. And I was sick of tragedies."

The waver to his tone hints at what or, rather, whom he speaks of.

Pulling away slowly, he bares himself to me with utter sincerity, and it's nothing but beautiful. "Am I completely healed? No. And I don't think I ever will be. But that's okay because I can finally accept who I am. I thought I needed to become a better man for you, but in reality, if you loved the man who I was…then I couldn't be so bad because you, you are so good."

"I'm not always good. I cursed you out more times than I can count," I counter with a small smile.

We have reached an understanding. It may have taken a year, but we're here now, and finally, the future is bright because it's a future together—well, I hope. I could be stubborn and harp on the past, but I'm done living in the shadows.

"So what happens now?"

Saint works in slow motion as he runs his finger down the

middle of my parted lips. "What do you want?"

That's a no-brainer.

My eyes flicker when he skims my bottom lip before gently pulling away. "I want you," I reply without pause.

He exhales, and I wonder if he thought otherwise.

"That's never changed. And whatever life you want to live, I'll take it because it's with you. You were right to allow us some time apart, but not because that allowed me to see what a mistake we were. No. It only showed me how strong we were to survive. And that's what we did. We survived."

Saint lowers his eyes because not all of us had that luxury. But if we can honor their memory by living for them that way, their spirit never dies. It will live on through us. Zoey, Sara, and Ingrid will never be forgotten.

"Now we just have to learn how to survive in this new world. Together."

A sudden silence envelops us, and my palms begin to sweat. Is Saint having second thoughts?

He reaches for my hand hesitantly and slips it under his T-shirt, coaxing me to lift it. With an eyebrow raised, I do, and when the tanned skin on his side is revealed, a gasp escapes me.

"You never left my mind. My heart. Or my body."

I don't believe it, but it's clear as…ink.

Blinking rapidly to brush away the tears, I smile.

"Now I'm not only a sinner." The reason being is because tattooed on his flank, on the opposite side of his sinner tattoo, is a word which stitches our story together.

Ангел.

He now has a balance between two worlds.

He can't promise me that his darkness will ever fade, but that's what makes us human. And that's what makes him mine.

I don't know who reaches for who first, but the moment our lips collide, nothing else matters but this. At last, I'm truly living because my heart is finally whole. I don't know what the future holds, but I do know that we will never give up.

When Saint lifts me, I happily comply, wrapping my legs around his waist. When his kisses grow sluggish, I moan in frustration.

Chuckling, he pulls away, rubbing his nose against mine. "What do you say we ditch this town and see where the roads or, rather, the *seas* take us?"

"You want to get back on a yacht?" My eyes widen.

"I want to go anywhere and everywhere with you… ангел."

How that name soothes my soul.

"We have so much to catch up on. And so many new things to uncover about one another. What better way to do that than sailing the seas with no direction? Time is no longer the enemy because we have a whole *lifetime* ahead of us."

I can't keep the tears at bay.

"It'll just be us against the world."

"Just how it's always been," I whisper.

"And besides, I think Harriet Pot Pie misses you."

The mere mention of her and the prospect of going back to the island have my lower lip quivering. It was there I felt safe. It was there we made a home. "Okay, let's do it. Let's go get my chicken. But more importantly...let's live."

Saint's grin is everything and so much more because finally...he looks happy. "I can't promise you it'll be hearts and roses, but what I can promise is that I give you me. All of me. Every flawed, vulnerable piece. Take it. It's yours."

"That's all I ever wanted."

He brushes his nose against mine. "Better pack your passport, Ms. Emma Miller. The world awaits us."

And it does...

His comment reminds me that Saint and Willow are no more. But when I get lost in those chartreuse orbs, I know that regardless of our names, of the obstacles we face, or where we are, he'll always be...forever my Saint.

How lucky am I?

THE DEVIL'S CROWN—Aleksei's story is coming in 2020!

ACKNOWLEDGEMENTS

I lost my beloved father in July, so completing this trilogy was tough. Many times, I thought I wouldn't be able to finish it. But I did it in honor of him. I wouldn't have been able to get through this difficult time without my family and friends. L.J. Shen, Elle Kennedy, Vi Keeland, Lisa Edward, Christina Lauren, Natasha Madison, Kylie Scott, SC Stephens, Helena Hunting, Tina Gephart, Jo Mantel, Kimberly Brower, Danielle Sanchez, Jenny Sims, Gemma, Louise, Ryn Hughes—thank you from the bottom of my heart for being there for me.

To my author family—Vi Keeland, Susan Stoker, Natasha Madison, BJ Harvey, Pam Godwin, Jay Mclean, Adriane Leigh, Helena Hunting, Penelope Ward, Christina Lauren, Stina Lindenblatt, Carrie Ann Ryan, Sawyer Bennett, Geneva Lee, Kristen Proby, Natasha Preston, L.J. Shen, Elle Kennedy, Jen Frederick, Audrey Carlan, Heidi McLaughlin, KA Tucker, Meghan March, Sarina Bowen, Kristy Bromberg, Beverly Preston, Lisa Edward, Rachel Brookes, Len Webster, Debra Anastasia—thank you for my beautiful flowers. I was so touched.

My wonderful husband, Daniel. I love you. Thank you for always believing in me. You're my favorite.

My ever-supporting parents. You guys are the best. I am who I am because of you. I love you. RIP Papa. Gone but never forgotten. You're in my heart. Always.

My agent, Kimberly Brower from Brower Literary & Management. Thank you for your patience and thank you for being an amazing human being.

My editor, Jenny Sims. What can I say other than I LOVE YOU! Thank you for everything. You go above and beyond for me.

My proofreader—Lisa Edward—More Than Words, Copyediting & Proofreading. You are amazing. I owe you dinner.

Sommer Stein, you NAILED this cover! Thank you for being so patient and making the process so fun. I'm sorry for annoying you constantly.

My publicist—Danielle Sanchez from Wildfire Marketing Solutions. Thank you for all your help. Your messages brighten my day.

A special shout-out to: Staci Hart, Mia Sheridan, Tijan, Aleatha Romig, Kat T.Masen, Danielle Norman, Carmen Jenner, Natasha Tomic, Lauren Grace, Sali Benbow-Powers, Lana Kart, Kimberly Whalen, Heyne, Random House, Kinneret Zmora, Hugo & Cie, Planeta, MxM Bookmark, Art Eternal, Carbaccio, Fischer, Harper Brazil, Bookouture, Egmont Bulgaria, Brilliance Publishing, Audible, Hope Editions, Buzzfeed, BookBub, PopSugar, Hugues De Saint Vincent, Romance Writers of Australia, Paris, New York, Sarah Sentz, Ria Alexander, Amy Jennings, Gel Ytayz, Jennifer Spinninger, Aurelie Dee, Vanessa Silva Martins, Rukaiya M. aka the future Mrs. Popov, Denise Reyes, Amz Bourne, Amalie—Amalie Reads, Megan—Steamy Reads Blog, Cheri Grand Anderman, Kim Nash, Lauren Rosa, Kristin Dwyer, and Nina Bocci.

To the endless blogs that have supported me since day one—You guys rock my world.

My bookstagrammers—This book has allowed me to meet SO many of you. Your creativity astounds me. The effort you go to is just amazing. Thank you for the posts, the teasers, the support, the messages, the love, the EVERYTHING! I see what you do, and I am so, so thankful.

My reader group and review team—sending you all a big kiss.

My beautiful family—Mum, Papa, my sister—Fran, Matt, Samantha, Amelia, Gayle, Peter, Luke, Leah, Jimmy, Jack, Shirley, Michael, Rob, Elisa, Evan, Alex, Francesca, and my aunties, uncles, and cousins—I am the luckiest person alive to know each and every one of you. You brighten up my world in ways I honestly cannot express.

Samantha and Amelia— I love you both so very much.

To my family in Holland and Italy, and abroad. Sending you guys much love and kisses.

Papa, Zio Nello, Zio Frank, Zia Rosetta, and Zia Giuseppina—you are in our hearts. Always.

My fur babies— mamma loves you so much! Buckwheat, you are my best buddy. Dacca, I will always protect you from the big bad Bellie. Mitch, refer to Dacca's comment. Jag, you're a wombat in disguise. Bellie, you're a devil in disguise. And Ninja, thanks for watching over me.

To anyone I have missed, I'm sorry! It wasn't intentional!

Last but certainly not least, I want to thank YOU! Thank you for welcoming me into your hearts and homes. My readers are the BEST readers in this entire universe! Love you all!

ABOUT THE AUTHOR

Monica James spent her youth devouring the works of Anne Rice, William Shakespeare, and Emily Dickinson.

When she is not writing, Monica is busy running her own business, but she always finds a balance between the two. She enjoys writing honest, heartfelt, and turbulent stories, hoping to leave an imprint on her readers. She draws her inspiration from life.

She is a bestselling author in the U.S.A., Australia, Canada, France, Germany, Israel, and The U.K.

Monica James resides in Melbourne, Australia, with her wonderful family, and menagerie of animals. She is slightly obsessed with cats, chucks, and lip gloss, and secretly wishes she was a ninja on the weekends.

CONNECT WITH MONICA JAMES

Facebook: facebook.com/authormonicajames
Twitter: twitter.com/monicajames81
Goodreads: goodreads.com/MonicaJames
Instagram: instagram.com/authormonicajames
Website: authormonicajames.com
Pinterest: pinterest.com/monicajames81
BookBub: bookbub.com/authors/monica-james
Amazon: amzn.to/2EWZSyS
Join my Reader Group: bit.ly/2nUaRyi

CPSIA information can be obtained
at www.ICGtesting.com
Printed in the USA
LVHW081441220919
631863LV00029B/512/P